SECOND CHANCES

By

LOUISE MERCER

SECOND CHANCES

By

LOUISE MERCER

Cover design by
Carly McCracken

Published By
Crimson Cloak Publishing

ISBN: 978-1-68160-763-4

ISBN: 1-68160-763-8

Edited by Denna Holm

Publisher's Publication in Data

Mercer, Louise

Second Chances

1. Fiction 2. Romance 3. Women's Fiction

CHAPTER 1

Emma had to admit it, she'd taken a wrong turn. Pulling into a lay-by, she threw her death trap of a car into reverse in the hope of getting back onto the right track. She rubbed at her aching eyes as her stomach rumbled. And even more importantly, her bladder felt close to bursting. As she released the pedal, the hideous car spat out a puff of smoke and completely cut out. Emma leaned her head against the steering wheel and felt like crying. Why her? Why did these things always happen to her? She took a few deep breaths to calm herself down. Okay, she could do this. She'd come this far. She could do the rest.

Releasing her seat belt, she checked her map to assess her options. She couldn't go back to Redsworth. After discovering her fiancé, Sean, had emptied her wedding account and bought a Ferrari of all things, she'd had no option but to leave him and the hotel he owned, her home and workplace. Instead, she thought about option two, her current venture. She needed a new life away from Redsworth. A fresh start, and money, obviously. The job she'd applied for in Thornhill Village offered both if she was successful at her interview tomorrow. Third option. Emma wriggled in her seat as jumping beans played havoc with her bladder. There wasn't a third option, which basically meant she had to be brave and continue with option two.

Winding down her window, she squinted through the persistent drizzle at the warm lights twinkling comfortingly from the nearby farmhouse. It may not be a lifeline, but hopefully it would offer her means to phone a mechanic and what she needed most, a bathroom.

Dragging her suitcase, Emma headed down the muddy path and prayed her luck would start to change. Each step echoed in the complete silence of the enveloping night, and she looked around nervously as she heard rustling in the trees and bushes.

Approaching the sprawling farmhouse, she pushed open the rickety gate and headed for the front door, cursing as the rose bush surrounding it ripped at her raincoat. With the absence of a bell, she rapped on the wooden door with her bare knuckles and waited with crossed fingers and legs for someone to answer. Breathing a sigh of relief as a light appeared, she peered under her hood as the door cracked open.

"I'm sorry. I know it's late." Emma squinted at the tall male figure outlined in the hallway. "My car has broken down and I wondered if I could use your phone and ring for help." She held out her mobile. "No signal."

"It's a bit remote around here." The man craned his neck to see her car in the layby, steaming as the rain fell hard on its bonnet. "Not a good night to break down." He glanced at her suitcase before frowning. "You're welcome to come in and use our phone if you wish, or if you want to head back to your car, I'll ring someone for you?"

Emma peered around the silhouette of the owner into the dark hallway. She had no idea what he looked like, but he sounded harmless. It was all the incentive she needed for her next question. "Actually, what I really want is a bathroom. Could I use yours, please? I'm desperate. I mean, totally, completely desperate."

"Oh yeah, sure." The man laughed at her crossed legs and frantic dance. "Upstairs. It's the second door on the left."

Emma didn't need telling twice. She risked leaving her suitcase on the doorstep and rushed up the rickety stairs. An empty bladder gave her the chance to re-evaluate. Of all the stupid things to do, she'd just entered the house of a complete stranger in the middle of nowhere. After drying her hands and reluctantly admiring the old copper bath, she checked her mobile again. Still no signal. With her phone in her hand as a potential weapon, she headed into the dark hallway where the owner still waited.

"Too much water and three hours stuck in a car." Emma screwed up her nose. "Sorry, too much information."

The man laughed. "No need to apologise. I wouldn't have lasted thirty minutes."

Emma leaned against her suitcase and stumbled as it fell open, shedding its contents over the doorstep. She swallowed back a squeal as her personal belongings were scattered for all to see. Hairbrushes, makeup wipes, tampons. Feeling beads of sweat form on her forehead, she dropped to the floor and grappled her things together, her face turning hotter as she tugged a sturdy pair of white knickers from under the man's feet and stuffed them into her pocket. Finally breathless and crestfallen, she pulled off her hood and tied back her unruly auburn curls. Could her night get any worse?

"Emma?" The man turned on the porch light and squinted at her face.

On hearing her name, she looked up into the dark eyes of the achingly familiar face.

"It is, isn't it? Emma Francis." The man rubbed a hand through his thick, dark hair. "Remember me? My brother Josh and I lived next door to you."

Emma closed her emerald eyes and cursed, *For frigs sake. Jack Sodding Seymour.*

CHAPTER 2

"Long time, no see. How are you?"

Polite chit chat? Emma thought. *Seriously?*

"What are you doing here?" Jack peered behind her. "Were you looking for me?"

As if. Emma stared at him, feeling pole axed. Those dark eyes, messy hair, and chiselled cheeks. He'd broadened out, but other than that, he hadn't changed. How many years had it been since she'd last seen him? She inwardly rolled her eyes at her own rhetorical question. It had been eighteen years, two weeks, and probably about five days since he had left Redsworth. Jack Seymour. Even saying his name still caused her toes to curl in shame and her disloyal hormones to clang around her body.

Jack grabbed the handle of her now zipped suitcase and pulled it into the hallway. "So, are you looking for me, or Josh?"

Eventually finding her tongue, Emma dragged her case back into the doorway. "Neither of you. It's a mistake. I mean, a coincidence."

"You mean, you've literally just broken down outside?"

"Yes," Emma confirmed with a hard nod. "Is that so hard to believe?"

Jack looked at her quizzically, his chocolate brown eyes dancing with something akin to amusement.

"Okay." Emma shrugged. "It is hard to believe, but it's true."

"So, what are you doing here?" Jack managed to snatch her suitcase handle and bang the door shut before she could protest any further.

Emma paused. How much should she tell him? She listened to the loud ticking of a grandfather clock as she formed an excuse. "I'm here on business."

"In Thornhill?" Jack headed into a large kitchen. Feeling inclined to follow, Emma trudged behind him, her eyes centred on his broad shoulders and the small mole on the back of his neck that she'd always wanted to kiss. "Do you want me to ring someone and let them know you've arrived? Your mum, dad? Your sister?" Jack's eyes quickly flitted to her ring-free hand. "Anyone?"

"No." Emma stuffed her hands in the pocket of her raincoat. "I'm here for a job interview. I've applied for the role of farm shop manager in Thornhill Village."

"Impressive." Jack switched on the kettle and pulled two cups from a cupboard, giving her a chance to look around. Soft grey painted cupboards ran the length of one wall, flanking an old Aga, while the large inglenook fireplace, lit to ward off the unexpected cold of the summer night, crackled comfortingly in the background.

"Sugar?"

"No, I'm not staying."

Despite her remark, Jack continued to prepare two drinks. He placed a hot cup on the pine-scrubbed table and encouraged her to sit. Weariness eventually taking hold, Emma pulled out a heavy chair, wincing as it scraped on the old, tiled floor. She'd have one drink and leave.

"Well, this is a surprise." Jack rubbed his stubbly chin. "How are you?"

"Fine."

"Fine?" Jack crossed his muscly arms as a small smile played on his lips. "In my experience of women, that's normally code for '*anything but fine*'."

Emma sipped the hot tea and cursed her eyes for watering as her tongue burned under the heat. "All is well in my life."

"Good, I'm glad to hear it."

Her body bristled at his casual response. Had he any idea how much he'd hurt her? Obviously not. At the tender age of sixteen, she had nursed the most heart-wrenching crush on Jack, the eighteen-year-old rugby captain, the most attractive and studious boy in Redsworth High. Over time, crushes come and go, but when the object of your attention happened to be the big brother to your best friend, Josh, and lived in the house next door, getting over him wasn't an option. Their childhoods had been intertwined. Josh taught her how to fight, climb trees, and make water bombs. Jack had taught her the call of the birds and how to fish. He'd also unwittingly taught her how to fall in love.

Closure eventually came with the news that his family were to move away. The last few weeks of summer they'd spent together had been bittersweet. She'd tried to make the most of it, but knew when the time came, it would hit her hard, and it had. Casting her mind back, she still wondered if her life would have been better if she hadn't told Jack how she felt just before he left. It would have saved her the hurt and humiliation.

Flick, her older sister, had been supportive in her own teenage way following the fall-out of her revelation. When not teasing her for having fallen in love with a boy who barely noticed her, she had stroked her hair and told her to let him go. Given time, her wounds would heal, and she would eventually learn to love someone else. She hadn't.

"Would you like a bacon sandwich?" Jack looked at her with concern. "You look shattered."

Back in the present moment, Emma shook her head. She was going to do something she should have done years ago. She planned to walk away with her head held high and her dignity intact.

"Look…" Jack shrugged awkwardly. "…if you genuinely have broken down outside, then I can see it's going to be a shock to—"

"Oh my God." Emma swallowed her hot tea and momentarily winced. "Do you really think I came to find you? Are you still so big headed?"

Jack glanced at her in surprise. "Pardon?"

Emma braced herself for attack, and then paused. It would do her no good to start arguing with the locals before she'd even been offered the job. She suddenly halted her thoughts. If she got the job, she'd be living in the same village as Jack. Her shoulders suddenly fell. What kind of a fresh start would that be? Having to see him every day? Her three-hour journey now seemed rash, without thought, and a massive mistake.

"Actually, I'm going to go." Emma stood up as the kitchen door opened, bringing with it a shower of rain drops and a tall blond-haired man.

"Friggin' weather. I'm wet through." He shook the rain from his curly hair before his bright blue eyes widened in recognition. "Oh my God. Emma Francis."

Despite her upset, Emma felt a grin form on her lips as she took in Josh's familiar slim frame. As brothers, they shared very little in common, physically or mentally. Whereas Jack had always been the sensible one, olive-skinned with dark, serious eyes, Josh had been like a playful puppy. Excitable and irresponsible, but extremely loyal.

"I'm absolutely stunned." Josh took off his wet coat and pulled her into a warm embrace. "What are you doing here?"

"Long story," Emma muffled against his t-shirt, happy memories of their childhood antics flooding her mind. "My car broke down outside your farmhouse."

"No way." Josh hung up his coat and sat at the kitchen table. "Seriously?"

Conscious of Jack staring at her suspiciously, Emma simply nodded.

“Well, I wasn’t expecting this tonight. So, who are you with?”

“I’m on my own.” Emma checked Josh’s empty ring finger before hiding her own. She’d glanced at Jack’s within the first few seconds of talking to him. The bareness had surprised her.

“She’s got an interview at Thornhill Hall,” Jack explained as he leant casually against the worktop. “The role of farm shop manager.”

“Ah, so working for the posh boy.” Josh nodded. “Mixing with the gentry.”

“Posh boy?” Emma frowned.

“He means Toby Montgomery,” Jack explained. “His family owns all the property around here. Thornhill is a privately owned village. Apart from my farm. They don’t own this.”

Emma cringed as she detected trouble. “Is he not nice?”

“Let’s just say it’s very much them and us with the Montgomerys,” Josh replied. “Unfortunately, I have to work for them. I have a joinery business and, as they own most of the buildings, they commission my work. Hey, you won’t know about Daisy, will you?”

“Daisy? Your wife?”

“No.” Josh laughed. “God forbid, I’m not married. She’s our sister. Sixteen and a handful. A shock arrival after we moved here, but we love her to bits. Talking of sisters, how’s Flick?”

“She’s fine.” Emma smiled. “Married, three kids. She’s done well for herself. So, where are your mum and dad? Do they live here too?”

“Nah.” Josh shook his head. “Mum died ten years ago, and we don’t hear from dad. He remarried and lives abroad.”

“I’m sorry,” Emma replied quietly. “I didn’t know about your mum.”

"Well, it's been a long time since we've seen each other." Josh rubbed his hands together, keen to move the conversation on. "So, where are you staying in Thornhill?"

"Something Horse." Emma pulled her phone from her bag and checked the address. "The White Horse, just for one night."

"That may be a problem," Jack replied with a grimace. "It's covered in water after a flood two nights ago. Did they not ring you?"

For the umpteenth time that evening, Emma felt like burying her head in her hands and crying. How could she explain that she'd been ignoring phone calls, especially those from her disgruntled wedding organiser, who was keen to know why no one had been paid for the imminent event? It hadn't escaped her notice that her ex-fiancé, Sean, hadn't been one of those callers, concerned about her welfare or whereabouts.

Sensing her upset, Jack sighed. "Do you want to stay here?"

Feeling like an unwanted dog that everyone took pity on, but no one wanted responsibility for, Emma slowly nodded. She didn't have any choice.

"She can have my room," Josh replied. "I can sleep on the sofa tonight."

"No." Emma shook her head vigorously, suddenly feeling awkward. She and Josh would instantly pick up where they'd left off, but it would be a different story with Jack.

"Well, if you want your own space, there's always the piggery."

"Piggery?" Emma halted, wondering if this was a joke.

Josh grinned, noticing her stricken expression. "It's nice. You'll like it. Plus, if you stay here, it will give us a chance to catch up on the last eighteen years. What do you say?"

"I'll pay, of course." Emma opened her purse and viewed the few coins. "How much for a night?"

"Don't be daft," Josh replied. "We're not taking money from you."

"How about I help out with a few things in the morning before my interview?" Emma looked around the kitchen at the disorganised worktops and soot-covered hearth. "That way I'll feel like I've earned it."

Josh glanced at his brother. "It's a plan, isn't it?"

Emma glanced at Jack as he shoved his hands in his pockets and stared at his feet. He looked about as joyous as she felt.

CHAPTER 3

Emma followed Josh as he pulled her suitcase through a dimly lit courtyard and across a muddy field. As they reached an overgrown hedge, the full moon illuminated a low stone building with a slate roof. Emma could just make out two white leaded windows either side of a plain wooden door.

He placed a key in her hand. "I've put some bedding inside and a few bits and pieces so you can make a hot drink. Do you want anything else?"

"No, I'm okay," Emma whispered, glad of the darkness to cover up her wobbling chin. She felt tired, emotional, and grubby, and desperately in need of a friend.

"Hey, are you okay?"

"Sure." Emma nodded. Now wasn't the time to start pouring out her heart. "I'll be fine. I'll see you tomorrow, okay?"

Alone in the darkness and feeling rather nervous at the unfamiliar sounds, Emma unlocked the heavy door and edged inside the piggery. Her mouth fell open at the homely sight that greeted her. A log burner stood centre stage against one wall, facing a sofa bed and small coffee table. She walked around, her eyes immediately drawn to the clean stove and well-stocked kitchenette. With running water at a stone sink, a small bathroom annexed off behind a wooden door, and a stack of logs and kindling in a basket, it seemed she had everything she needed for a night's stay. Drawing the curtains, Emma locked the door, feeling surprisingly safe and secure for such a remote abode.

Instinctively checking her improved phone signal, she jumped as it shrilled into life.

"You are kidding me," her sister gasped as Emma explained her eventful evening. "The Seymour family?"

"Yep," Emma replied as she filled the old copper kettle and put it on the stove. "I knocked on the door and there he was."

"Wow, Jack Seymour. Now there's a name I've not heard in a while. Is he still as gorgeous?"

"So, so," Emma lied.

"Married?"

"I've no idea," Emma lied again as the kettle started to whistle. She took a cup from the kitchenette and made herself a drink before settling on the sofa with a well-placed blanket over her knees.

"And how about Josh? You two were like brother and sister. Is he still as cheeky?"

"I get the impression he is." Emma smiled as she recalled his scruffy t-shirt and ripped jeans. "I don't think he'll ever change."

Flick paused for a few seconds. "You don't have to do this, you know. You can come and stay with me. I know you were glad Sean gave you an excuse to leave him, but I also know it's dented your confidence. You simply made the mistake of trusting him."

"And I lost everything. My home and my job. I put all my eggs into one basket by working for that bastard."

"You've not lost us," Flick replied firmly. "We're still here. If you don't get that job, promise me you'll come straight to us."

"I promise." Emma coughed, hoping to disguise the lump of emotion at the back of her throat. "Anyway, did you know they have a little sister?"

"No way. How old is she?"

"She's sixteen. I haven't met her yet, but Josh said she's the spitting image of Jack."

"Gorgeous then," Flick replied drolly. "And good at flirting. The thing was, he was kind and mature with it."

"Was, being the operative word," Emma replied hotly. "He eventually showed his true colours after he read my love letter. Talk about making a fool of myself."

"You make my school days go faster," Flick recited dramatically. "My summers last longer—"

"Okay, okay." Emma cringed at the words she'd tried so hard to forget. Not only had she written him a love letter he ignored, but she'd also suggested one last evening together that he never turned up for. "I'll never forgive him," Emma huffed. "A whole hour I waited for him while all my schoolmates jeered at me. Each time the town clock struck another fifteen minutes, they started to laugh. Worse still, they couldn't wait to tell me the day after that he'd been inside the cinema all along … with another girl. And I ended up with that nickname. No wonder no one in Redsworth fancied me after that."

"Frigid Francis." Flick giggled. "It was catchy."

"Hey, you're meant to be on my side," Emma grumbled. "It's because of him I never dated. Every relationship I've had has been with someone I already know. I'm so glad I gave him that insulting letter as they were leaving for the Cotswolds. A barf bag. That's what I called him. He deserved it."

"But that was almost twenty years ago. If you're going to be living in the same village as him, then you need to let this go. You were both kids back then. You're adults now."

Emma rubbed her eyes tiredly. She knew Flick had a point. It had happened a long time ago and any other person with a life would have forgotten about it by now.

"It's strange he stayed on the farm," Flick continued. "I thought he planned on going to University."

"Well, he obviously didn't go to University because he's just a farmer."

A loud banging on the door caused Emma to jump and spill her tea down her jeans. Her heart banging against her chest, she peered cautiously around the curtains.

"I've tried fixing your car but it's as dead as a dodo and probably not worth the repairs." Jack held out her car keys. "If you want to help out in the morning, we start work at five-thirty."

Emma edged forward. "Five thirty as in…?"

"The morning," Jack clarified. "By the way, I did go to University. I studied agriculture. I got a first. Quite good for just a farmer."

Oh bollocks.

*

After cleaning her teeth in the small bathroom, Emma climbed under the thick duvet, hoping it would offer some comfort and protection against the feelings of loneliness. Why had she been so foolish? She'd trusted Sean, or had she? Was there a reason she'd kept all her other bank accounts separate from him? Turning over restlessly, she had to admit to some feelings of relief caused by his actions. Marrying Sean would have meant marrying his money troubles. Just because he supported her after the death of her parents didn't mean she owed him her life, but at least it meant she had belonged to someone. Now she felt like an abandoned piece of a jigsaw puzzle fitting into nobody's picture. Turning off the small lamp, she turned her head into her pillow and let the tears flow.

CHAPTER 4

Even from under her duvet, the sun made its presence known. Momentarily confused by what had awoken her, Emma opened her eyes and squinted around the warm room. Yesterday's events came flooding back and she buried her head under her pillow and groaned. How had she hit rock bottom so quickly?

About to fall back asleep, she jolted at the shrill squark that pierced her eardrums. Angry at the rude interruption, she dragged herself out of bed and tugged back the curtains. A rooster? Seriously? Stepping outside into the brightness, her jaw dropped at the acres of undulating landscape before her. Luscious green hills and fields rose and fell as far as the eye could see, all shimmering under a fine veil of morning mist. Grazing cows interspersed the view along with the rooftops of churches, farms and tiny cottages, smoke trailing lazily from their chimneys, even at this unearthly hour.

Emma glanced at her watch as the rooster crowed again. Quickly rummaging through her suitcase, she pulled on an old t-shirt and pair of denim shorts and pushed her feet into her trainers before looking down at her pale freckled legs and replacing the shorts with jeans. Eighteen years later, she still cared how she looked in front of Jack Seymour and she really shouldn't. Finally accepting she'd done what she could with her wild curls, she followed the cacophony of birdsong across a field and into a well-presented courtyard surrounded by yellow stone outbuildings. She looked around, amazed by the abundance of wildflowers and apple trees that cocooned the farm from the vastness of the rolling hills.

Approaching the thatched farmhouse, she tentatively tapped on the kitchen door, feeling a bit of a fool for the earliness of the hour. No one got up at this time of day, did they?

Jack opened the door and beckoned her inside. The soft lull of a radio and the comforting smell of bacon soothed her nerves, until the unmistakable, knee-wobbling fragrance of his woodsy shower gel intensified them again.

"Breakfast?" He pointed to the stove where a full plate of sausages, eggs, and bacon sat within her reach.

She glanced at the dirty plates on the table, curling a piece of hair around her finger. "I'll just have a piece of toast."

"You'll need a proper breakfast. Farming is hard work." Jack placed the full plate in front of her. "A slice of toast is for townies."

Lowering her eyes, Emma cut into the thick slices of bacon and dipped them into the golden yellow egg, her taste buds bursting with joy. Did food always taste this good or did the country air really change your senses?

"Are you ready to start work?"

Chewing on her last piece of toast, Emma stood up and put her empty plate into the sink and turned on the tap. He obviously had a strict timetable. "What do you need me to do?"

Josh interrupted her question by bounding into the room with his usual vibrancy. Judging by his dirty t-shirt and mud-stained jeans, he'd also been up for quite a while. He poured himself a coffee from the simmering percolator. "Sleep well?"

"Yeah, sure," Emma lied. They wouldn't want to know that she'd sobbed into her pillow for hours before falling into a restless sleep. "It's very quiet around here, isn't it?"

"When Daisy's asleep it is." Jack nodded to her jeans. "You'll need overalls. There's a spare pair in the parlour."

Emma's eyes widened as two curious chickens wandered into the kitchen and pecked at a few crumbs under the table. She glanced at the two brothers, who continued drinking their coffee. "I don't need overalls. I don't mind getting dusty with housework."

"Housework?" Jack furrowed his brow. "You're helping me milk the cows."

Spluttering on her coffee, Emma watched as a throng of black and white lumbering bodies made their way past the kitchen window, led by a stooped figure in a flat cap.

"I'll need to get going." Josh stood up and waved to the old man outside. "I'll meet you for dinner after your interview and see how you've got on. We're quite close to the village. There's a stream that runs by the side of the farm. Follow the path and it'll take you straight to Thornhill Hall." He ruffled her hair as he walked past. "Good luck with milking. Jack will show you the ropes."

Her stomach in knots, Emma followed Jack into a large honey stone building off the courtyard into a parlour full of gleaming white tiles and milking machines. A large gully ran down the middle, currently empty and as clean as the rest of the room. To her left, their great bodies pushing and steaming against a metal gate, stood the herd of cows she had spotted moments ago, their tails swishing as they mooed menacingly.

"Wash your hands at every opportunity. I don't compromise on cleanliness." Jack handed her a pair of brown overalls, which she stepped into and buttoned up before rolling up the legs. She glanced down at herself and sighed. *Great, I look ridiculous.*

Warning her to keep a distance, Jack pulled back the bolt and swung open the metal gate. The cattle ambled in calmly and slowly, almost as if they knew the process. Emma watched with fascination as they made their own way to the milking machines, walked into the harnesses, and munched away at troughs of fresh grain and hay.

Jack handed her a long pipe as he started to fix milking teats on a line of cows. "This is iodine. Do you know what to do with it?"

Emma took the pipe with as much confidence as she could muster. Her working life in hospitality had been about facing challenges. Double-booked rooms, famous hotel guests wishing to remain anonymous, romantic proposals, surprise birthday parties. She'd organised them all. If she could do all that without breaking into a sweat, she could figure this one out.

Looking hesitantly at the pipe in her hands, and aware of Jack watching her closely, she quickly pictured cattle in fields. With a vision in mind, she approached the first cow and pressed the gun leaver at its backside. Trying to ignore the pools of orange fluid filling the once clean gully, she made a perfect cross on its hind.

"What the bollocks are you doing?"

Emma lowered the pipe as Jack looked on in bewilderment at his orange tinted cow.

"I'm making a cross," Emma shrugged. "So, you know it belongs to you."

Jack covered his face with his hands. "Iodine is to disinfect their teats prior to milking." He rubbed at the large orange mark on the cow's backside. "It's not body paint. Surely you know the difference?"

"Oh yeah," Emma replied drolly, trying to hide her embarrassment. "We milked loads of cows as kids. Don't you remember our sessions after school?"

Jack simply rolled his eyes. "I didn't ask for sarcasm."

'And I didn't ask to be stood up!' Emma reigned in her caustic remark as she recalled Flick's advice. Life would be hard enough in a new village without enemies. "Actually, I can see what you're doing. Shall I do that while you do something else?"

"No, it's not safe for you to be alone with cattle when they barely know you." Jack examined the gauges and dials on the large tanks of milk. "They can behave unpredictably."

Sighing with frustration and tiredness, Emma ignored his comment and picked up a suction claw. Copying Jack, she placed it on the teat of a cow and looked around for what to do next. A button, a switch? There must be something to trigger the milking. Turning her back on the cattle, she tripped over a metal bucket, wincing as it clanged on the tiled floor. The cow she'd been attending to kicked up its back legs, sending her scuttling full length across the floor.

Before Emma had a chance to cry for help, Jack scooped her into his arms and held her close. Instinctively, she turned her head towards his chest, just as she'd done many years ago, after falling off her bike and breaking her wrist. He led her to a corner of the parlour, where he placed her down, his large frame protecting her. Eventually calming the cow enough to approach it, he led it back into its stall and closed the gate before turning to her, his eyes filled with concern. "Are you hurt?"

"No." Emma brushed back her curls with shaking hands. "I'm fine."

His eyes swiftly scanned her for cuts and bruises. "You were very lucky there. That cow wasn't fastened into the stall. You freaked her out. This isn't a place to disobey orders. The cows need to trust you, and you need to trust me. Is that a deal?"

Emma simply nodded.

"Okay." Jack put his hands on his hips and breathed out deeply. "I can't deny it shook me up. I'd forgotten how danger prone you were. I needed eyes in the back of my head when you were a kid, and it seems not much has changed." He picked up his water bottle and took a large drink before looking around. "Do you want to sweep up the cow pats instead? I think we'll get along better if you don't try killing us both."

Muttering under her breath, Emma grimaced at the steaming piles of muck and thanked her lucky stars that she didn't intend to stay here. Milking and farming were obviously not her forte. She gritted her teeth as splatters of cow muck spread around her legs as she swept, filling her nostrils with its pungent smell. Who on earth would choose to live here and do this?

"Emma, I'd move if I were you."

"I am moving. I'm working as fast as I can." Emma gasped as a warm dollop of cow muck slid slowly down her hair and face. The cow it came from swished its orange-coloured tail happily.

Jack sighed and rubbed a hand across his forehead. "I meant move to one side. Never mind. Go and have a shower. I'll sweep up later."

CHAPTER 5

"Why do these things always happen to me?" Emma grumbled as she shampooed her hair for the fifth time to eradicate the offensive smell. Eventually accepting the ancient shower would offer her no more cleanliness, she headed to the piggery and hastily dressed in her only skirt and blouse.

Sitting down at her makeshift dressing table, she grabbed handfuls of her frizzy hair and stared at it despondently. She'd planned on looking elegant for this interview. Smooth curls, perfect makeup, sleek city heels. The reflection in the mirror said otherwise. Pulling back her wayward hair, she slapped on a coat of lip gloss and jabbed herself in the eye with the mascara wand. If she added socks, she wouldn't be a million miles away from the schoolgirl who'd crushed after Jack at the tender age of fifteen.

After giving her reflection a well-needed pep-talk, she picked up her interview notes and set off in the direction of the village. The narrow country lane Josh had alluded to wasn't difficult to find. The trickling stream bubbled gently over rocks and stones, as if showing her the way, and the leafy trees provided much needed shelter from the heat of the late morning. As promised, within ten minutes of leaving the piggery, she found herself in a typical Cotswolds dream.

Standing on the village green near a large duck pond, she admired the uneven row of stone cottages and shops with their blooming gardens. Rows of bunting hanging between lamp posts flapped gently against the summer breeze, while the smells of burgeoning hanging baskets attracted interest from tourists and bees alike. Emma stood still and took in the bucolic riches of the countryside. The red telephone boxes, the gentle peel of laughter from the beer garden of the thatched pub "The Dusty Mouse", and the old hall that presided majestically over the village. Even the neglected barn set slightly off the green with its arched double doors and wooden pitched roof held its own romantic charm.

Feeling an anomaly in her suit and heels amongst the sunhats and sandals, Emma took off her jacket and re-read her interview instructions. She walked up the gravel driveway on wobbly legs towards the ivy-clad Georgian Hall and waited impatiently in the cool reception for someone to greet her. Her life hung in the balance of this next hour. It was make or break time. Being offered this job would grant her security. It came with accommodation, good pay, and as far away from Sean as she could get. She rehearsed her answers in her head as the butterflies in her stomach flitted around. If she didn't get the job. Well, she didn't want to think about that.

A young woman guided her down panelled corridors past many antiques and oil paintings. Money oozed out of the thickly carpeted floors and her insides turned to water with newfound nerves. Middle class, she was not. Like Jack and Josh, she had been brought up with nothing. She eventually found herself in a sun-filled office that overlooked private gardens where a young man sat alone.

Toby Montgomery, as he introduced himself after shaking her hand, surprised her. She'd been expecting an older, serious-looking man, but instead found a handsome blond of her own age, wearing a white linen shirt and casual blue jeans, sitting on the corner of his desk. With his quiff of sun-streaked hair and chiselled cheek bones, he epitomised suave. He invited her to take a seat before quickly scanning her application and smiling with startling lavender eyes.

"So, Emma, tell me a little bit about yourself."

Emma shifted in her seat, slightly thrown by his attractiveness and unusual irises. "My professional background is mainly in hotels and restaurants. More recently, I worked in—"

Toby smiled and held up his hand. "Let me stop you there. I'm interested in you. What do you like doing? What's your passion? What gets your heart beating and your mind racing?"

Emma stared blankly. What did she like doing? She had no hobbies or interests. As for passion, did that really exist? Did people seriously wake up with such joy that they jumped out of bed, eager to go somewhere or do something? Heart beating? Mind racing? Her palms started to sweat as her mind remained empty. Nothing. She had nothing.

"Would you like a drink of water?" Toby asked gently. "I'm very sorry. I should have offered you a drink from the start."

Emma nodded and managed to whisper a thank you as he slipped off his desk and left the room. She let out a deep breath of nerves. Jesus, what on earth was she doing here? What could she offer a place like this? She'd never worked for the middle class before. She'd looked after them as guests, obviously, but her employers had been like her; keen to keep their jobs and move up the ladder. None of them had owned the estate, and certainly none of them had looked as good as him.

"Would you like the window open?" Toby walked back in looking calm and collected, bringing with him a heady oriental aroma. He placed a glass of sparkling water by her side and the remainder of the expensive bottle.

She looked up to see him smiling with his unusual eyes as he resumed his position on the desk. Had he sat there to appear non-aloof? Casual? Approachable? His understanding gaze certainly said so. She'd never been interviewed by anyone like this before and she sensed that her pre-prepared answers would not cut it here. This guy oozed confidence, and he would expect the same of his staff. Well, if he wanted to know the real Emma, she would give it to him.

"In answer to your first question, I'm afraid my life experiences haven't offered me hobbies and interests; instead, they have provided me with strengths."

Emma waited for his hand to go back up, but instead found him moving expectantly to the end of his desk.

"Not everyone sees those strengths as attributes, mainly because they are ones of survival and to most, that's a basic gift. While others around me have been busy filling their social media with new relationships and job promotions, I've been keeping my head above water and that has involved more skill and determination than any hobby. How do I prove that? Well, for example, two days ago, I left my fiancé and my job. Most people would crumble under that kind of pressure, but I've not had that luxury. I could either drown under life's waves or I could swim. I've chosen to swim. I have no idea where my future will take me, but I know I'll navigate it with pride and dignity, and those are attributes that cost nothing. I guess what I'm trying to say, Mr. Montgomery, is if you're looking for someone who can do this job while you get on with yours, then I am undoubtedly that girl."

Exhilarated, Emma stopped, her words surprising herself. Her back straightened up without effort, and she felt the first stirrings of excitement at her new future without Sean. It didn't matter so much now if she didn't get the job, as she knew she would survive.

Toby eyed her thoughtfully. "So you have no notice period to serve?"

"That's correct."

"The address on your application is for a town quite a distance from here. Where are you currently staying?"

"I'm staying with a friend in the village. That address is my sisters, and the best to use for now." Toby didn't need to know she had no fixed abode and was living in a piggery with her once best mate and her old high school crush.

"When can you start?"

Emma's jaw fell open. "Seriously, after just one question?"

"Seriously." Toby's lavender eyes twinkled. "You've impressed me."

Shaking her head in amazement, Emma laughed. "I can start tomorrow if you need me. Is this a job offer?"

"It is. You're the last person to be interviewed and by far the best." Toby slipped off his desk and sat in the chair opposite. Emma didn't miss the significance of this. Before they had been informal, now they were formal. "I've never been surer of anything in my life. You've just ticked every box."

Her feet dancing under the table in excitement, Emma thought about her own questions. "Where is the accommodation that comes with the role? Is it in the village?"

"Ah." Toby grimaced. "There is no accommodation. That was an error in the advertisement. Our Parish Council isn't the greatest at factual content. Is that a problem?"

Emma's shoulders slumped. She'd come all this way for a clerical error. Now what?

"Could you possibly stay with your friend until a property becomes available?"

She cursed under her breath. Everything had been going so well. Talk about a curveball. However, did she have any choice? "I'll sort something out," Emma eventually responded.

"Wonderful." Toby stood up and shook her hand warmly. "I can't tell you how pleased I am. You are like a breath of fresh air. I can meet you outside the barn on the village green where the farm shop is situated tomorrow morning and take you through what needs doing." He opened a drawer and took out a business card, writing down all the relevant details on the back. "We'll be working together closely on this venture. Will that be okay?"

Emma gave her best smile, feeling more positive by the minute. That was perfectly fine by her.

CHAPTER 6

"Well done." Josh congratulated her as they sat under the shade of a much-needed parasol outside the White Rabbit village bakery. "I knew you'd smash it."

Emma returned the high five as she admired the Mad Hatter-themed window display of exquisite cakes and pastries. Whoever owned this place certainly knew how to attract customers of all ages.

"You look disappointed. What's the problem?"

"The job doesn't come with accommodation." Emma perused the menu decorated with miniature rabbits and clocks. Each section was labelled with either '*Drink me*' or '*Eat me*'. "The advert said it did."

"Ah, that will be our very unreliable Parish Council. They can't get anything right, but accommodation will be a problem if that's what you're after. People move to Thornhill for a better standard of life, and they stay here. The remainder of the rooms are booked by tourists and will be all summer."

Emma's resolve melted like ice cream on a hot day.

"Look, let me have a chat with Jack about you staying in the piggery. He desperately needs help. Clive, our farm hand is getting on in years and needs to rest, but he refuses to take it easy because he knows he's needed."

Thinking back to this morning's disaster in the parlour, Emma shook her head. "I can't, Josh. I'm no farmer. I know my limits and that's beyond me." She didn't add that being so close to Jack would cause further complications. She cringed each time she thought about that love letter. Thank God Josh had never known about it.

"So, what's your suggestion? Where would you stay otherwise? You've accepted the job. You need somewhere to live."

"I know." Emma sighed. "What a mess."

"Let me speak to Jack," Josh said kindly. "You two were always close as kids. We'll sort it out." He raised a hand and pointed to the sunny sky. "It's a nice day, and you've just smashed an amazing interview. Let's talk about something else. Tell me about the last eighteen years. What's the highlights?" Josh pointed to the white mark around her ring-free finger. "Or the low lights."

Emma rolled her eyes at his lack of tact. He'd never beaten around the bush in his life. "There's not much to tell. After you left Redsworth, I went to college and eventually onto University. I studied hospitality and worked my way up in the hotel industry."

"Well, that's a good overview of your professional career. I was kind of hoping you'd enthral me with a torrid sex life."

Emma had to laugh. "I'm afraid there isn't one. My road map is simple, with very little in the way of deviances." She took a deep breath; she'd have to tell him at some point. "Mum and Dad died."

Josh closed his eyes and silently cursed before taking hold of her hand across the table.

"It's okay." Emma nodded, reassuring herself more than anyone else. "I've coped so far, but I know how close you were to them."

"So, is that why you're here with us?"

"No, I genuinely didn't come looking for you. Although thinking about it, Thornhill probably rang a bell, but not consciously. The reason I'm here is because I made the mistake of trusting someone with my heart. To cut a long story short, I moved in with him, and to cut the story even shorter, two days ago, I moved out."

"Ah," Josh sat back in his chair and nodded. "I figured a man had to be behind all of this. So, what did he do? Dip his nib in someone else's ink?"

That explanation suited Emma just fine. In fact, it made her story more plausible. She would confide in him at some point about the Ferrari and the wedding. Just not today.

"Well, you've got something in common with our Jack then. A failed relationship. His personal life is what you would call complicated." Josh signalled to the woman behind the counter that they were ready to order. "If you're working in the farm shop, you'll need to get to know Milly. She runs this place, but I'm warning you, she's not as sweet as she looks."

Emma craned her neck to get a better look at the petite young woman with the long dark hair and ankle-length yellow sundress. "She looks okay to me," she replied, liking the look of her pixie face and big blue eyes. "What's wrong with her?"

"She's a mini rottweiler," Josh murmured. "Prepare to be bitten."

Milly took their orders before staring at Emma curiously. "If you're his girlfriend, you're best ordering your own food."

Josh scowled. "Very funny. She's not my girlfriend and we just want two coffees and two choux buns."

Milly raised her eyebrows at Emma, as if confirming the order.

"That's fine with me." Emma smiled in response as she bit back her intrigue. "And I'm definitely not his girlfriend. Just an old school friend."

"Wise woman." Milly shook Emma's hand with a welcoming grin. "It would have to be someone brainless to take him on. So, what's a nice girl like you doing with an idiot like him?"

Josh rolled his eyes as Emma started to laugh. "I'm staying with him for a few nights until I can get somewhere permanent to live. I've just been offered the role of manager of the farm shop."

"Cool." Milly nodded approvingly. "New blood. This village needs it. It's a shame I didn't know earlier about your arrival. I've just rented my spare room out to someone."

"You wouldn't want to live with her," Josh replied quickly as Emma's face fell. "She needs all her free space for her cauldron. Sorry, did I just say that out loud?"

Milly tutted before turning back to Emma. "If you get fed up with talking to this knob head, give me a shout. I'm much nicer than he is, and I'm better looking, too."

Emma laughed at Milly's sassy smile as she headed back to the bakery. "I really like her. What's the story between you two?"

"Let's just say it was a date that went very wrong. I took her out one evening to an artisan food market. Think twinkly lights, soft music, meandering around cobbled streets full of quaint stalls. Things were going well until I kissed her."

"How bad at kissing are you?" Emma asked, trying to keep a straight face. "I know we never shared that delight, but I had the impression you were educated in that department from your brother, at least."

"Hey, I'm good at kissing." Josh huffed. "At least that's what I've been told."

"So, what did she do? Smack you with her handbag?" Emma had to grin at Josh's closed expression. "Oh, come on. What happened? Spit it out."

"She vomited."

Snorting into her hands, Emma laughed. "What did you do to her?"

"Nothing. I literally just kissed her. About five minutes later, she vomited all over my jeans, and then she disappeared for ages. I told her not to drink so much cider. I had to travel home on the train covered in the contents of her stomach, and she's barely spoken to me since. In fact, she goes out of her way to make my life as awkward as possible. She's a pain in the arse. I feel sorry for any guy who takes her on."

Milly may be strong minded, Emma thought with amusement as she bit into her chocolate filled choux pastry, but she could certainly bake. As for attention to detail, she had it completely nailed down, right from the Queen of Hearts napkins to the delicately iced clocks on the complimentary shortbread biscuits.

"Come on." Josh left money on the table as they cleaned their plates of any remaining crumbs. "I'll walk around the village with you, make sure you know your way around. Not that it's exactly a metropolis."

Emma gazed upon the small stone shops, all boasting pastel painted doors, their bay windows filled with sun hats and postcards. There may not have been much in the way of high street shops, but as for an idyllic countryside, this place had it in abundance.

She stopped halfway around their short tour to buy ice creams from the wisteria-covered Post Office. "So, Joshy boy, seeing as we're getting to know each other again, do you have a girlfriend?" Emma paused. "Or a boyfriend?"

"I'm not gay," Josh confirmed with a slight smile. "But in answer to your question, I'm happy being single."

Aiming to act casual, Emma asked the burning question, "And Jack?"

"He wouldn't touch a serious relationship if it was covered in gold, not after what happened to him. He's still as popular with the ladies though. He shovels cow muck for a living, and they insist on falling at his feet."

Emma glanced at her friend's tanned face and ruffled blond hair. Josh, as expected, had grown into a good-looking man. If she didn't see him as a very annoying brother, she may have been interested. "Are you jealous?" she teased.

"Hey, I have my charms too," Josh replied with mock offence as he flexed his biceps. "I'll have you know I'm quite a catch around here."

"Except you don't want to be caught?"

"Exactly." Josh laughed as he ate the last of his ice-cream and licked his messy fingers. "The problem with women is that they try to fix you, and I don't want to be fixed. My un-ironed clothes are a style."

"They're scruffy." Emma giggled at his moth-eaten t-shirt. "But you're right, they have an appeal. So, what have you been doing for the past eighteen years?"

"Building up the joinery business mainly. It was something I got into after leaving school. I started doing a few jobs around the farm and it turns out I have the knack for it. Basically, I'm self-taught."

"The farm is in good condition," Emma conceded. "But I guess if you live there, you want to look after it."

"Technically, I shouldn't be living there. I did have my own cottage in the village, but I had to move out. I couldn't afford the rent."

They strolled peacefully around the remainder of the village, catching up on each other's news as Josh pointed out places she'd need to know. It reminded Emma of their teens, when they had shared their wishes and dreams. He'd wanted to be an adventurous explorer back then, inspired by action movies. She could still recite *Raiders of the Lost Ark* in her sleep. He'd always claimed he was tough, trying to live in his older brother's shoes, but then they'd watched her favourite actor in his best film, *Ghost*, and his pretence had unravelled.

"So, you like the place?" Josh asked as they found themselves back on the village green. "Do you think you've made the right decision taking the job?"

Emma breathed in the peaceful landscape, where even fresh bedding on washing lines blew at a gentle pace. This is exactly what she needed. Somewhere quiet she could heal and find herself again.

"Come on." Josh put his arm around her shoulders. "Let's go speak with Jack."

CHAPTER 7

If she could have rolled her eyes and got away with it, Emma would have done so, but that wouldn't help her in this endeavour. She needed the piggery, and as much as she hated to admit it, Jack held the cards to that happening. Her common sense told her she should be grateful, but instead, she just felt humiliated.

"I can't believe you felt you had to ask." Jack picked up a bale of straw and threw it near the chicken pen before heading towards the kitchen. "You should know me better than that. Of course you can stay, but I want nothing to do with Toby Montgomery."

"You won't need to," Emma replied, following him into the welcoming coolness of the farmhouse. "It's me who's working with him, not you. Anyway, why don't you like him? He seemed fine to me."

When Jack didn't reply, Josh intervened. "There's bad blood between the families because we won't sell the farm to them. That basically sums it up."

"You're not on about the Montgomerys again, are you?"

Emma turned to see a young girl skip into the kitchen wearing a pink cotton top and denim shorts that showed off her long slim legs. With her big brown eyes, dark hair, and olive skin—just like her elder brother's—this had to be Daisy.

"Are you going to say hello to our new guest?" Josh prompted his sister. "This is Emma, my best friend from my years in Redsworth. She's going to be staying in the piggery for the time being."

"Oh, cool." Daisy pulled her long dark hair into a ponytail and gave Emma a friendly grin. "Some female company at last. Perhaps you can talk them into letting me stay out tonight, because they don't understand what it's like to be sixteen."

"I remember it very well," Jack replied with mock sternness as he stretched his long legs under the kitchen table. "I also remember what I got up to at that age, and for that reason, you're home by ten and no later."

Daisy tutted dramatically, causing Emma to smile. With her petite frame and stunning features, she could understand Jack's protectiveness. For a moment, it brought back a pang of nostalgia. He used to look out for her, too. A long time ago.

"Why were you talking about the Montgomerys?" Daisy headed over to the fridge and stuck her head inside, her voice muffled as she eagerly searched the shelves.

"Because Emma will be working for Toby," Jack replied. "In the new farm shop."

"Really?" Daisy paused in her search and looked at her brothers sceptically. "And you're supporting that?"

"Let's say we're setting some ground rules." Jack glanced at Emma before turning his attention back to the papers in front of him. "What have you done today, Tilly Mint?"

"Almost everything you asked," Daisy replied dryly. "I fixed that section of dry-stone wall and painted the fence, but I didn't have time to clean the other barn. We need more hands on this farm."

"This is where Emma can help," Josh replied. "She's offered to assist in the parlour so you can concentrate on setting up the cheese business again."

"In the parlour?" Jack raised his head in alarm. "I don't think so."

"Actually…" Emma tentatively raised her hand. "…I didn't offer to work in the parlour. What's this cheese thing?"

"Mum's old business in the other barn." Josh pointed to a smaller stone building with a slate roof and dove cote walls. An old rose rambled around the windows, making it appear less ramshackle and more enchanting. "She sold the cheese we made from there. Daisy is aiming to get it up and running again. The parlour is where we need the most help though."

"It's not happening," Jack replied firmly. "She can help Daisy with the cheese shop. That's my final answer."

Emma stared at him challengingly. Throughout her youth, he'd always seen her as Josh's little friend. The annoying kid who hung around with them, falling over, cutting her knees, and having to be pulled out of all kinds of scrapes. Perhaps it was time to show him she'd grown up.

"She's a quick learner," Josh said, continuing to fight her battle. "You remember Emma from being young. Nothing phased her. I mean, come on, you both got on so well as kids before we left Redsworth. What's changed? I've got to say, it sounds to me like there's some tension between you two."

Emma felt her toes curl as Jack continued to stare at her, and she secretly pleaded with him to keep quiet about that stupid love letter. She understood the contents of it must have embarrassed him. If he'd thought she only ever saw him as a friend, then reading it would have given him one hell of a shock, and judging by his sharpness with her since her arrival, one he hadn't forgotten, but he had to leave her with some dignity.

"There's no tension between us," Jack replied. "However, my answer is still no. She's not cut out for farm life."

"I beg your pardon?" Emma said, her relief at his discretion replaced with indignation. "You think this is too hard for me?"

"Yeah, I do." Jack shrugged unapologetically as he glanced at her sombre interview outfit. "I'm not trying to be argumentative, but I've never seen anyone as out of place on a farm in my life."

"Right." Emma threw down the gauntlet as her cheeks burned with irritation. "Did you say five thirty in the morning? I'll be there, and I'll show you exactly what I'm made of, and don't try to stop me because I'll do it regardless."

Jack opened his mouth to respond before shaking his head in resignation. "Whatever. I don't know why I'm bothering to argue. You always were a stubborn so and so."

"And that's the pot calling the kettle black," Josh mumbled, his eyes flitting between the pair suspiciously. "Well, I'm glad we've got that sorted."

"Hey, you'll be able to come to the summer ball with us," Daisy said excitedly as she ripped the top off a yogurt pot. "It's the only thing the Montgomerys do well. They host one during summer, autumn, and winter to thank the locals for their hard work. Do you want to come with us? Or you could be a miserable bugger like my big brother and not go at all."

"You know why I don't go," Jack replied with a warning glare.

"Well, I'm going." Daisy scraped out the yogurt pot and threw the dirty spoon in the sink with a clatter, causing Jack to roll his eyes. "It's really dressy."

"Ah." Emma paused, thinking about the creased t-shirts, shorts, and jeans still unpacked in her suitcase. "How dressy?"

"Very," the young girl replied. "But don't worry, my friend is the same size as you. She'll lend you something to wear. She's a lot younger, but we'll get round that."

Emma caught Josh's eye and smiled at the unintended insult. Kids had no filter.

"Well, you lot can sit here talking about parties, but I've got work to do." Jack nodded to Emma as he headed back onto the courtyard. "Five thirty tomorrow morning. Are you sure you're up for this?"

"Just watch me." Emma smiled sweetly. "I'll surprise you."

*

After speaking with Flick and filling her in about the job offer, Emma pulled her suitcase from a corner of the room and unzipped it. She hadn't expected to do this, to make a home on this farm. Putting her clothes into a chest of drawers and finding space for her other belongings, she eventually sat down on her doorstep and admired the sun as it started to set, turning the landscape into a kaleidoscope of pinks, crimsons, and purples. There had to be worse places to live, she mused, looking down upon the rolling hills as the scents of wild honeysuckle and viburnums invaded her senses.

The cold air eventually forced her inside, and Emma threw a match on the log burner, turning the paper twirls a comforting orange. Making up her sofa bed, she curled up under her blankets with a hot drink, feeling safe and secure amongst her familiar belongings.

She knew the significance of this. Her agreeing to take on this role meant a final goodbye to Redsworth. Sean wouldn't take her back now, even if she wanted him to, and she didn't. She'd agreed to marry him simply out of a wish to belong to someone, but there was belonging and there was being owned. She could see that now.

Looking around the small room, she suddenly smiled. She'd come a long way in the past few days, and she still had far to go, but she'd survive. As for tomorrow, she'd show Jack just how tough she could be. She put down her cup and turned off her bedside light, listening to the unfamiliar sounds of the countryside. If he still remembered the sixteen-year-old with the Ribena mouth and baggy socks, then he'd be in for a shock.

CHAPTER 8

Forced out of her cocoon by the loud rooster, Emma made a cup of tea and quickly dressed in an old pair of jeans and a faded brown t-shirt. She wouldn't give Jack any reason to raise his eyebrows at her non-farming clothing today. In fact, she felt determined not to give him any reason to find fault with her at all. With this in mind, she pulled her curls into a disorganised bun and slipped her feet into her trainers before heading towards the farmhouse.

The radio could be heard playing quietly in the kitchen. She peered cautiously through the open door to find the warm room empty. If it wasn't for the used breakfast plates and uninvited hens clucking under the table, she'd be forgiven for thinking she'd been the first to arrive.

"There you are." Jack pushed open the door behind her, causing her to jump. "Come on, we've got work to do."

She followed him into the parlour, grimacing at the earthy smell. He threw her a fresh pair of overalls and went to examine the large milk tanks.

"Right, you're going to learn how to milk a cow today." Jack encouraged her to wash at a small sink before throwing her a roll of tissue. "By hand."

"What!" Emma looked at him incredulously. "Are you being serious? All of them?"

"Not all of them," Jack bit his lip in what may have been amusement. "When I know you understand what you're doing, I'll train you to use the machinery."

He led her over to a cow tethered to the wall with a rope. Emma approached hesitantly, the incident from yesterday morning still fresh in her memory.

"She's the most placid of my cattle." Jack smacked the cow on its hind as it turned to view Emma with soft, curious eyes. "You'll have no trouble with her."

She concentrated as Jack cleaned the teats, squeezing them effortlessly. Her eyebrows raised as milk flowed into the metal bucket below.

"Looks easy." Emma nodded, trying to not pull a face at the huge udders hanging underneath the distended stomach. "I can do that."

"Fine." Jack kicked a small milking stool her way. "Hand milk her and let me know when you're done."

Emma sat on the stool and resisted biting her thumbnail. Was he watching her? Her neck ached with trying not to look. Five seconds later, she risked a peek only to find him writing notes on a clipboard. Of course he wasn't watching her. She cricked her neck and returned to the cow. Okay, just squeeze, nice and gently, like he did. There was nothing weird about this at all. This is how they milked years ago, wasn't it?

Ten minutes later, her bucket remained empty, and her thumb had started to hurt. Jack's line of cows had moved on, ready to go back to the field, and she still wrestled with one teat.

"Done?" Jack approached and stared into her empty bucket. "What's the problem?"

"This!" Emma rubbed her sore muscles in her hand. "It doesn't work."

Jack laughed at her frustration before bending down and squeezing milk into the bucket with an ease that just wasn't possible. "Where's the stubborn kid that wouldn't go home until she'd beaten me in a race? Try again."

Groaning, Emma bent down and rubbed her aching back. Despite the gathering heat haze already forming over the fields, the parlour felt cool, especially when sitting in one position near a cold floor. Once again, she squeezed, to no avail. Standing up, she attempted to stamp some life into her aching limbs.

"Giving up?" Jack glanced her way as he pulled back the holding gate and maneuvered another batch of cattle around. "Is it not easy work, for just a farmer?"

"Sod off," Emma muttered. Did he genuinely wish to make her life a misery? Admittedly, she'd called him a barf bag, but if anyone should be feeling angry, it should be her. He'd left her standing there like a prat in front of her school friends. It was his fault she'd turned down so many dates, and it was his fault she'd never fully fallen in love again.

She sat back down on her stool and closed her eyes before giving herself another pep talk. She needed to concentrate on the task in hand, otherwise she'd be homeless and jobless again. Right, cows got pregnant, they produced milk. Nature shouldn't be this hard. Plus, she'd had worse experiences than this and survived them. In fact, considering everything she'd been through in the past few days, this shouldn't be hitting the Richter scale at all. Pulling back her shoulders, she flexed her neck and tried again.

"Oh my God!" Emma jumped up, knocking over the bucket as milk flowed onto the floor. "I did it." She turned to Jack excitedly. "I've just milked a cow!"

"Good." Jack walked past her with barely a flicker of emotion. "Now fill that bucket."

She stared at him in dismay. "Are you kidding me?

"Does it look like it?" Jack replied with a perfectly straight face. "Thankfully, we have generators in the back of the parlour for power cuts, but if they failed, we'd need to milk by hand. All day if needs be."

For the next hour, her hands, arms, and neck ached, but she milked and milked until the bucket almost spilled over. Sweat clung to her back and the curls that had come loose from her bun matted on her forehead, but she didn't care. She'd show him.

Eventually she stood up on numb legs as the muscles in her calves spasmed, causing her to stumble. She leant against a wall for support whilst rubbing her aching hands.

Walking past, Jack casually picked up her milking bucket and threw the contents down a nearby drain. Emma gasped as she watched the white liquid disappear down the grid. "Why did you do that?" she shouted, hands on hips, her red face contorted in fury. "I spent ages filling that bucket."

"I don't take risks on my farm with unprocessed produce." Jack handed her a cleaning cloth. "Now you can learn how to sterilise the equipment after milking and your morning's work should be done."

Emma snatched the cloth from his hands and cursed her stupid car for breaking down outside his farmhouse. If only it could have lasted another mile, she'd have been at the mercy of Toby Montgomery and his sumptuous sofas. Bloody typical.

*

The walk along the bubbling steam helped to soothe her mind and aching muscles. She knew things would become easier the more familiar she became with the routines, but right now she could only feel weariness. Leaving the thicket of trees, Emma entered the bustling village green where tourists and locals meandered in shorts and t-shirts, morning newspapers tucked under their arms as they walked their four-legged friends. For them, their day had only just begun; for her, it felt like mid-afternoon.

"Hello, stranger." Toby approached from the other side of the duck pond, wearing a light blue shirt and cream chinos. He warmed her with his welcoming smile. "Are you ready to start your first day?"

"My first day started before five o'clock this morning," Emma walked with him towards the old barn, suddenly regretting her choice of denim shorts and a white t-shirt. At the time, they'd seemed fresh and casual, but now, in comparison to Toby's outfit, they looked cheap. Seeing his questioning look, she paused. He'd find out about her living arrangements at some point. "I'm staying with Jack Seymour on his farm. I've been up since five this morning helping him in the dairy parlour."

"Oh, right." Toby frowned deeply. "So, he's the friend you mentioned yesterday. Are you two…?"

"Oh, God no." Emma laughed, finishing his sentence. "You couldn't be further from the truth. We've not seen each other for almost twenty years and we're not quite as compatible as we once were. Let's just say relations are a little fraught between Jack and me."

"That doesn't surprise me." Toby diverted his path and headed towards the bakery. "I take it he's told you we don't see eye to eye?"

Emma raised her eyebrows with a slight smile to convey her reply.

"I had hoped the passing of my father would be the end of it, but he still holds a grudge."

"I'm sorry." Emma stalled. "I didn't know you'd lost your father."

Toby nodded. "A few weeks ago now. He ran this village. My family owns all the properties around here. With his passing, it means I take over."

"Huge responsibilities then?" Emma replied, looking around her at the immaculate cottages. "Aren't you daunted?"

"Nope, I can do this with my eyes closed." Toby disappeared inside the already busy bakery and came out with a warm blueberry muffin and a hot latte. “Anyway, less of my woes. You look like you need some sustenance.”

Taking the offerings, Emma cringed. He hadn’t even said hello properly and she’d already started to moan about her life on the farm. Not exactly appropriate for her first day.

“I didn’t expect this.” Emma broke off a corner of the muffin and nibbled it with as much delicacy as she could muster, given her empty stomach. “I wasn’t looking for sympathy.”

“I know you weren’t. I’m simply trying to be supportive.” Toby smiled as she groaned with pleasure at the strongly flavoured coffee. “Jack should be looking after you, not treating you like cheap labour, but that’s him all over. Self-centred.”

Realising she could potentially be stepping on dodgy ground, Emma looked for a change in subject. “So, the barn?”

“Yep,” Toby swapped her coffee for a large set of keys that lay heavily in her hands, reminding her of the responsibility she had taken on board. “Do you want to do the grand unveiling?”

The minute the large door opened, excitement filled her. She breathed in the sweet smell of straw that lingered from years of the barn being an instrumental part of farm life. After taking in the beauty of the dusty wooden rafters, sun speckled windows, and powder-covered slate floors, her eyes eventually fell on a smiling Toby.

“What do you think?” he asked.

Emma spun around, admiring the old mezzanine level. “I love it.”

“I knew you would.” Toby crossed his arms and looked upwards at the vaulted ceiling, providing Emma with an opportunity to study him. It couldn’t be denied; he was a cute looking guy. Those unusual lavender eyes against his bronzed skin gave him a Californian beach look. Toned, tanned and healthy. Others would say, rich looking. Did his position intimidate her? A little, but it also added an extra sense of excitement. She walked slowly around the barn, examining the shelves, dressers, and chests of drawers that had stood untouched for years. This felt more her thing, dealing with people and customers.

Now on more familiar ground, she started to weigh everything up. Refrigerators, fruit baskets, ways and means of displaying goods outside. Ideas swarmed, causing spurts of excitement. Any doubts she'd had about taking on this role suddenly evaporated away like the mist on the hills this morning.

"What are you thinking?"

Toby's voice interrupted her thoughts and she turned to him with a wide grin. "I'm thinking I need to get busy. We've contracts to organise, shelves to fill and customers to entice. I'm thinking of ladders outside with potted plants and fresh herbs. Hanging baskets made by locals, a corner dedicated to handmade crafts. We can arrange to stock local wines, jams, gins even."

Toby laughed at her eager expression. "I knew you were the girl for this job the minute I set eyes on you. This village is attracting more and more interest every year and we need to move with the times. Dad had plenty of enthusiasm, I'll give him that, but he was archaic in his approach. I'm looking forward to shaking things up a bit." Toby shrugged with fake nonchalance. "It's a hard job, but someone has to do it."

Emma laughed at his ability to make fun of himself. "Does that not fill you with dread? Being the public face of a village as popular as this?"

"Not really. I've always known it would pass to me one day. Officially, from tomorrow evening at least. That's when the will gets read and the title passes over. I guess it's a bit like being part of a royal family. It's a role you're born into." Toby passed her a winning smile. "Anyway, who's asking the questions here? Aren't I supposed to be finding out about you?"

"You've already interviewed me," Emma replied breezily. "You had your chance."

"Ah, a girl with confidence. I like it."

Emma smiled to herself as she walked around the room. This was exactly what she needed. Someone to boost her self-belief.

Whether Toby had attempted to flirt with her or not, she didn't know, but his interest in her felt refreshing.

"You've got me for another hour, so what else would you like to know?"

Only an hour? Emma hoped the surprise didn't show on her face. Did he plan to leave the rest to her completely?

"I'd have stayed for longer but we've the summer ball to organise for tomorrow night and I'm afraid I'm running out of time." Toby paused and looked at her hesitantly. "Forgive me, I'm talking about an event you've probably not received an invite to. If you're free, would you like to join me?"

"Erm…" Emma wondered how Josh would feel if she went with Toby Montgomery himself. "I'm not sure…"

"Eight o'clock. Don't worry about not having an official invite card. That won't be an issue." Toby held his arms out and shrugged. "After all, I own the hall."

Emma blushed like a teenage girl. How could she possibly refuse?

*

By mid-afternoon, she'd achieved what she set out to do. The furniture had been scrubbed clean and now stood drying in the warm air, ready to be positioned, and the floors and windows now sparkled after their vigorous attack with vinegar and warm water.

With the radio playing softly in the corner of the room, the sounds of laughter floating in through the open doors, and the frequent friendly head popping in to welcome her to village life, it had been a pleasurable, if not relaxing, day. Taking an opportunity to drink in the fresh air, she stood in the doorway of the barn and watched families gather by the pond with their picnics.

"You look part of the village already." Josh laughed as he carried a large rucksack. "According to my brother, you missed breakfast this morning. He's made you a sandwich."

Josh sat down on the warm grass, removing his t-shirt to bare a tanned, toned chest. "I'm here to start any work you need in the barn. How's your day going so far?"

"Started bad, getting better," Emma mumbled between mouthfuls of sandwich. The muffin this morning had filled a corner, but her hard work had resulted in a very empty stomach. Feeling a little cheeky, she rummaged in the bag, relieved to find fresh fruit, yogurt, and a large piece of fruit cake. She looked at it longingly.

"Go ahead, all that's yours. I've got my own." Josh lay on the grass and squinted up against the blue sky. "This is like the good old days, isn't it? You and I, eating outside."

Emma smiled at the memories. It had taken her a long time to open her mind to the '*good old days*' since the passing of her parents. Time was a great healer, they said, but time also meant it created a distance, and as the years went by, she fought to remember each detail. Sometimes it felt like they were slipping through her fingers.

"How are you finding the locals?" Josh asked as he rolled to his side to face her. "There's a lot of loyalty around here. Kick one and we all bark. Apart from that lot, of course." Josh pointed towards the hall. "I bet the first thing Toby does is increase the rent prices. I don't think he realises that higher rent means we have to charge tourists more, which in turn means they go elsewhere."

Emma decided not to reply. She didn't want to be the piggy-in-the-middle.

Catching her hesitancy, Josh rolled his eyes. "I know. I'll change the subject. Have you had a chance to think about the summer ball yet? Are you coming?"

Biting the inside of her cheek, she decided to get it over with. "Actually, Toby invited me to go with him."

"Ah." Josh nodded. "I figured he might. Does he know you're staying on our farm?"

"I told him this morning." Emma nibbled the end of her thumbnail. "Is it a problem, me going to the ball with Toby?"

"Nah, I'm not fussed, but tread carefully with Jack, especially if there's a potential relationship going on with the posh boy. It won't go down well."

"Why?" Emma asked with surprise. "Do you think Jack would be jealous?"

"Of you and Toby?" Josh burst out laughing. "Jack wouldn't give two hoots about who you dated. No, I meant he'll not want Toby linking into our lives."

Emma's cheeks burned with humiliation as she pretended to laugh along at their crossed wires, while desperately searching her head for a conversation changer. "Did you say Jack wasn't interested in relationships? What happened?"

"It's all a bit of a mess." Josh paused before sitting up and picking a few blades of grass off his elbows. "He doesn't talk about it very much because it upsets him. You remember Jack, always protective of his emotions. Do you know he has a four-year-old son?"

Putting down her piece of cake, Emma stared at Josh in surprise. "Come again?"

"I know. It's a shock, isn't it? His name is Caleb. Jack is divorced from Joanne now, and I think that's the best thing for them both, but she uses the child as a bargaining tool for money. He's a lot on his plate because of her. The fact he has a child isn't common knowledge in the village, by the way. I'm only telling you because I trust you not to blab." Josh looked up as his sister headed towards them across the green. "Daisy knows some of the story, but not all of it."

"I'm hungry," Daisy interrupted as she plonked herself down at the side of her brother. "Can I have some money?"

Josh groaned as he felt for his wallet. "I don't know how you stay so slim considering the amount you eat. Buy something healthy please or I'll have Jack on my case for letting you eat junk."

Emma watched Daisy skip towards the bakery in her tight shorts and cropped top and waited for Josh to continue with his story.

"She takes after Jack. She's clever. Mum would have been proud of her."

Realising the subject of Jack and his marriage wouldn't be resumed, Emma followed his line of conversation. "What happened with your mum?"

"Heart attack. There was no warning. She just dropped dead in the courtyard. The thing is, she'd worked for months to build that cheese business, and the week after it opened, she died. It was Daisy I felt for. She was only six."

"So you two have brought her up?"

"Jack mainly. She sees him as a father figure since Dad left. It works, and to be honest, between us both, we manage. She's not a bad kid, she's sensible, but I often worry she keeps a lot to herself. We've encouraged her to be open with us about anything, girly stuff, school problems, but some things she'll not want us to know."

"Has there been no woman in Daisy's life since your mum passed?"

"Not really. Joanne didn't show her maternal side, although I appreciate she didn't expect to be bringing up a grief-stricken kid. When you're newly married, having a six-year-old sleep between you who wets the bed and cries all the time doesn't help. It's one of the reasons Jack doesn't talk about Joanne. He doesn't want Daisy dwelling on those times."

"I think your sister is very lucky to have you guys," Emma said with meaning. "I grew up with you two, remember?"

Josh smiled gratefully as Daisy returned with a bag of donuts and sugar all over her sunburnt nose. “Milly’s bringing over coffee in a minute. She said her shower’s not working properly.”

“Great,” Josh mumbled. “I know what I’ll be repairing this week.”

“Better than setting up a cheese business on your own,” Daisy grumbled with jam on her lips. “I don’t know what I’m doing.”

“It doesn’t matter,” Josh reassured her. “Your brother makes the cheese. We just want you to have a go at setting up a website and advertising the product. This is all part and parcel of what farming is. You know that.”

Daisy pulled a face as she looked towards the barn with the doors flung wide open. “Can I work here with Emma for today? I’m bored of being on my own, and she might be able to teach me stuff about selling.”

“You’re manipulative.” Josh ruffled his sister’s hair affectionately. “Is that okay with you?”

“Sure,” Emma replied. “But I don’t want to cause any problems. Jack’s fed up with me enough at the moment.”

“Two lattes,” Milly interrupted, her tongue stuck out in concentration as she approached the small group. Just about to hand them over, a small dog ran behind her and barked loudly, causing Milly to jump in fright, and one of the cups to fell into Josh’s lap.

“Shit!” He brushed frantically at the hot liquid soaking into his groin. “Jesus, what the hell is up with you? It was a friggin’ dog, for God’s sake, not a bloody bomb. This is precious cargo in my underpants.”

“Oh, sorry.” Milly shrugged with a sarcastic smile. “I didn’t know you’d grown a pair of balls.”

“One thing I know for sure, you’ll never find out.” Josh gingerly pulled the top of his shorts away from his stomach and looked down. “Phew, no damage done.”

Emma pretended not to notice Milly's shaking hands as she picked up the empty cup. "When does your new roommate move in?"

"Oh God, it's been a complete disaster," Milly mumbled as she wiped her wet hands down her long sundress. "He turned up this morning and let's just say he wasn't at all what I expected. I'll tell you about it later. Anyway, I rang the agency and I've got another one coming tomorrow. A dentist. Fingers crossed this one is normal."

"Do you do normal?" Josh murmured as he sat back down in his soaking shorts.

"With all due respect, you're the one in the wet pants." Milly grinned as a group of teenage girls started to titter as she walked back to her bakery. "Don't forget my shower," she shouted from across the green. "And make sure you go to the toilet before you come out next time."

Josh lay back on the grass and stuck his finger up in her direction. "I don't know who will be brave enough to date her, but God help them."

They worked solidly side by side for the next few hours. Emma organised furniture as Josh hung shelves and added new electric sockets. Even skirting boards and window frames were replaced, lifting the appearance of the interior, while Daisy proved her weight in gold, writing down the names of potential farm suppliers and their contact numbers, making it easier for Emma to build up much needed relationships. So far, everyone in the village had been welcoming, and Toby had shown himself to be supportive and helpful. Not to mention gorgeous. She didn't want to speak too soon, but it seemed she may have fallen on her feet.

Josh put his phone down after answering a call. "I've got to head off for another job. A burst pipe in the church hall. I'll not get a chance to come back today. Are you going to be okay on your own?"

"Actually, can I go too?" Daisy glanced at her watch and quickly sent a text, already heading out the door in her haste to leave. "My friends are meeting up later and I want to go with them."

"Make sure you tell Jack where you're going," Josh shouted before turning back to Emma, frowning. "This is a lot of hard work for one person. Is Toby not meant to be part of this project?"

"He had to organise the summer ball." Emma shifted a large wicker basket nearer to the door. "He said he'll come across later."

"Well, make sure he helps you," Josh replied as he heaved his bag onto his shoulder. "He's known for shirking his responsibilities. And don't get taken in by his charm."

Emma nodded patiently. She trusted Josh, she always had, but she needed to make her own mistakes and discover people's personalities for herself. Finding herself alone again, she stood in the middle of the barn and appreciated the peace and silence. She breathed in the warm evening air that floated in from outside, carrying with it the scents of freshly mowed grass and suntan lotion. For as long as she lived here, she would never take any of this for granted.

"Snoozing on the job?"

Emma jumped, expecting to see another curious villager.

"I see you've been making friends already." Toby nodded towards the windowsill where welcoming gifts sat. "I'm surprised you're still here."

"Lots to do." Emma glanced at his clean clothing before self-consciously brushing at her bruised and dirty knees. This is not how she wanted to look in front of a man like this. "Although I'm just about to lock up."

"Perfect timing then." Toby nodded to the packed beer garden where people spilled onto the village green. "Come on. Let me treat you. I insist."

Following him to the only free table, Emma took a seat while he went inside to order their drinks. Expecting him to be a while, given the amount of people waiting to be served, Emma took her phone from her bag and quickly messaged her sister. It made a change, she thought, to be sending a genuine smiley emoji.

"I forgot to ask what you wanted." Toby placed a tray of drinks onto the table. "I figured you looked like a vodka kind of girl."

Emma glanced at the lengthy queues still near the door. "I thought you'd be ages."

"Perks of the job." Toby took a deep drink from his beer and pointed to her glass. "Do you like vodka?"

"Yeah, sure," Emma lied, aware of annoyed looks from those still waiting to be served. She turned her back on them and tried to relax. "How did your plans go for the summer ball?"

"Great." Toby leant his elbows on the table and gave her his full attention. "I've moved the seating plans a little so we can sit together. I figured, other than Josh, you wouldn't know anyone else there." He pulled a menu from his pocket and pushed it across the table. "Let me know what you'd like to eat, and I'll order it for you tonight."

Emma perused the food quickly, her stomach rumbling as she read the delicious choices. Did this guy really want to go with her? Surely someone like him would already have a date.

"We've not had much chance to talk since you arrived." Toby glanced at her choice of fresh salmon with pan-fried potatoes and put the menu back in his pocket. "I thought the ball would be a good chance for us to get to know each other. We'll be working closely together. It helps if we know what makes each other tick."

Emma laughed nervously. "Well, there's not a lot to my ticking."

"I'm not too sure about that," Toby mused as he eyed her inquisitively. "I admire you."

"You admire me?" Emma almost spat out her vodka and tonic. "Why?"

"I can't believe you need to ask that question," Toby held out his hands towards her. "Look at you. You've spent all day working in the heat and still manage to look as good as you do. Plus, you're creating miracles with the farm shop. I think luck has just fallen on my side."

Emma had to smile as she reacted to the flirtatious comment. It had been a long time since anyone had looked at her in that way or flattered her so effortlessly.

"So, come on, tell me more about yourself. How do you know Jack Seymour for a start?"

"We grew up together. As kids, the three of us were inseparable, especially Josh and me. Jack's slightly older than me, and back then two years made a lot of difference."

"Were you romantically involved?"

"No, never." Emma hoped her face didn't show any signs of regret. "We didn't have that kind of relationship, and we definitely don't these days."

"What happened?" Toby leaned forward sympathetically. "You can tell me. I'm discrete."

Emma took a breath and then paused. She hadn't even confessed this to Josh, so best to be as vague as possible. "Just a misunderstanding over something that happened many years ago. It should all be water under the bridge by now, but I don't think either of us can let it go."

"He can hold a grudge, I'll give him that, but that's farmers for you. They've not much else to occupy their minds."

About to retaliate with a defensive response, Emma bit her tongue. It wasn't her job to protect Jack Seymour. After all, he hadn't exactly been easy on her today.

"Jack's one of those who thinks he can have it all. He failed at his marriage though. I bet he hasn't told you that."

Feeling uncomfortable about the shift in conversation, Emma simply shook her head.

"Has he mentioned her to you?"

"No," Emma replied truthfully. "I don't see much of him, to be honest. I'm staying in the piggery, so we only cross paths during morning milking."

"Piggery?" Toby looked at her incredulously. "Did he not offer you a proper room?"

"It's quite nice, actually." Emma thought about the small windows that faced the never-ending hills and valleys. "I like it."

"You deserve better than a shed though." Toby picked up his pint and almost downed it in one huge gulp. "I wish you'd have said you were living in those kinds of conditions. I would have offered you a room in the hall."

Momentarily tempted, Emma shook her head. "You know, I kind of like having my own front door, but thanks for the offer. I really do appreciate it."

"Anytime." Toby's lavender eyes twinkled, complimenting his perfect teeth. "Someone like you deserves to be treated well. I expect you're the kind of girl who works hard and plays hard. You have an intriguing excitement to you. It draws me in."

Emma bit back a smile. He was definitely flirting. A combination of vodka and an empty stomach caused shivers of excitement to run through her body. Never in her wildest dreams had she imagined a guy like this would be interested in a girl like her. Yet going off his attentive expression, he certainly did.

"Have you heard of Featherby's?"

"Yes, I have." Emma bit her bottom lip as she frowned. "A Michelin starred restaurant?"

"Yep, or due to be, with the right people behind it. Me being one of them. How do you fancy going there one evening? Champagne, fine food, excellent company."

Emma twiddled one of her curls around her finger and smiled back. She couldn't help it. He brought out the feminine side to her.

"I'll book us a table then for one evening. The desserts are delicious."

Feeling a blush rise to her already warm cheeks, Emma mentally gave herself a thumbs up. She'd never played it cool in her life, but with him conversation came so naturally. She could flirt forever with this guy and still feel sexy and desirable.

"Another drink? One for the road?"

"Unfortunately, I'm up early," Emma replied regretfully. She would have loved to have stayed for longer. Dusk had started to set over the hills and fields, bathing everything under a warm apricot blanket. Birds chorused each other from the safety of their treetops and this man seemed to hang onto her every word.

"My loss." Toby shrugged as he stood up and helped her into her fleece. "I'll see you in the morning in the barn. Just let yourself in now you have the keys." He cocked his head to one side and smiled at her gently. "I'm glad you came to Thornhill, Emma."

So am I, Emma thought happily as she restrained herself from skipping across the green. *So am I.*

CHAPTER 9

Emma stretched her arms as the rooster continued to crow. She'd slept beautifully. No cars beeping, no dogs barking, no Sean snoring. It had been just what she needed.

Taking advantage of the early hour, she boiled a kettle of water and cleaned around the small piggery. Taking down the slightly dusty curtains, she rinsed them as best as she could in her small sink before hanging them outside on a makeshift washing line. Feeling like Julie Andrews in the *Sound of Music*, she continued to clean while thinking about the summer ball with Toby Montgomery. Tonight would be the start of something wonderful; she could feel it in her bones. After soaking all the cutlery in the kitchenette, she closed her door and headed towards the farmhouse for breakfast.

"Good morning, Sleeping Beauty." Josh stood near the Aga, managing frying pans full of bacon, eggs, and sausage. "A good breakfast is highly recommended if you're going out tonight. It will line your stomach."

"We need to check those milk tanks again," Jack interrupted as he came through the door dressed in a black t-shirt and fitted jeans that clung to his toned body.

Emma glanced at his behind before dragging her eyes away. How many times had she taken sneaky peaks when he hadn't been looking? She'd even watched him on the rugby pitch, from the back benches, of course. The popular girls in their short skirts had sat at the front. The ones he had dated.

"I'll have a look after I've finished the shelving in the farm shop later." Josh ladled food onto warm plates and handed them around. "Clive said he'll call in and say hello to you. He's our farmhand. You'll recognise him because of his piglet."

"Piglet?" Emma questioned.

"Yep, he's like Doctor Dolittle. He attracts any animal in need. So, the summer ball, are you all sorted?"

"Yeah, I think so." Emma reminded herself to look at the dress Daisy had suggested for her. She still hadn't seen it. "I need to try and tame my hair without straighteners. God only knows how."

"What did they call you at school?" Josh frowned. "You had a nickname, something to do with your curls."

"Worzel." Jack bit back a smile as he grabbed a piece of crispy bacon off her plate.

"That was it." Josh laughed as Emma placed a hand on her messy bun. "Worzel Gummidge. You've not changed much."

Thanks, Emma thought as she tucked into her breakfast. Now she knew where to come for a confidence boost.

After swilling off the dishes and sweeping the kitchen floor, Emma followed Jack into the small cheese parlour. The neat wooden shelves filled with cheese molds all carefully labelled intrigued her. With notes scattered around the worktops and a large comfy chair in the corner, she could already tell this is where Jack preferred to spend his time.

"Wow, this is seriously cool. It reminds me of Dad's old shed."

"I'll admit, this is my thinking place. You're very honoured. I don't normally allow anyone else within here. The cheese dairy is my territory." He picked up a clipboard and his overalls before heading into the milking parlour, where the cows waited patiently for entry.

This time Emma didn't flinch when he opened the holding gate and let in the cattle. Instead, she filled up the troughs of hay and disinfected the cows ready for milking.

"Did you walk home alone last night after seeing Toby?"

"Yep." Emma patted one of the cows on its flank as it nudged her for attention. "But I had a torch on my phone."

"Torch or no torch, Toby should have walked you back. It's not like he doesn't have the money to put you in a taxi either. Letting you come home alone was irresponsible."

Emma followed him to the other side of the parlour, keen to set some ground rules. "If you've got a problem with me spending time with Toby Montgomery, then we need to resolve it now, because I'll be working with him closely over the next few months, and I think you ought to know that he's asked me to the summer ball, and I've said yes."

"I gathered." Jack turned to her and sighed. "Do you know what you're doing with him?"

"I beg your pardon?" Emma bristled. "That's none of your business."

"Well, I think it is." Jack leaned over her to fasten a stall, and Emma couldn't help but breathe in his intoxicating aroma of shower gel and aftershave. "While you are living and working here, I have a responsibility to look after you."

"I can look after myself, thank you very much," Emma replied tartly. "And in answer to your question, I do know what I'm doing with Toby. I'm not totally naïve."

"I'm not saying you're naïve, more that he's very persuasive."

"Meaning?"

"I mean, just be careful. I know how men's minds work."

Feeling taken aback by his audacity, Emma sniffed haughtily. "I can handle men, okay? Don't forget, I grew up watching you flirt with everything that moved."

About to defend himself, Jack suddenly shrugged. “Fair point, but perhaps that makes me better placed to say something to you.”

“Are you jealous of him?”

“What?” Jack folded his arms and laughed. “That suit-wearing idiot?”

“Oh my God!” Emma put her hands on her hips with exasperation. “Toby is really friendly and a gentleman. He is kind and caring and considerate.”

“Whereas I’m a maggot barf face with no personality that you hope never to see again?”

Emma froze. She’d been expecting this, just not today.

“Oh, come on. Let’s stop ignoring the elephant in the room.” Jack leaned against the parlour wall and crossed his arms. “That letter must have taken some guts to write. I remember you as a kid. I was shocked.”

Closing her eyes, Emma prayed for the floor to open up. On a cringe level, this would be a definite ten.

“Why did you write it?” He stared at her intently, watching emotions pass over her face.

“Are you really asking me that question?” Emma looked up at him incredulously while cursing him for being so tall. “I was sixteen. Hormones. Life. I don’t know. It was a stupid thing to write.”

“What brought it on?”

“What?” Did he expect her to list all the reasons she’d fallen in love with him? “I’m not going to answer that, Jack. I think you’re being unfair.” Emma’s cheeks heated up, her voice breaking from strong emotion. “It was a long time ago and I’d rather forget about it.”

“I guess you’re right. I shouldn’t drag up stuff that’s in the past.” Jack rubbed at his lower lip before nodding. “Will you accept my apology?”

Emma stood by his side and thought about the years of hurt. His rejection had shaped her in so many ways. Her self-confidence had taken a hit and her ability to trust questioned. She'd adored him and he'd turned his back on her when she needed him the most. However, that was almost twenty years ago. She'd changed. He'd changed. She thought about Josh's words yesterday. He had enough problems with his ex-wife and his young son. Maybe she needed to take Flick's advice and let this go.

"I'll be honest. I'm keen to put this behind us." Jack moved away from the wall before turning to her thoughtfully. "Do you still feel the same way?"

"No!" Emma shook her head vigorously as he stared at her. "Absolutely not."

"Thank God. That's a positive. I was dreading you saying yes."

Emma curled her toes up inside her trainers. Well, she had wanted closure, and she just got it, but oh Jesus, the shame.

"I guess we all do stupid things when we're young." Jack chewed the inside of his cheek as he sighed. "I've done a fair few myself. I'm glad we've cleared the air though. That letter has bothered me since the day you arrived on this farm."

"Okay," Emma snapped as she swept cow dung into the gully. "Point taken. Can we move onto another topic of conversation?"

"Fine," Jack muttered as he dodged her vigorous sweeping. "So, have you got comfy shoes for tonight? You'll be doing a lot of schmoozing."

"Schmoozing?" Emma leant on her broom and looked up in confusion. "Why?"

"You're not going to be sitting in an intimate corner getting to know each other. He'll need to mix. I admit they put the ball on to thank the locals for their hard work, but it's also a business opportunity for them."

Emma hadn't considered that. She suddenly wondered about her outfit. Would it be appropriate? She should have given this more thought.

"And you need to watch your P's and Q's."

"What?" Emma bristled. "What's wrong with my language?"

"Nothing. I understand you perfectly. I come from Redsworth too, but they're not used to Northern accents around here."

"Are you trying to say I sound common?" Emma could feel her temper rise and she turned to Jack in time to see him biting back a smile. "Are you winding me up?"

"Nope. Never."

Emma returned to her sweeping, now feeling uneasy about tonight's event. She'd never socialised with the middle class before. Should she curtesy?

"You'll get to meet his mum too," Jack continued. "She's not too bad, actually. She comes from a working-class background, so she understands real life, certainly more than her son or her husband ever did."

Emma sighed deeply at the sly dig. No wonder Toby didn't like him.

"Where's he going to meet you? In the hall?"

"Yes," Emma replied shortly. "Do you have any more disparaging remarks you'd like to make about him before I head off?"

Jack pretended to zip his mouth shut, an amused smile playing on his lips. Emma watched him with frustration. Smug. That's how she'd describe him right now.

"I'm done." She threw the broom to the side of the parlour as she wiped her dirty hands down her overalls. "I'll see you tomorrow morning."

"Have fun tonight, Cinderella." Jack laughed as Emma threw a roll of tissue his way. "Remember, Josh has offered to be your pumpkin, just in case Prince Charming lets you walk home alone again."

"Piss off, Jack," Emma shouted back. "At least Prince Charming turns up for his dates."

*

Her hair still damp after showering, Emma stood in the piggery and pondered on their argument. She hated confrontation, it unnerved her, and it always cast a cloud over everything else.

After dithering over what to wear, she eventually chose her only summer dress in the hope it would cheer her up. She pushed her feet into her trainers and concentrated on her hair. Up or down? Either way, she resembled a poodle as her curls dried naturally in the warm air. '*Worzel*'. No wonder they'd nicknamed her that. Applying mascara to her long lashes, she added a small amount of lip balm before spraying herself liberally with body spray. That would have to do, and tonight needed to be a separate problem.

The shelter of the tree canopies lining the bubbling stream kept her cool as she headed into the village, but once onto the green, the heat made its presence known. Even the bunting strung between lamp posts didn't dare move for fear of sunstroke. Taking the heavy keys from her bag, she unlocked the door to the barn and walked inside, allowing its coolness to envelop her. Opening the windows, she sighed with contentment as the sounds and smells of a warm summer drifted inside. This was her new life. She worked here. This barn belonged to her. She needed to concentrate on those positives, and not on Jack.

Turning on the radio, she picked up Daisy's folder of contacts and went through them carefully. Many people wanted to support local businesses. A shop like this one should be an extension of the community, not something new, therefore she needed to understand what they could offer her, and what she could offer them in return. After a few hours of research, she felt confident enough to ring the farmers and other suppliers. Dairy, eggs, meat, fruit, vegetables. Even homemade wax candles and local arts. They'd all have a place in her barn. Satisfied with the agreed contracts and delivery times, she chose a cupboard for a counter and started to organise all her papers and stationery. The comfort and familiarity of these basic tasks soothed her like a warm blanket on a cold night. Spying an old milk bottle near the door, she filled it with water and headed outside to cut handfuls of scented wildflowers. Placing the makeshift vase on her counter, she stood back and admired the effect. Now she felt more optimistic.

"You've beat me to it, I see."

Emma turned around happily as Toby presented her with a small cash machine, which he placed on her carefully organised desk. Nodding to the milk bottle, he smiled. "I'll bring you over a vase if you need one."

"No, I like its simplicity." She studied his tense expression closely. "Are you nervous about today? You take over the role of managing the village, don't you?"

"I do. We've got the reading at four o'clock, and then it's all guns blazing for the ball. You'll be sitting with me, by the way, and my family."

"Your family?" Emma swallowed deeply. "We won't be sitting on our own?"

"No. We have the top table. It's tradition. Speaking of which, my father always did a speech before the entertainment. This year it will fall to me."

"That must be difficult," Emma sympathised.

"Not really. I've listened to loads of opening speeches. So, how's the morning going?"

"Great." Emma frowned slightly at his last comment. "The deliveries are coming this afternoon and the contracts will be signed. Do you want them in your name or mine?"

"Put them in your name. I can't be bothered with the paperwork."

"Fair enough. Josh will be here soon to finish off the shelving and electrics. Then we're good to trade."

"I'm impressed." Toby walked around the barn, checking the vintage cupboards, dressers, and old wicker baskets. "You're going for a country look, I see."

"Yep." Emma nodded. "That's the theme."

"Do you not think it will be a bit twee?"

"No, not at all. People come here for the halcyon tranquillity. Most of these visitors are photographing the red telephone box and thatched cottages. They want England on a plate and I'm going to serve it to them. I mean, how many visitors do you get on average per day?"

"Erm…" Toby furrowed his brow as he looked outside the window. "It differs with the weather."

"Well, yesterday I took a few notes while I worked. Admittedly, the sun is out, which will increase your footfall, but I calculated around fifty people who sat on the green yesterday eating picnics. That's fifty potential customers to this shop each day if we market it well. Sensible prices, good food surrounded by the country look they are hoping for." Emma pointed to the milk bottle full of scented blooms. "See what I mean?"

"I do." Toby rubbed his chin thoughtfully. "You obviously know your stuff."

"And that's why I got the job, isn't it?"

"Naturally." Toby's eyes twinkled as he took in her summer dress that stretched over her full breasts and small waist. "Why else?"

Emma felt herself melt under his sexy smile. If he looked this good in jeans and a plain shirt, God help her tonight when she met him in a suit.

"Oh, I meant to ask. What are the plans for later? I mean, where are we meeting?"

"Normally, I'd offer to pick you up..." Toby rubbed his hands sympathetically. "...but with my new role and everything, I'm going to be a bit busy, so I'll order you a car. Does that sound okay?"

"A car?" Emma raised her eyebrows. "I don't expect that. I can make my own way there. I meant, where shall I meet you?"

"In there, at eight o'clock?" Toby glanced at his watch as a black car drove smoothly towards Thornhill Hall. "Looks like the family has arrived. Are you going to be okay on your own here today?"

"Yeah, sure." Emma rearranged the cash machine on her counter. "You can leave all this to me. It's in hand."

Feeling like a giddy lamb in spring after her flirtatious encounter, Emma continued with her decoration for the barn as deliveries started to flood in. Boxes of fresh vegetables and fruit arrived thick and fast along with meats for the refrigerators. Carrots and leeks with the dirt still hanging from their roots. Red juicy apples newly picked from their branches. They all filled the wicker baskets and wooden crates she'd prepared. As for the cupboards and dressers, they soon groaned under the weight of homemade jams and chutneys.

"Now this is a sight for sore eyes. Am I too early to buy something?"

Even before she could turn around, Emma knew her customer. The old man greeted her in a strong Gloucestershire accent, his pale blue eyes twinkling under a thatch of white hair as he twisted a flat cap in his hands. "I'm Clive, and you must be Emma."

"How did you guess?" Emma smiled as she wiped her hands down her dusty sundress and returned the friendly handshake, laughing in delight at the plump piglet that trundled in behind him.

"This is Pickles." Clive gazed fondly at the little animal as it snuffled around the barn. "He's my best mate and confidant. I can tell him anything and he doesn't repeat it." Clive chortled at his own joke as he looked around the barn. "It's nice to see this place open again. I spent many happy hours here as a kid. There was a ladder back then that led to a mezzanine level. It attracted many young couples on a cold night, especially when full of hay."

"You included?" Emma raised an eyebrow knowingly.

"A gentleman never tells." Clive tapped the side of his nose. "But Betty and I, God rest her soul, we named our first-born after the old tractor they often parked in here. I've never told him that though. I don't think he'd ever forgive me. So, I hear you're helping Jack on the farm."

"I'm trying to pay my way." Emma inwardly sighed again at their earlier argument. "I don't like freeloading. I need a place to stay, and he needs assistance."

"A match made in heaven?"

"Not exactly," Emma replied with a grimace. "I've not proved myself to be much help so far. In all honesty, I think he finds me a hindrance."

"You'll get used to it. Farming is a very different way of life if you've been brought up in a town."

Emma nodded to herself, not missing the fact that Clive hadn't contradicted her. She mused on how that felt, for Jack to consider her a hindrance. Did it hurt? No, it had been what she expected after all these years. She opened a bottle of lemonade and encouraged the old man to sit on the bench under the barn window.

"How are you settling into village life?" Clive asked as he sipped his lemonade noisily. "I hear you've impressed the locals already. Especially a certain young man who's got your dance card signed for tonight, if the gossip is to be believed."

"I hope I'm not making waves by going." Being the centre of tittle-tattle, or worse still, accused of brown-nosing, filled Emma with a sense of insecurity. She needed friends right now, not enemies.

“No, not at all. I think people are just curious. Toby can be a little aloof at times.” Clive nodded towards the hall as the piglet jumped onto his knee and settled down comfortably. “He’s got big shoes to fill.”

“His father’s?”

“No.” Clive pursed his lips as he shook his head. “His father was a cold man, motivated by money. I mean his grandfather, Bartholomew. Now, he was a decent chap. If you went to him with a leaking roof, you’d have it fixed within the hour with a loaf of bread and a packet of butter on your table as an apology for it happening in the first place. A gentleman.”

“So you knew him?”

“Aye, we grew up together. He didn’t see a class system. His mates weren’t judged by their clothing or education. Unfortunately, though, his son and heir thought differently, and so when Bart finally fell off the earth, the prices went up, and they’ve been a succession of money-makers ever since. Bartholomew would turn in his grave if he knew the legacy his son had left behind.”

“I know Jack doesn’t like them.” Emma smiled ruefully. “It’s caused a bit of friction, me working here and going to the ball tonight.”

“Aye, well, Jack’s farm is worth a lot of money if he sold it. There’s the land for a start, and then the business on top of that. Everyone around here knows if you want quality dairy, you go no further than Seymour’s Farm. He’s worked hard to build that reputation and he’s kept it. Unfortunately, he only just breaks even. He doesn’t have enough cattle for it to be a financial success, but if he did, there would be no stopping him.”

Emma considered the old man’s response. “I didn’t realise it was such a sought-after business.”

“Oh, it is, and that’s what annoys the Montgomerys, because they don’t own it. There’s a lot of other underlying problems there as well, caused by jealousy.”

“Jealousy? Because of the farm?”

"No. It goes deeper than that. There's always been rivalry between the two families. It started before my time with Bart's father, over ninety years ago now. He was head of the family at the time and ran the village. Obviously, back then, bank accounts weren't common, so physical money exchanged hands. Anyway, it transpired that many of his luxuries came from the pockets of the locals. Theft, basically. Jack's great grandad found out and outed them, and the Montgomerys lost their reputation and their name. They've never quite recovered. In a village like this, secrets are never fully buried. They carry on through generations, like Chinese whispers, tweaked and edited to suit the audience. That's when the bad blood started between the Seymours and Montgomerys. Do you want to know more? Have you the time to sit with an old man while he rattles on?"

"You've actually caught my interest." Emma settled herself on the bench, enjoying the historic gossip as she looked out over the ivy-clad hall with its solid walls.

"Well, around twenty years later, Jack's grandad had an affair with Bart's wife. Think Lady Chatterley's lover, although a nice young girl like you probably won't understand the reference."

Emma smiled to herself. She could recite most chapters of that book in her sleep.

"Bart was a good friend of mine. He was gutted when he discovered what they'd been up to; however, he had the family name to protect and therefore he took no retribution. There was gossip though, and many said Bart's son wasn't his. Toby's father had to live with the slight all his life, that he may not be a true Montgomery. I think that's what made him such a bitter man, a huge contrast to his father."

"And was he his son?"

"Yep. The family trait was there, the lavender eyes, but a slur is a slur. Unfortunately, the bitterness continued in the generation below them. Toby's father fought for the Seymour land and lost. Now there's a new feud between the existing pair."

"You mean Jack and Toby?"

"Aye." Clive sighed deeply. "It's been tit for tat between those families for far too long. A deep inset hatred exists in the Montgomerys for what the Seymours did to their name. When Jack and Josh came to live here, I knew the problems would continue. Toby was a sullen child. He struggled to be accepted socially amongst his friendship groups, and then along came a dark-haired strapping lad who all the girls immediately flocked to, including Toby's girlfriend. They've fought like cats and dogs ever since."

"Is she telling you about her posh new boyfriend?" Josh interrupted as he lolloped across the village green with his tools and ladder.

"He's not my boyfriend." Emma shaded her green eyes from the sun as she absorbed the old man's words. No wonder Toby didn't like Jack, if he'd stolen his girlfriend. "Tonight isn't an official date."

"If you say so," Josh teased as he clapped the old man on the back affectionately. "Are you not joining us tonight, Clive? I seem to remember you had a good pair of dancing feet on you."

"Those days have passed me by." Clive looked down at his worn boots. "I'll be at home tonight with a pork pie by my side and a glass of whisky." He gently nudged the small bundle of soft fur in his lap. "Anyway, if ever you want to know the history of this place, just give me a shout. When you're old and useless like me, chatting gives you a purpose."

Emma smiled as the old man trundled his way back across the green with the small piglet trailing close to his heels. She could see why the Seymour family was so fond of him.

"He's a character." Josh sat by her side and offered her a drink from his flask. "He's been like a dad to us over recent years. Even when Betty died and his son asked him to move in with them, he wanted to stay here. He's a more permanent fixture than the house itself. Anyway, tonight. I'll be leaving just before eight o'clock with Tilly Mint. Do you want to join us for the walk down?"

Envisaging a nice stroll by the stream to calm her nerves, Emma suddenly sighed. She'd have to go in the car Toby had ordered for her. Feeling a bit self-conscious about the extravagance, Emma shook her head. "Nah, it's okay. I don't know what time I'll be done here. You two make your own way there."

Emma looked across the green towards the White Rabbit bakery, where customers waited patiently for an empty table. "So, do you have a date for tonight?"

"Nope." Josh headed inside the barn and set up his ladders before starting to measure the walls for new shelving. "I prefer to browse, so to speak."

"Are you seriously telling me you've never had a serious relationship?"

"What is it with women?" Josh came down his ladder and sighed. "They see a single man and they instantly want to set him up with someone. I thought you knew me."

"So did I." Emma gazed at him thoughtfully. "You always wanted a big family."

"I also used to sit on a climbing frame and pretend I was Indiana Jones. The truth is, I've dated women, but none of them have ever intrigued me. I don't even have a type, but I know what I want."

"Which is?"

"I want someone I can be myself with. I'm not an academic or someone who will reach for the stars. Give me a designer shirt and I'll ruin it within days, but give me a pile of bricks and I'll build you a house. I'm a simple man, but women find that boring. They want successful men with big wallets and even bigger attitudes. I want a pint at the Mouse and a weekend near the sea." Josh pinched her nose with his pliers as he walked past. "See my problem?"

"I'd quite like a weekend by the sea," Emma mused. "Do you want to marry me?"

"I can't. You're marrying Jack, remember? You asked him once."

"I did?" Emma pretended to rearrange the flowers on her counter. "What did he say?"

"He said you'd never be old enough. In all fairness, I think you were running around our garden in your knickers at the time, having a water fight with me."

Emma lowered her head and laughed. "I remember that, vaguely."

"I think it was your seventh birthday. Your mum sat at the side of my mum and they both did that *'aww'* thing." Josh paused momentarily. "I wonder if they're still watching us."

Emma smiled as she looked out the window at the clear sky. She'd wondered about that herself, quite a lot.

"But life goes on and we grow up. Speaking of which, do you remember that purple velvet jacket I wore all the time during my teens?"

"Yeah, I do," Emma replied. "You belonged on the set of Joseph and his technicolour dream coat."

"Very funny. Well, apparently, it's now classed as vintage. Daisy's borrowing it tonight. Actually, I was going to ask you a favour, if you don't mind. Something to do with Tilly Mint."

"Ask away." Emma unwrapped bags of coins to use as her float and added them to her new cash desk. "Is she okay?"

"She's fine, but this cheese shop is getting her down. She picked it up as a project about four months ago, but she doesn't really know what she's doing. Granted, she has enthusiasm, and I can't deny she works hard, but over the past few days, I've noticed she's finding excuses not to do it."

"She's overwhelmed?"

"Exactly. I wondered if you could give her some pointers, or gentle guidance. Make it sound like they were her ideas in the first place."

Emma smiled to herself. It would be an honour to make his mum's wishes come true. "She's a lovely girl."

"She is, most of the time. By the way, Daisy said if you go to her bedroom after work, she'll give you a makeover for the summer ball. Hair included. She also said to give her plenty of time. Her words, not mine."

*

By mid-afternoon, the small traffic jam caused by vans eager to deliver their produce had disappeared, and Emma found herself left with piles of boxes and crates. She looked into them eagerly. Homemade scented candles, intricately woven wicker hearts, and delicate jewellery. At this rate, she'd need to expand before they'd even started trading.

Up went water paintings by local artists alongside wood carved clocks. Hand painted crockery stood proudly by matching place mats, and printed tea towels were folded next to vases of fresh flowers. Finally, she strung twinkly lights throughout the shelving to give it all that welcoming glow. Standing back to admire her work, she almost felt like crying with pride. She had achieved exactly what she'd aimed to do.

"Wow." Milly lumbered through the door, her arms full of cakes and freshly baked bread. "This is something else. It's like an Aladdin's cave of homeliness. I could live here."

"That's the exact effect I've been aiming for," Emma replied happily. "I'm glad you're here. Can I arrange a contract with you for muffins and coffee each morning for the farmers who deliver to me? I'm trying to build loyalty and good custom and I often find it's the small touches that help."

"Yeah, sure. They'll appreciate that around here. Most people are friendly."

"Speaking of friendly, have you found your perfect lodger?"

"Oh, don't even go there," Milly groaned. "The Parish Council messed up my advert. They sent the vacancy to a website that has a particular reader, if you catch my drift. No wonder I'm attracting weirdos who are expecting more than just a roof over their heads." Milly rolled her eyes before she started to smile. "The bloke who came the other day had a suitcase with him which I already found suspicious. He opened it, took out a Policewoman's outfit, asked me to wear it, arrest him and spank him for being a bad boy…"

Emma snorted with laughter. "What did you say?"

"I told him I had twenty-four cupcakes to ice, and could he put his clothes back on, hide his truncheon and leave. Do you want to know what the dentist asked for?"

"Dare I ask?" Emma wiped tears from her eyes. "I assume he didn't want just lodgings either?"

"He wanted to gargle for me with mouthwash after I'd cleaned his teeth with a fake dentistry set."

"That doesn't sound too bad," Emma added tentatively.

"It is when they want to wear your underwear while you do it." Milly straightened herself up and sighed. "Are you sure you don't want to move in with me?"

"If I could afford to pay you rent, I would. Unfortunately, I need to milk cows and sweep up muck to earn a roof over my head." Emma rubbed at her still painful thumb from yesterday's hand-milking. "It's not very glamorous, is it?"

"At least you're doing it for the most eligible bachelor in this village." Milly nodded towards her hand. "Is it sprained?"

"I think so." Emma winced. "Any suggestions?"

"Yep, a cold compress." Milly examined her thumb by gently moving it. "It's not broken. Have you been applying repetitive pressure to something?"

"How do you know that?"

Milly leaned forward conspiratorially. “I used to be a doctor. Keep that between us. I don’t want the village turning up and asking me how to treat haemorrhoids.”

Emma looked at her new friend in surprise. “What’s a doctor doing running a bakery?”

“Pushy parents. They wanted a daughter with a good career who would earn lots of money, find a cure for all diseases, and earn a Nobel Peace Prize.”

“Not your thing?”

“No way.” Milly looked across at her bakery. “This is what I wanted to do all along. Hence my need for a lodger. It’s expensive to live here, but my parents don’t see it as a career and therefore they refuse to support me, emotionally or financially.”

“That can’t be easy,” Emma sympathised. At least her parents hadn’t been in touch for a good reason. Milly’s family not speaking to their daughter came from choice, and that knowledge must hurt.

“I’m better off on my own.” Milly shrugged. “I’ve learned to be independent, and I don’t regret it. That’s why I understand your need to earn accommodation. At least Jack will have your back while you’re doing it. Did you know he used to be married?”

Emma nodded, careful not to break Josh’s confidence on this matter.

“Joanne used to look at me like I was something she’d stepped in. I’ll be honest, I don’t know why he stayed with her, apart from her looks, of course. Tall, dark, sultry, his usual type. Anyway, one night at the summer ball, she just stood up and walked out on him, and no one has heard of her since.” Milly craned her neck to see more cars arrive on the hall driveway. “At least Toby will be in high spirits tonight. How’s he taken the news that you’re living with the Seymours?”

“Okay. I’ve not hidden it from him. He knows we’re all childhood friends.”

"Just a word of warning. Toby is very jealous of Jack. If he thought you were getting friendly, he probably wouldn't react well."

"Well, he's nothing to worry about," Emma replied casually. "Because that's highly unlikely to happen. Jack sees me as a hindrance from his past. I can't see anything changing that."

CHAPTER 10

After ensuring she'd done all she could for her opening day tomorrow, Emma locked up the shop and turned to face her barn. A few days ago, she'd felt apprehensive about this role, and now she couldn't wait to get back inside. Proof, if needed, that she'd made the right decision.

Hidden amongst the thicket of the stream bank, she allowed herself to skip, something she hadn't done in many years. Tonight would be amazing. Okay, she'd be sitting with Toby's family, but surely they'd get some time to themselves. Shaking her head at her dreamlike state, she grinned to herself. Toby ticked every box of what she needed right now. Young, flirtatious, non-serious, and easy on the eye. Everything Sean hadn't been. Not for the first time, she viewed that Ferrari as her lucky escape.

Approaching the farm, she opened the gate and walked straight into the kitchen. Looking around the empty space, she cocked her head to one side and listened to the music coming from upstairs.

"Come on up." Daisy beckoned from a perfume-fogged landing. "I've got everything ready for you." She pulled a chair from under a dressing table and encouraged Emma to sit. "So, are we going for full glam?"

"No!" Emma looked in alarm at the selection of glittery eyeshadows. "Subtle. I want the 'barely there' look."

"Oh, fair enough." Shrugging with slight disappointment, Daisy plugged in her curling wand. "I thought purple eyeshadow would have gone well with your yellow dress."

"Yellow?" Emma turned around quickly. "With my hair colour?"

"Joking!" Daisy snorted. "Your face, it's a picture. You can put the dress on once we've done your makeup. Now sit back and let me work my magic."

What seemed like hours later, Daisy zipped up the back of the dress and stepped back to allow Emma to see herself in the full-length mirror. For a few seconds, she simply stood and gazed at her image. The emerald dress fitted to her small waist and full breasts before flaring in soft folds to her knees, the strapless design showing off her slightly tanned shoulders. She angled herself to see how far the neckline dipped. Enough, but not too much to be inappropriate. With shiny auburn curls flowing down her back, her makeup shimmering softly to emphasise her green eyes and full mouth, the girl from Redsworth was gone, and in her place stood a confident, sensual woman.

"Wow." Emma finally let her arms drop to her sides. "I don't know what to say. I didn't expect to look like this."

"Why not?" Daisy asked as she turned off her curling wand. "It's just you, with makeup."

The unintentional compliment caught Emma by surprise, and to her horror, she felt her eyes start to water. Busying herself to hide her moist lashes, Emma looked at her trainers and cringed.

"Don't worry, I have shoes too. I checked your size yesterday. You're the same as me." Daisy handed her a pair of cream pumps before picking up Josh's purple jacket and delving into the pockets, pulling out all sorts of papers and throwing them onto her bed. "Right, I think we're ready. Are you still not walking down with us?"

"No, there's a few things I need to do first." Emma glanced quickly out the window, relieved not to see a car waiting outside. "Shall I see you there?"

"Fair enough. I don't think Josh is ready yet anyway. I can still hear the shower running." Daisy skipped down the stairs before turning around to watch Emma walk across the landing.

"Toby's face is going to be a picture when he sees you. He won't believe his luck."

CHAPTER 11

The drive in the smooth, sleek car did nothing to calm Emma's nerves. The walk would have been better, but grumbling made her feel ungrateful. Climbing out of the seat, assisted unnecessarily by the chauffeur, she made her way inside the hall and stood near the reception area as instructed. Momentarily fearing she had overdressed, she felt relieved to see many evening gowns and men in full suits. Tucking her borrowed bag under her arm, she tried to blend into the crowd, feeling like an imposter against the groups that congregated together excitedly, their voices low and whispered. As the minutes ticked away, her nerves continued to build. Where was Toby? She fidgeted with her watch as people passed by, some looking at her sympathetically, while others gave her a friendly nod and encouraging smile.

Checking her phone again, Emma sighed. No messages and she couldn't ring because she had no private number for him. As for where he lived. He lived here. Somewhere in the hall.

As guests started to file into the ballroom, ready for the evening meal, Emma felt her shoulders slump. Surely, he wouldn't stand her up. Having this happen to her once in life was bad enough, but twice. Walking up the sweeping staircase to give her height advantage, Emma stood on the softly lit landing and looked down over the dwindling guests. Her eyes picked out various figures, but none of them were Toby. Glancing towards the doorway again, she did a double take. Surely not?

She watched Jack also roam the reception area, like her, seemingly desperate to find someone. As if aware of her gaze, he lifted his head and looked up the staircase. His eyes initially passing her by, they quickly drew back before widening. Standing still for a few seconds as he stared at her, he eventually climbed the staircase.

"I didn't recognise you. Are you okay?"

"Yeah, of course I'm okay." She placed a hand above the top of her dress to cover her cleavage. "What are you doing here?"

"I decided to see what all the fuss was about." Jack glanced at her bare shoulders. "No Toby?"

"He's been delayed." Emma lifted her chin high, hoping he'd leave her in peace to suffer her humiliation alone. Tears were already threatening, and she felt determined not to let them fall, especially in front of Jack. Glancing at the clock, she prayed for Toby to turn up.

"Shall we go through then?" Jack pointed to the ballroom. "It's better than standing here."

Anxiety heightening her frustration, Emma felt herself snap. "I'm waiting here. You go through. I don't need a chaperone."

The nine chimes of the grandfather clock struck hard into her heart. One whole hour. Was she really so unforgettable and unimportant that men did this to her? Humiliation spread through her from her toes upwards as she recalled that awful chant *'Frigid Francis'*. She'd just been transported back eighteen years, except this time Jack had turned up, just not for her. The irony would be laughable if it didn't hurt so much. Her phone suddenly beeped, and she pulled it out of her bag, relief spreading through her as she recognised Toby's work number. However, her reassurance didn't last as she read the brief text, *'Sorry, urgent business. Not able to attend. Have fun.'*

"Well?" Jack looked at her. "Any news?"

"He's not coming," she managed to say, her throat thick with tears. She looked around at the elegantly dressed guests, laughing and linking arms with their significant others. Why her? Why did it always happen to her? She desperately wanted to cry. All her efforts had been for nothing. Her hair, makeup, the dress, all a waste, and worst of all, after all her boasting, she felt a complete and utter fool in front of Jack.

"I'm going home," she murmured, fumbling with the keypad on her phone.

Jack shook his head as her eyes filled with tears. "No, you're not."

"Don't tell me what to do," Emma retorted, aware of her chin wobbling dangerously. "I'm not on your farm now."

"I'm not telling you what to do," he whispered as he placed a hand on the small of her back and guided her towards the ballroom. "You'd never listen to me anyway, and please don't swear at me. It's not that kind of place."

Emma pulled on his arm angrily, half expecting him to shout at her, but instead he bent his knees and looked her in the eye. "What's the worst that could happen? Come on, you're here now. You may as well stay for a while."

He linked her arm and led her into the vibrant room. Despite her upset, Emma looked around in amazement. She felt like she'd entered a set straight from Cinderella's ball. Tables were topped with pristine white cloths, while lines of silver cutlery and arrangements of roses fought for space, all giving off a heady floral scent as they shimmered against the many candelabras. The deep red walls and old oak panelling added to the romantic mood, oozing intimacy, and sumptuousness.

Jack guided her to the bar and caught the attention of the barman. He handed her a glass of red wine and studied her carefully. "Don't cry. You'll ruin your makeup."

Emma took a sip of her drink, avoiding his eye. She felt ridiculous in this unfamiliar outfit. "I still want to go home."

"Okay, if you feel the same after your drink, I'll walk you home myself."

Emma nodded miserably as she picked at her freshly painted nails. "Why are you here? You didn't explain."

"I didn't see the point in explaining. You never take any notice of me anyway." Jack leant against the bar. "How's the wine?"

"Okay. I mean good. How did you know I liked red wine?"

"You mentioned you'd bought a bottle to settle down with one evening. Unlike you, I do listen. Look, why don't you stay for the meal at least. You might enjoy it."

Emma glanced at the table plans near the door and shook her head. What had Toby expected her to do while attending alone? Walk over to his mother on the top table, introduce herself as the new manager of the local farm shop and pull up a chair?

Jack caught her line of vision. "Wait here. I'll be back in a few minutes."

She stood by the bar cradling her glass, desperately trying not to meet anyone's eye. They would all be laughing at her, the new girl thinking she could run with the posh family.

Jack soon returned and ushered her towards a small table in the corner of the room. "I know you want to go home but I'm starving. Come on, sit with me."

Despite her hesitation, Emma followed him. She felt weary and tearful, and another argument with Jack didn't feature high on her agenda. Pulling out a chair, she sat by his side and stared at her empty wine glass. Now she just felt uncomfortable. Not knowing what to say, she picked up a napkin ring and spun it around in her fingers, the silence between them more deafening than the laughter around the room. She sighed, thinking she should have opted to go home.

"Do you want another drink?"

"No." Emma stopped playing with her napkin and looked up to find Jack staring at her. No doubt he struggled to find a conversation starter too. She looked at her empty glass and shrugged. "Well, maybe one more."

As the waiter replenished their drinks, Jack took the napkin out of her hand and pointed to her phone. "Did he not explain?"

"No, and to be honest, I don't care." Emma went to rub a hand over her eyes and stopped herself just in time. She would have spread mascara everywhere. "Well, obviously I do care."

"He might have a good reason."

"Go on, say it's because his diamond-encrusted shoes were pinching his toes."

"I could," Jack mused as his lips lifted. "But to be honest, I don't fancy wearing that glass of wine."

Emma had to smile. Diplomacy didn't come easy to him where the Montgomerys were concerned.

"Daisy's done your hair, I see. It looks good."

"Thanks." Emma cringed as she looked down at her dress. "She lent me this as well. It's too revealing for me though."

"If you say so." Jack swirled his glass of whisky. "I'll be honest, there's not much occasion to get dressed up around here. My suit gets an outing once every few years. One day I'll put it on and it'll either be moth-eaten or two sizes too small."

Emma watched him look around the darkened room. "You said you don't come to the hall. Is it because of Joanne?"

"It sounds like you already know the answer to that one." Jack looked at her, a slow smile on his lips. "It's okay. Josh told me he mentioned her and my son to you."

Emma watched his fingers tap the side of his glass as he waited for her next words.

"I can tell you're dying to ask, so I'll give you the truth before the jungle drums twist everything up. Basically, we married too young. I fell for her hook, line, and sinker without a thought for our differing lifestyles. Within a year, she was asking me to sell up and move to the city, but that wasn't the life I wanted at all. Things got worse after Mum died. She started to resent me and the farm. I honestly thought a family of our own would fix it, but when one finally did come along, she told me she didn't want to spend her life in the hills bringing up babies. I was in here when she told me she was leaving and taking my unborn child with her. She just stood up and walked out."

Emma sat back in her chair, feeling childish for her earlier strop. Her issues with Toby were nothing compared to this.

"One minute I was on top of the world, and the next I found myself at the lowest point possible. She hated me for trapping her." Jack moved their napkins as the first course of their food arrived. "She was fickle. One minute she was all over something, and the next it was boring. I never got to grips with what she really wanted out of life, and I don't think she did either."

"How often do you see him, Caleb?"

"Never."

"What?" Emma lowered her soup spoon. "Ever?"

"Nope." Jack sighed deeply as he pushed his bowl away. "I don't even know where she lives now. She took out a court order against me after I kept messaging and ringing her. She called it harassment. I think she was right."

Emma put her hand out to his. She'd thought of Jack so many times as she grew up, but she'd never envisaged him suffering like this. "I'm so sorry."

"Hey, it's my fault. I should have given her the space to come to terms with everything. The first year was hard. I kept thinking about my child, but after a while, I learned to deal with it better. I always send extra money for birthdays, Christmas, and Easter, basically any occasion where a kid should be spoiled. He's never far from my mind, but let me tell you, child maintenance isn't cheap. Every month I struggle to send her what she needs."

"So, you pay every month for a child you're not allowed to see?"

"Basically, yes. I get the odd photograph, but that's all." Jack took a picture from his wallet and handed it over. "He looks like Joanne. I go without many pleasures in life to support a kid I've never held."

"That must be so hard," Emma replied softly as she gazed upon the young child with a mass of brown hair and equally deep brown eyes. "Life can be cruel at times."

"It can." Jack leant his elbows on the table and gazed at her thoughtfully. "Anyway, now you know my sob story, what's yours?"

"Mine?" Emma pointed to herself as she handed back the photograph. No way could she admit how she'd been fooled so easily by Sean. "I don't have one."

"So, what are you doing here? Why leave a good job and a home for an uncertain future?"

"I fancied a bit of excitement." Emma shrugged. "That's all."

"Bullshit." Jack sat back in his chair. "I know you too well. Shall I tell you what I think?"

Emma sighed. "Go on. Let's hear your character analysis of me."

"I think you've been badly hurt. Someone has abused your trust and left you financially insecure and, quite possibly, if I may be so blunt, left you homeless? Am I right?"

Emma looked at Jack in shock. "Did Josh tell you?"

"Nope, he told me your fiancé had been unfaithful, that's all."

"So, how did you know?"

"A hastily packed suitcase. Agreeing to live in a piggery. Travelling two hundred miles on a whim for a job in a village you knew nothing about. It all smacked of becoming unanchored."

Emma felt her eyes fill with tears. Unanchored is exactly how she felt. How on earth had he guessed all this?

"Hey." Jack gently touched her arm. "I didn't mean to upset you. If it's any consolation, I didn't see the writing on the wall either."

Emma looked into his sympathetic eyes, suddenly transported back to her teens when she'd sit at the side of him on a park bench and wish he'd notice her. God, she'd loved him back then.

"My ex used our wedding account to buy a sports car." Emma pushed a curl behind her ear. She'd not talked about this to anyone but Flick. "I also suspected he was seeing someone else and, judging by his recent silence, I think I must have been right. When I discovered his betrayal over the car, I scratched the side of it, punctured the tyres and called him a useless wanking bastard."

Jack put his head back and laughed. "And that, unsurprisingly, left you single and homeless?"

"Yep." Emma played with the edge of her dress before starting to laugh. "You couldn't write it, could you?"

"I'll be honest, I was expecting another woman, or irreconcilable differences over money. A sex change even." Jack shook his head with mock consternation. "But a sports car? Well, that's blown my tale of woe out of the water."

Emma laughed at his attempt to lighten the mood. "It wasn't even a new one. It was second hand, and it had those awful stickers in the window, you know, his and her names. Obviously, Russell and Paula were fed up with it too."

Jack laughed. "I can see you now, driving around Redsworth, top down, with Emma and Sean plastered on your front window. What was his surname?"

"Dimmer." She started to laugh. "I know what you're going to say."

"Emma Dimmer?" Jack looked at her incredulously. "That's an electric fitting, not a name. How could you have possibly thought that would work?"

"I don't know." Emma giggled, wiping her eyes with mirth. "I guess I tried not to think about it."

"I left you alone for eighteen years and look what happens. You do realise you had a lucky break, don't you? You could have been driving around in a battered Ferrari with three kids in the back called '*Switch Dimmer*, '*Light Dimmer*' and '*Lamp Dimmer.*"

"Stop it." Emma laughed as she doubled up on her chair. "I'll wet myself laughing."

"You deserve the humiliation." Jack shook his head at her. "What happened to the lad you were seeing at school? Scott something?"

"Ah." Emma nodded. "Now he had a sensible name. Walker."

"You could have had three baby walkers by now."

"Do you ever give up?" Emma used the napkin to clear any mascara under her eyes. "For your information, he was getting too serious, and I was too young."

"Then you met the Ferrari guy?"

"No, I lived in Brighton for a few years. I worked in boutique hotels and moved my way up in the hospitality industry. I even managed a seafront hotel for a long time. I loved it."

"And then what?"

"And then I came back to look after Mum and Dad." Emma forced the words off her tongue. "They died five years ago."

Jack closed his eyes briefly. "Josh mentioned it. I didn't want to bring it up and upset you. Your mum and dad were great people. I've so many good memories of them."

"Likewise. You know how it feels." Emma shrugged to indicate moving the conversation on. "And then I met Sean. So how about you? What did you do after leaving Redsworth?"

"I went straight to University. I could have carried on studying, but my heart was in farming. Boring, I know, especially in comparison to your life."

"I don't think it is." Emma thanked the waiter as he brought them more courses. "It's harder work than I realised. You were right. I think I expected to be pushing wheelbarrows and collecting eggs, not getting pooped on."

"That was funny." Jack winced as she hit his arm. "Hey, do you ever hear from Jono? You remember, the fullback on my rugby team."

"Yes, his sister, Sally, is a good friend of mine. Why?"

"No reason, just wondered."

Emma folded her arms. "What are you hiding, Seymour? What do I not know?"

"Only that he fancied you rotten." Jack picked up a beermat and turned it over in his hands. "I was just curious if he ever told you. He once asked me if I'd set you both up on a date."

"Seriously!" Emma almost spilled her wine with shock. "Why didn't you tell me?"

"Because he was eighteen and you were sixteen."

"So?" Emma held out her hands, waiting for a further explanation. "Why would that matter?"

"Because he didn't want to take you fishing, like I used to do. He was expecting something … slightly more grown up."

"I could have handled him." Emma shook back her hair, feeling rather pleased at this new revelation. "For your information, I was very mature at sixteen."

Jack raised his eyebrows slightly, causing her to blush. *That bloody love letter!* Okay. Maybe not that mature … but still.

"Plus, it would have felt weird. You were Worzel. You always looked wired for action with a mouthful of toffee and dirty knees."

Great, Emma thought. *No wonder he stood me up*. "You should have told me about Jono. I could have been married to him by now."

"But I didn't, and you're not."

Emma shook her head at his smugness. "You do realise you've changed my road map by not telling me? He may have been my soul mate and now I'll never know."

Jack tapped her glass, encouraging her to drink as he ordered more wine from the waiter. “Have you considered that I may have altered your road map for the better?”

“How?” Emma pointed to herself. “Look at me. I’m thirty-five. I’m single. I’m living in a piggery. Two weeks ago, I was homeless and jobless. I look like Worzel ninety percent of my life, and the remaining ten percent, I’m covered in cow muck. How is that better?”

“Why do you always put yourself down?”

“I don’t.” Emma sat back in her chair. “Do I?”

Jack nodded to her outfit. “Well, you don’t look like Worzel tonight, and you’re not covered in cow muck.”

“I still got stood up.” Emma sighed and puffed out her cheeks. “If you’d given me that number, Romeo, I could have been happy by now.”

“Romeo?”

Emma winced. That hadn’t meant to come out. Drinking always loosened her tongue. Still, she’d started now. “You never had any trouble attracting the ladies. Captain of the rugby team, flirtatious, always snogging behind the science block.”

Jack cringed at her description. “I’ve grown up since then.”

“But you still date?” Emma watched his expression closely.

“I still date.” Jack took off his jacket and loosened his tie, causing his familiar spicy fragrance to breeze Emma’s way. She breathed it in deeply. “But I keep things light. I’ve got Daisy to think about now. I don’t want women entering her life and then leaving. She needs stability.”

“I get that.” Emma nodded as she accepted her dessert from a passing waiter. “So, no one in the village has ever taken your fancy?”

“Like whom?” Jack’s eyes twinkled.

“I’m just curious. I mean, you’ve got a nice little set up. A barn full of hay. You could even teach her how to hand milk cows.

Women love hard work. Seriously, don't let them tell you any different."

Jack put his head back and laughed, his eyes lighting up as he stared at her with an intense gaze.

Emma smiled back as she ate the last of her dessert. She'd just made him laugh. Properly. The sensation of engaging him felt heady. How many years had she spent wanting this kind of reaction from him? Okay, stop. Those kinds of thoughts were in the past. She felt her cheeks redden as he rolled up his shirt sleeves. God, he smelled good.

"Anyway, you should be concentrating on your own relationship." Jack nodded to the top table where the occupants sat with faces as straight as their backs.

From her position in the corner of the room, Emma eyed them curiously. Apart from one woman eating the last of her dessert while talking to someone else, the table seemed devoid of life. Emma looked at Jack, who simply raised an eyebrow as he drank the last of his whisky.

"He's got money. He'd never make you milk cows."

Emma laughed lightly at his joke. She was on dangerous territory here, she knew that. Those teenage feelings weren't as deeply buried as she'd hoped, but she did know her heart wouldn't survive another Jack-shaped hole in it.

"Hey, are you okay?" Jack glanced in concern at her flushed cheeks. "You look a bit warm. Do you want to stand outside?" He placed a hand on her lower back with a gentleness that belied his frame. The quietness of the open air when it hit her contrasted with the vibrancy of the room they'd just left, and her ears rang as they adjusted to the change. He placed his coat around her shoulders as he leant against a wall. "Feeling better?"

Emma nodded as she breathed in the night air and looked upon the silent village green. Even the Dusty Mouse stood in darkness after calling last orders. She pulled Jack's suit jacket closer around herself, revelling in the fragrance she caught from its collar. She glanced at his twitching lips, then laughed at herself in the oversized outfit. "I look like Worzel again, don't I?"

"No. You don't."

The fire door banging shut jolted them both, and Emma turned to see Josh staggering towards them, a whisky glass in his hand.

"I thought I saw you both," he slurred, placing his arms around Emma. "You look pretty good when you scrub up. I'd fancy you myself if the thought of kissing you didn't make my toes curl."

Jack rolled his eyes as his brother propped himself up against a wall. "Where's Tilly Mint?"

"Inside, flirting with a bunch of boys."

Jack rubbed his chin. "She'll be the death of me."

"She's having fun." Josh put his empty glass on the step and pulled a tankard from his pocket. "What are you doing here, dear brother? You hate this place."

"Just thought I'd turn up and have a look around."

"You mean you heard the news and came to gloat." Josh handed Emma the tankard and encouraged her to take a drink. "I take it Toby didn't come to face the music."

Emma winced as the whisky burned her throat. "What music?"

"You don't know?" Josh staggered forward with surprise. "It's all over the village. His mother won't give him the reins to run this place. She says he must work for them. He's well pissed off. Serves him right." Josh put his head back and closed his eyes. "Are you walking home? I think I need to go to bed."

Like a jigsaw from a different angle, pieces started to fall into place. Toby not turning up, the gossipy heads, the sullen top table.

"I'll go and find Tilly Mint." Josh staggered as he pushed himself away from the wall. "See you in a few minutes."

Emma turned to Jack as he bit his lip. "You knew, didn't you, and that's why you came tonight?" Emma felt her insides shrivel with shame. For one second, she'd allowed herself to believe that Jack Seymour had chosen to be in her company. Now she realised he'd simply felt sorry for her.

"I couldn't leave you standing alone to be ridiculed. It felt cruel."

Emma pulled his coat tighter around herself to hide the hideous dress. She couldn't trust herself to speak. *Oh, the irony.*

"Come on, let's get walking. The other two will catch us up." He put his arm around her shoulders. "Don't cry. No man is worth tears."

Crossing the village green, Emma's face crumpled. Toby's no show didn't hurt half as much as knowing Jack had felt forced to sit with her.

"Hey, come on." He pulled her to him as she sobbed against his shirt. "Talk to him tomorrow. You'll sort it out."

"Why is it always me?" Emma cried, her voice muffled against his chest. "Why didn't he turn up for me?"

"I don't know." Jack stroked her hair gently. "But he's a bloody fool. I know that."

CHAPTER 12

"Can she make any more noise?" Josh groaned as Daisy's bedroom door slammed shut for the third time. "Does she not realise five thirty in the morning and a hangover don't sit well together?"

"Serves you right for drinking all that whisky on the walk home." Jack handed his brother two painkillers and a strong cup of coffee. "Never mix your drinks."

"Oh, shurrup." Josh rubbed his eyes. "You're not looking that great yourself."

Emma ate her toast in silence as Jack pushed a cup of coffee her way. She knew her eyes would be puffy from crying, but she could blame that on the wine. As the rooster continued to crow, she looked outside at the washing line, where Jack's shirt hung in the morning sun. Even from this distance, she could see the mascara stains still on it. At what time had he washed that? After he'd left her at the piggery, no doubt cursing the amount of makeup she'd put on her face? If the floor could open up and swallow her, she'd welcome it with joy.

"I'm sorry about last night, Emma." Josh knocked back his pain killers and grimaced. "I thought you knew. I should have broken it to you more gently."

Wanting to put the sorry night behind her, Emma shrugged. "It's okay. I'd have found out one way or another. Best it came from someone I knew."

Jack turned to the frying pan as thick slices of bacon sizzled away.

"I can't believe he stood you up," Josh continued. "He should have at least rung you. I mean, I get he's pissed off, but you were his date. Do you want me to have a word with him?"

"No," Emma replied quickly. "I have to work with him, remember?"

"I wish you hadn't taken that job now." Josh folded his arms angrily. "Well, he didn't deserve to spend last night with you. You looked amazing, by the way. Didn't she, Jack?"

Jack turned over the bacon quickly, jumping as the fat splashed his arm.

"You okay, mate?"

"Yeah, I mean. Yeah, she looked good."

"I'd like to see him doing this job. I know for definite he won't be up at this hour." Josh winked at Emma. "Farmers are quick risers, aren't they, Jack?"

"Josh…" Jack looked at his brother disapprovingly. "…let's not get rude."

Emma felt a smile lift her lips as Jack mouthed a '*sorry*' her way. Josh had always been inappropriate. She was more than used to him.

"Clive is coming this morning." Jack sat down at the table after making everyone a bacon sandwich. "He's bored, poor chap. Retirement doesn't suit everyone. I'm trying to think what jobs I can give him to keep him out of mischief. I caught him fixing tiles on the roof of the parlour yesterday afternoon."

"He needs a new distraction," Josh agreed as he finished off his breakfast and burped loudly. "Right, do you need a hand with the milk tanks before I head to work?"

"Nah, I'll manage them. I've finally ordered new ones, although I'll probably still be paying for them when I turn sixty."

Jack threw their empty plates into the sink and nodded to Emma. "Are you ready?"

The coolness of the parlour was a welcome relief to the already heady temperatures. As the earthy scent hit them both, Jack bent over and rested his hands on his knees.

"Are you okay?" Emma put a hand to her mouth and tried not to laugh as he gulped. "Do you need a bucket?"

He wiped his forehead and stood up with a hangdog expression. "There was no way I was going to admit to feeling rough in front of Josh. He'd take the piss for weeks."

"I must admit, I'm a bit worse for wear." Emma filled the hay troughs, ready for the cattle to come through. "It must have been that whisky."

"And not the three bottles of red wine we drank?" Jack rubbed his temples. "How were you last night?"

"So, so." Emma lowered her head. In the light of day, back in her normal shorts and t-shirt with her face bare of makeup and her hair back in a bun, she didn't want to be reminded of last night's disaster. Thankfully on the walk back to the farm, Jack hadn't mentioned her upset or drawn attention to the makeup stains on his shirt. He'd simply walked her to the piggery and watched her head inside before retreating to the cosy farmhouse. She'd sat for ages on her bed, taking off her makeup and brushing out the glossy curls. They belonged to a night that had offered her only hurt and confusion.

"How are you feeling about seeing Toby today?"

"I don't know." Emma pulled back the holding gate, realising only moments later that she hadn't flinched as the cattle's lumbering bodies pushed against her. "He embarrassed me, and he caused you a lot of inconvenience."

"Did he?"

"Well, yeah, you had to sit with me all night. The thing is, even though I'm annoyed with him, I understand why he didn't come. Everyone would have been talking about it, and I know he's not that popular around here."

"But you like him?"

Emma shrugged. "He's always been fine with me."

"Apart from standing you up."

Inwardly tutting, Emma felt a slight annoyance. Jack had made a fool out of her once, too. He had no right to criticise.

"I'm sorry." Jack closed his eyes. "I'll try to be less harsh. I agree, last night can't have been easy for him."

Emma directed some of the cattle into the milking stalls and closed their gates. "I know he can be obnoxious. I've seen it myself over the few days I've worked with him, but I genuinely think he's just misunderstood. Clive said he struggled as a child to fit in, and I think he carries his insecurities around with him and they make him appear aloof. With me, he's attentive, complementary, and kind. I feel good about myself when I'm with him."

"He gives you confidence."

"Yeah, that's it." Emma nodded as she resumed her milking duties. "I just want to be…" She paused suddenly feeling embarrassed. Sex talk with Josh felt natural. They'd swapped many hints and tips about moments under the covers, but she'd never, ever talked about anything like this with Jack.

"Flirted with?" Jack smiled. "Don't be embarrassed. It's only natural."

"Well, yeah." Emma turned around so he wouldn't see the rising colour on her neck. "That's it. In a nutshell."

"I understand." Jack watched her as she fitted milking claws onto the cattle. "I just want you to be careful, that's all, but I promise not to be as selfish with my comments about him in the future."

Emma continued to disinfect the next herd. Jack could be many things. Selfish wasn't one of them. Turning to contradict him, she watched him puff out his cheeks and place his hands on his hips, his face decidedly green. Guilt flooded through her, knowing it was her fault he felt this rough. “Are you sure you’re okay?”

“Never felt better. I just want to vomit.”

“Go ahead.” Emma laughed as he placed a hand against the wall and groaned. “I won’t judge. In fact, why don’t you sit down, and I’ll do the milking. You tell me what to do and I’ll follow your instructions.”

“You’re actually going to do what I tell you?” Jack gingerly lowered himself onto a hay bale and took a long drink of water from his bottle. “That’s a first.”

“Listen, lightweight, I can turn my hand to anything.” Emma checked the milk lines for flow. Seemingly happy, she released a batch of cattle and prepared the stalls for the next cows.

“You’ve picked this up quick.” Jack frowned, watching her work. “How long have you been here? A few years?”

“I had a good chat with myself after the hand milking fiasco,” Emma picked up the broom and moved a splatter of dung into the gully.

“Hey, that wasn’t a fiasco. You did well. Most people are squeamish about stuff like that. I’ll give you your due, you got stuck in.”

“It’s about finding commonality, isn’t it? Okay, this parlour is a very different environment to what I know, but strip back the surroundings and the basics are the same.”

“How?” Jack asked as he took another swig from his bottle.

Emma glanced at him and paused. She needed to stop exposing the thoughts in her head. It only led to ridicule or allowed others access to her feelings. “Ignore me. I’m talking rubbish.”

“Seriously, I’m genuinely interested.”

Watching him rub his tired eyes, Emma shrugged. They were both at a disadvantage this morning; what the hell. “Well, I decided to see the cattle as guests and the stalls as bedrooms. I change the sheets, keep the rooms clean, watch out for unusual behaviour and try not to double book. Once I did that, the rest came to me naturally."

"I dread to think what analogy you put to cleaning the teats, but hey, if it works for you."

"I knew you'd laugh." Emma felt heat rise to her cheeks. "I told you it was daft."

"Actually, it shows an intelligent mind. Single minded people can only focus on the task in hand. They can't take in the bigger picture or use their strengths to improve a situation. I think your analogy is ingenious."

"Really?"

"Stop doubting yourself." Jack put his head back and drank the last of his water. "Do you know what your problem is? You've no self-confidence. You enter situations already on the back foot. You are by far smarter and stronger than you think you are."

"You would say that," Emma replied quietly as she patted a cow on its hind to move it along.

"Why would I?"

"Because we grew up together and you're slightly older than me, so you think you need to use your nurturing instincts to bolster me along."

"I'm only two years older than you, and we've both changed since we were teenagers."

"Have we?" Emma frowned. "I'm still the same, I think." She looked down at her freckled, slightly tanned legs. "I look the same, don't I?"

Jack bit back a smile. "In some ways."

"So, you think I should be tougher on Toby, is that what you're trying to say?"

"I thought his actions last night were disrespectful, but I take on board what you say. I'm not in his shoes and he has suffered a public humiliation," Jack bit his lip hesitantly as he sat on the hay bale. "So, are you and him an item?"

"I don't know. I think, maybe. He's never actually said so."

"But you're hoping there's a possibility?"

"I guess. Look, I know you don't approve of him, and I'm not asking you to, but it would be great if you'd support me so we didn't have to fight over it."

Jack slowly nodded. "I know, and I don't want to argue with you either. Life is tough enough right now. However, I know Toby. I know him well. I do still have my concerns, but I promise you I'll keep my trap shut. I also want you to know if things get difficult, then I'm here for you. Does that seem fair?"

"Things won't get difficult. I can handle myself."

"I know you can." Jack stood up and took the broom from her hand. "Why don't you go and get ready and leave this to me? Isn't it your opening day today for the farm shop?"

Emma nodded. She'd almost forgotten about the barn. Toby's no show had shrouded her excitement.

"Go find Toby, speak with him and settle your mind. It seems to me you know what you want. So go and get it."

Wiping her hands on a towel, Emma suddenly wondered what she did want. In all honesty, she didn't want to dwell on those thoughts.

CHAPTER 13

"She did what to your toenails?"

"She inspected them." Milly opened the oven doors and took out a batch of chocolate chip muffins, causing her rosy cheeks to go even pinker. "I thought she was going to give me tips on nail care, but she started to do a fungal test on them." Milly raised her gloved hands in astonishment. "Right there in the middle of my own front room, she asked me to cut a piece of my nail off and put it into a sample tube so she could analyse it, and get this, then she'd tell me if I was an acceptable flat mate. The cheek of her. Not just that, she asked me if I suffered from thrush, because she didn't want to flat share with someone who had yeast infections."

Emma burst out laughing. After the stress of last night, Milly's honesty and self-deprecating humour was just what she needed. "What did you say?"

"I told her I didn't think we'd get along." Milly pulled a face. "I didn't know what else to do. I was wearing one shoe and had my foot up on the table, and she was brandishing a pair of nail scissors. She looked so shocked, I almost felt sorry for her, until I caught her sniffing my cushions. I'm going to end up like her off '*single white female*' at this rate." Milly brought over two warm muffins and sat by Emma's side in the sunny bay window seat. "I need some normal company. Why don't you come here tonight? We can share a pizza and a bottle of wine and watch a movie?"

Emma nodded. "Definitely. Count me in. Friends are never lost."

"Talking of friends, at least you've landed on your feet with Jack. He turned up last night, didn't he?"

"How early does gossip start to spread in this village?" Emma laughed. "I haven't even opened the farm shop yet."

"Quickly, especially when the object of the gossip is a very handsome farmer wearing a tuxedo in Toby's hall."

"Oh God." Emma smacked a hand to her forehead. "You know, I've only just realised that's another reason he doesn't go in the hall. It belongs to Toby."

"Exactly, and all the profits go directly to his family. Jack ordering drinks last night raised a few eyebrows. The oldies around here think he stayed just to piss Toby off."

Emma didn't reply. She had wondered the same thing herself. Why else would Jack sit in the hall all night with her? He must have known people would talk.

"No one's seen Toby since the news broke," Milly continued. "Did he tell you about it?"

"He didn't tell me anything. He just sent me a text saying he wasn't coming."

"A text? Is that all?" Milly harrumphed. "Cheeky bastard. I take it you're going to have words with him?"

"I don't know." Emma puffed out her cheeks with frustration. He'd made a fool out of her last night, and so far, she still hadn't received an apology. However, she needed to give him the benefit of the doubt. She couldn't go joining the anti-Toby campaign without hearing his side of the story first. Plus, and she hated to admit this about herself, she liked his attention. Sean's actions had hurt her more than she'd realised. They'd left her feeling insecure and vulnerable and, if she had to be honest with herself, unattractive.

"I'm pressuring you, I can tell." Milly touched her arm gently. "I'm sorry. It's your life. If you like him and he likes you, then it's no one else's business." She stood up to serve a few early customers with her freshly baked bread before sitting back down in the window seat. "So, do you want to know what happened to Toby?"

Emma nodded. "I guess I need to. Forewarned is forearmed."

Milly checked to make sure no other customers were loitering before starting. "I heard this from their receptionist this morning when she came in for her usual coffee. His mother is concerned he's not responsible enough to take over the role, and she's fed up with the family name being associated with negativity. I don't think arguing with the Seymours has helped, but we'll not dwell on that. She's started a probation period for him while she's away in Scotland visiting family. He has to prove he can do the role by showing his maturity and by making the shop a success."

"I thought I was managing the farm shop?"

"That's why I wanted you to know." Milly looked out over the village green towards the barn. "He may need to be more involved in it."

Emma grimaced. The past few days working on her own had been hard, but she'd secretly enjoyed not having to compromise on her ideas. She had built the shop her way and now she looked forward to running it independently.

"Does that bother you?"

"A bit," Emma admitted. "It's become my baby."

"I know the feeling." Milly looked around her bakery with pride. "This place is only tiny, and I can't extend it because it's a listed building, but it's mine. Well, technically it's not mine, the Montgomerys own it, but I pay for it."

Emma chewed the inside of her cheek thoughtfully. She would have to bite the bullet and see how things went on their opening day. Her ideas for running the barn were strong, and her experience stronger. She already understood her demographic, just by paying attention. In theory, if he listened to her, it wouldn't fail. Raising her eyebrows, she laughed at her own naivety. She'd just fallen into the same trap as she had with Sean. Mixing business with pleasure. She just hoped this relationship would have a better outcome.

*

Biting her fingernails nervously, Emma glanced at the clocks on the wall and then at the long queue snaking outside the barn, waiting for the doors to open. Should she be the one to begin trading? Surely Toby would want to make it official, or Mrs. Montgomery, although she appreciated his mother may have already left for Scotland.

Seeing some of the customers start to look impatient as they checked their own watches, Emma decided to take matters into her own hands. Bending down, she undid the bolts and flung the doors open wide, a bright smile on her face as the line entered and immediately started to browse. She'd deal with the wrath of Toby if, and when, he turned up. For now, though, she had customers to serve and a reputation to keep. She may have been the girl who Toby stood up, but she was still the girl who'd got this business off the ground.

Two hours later, her legs were wobbly with hunger, but nothing could detract from the happiness of seeing the barn full of shoppers. Taking note of her best sellers, she rushed around restocking shelves and crates while trying to keep the queues to a minimum. The balancing act came naturally to her, and, as midday approached, she prepared herself for the dinner time rush.

Her morning preparation didn't go to waste. As she'd expected, the cooked meats, olives, houmous and sun-dried tomatoes in her deli selection flew from the shelves along with plump fruits and bottles of freshly squeezed orange juice. Her customers eagerly bought before searching for the perfect spot on the village green, some under the much-needed shade of the apple trees and others under the hot rays of the scorching sun.

Four hours later, the balls of her feet burning and her stomach still recovering from the hastily eaten sandwich she'd managed to cram in, she turned her shop sign to 'closed' and took off her trainers, allowing her tired feet to cool on the floor of the barn. The small knock at the heavy wooden door caused her to inwardly groan, and she peered through the window. Seeing Toby, his head low, she felt the first stirrings of frustration and compassion, all in one go.

"Hi." He shrugged sheepishly, walking inside, and locking the door behind him. He stood in front of her, his hands in his pockets as a smell of stale alcohol surrounded him, providing some answer to his no show this morning. Emma understood his behaviour, but after being on her feet all day, her tolerance and sympathy levels had vastly reduced.

"How are you?" Emma poured him a glass of cold water and passed it over the counter.

"I've been better." Toby sighed, his lavender eyes dull and lifeless. "I take it you've heard the news."

"That you've not inherited the role?" Emma nodded. "I did."

Toby rubbed his stubbly chin. "This village will be having a field day. No doubt it's their main topic of conversation. Any sign of scandal and they pick at it like a sore scab."

Emma didn't reply. There seemed little point.

"I don't know why she's done it." Toby raised his arms and looked around. "I mean, running this village isn't rocket science. People pay us rent. Things break, we arrange to get it fixed. We keep the place looking good to attract the tourists and the remainder runs itself. I feel completely victimised. None of my predecessors had to prove their worth. I don't see why she's making an example of me."

Emma stayed tactfully quiet. She assumed there'd be a lot more to the role than he'd just stated, but it wasn't her place to say anything.

"I need to work with you in here." Toby looked around, not commenting on the cleanliness or how quickly she'd restocked the shelves, but he did glance at the till and the money all bagged up, ready to be taken over to the hall. "And I have to find a way of improving local businesses. It's part of the terms."

Emma nodded. They needed to talk about their working together and set agreed boundaries.

Toby suddenly looked at her bare feet and closed his eyes. "Forgive me. I should be saying sorry, not dumping all my problems on you. My actions last night were unforgivable. I take it you didn't stay?"

"No, I stayed," Emma replied quietly, relieved he'd finally acknowledged his behaviour. "Did none of your family tell you?"

"In all honesty, I haven't spoken to any of them since last night, and by the time I'd sobered up, they'd all left for Scotland. Did you sit with Josh and Daisy? I know they normally go."

"I sat with Jack, actually." Emma watched a darkness flood Toby's face, causing her to consider her next words carefully. "He came so I wouldn't be sitting alone."

"That's nonsense," Toby growled. "He came to celebrate my downfall. He's never stepped foot in that place since his wife left. Anyway, I thought you didn't get along with him. You said he's obnoxious."

"Let's just say I didn't have a choice." Emma could feel her frustrations begin to build. Could he not put his own issues to one side and see how he had embarrassed her? "I'd made the effort to turn up, wear a dress, do my hair. I even wore makeup. Did you expect me to go home and wait for you to ring me?"

Toby stared at her thoughtfully for a few seconds. "So, Jack was your knight in shining armour?"

"He prevented me from looking like a total idiot, yes."

"My back was turned, so he stepped right in and took my date."

"No." Emma put her head back and groaned. "Jack isn't interested in me in that way, okay?"

"Are you sure?" Toby sniffed. "It's not like him to swallow his pride. Any opportunity to belittle me and he'll take it."

Refusing to be drawn in, Emma brought the conversation back to her. "Look, I think you're missing the point here. I feel like you should apologise to me. Properly."

Toby acknowledged her words with a slow nod. "You're right. I'm being selfish. I should have turned up and given you an explanation." He walked around the counter and held out his hand. "I'm very sorry. Jack was obviously a very lucky guy, getting to sit with you. If anything, I should be thanking him for taking care of you."

Feeling slightly appeased, Emma felt her resolve start to melt. He'd apologised with maturity and found the courage to thank Jack as well. Knowing the history between them both, those words would have taken some guts to say.

"Thank you," Emma replied, keen to get things back to some kind of normal. She had to work with this guy, after all. "I accept your apology."

His usual aplomb, that Emma admired, returned with each breath and she felt last night's tension and hurt drain away. He'd suffered a crushing disappointment, yet still managed to turn up to see her.

"I haven't said anything before now because I didn't want to come across as inappropriate." Toby swallowed deeply and fiddled with his watch. "But I feel there's a connection between us. You're a very strong, talented young woman. I mean, look at this place, everything you've done. It's amazing. You're amazing. Professionally, we have to work together, and I'm really looking forward to that, but part of me is hoping we can get to know each other outside of work too."

Emma felt a jolt of excitement run through her. So, she was right. He did like her. The confirmation boosted her low self-esteem, and she didn't miss the quick glance he gave to her tight t-shirt. It felt so good to have someone appreciate her for what she was.

“I’d love to take you to Featherby’s one evening.” Toby cocked his head to one side. “Would you like that?”

“Definitely.” Emma smiled, meeting his twinkly eyes. “We could go tonight. Oh.” She suddenly tapped the side of her head. “I’m sorry. I can’t. I’ve just remembered I’m going to Milly’s for the evening to watch a movie. Could we do another night? Tomorrow, maybe?”

“I can’t tomorrow,” Toby replied regretfully. “I’ve got a meeting with my accountant. In fact, why don’t you take the day after tomorrow off? That can be your rest day.”

“Thank you.” Emma bit the end of her thumbnail as a smile stretched across her face. A bit of gentle flirtation never hurt anyone, and, another major plus, it would take her mind off Jack.

CHAPTER 14

"I've told you, I can't tonight." Emma wiped down the kitchen table, ready to serve the cottage pie bubbling in the Aga.

"Why not? Hair of the dog, and it'll celebrate your first day in the farm shop." Josh grinned at her mischievously, his blond curls bouncing energetically. "I've heard it was a roaring success. You must be buzzing."

Emma smiled to herself. She was buzzing. All over.

"And you've had that dickhead to deal with. Come on, you used to love a night out. It'll be like the good old days. Except this time, we'll be drinking alcohol and not cherryade."

"I think my liver would prefer the cherryade." Jack walked into the kitchen and helped her to set the table. "How was your first day?"

"Great." Emma tried to ignore how her face automatically smiled when she saw him. "I had loads of customers. I'm really happy with how it's going."

"And Toby?" Jack put a knife and fork by her placemat. "Did he turn up to apologise?"

"Yeah, he did." Emma deliberately opened the Aga to take out the cottage pie so she wouldn't have to say anymore.

"Never mind about Toby," Josh wheedled. "I'm trying to get her to come out with me tonight."

"I've told you, I can't," Emma replied. "I've made plans."

"Toby, I take it." Jack took the warmed plates from the oven and set them by her side. "Where are you going?"

"I'm seeing Milly, actually." Emma dished out the cottage pie along with fresh vegetables she'd bought from her own shop. "She's had bad luck trying to find a lodger and I think it's getting her down."

"Why is she trying to find a lodger?" Jack asked. "I thought the bakery was doing well."

"It is from what I can see. I think some of her downfall is that she doesn't have much of a seating area for customers." Emma took a mouthful of food and chewed on it thoughtfully as an idea formed in her head. She needed to speak to Daisy about it first, though.

"If you want to go to the Mouse tonight, invite Milly along," Jack suggested.

"Hold on." Josh swallowed his food quickly. "I don't want Milly there. She'll take the piss out of me all night."

"That's because you're always insulting her," Emma replied, feeling protective of her new friend. "She's great fun. You should give her a chance. You may find you actually like her."

"And pigs will fly," Josh muttered as he finished off his meal. "I was looking forward to this night out and now you've pissed on my parade."

"Well, could you at least try to be friendly to her?"

Rolling his eyes, Josh eventually nodded. "I promise to be civil. Will that do? Jack, if you come too, then I won't need to talk to Milly."

"I wasn't planning on coming out." Jack glanced at the clock. "I had a late one last night."

"Aww, come on." Josh looked at his brother pleadingly. "You can't leave me alone with two women. I'll do you a deal. If you come tonight, I'll help you milk in the morning."

Jack lowered his head and laughed. “I don’t know why I’m bothering arguing with you. You’ll get your own way eventually. Fine, I’ll come out.”

“Right answer.” Josh stood up and sniffed his armpits. “I’ll have a shower in the morning. I can’t be bothered tonight.”

“Actually, I’ll have a shower now, if that’s okay?” Emma dried the few dishes left on the drainer. “I may as well make the effort if we’re going out.”

“Does that mean you’re wearing that green dress again?” Josh asked cheekily. “The low cut one? Toby will get jealous if you keep wearing all your best stuff when you’re with my brother.”

“Josh,” Jack warned quietly. “Behave.”

“I’m only stating a fact. Have you checked with him that you can come out with us?” Josh gave a mischievous wink. “If he thinks Jack has his sights set on you, that would wind him up.”

“That’s a ridiculous notion.” Jack pushed his chair back forcefully and picked up his boots. “I’ll see you later.”

*

Josh’s head swivelled as girly laughter erupted from the table behind them. Emma gave him a nudge to bring his attention back to Milly.

“So, I’ll just have to wait to see if anyone else is interested in my spare room,” Milly continued. “I guess it’s better than all the perverts I’ve been interviewing expecting sexual favours.”

“What?” Josh turned towards them. “Sexual favours for what?”

“Never mind.” Milly shook her head with annoyance as she arranged her summer dress around her ankles. “You’re more interested in the table behind you. I wonder why that is.”

Josh grinned. "Because they're having fun. Try it. Lift your lips. It's called a smile."

"I know how to have fun," Milly tutted. "Just not with you."

"Oh, come on." Josh winked, his blond curls bouncing around his mischievous eyes. "Your idea of fun is organising your cupcakes in colour order. When was the last time you let your hair down?"

"Hey, children." Jack laughed at their heated expressions. "Why don't you two try to forget the past and reintroduce yourselves? Start with an interesting fact about each other. Josh, you go first."

"I'm not doing this." Josh folded his arms. "It's childish."

"And you're not?" Milly smiled sarcastically. "You won't have an interesting fact, anyway."

"And you do?" Josh retorted.

"Actually, I do. What's yours?"

Pausing momentarily, Josh scratched the back of his neck. "I can swim under water for seventy seconds."

Milly looked to Jack for confirmation, who simply nodded.

"See," Josh replied, a hint of relief behind his eyes. "And don't say you can do it for longer, because not many people can."

"I wasn't going to say that, because I can't swim." Milly shrugged casually. "I think it's a skill you need to learn as a kid."

"You can learn to swim at any age," Jack replied. "You just need confidence. There's a lake near here that's not too deep and it's very secluded. It would be the perfect place to learn if you wanted to."

"Josh can teach you," Emma interrupted, feeling pleased to find something to connect the pair. "He taught me."

"Whoa." Josh wiped beer froth off his top lip. "No way."

"No way, doubled." Milly looked up incredulously. "You can strike that one off your list. It isn't happening."

"I'm not even offering," Josh replied drolly. "Anyway, what is your interesting fact? Can you kiss without puking?"

"Very funny," Milly tutted.

"So, go on, what is it?" Josh leaned forward on his elbows. "Are you a member of the Mafia?"

"No." Milly took a long drink of her gin and tonic. "I was a member of the military for five years, serving in Iran as a doctor."

Josh paused before shaking his head and laughing. "Nah, you almost had me there. You, in the army, that's just ridiculous. You can't even swim."

"I beg your pardon?" Milly banged her glass on the table furiously. "What's so unbelievable about me being in the army?"

"Look at you for a start." Josh pointed to her pink printed dress and sparkly sandals. "That's not exactly camouflage, is it? Well, I suppose it matches your twee cake stands. You blend in with those." He nodded to his brother. "What do you think?"

"Hey, you can leave me out of this one," Jack replied with a grin. "Milly may be petite, but I don't want to get on the wrong side of her."

Taking Jack's lead, Emma also stayed silent, but she made a mental note to ask Milly more about her old career tomorrow. People didn't leave a job like that without good reason.

"And just to clarify…" Milly sniffed haughtily. "…you don't need to be able to float to be a doctor. Anyway, I have no intention of wearing a swimming costume in front of you."

"Believe me, I'm not interested in your body." Josh gave her a challenging smile. "But I can teach you how to swim. So, tomorrow night, we're going swimming. All of us."

Emma swallowed her wine quickly. "The four of us?"

"I ain't going if you're not going." Milly looked at her threateningly. "You can't let this idiot drown me."

Emma nodded, wondering how she'd managed to get herself embroiled in swimming with Jack. She'd have to buy a costume and shave her legs properly and, oh God, other parts that had been neglected for far too many months. The last time she'd worn a costume in front of Jack, she'd been around seven years old. Thinking back, she'd probably had a crush on him even then. She vaguely remembered him throwing water bombs at her, his face filled with regret as she started to cry.

"Are you asking Toby?" Milly raised an eyebrow as Emma looked up. "Just wondering, seeing as you two are getting close."

Emma shifted in her seat. By rights, she should ask Toby. It would cheer him up after his recent upset, and it did sound like a couple's thing to do, but somehow, she couldn't imagine Toby frolicking in a lake. If he fancied a swim, he probably had access to a private spa with a bar that served cocktails with tiny bowls of olives by the side. He definitely preferred the more luxurious side of things, not that she considered that a negative. As long as he knew how to have fun and had the ability to make her laugh, then the rest was just materialistic.

"He'll need to bring his butler to iron his speedo's." Josh laughed before wincing as his brother kicked him under the table. "Aww, come on. You can't invite Toby. It will be an odd number."

"He'll probably be busy anyway." Emma shrugged casually. "Plus, as much as we enjoy each other's company, it's also good to spend time apart."

"So, you're seeing him officially?" Milly asked.

"Not officially." Emma recalled Jack's comment earlier, a relationship with her being a ridiculous notion. "However, there's a mutual attraction, I can't deny that. He's made it clear he wants more than just friendship, and I'm happy to see where things go. I've had enough of the type of men who need support. It's time for me now."

"Well, good for you." Milly chinked her glass against hers. "It's refreshing to hear a girl who's striving for what she wants. I hope you and Toby make a go of it."

Not able to help herself, Emma turned her head and pretended to look at the other tables, catching Jack's eye deliberately in the process. He smiled at her before raising his glass slightly. Perhaps he'd accepted her relationship with Toby after all.

"Hey, talking about posh boys." Josh leaned forward across the table. "Don't look now, but Toby's over there, looking at you."

"Where?" Emma strained to keep her head still.

"Your three o'clock. I don't think he realises I've spotted him. He's got a hell of a face on him. If looks could kill. Does he know you're out with us?"

Emma shrugged, feeling slightly uncomfortable. "He thinks I'm at Milly's, watching a film."

"He won't like you being sat with me," Jack warned. "Do you not want to nip over to him now and explain what's happened?"

"No." Emma shook her head vigorously, suddenly understanding why people felt they ought to apologise for a badly behaved child or pet. "Toby isn't immature. He'll simply be curious about my change in plans."

"Shall we invite him over?" Milly asked. "He's definitely staring at you."

"How do you know he's staring at her?" Josh asked sarcastically. "Oh, don't tell me you've got surveillance cameras fitted to your headband that the army gave to you."

Milly pointed to the compact mirror in her hand as she applied her lipstick. "I thought you'd have figured this one out, knob head. Oldest trick in the book."

Josh tutted before rolling his eyes in frustration. "He's gone now anyway. That was a bit freaky."

"Are you sure you don't want to nip over and talk to him now?" Jack repeated. "It might be a good idea before he gets ideas in his head."

“I’m perfectly sure,” Emma replied firmly, then she drained her glass and stood up. “You and I are friends with no romantic involvement whatsoever. What’s he got to be jealous about?”

“Nothing, I guess.” Jack sighed as he stood up and picked up his fleece. “As you say, we’re just friends.”

CHAPTER 15

"I told you my brother wouldn't leave a beer garden while they're still serving." Jack pulled a torch from his pocket to light the bank at the side of the stream. "It's the only thing he has in common with Milly."

"Did you know she was a doctor in the army?" Emma asked.

"I had an idea about her medical background, only because she's assisted in the village with a few emergencies. Why did she leave?"

"She said it wasn't the career for her," Emma replied. "But I think there's probably more to it. I didn't want to ask her that question tonight. She's so down to earth and honest with her feelings, yet around Josh she's a closed book."

"And he's the same with her. Very defensive."

Emma nodded, aware of Jack close by her side, his breathing, and footsteps perfectly in line with hers. "It was a good night though, wasn't it?"

"Yep, I enjoyed it." Jack walked ponderously by her side as he lit their way. "Please don't think I'm trying to labour the point, but I just wanted to say I'm sorry for going on about Toby tonight. I was just worried he'd react badly to you being with me."

"It's okay," Emma replied, trying to hide her sharpness. Why did everyone keep going on about this? Did they doubt her abilities to handle a relationship? "I wasn't just with you. We were a group of four and he's no reason to be concerned. Has he?"

"No. It's just he can be very unpredictable at times. He's overreacted in the past, especially around me. I don't want you bearing the brunt of any of his jealousy. I'm sorry for going on about this. I genuinely am trying to be supportive."

"I know, and I am listening to you, but he's not at all the ogre everyone paints him out to be." Emma jumped as a fox ran straight in front of them, putting her hand over her heart. "That was close."

Jack laughed lightly as they continued to walk. "The wildlife is quite brave in the hills. Don't worry, I've got you covered."

Emma's heart rate doubled at the thought of Jack protecting her, and she cursed her reactions. She'd put him on a pedestal, she knew that, and despite him standing her up all those years ago, it wasn't enough to knock him off.

"Can I ask you a personal question?"

"Dare I refuse?" Jack's eyes twinkled in the dark as he lit the way.

"Why did you steal Toby's girlfriend?"

"Ah. I thought this might come up." Jack pushed a thicket of thorns out of the way as they walked along the trickling stream. "When I arrived here, Toby had a girlfriend, a quiet kind, but she had a knowing look in her eyes that I recognised immediately. She wasn't at all the sort of girl who would settle down in a village."

"So, you had some fun with her?" Emma asked, as she mentally rocked Jack off the top of his plinth.

"No, I put her straight after she tried to kiss me. I warned her off, which she didn't like, so she told Toby I'd tried it on with her. He thumped me and in return I pushed him into the duck pond."

"You pushed him into the duck pond?" Emma stopped and stared at him. "Really?"

"Yeah, I know, very big of me. I'm not proud of myself."

"And that's when the arguments began between you?"

"More or less. I later found out he'd planned to ask her to marry him. I felt awful about that, but after a while, I realised I'd done them both a favour. She'd have been unfaithful to him at some point."

"Poor Toby." Emma tried not to picture him floundering in a duck pond. "He doesn't seem to have much luck, does he?"

"Well, he's got you."

Emma looked up at Jack, expecting to see a mocking expression, but instead found him concentrating on the path ahead. Not knowing how to take his comment, she decided on a safer subject. "I've been thinking about the cheese shop Daisy is trying to start up again. Do you think she'd be open to some suggestions from me?"

"I don't see why not. Why, what are you thinking?"

"The only reason Milly needs to take in a lodger is because she's not earning enough money. She has the ability to bake on a bigger scale, but she needs somewhere to sell it. I'm wondering if she'd go into business with Daisy and they could combine their produce. Cheese, home baked crackers, breads, and chutneys. I really do think it would work. Clive could help out too. It would give him something to do."

"It's not a bad idea." Jack opened the gate to the farm and allowed her through before closing it behind them. He glanced at his watch. "Have you time for a beer? I'm actually interested in your suggestion."

Heading into the kitchen, Jack took two bottles from the fridge and pushed one towards her. "So, what are your thoughts on how it would work?"

"Have you got a pen and paper?" Emma moved the table mats out of the way and sat down. She took the lid from a pen and started to draw columns. "In comings, outgoings. I take it you're on top of them."

"Every penny." Jack leaned against the counter and watched her thoughtfully.

Emma tapped the pen against her lip. "Farmers markets are good research for this kind of thing. Find out what customers want seasonally and then make your produce based on expected demand. You could even add spirits to complement the food. Ports, red or white wine, that kind of thing. Bespoke luxury hampers to suit any budget with Milly's cakes included."

Emma looked up to find Jack staring at her, a small smile playing on his lips. "You used to sit like that when you were doing your homework at our kitchen table. Tongue out with ink on your nose."

"What?" Emma rubbed at her face, groaning as a black smudge appeared on her fingers. "Why didn't you tell me?"

"Because it suits you." Jack turned the piece of paper his way and nodded at the series of tables. "It's viable."

"Of course it is. Luxury foods are a big thing these days. They attract a very wide demographic."

"And you think Milly will go along with this?"

"I think she'll bite your hand off."

Jack sat down thoughtfully. "And what about Toby?"

Emma frowned. "What about him? This has nothing to do with him."

"Technically, it doesn't, but he'll not take kindly to you passing ideas onto me, not when he's got to come up with a way of improving local business himself."

Emma furrowed her brow. Jack had a point. It would be rubbing his nose in it.

Jack shrugged. "Unless we say it's my idea."

Emma breathed a sigh of relief. For a moment there, she'd felt trapped between them. "Anyway, I'm doing this for Daisy. It will help to take her mind off her exam results. Doesn't she get them in a few days?"

"Yep, this Thursday." Jack bit his lip as he continued to look at the figures. "I'm impressed. You know your stuff."

“Years of working with the public.” Emma took another sip of her beer while sitting back in her chair. She’d done it. She just proved to him she’d matured.

“Another beer?”

“I’d best not. Another early morning tomorrow, and then swimming. We’ll be shattered.” Picking up her handbag, she felt her heart miss a beat as a humongous spider crawled leisurely across her trainers as if it deserved to be there. Panicking, she kicked her foot out, causing the gigantic spider to scuttle up the inside of her jeans. The shock and panic of seeing the large arachnid disappear into her clothing rendered her speechless until she felt its eight legs explore her lower calves. Her breath spasming against her chest, she dumped her bag on the floor and shot out of the kitchen and up the farmhouse stairs. Slamming the bathroom door shut, she yanked down her jeans and held in a terrified scream as the equally petrified spider made its bid for freedom behind the toilet. Fear of it attacking her again, she jumped into the bath with her jeans pooled around her ankles and peered over the edge as she attempted to calm her breathing.

“Emma?” Jack knocked gently on the bathroom door. “Are you okay?”

Breathing in through her nose and out through her mouth, Emma attempted to respond without hysteria. God only knows what he thought of her rushing off like that. Only seconds earlier she’d been businesswoman of the year, and now look at her, sitting at the bottom of a copper bath in a pool of undrained water with her jeans sagging around her feet.

“Are you not feeling well?”

Knowing she had to respond to him at some point, Emma wrestled the wet denim up her calves before giving up. She’d have more luck trying to shovel jelly into a sausage skin. She looked around desperately for a robe or a towel, something she could wear while she opened the door, but apart from a small hand towel, there was nothing.

Jack knocked again. “Okay, you’re worrying me now. What’s wrong?”

"Nothing," Emma managed to squeak as she attempted to thread her feet out of her jeans while keeping an eye out for the spider at the same time. "Just a small issue." Her foot suddenly slipping in the pool of water, she screamed out loud as she went crashing into the bath, her tangled legs in the air.

"Right, I'm coming in." Jack rattled the handle. "I don't care what state you're in."

"No," Emma shouted in panic as the door opened slightly. "I'm not decent. Just give me a second. I've had an accident."

She grimaced as her choice of words sank in. She grimaced even harder at the long pause that followed.

"It happens to the best of us. Shall I bring you some spare clothes?"

Emma held a hand against her forehead and muttered obscenities under her breath. Why did these things always happen to her? Realising the truth would now be much less embarrassing, she pulled off her jeans and sat in the bath as Jack peered around the door.

He bit his lip in an attempt not to smile as she sat with her knees hunched up to her chest. "Do we need a mop?"

"It wasn't that sort of accident."

"Ah." Jack winced. "That sort of accident."

Closing her eyes, Emma wondered how deep a hole she could dig for herself. "Actually, it was a spider."

"A spider?" Jack looked around the bathroom, slightly alarmed. "I'm not following you."

Emma's cheeks flamed red as she attempted to cover her freckled thighs. "It got into my jeans. I jumped in here because the spider is on the floor, but I didn't know there was water in the bath, and I sat in it."

"Where's the spider?"

"I don't know." Emma reached for the robe Jack handed to her. "On the floor, I presume."

Jack looked down just as the gargantuan arachnid came out of hiding. As it rapidly approached his feet, he yelped and jumped in the bath with Emma.

"Now who's being brave?" Emma asked drolly as he stood beside her.

"You didn't say it was that big." Jack laughed nervously as the eight-legged creature made its way leisurely across the tiles. "Now what do we do?"

Emma suddenly snorted with laughter at the sight of them both cramped into one small bath, their feet immersed in an inch of water. Whatever she'd imagined tonight would bring, this would never have made her list of possibilities. As tears started to roll down her cheeks, she held onto Jack for support, causing him to start laughing too.

"Stop it." Jack wiped his eyes. "We need to get out of here at some point. Why is it that I always find myself in awkward situations with you?"

"Hey, you jumped into here. I didn't ask you to." Emma giggled as her feet started to slip again. "So, you're scared of spiders too?"

"Me?" Jack pointed to himself as he tried to hold her up. "Don't be daft. I'm a farmer."

Footsteps coming up the stairs halted their conversation and they both waited expectantly for the door to open.

"Why are you in the bath?" Daisy looked at them in confusion. "I could hear you both laughing from miles away. And why is Emma wearing your bathrobe?"

"You wouldn't believe me if I told you." Jack pointed to the cup holding their toothbrushes. "Do us a favour, capture that mutant tarantula on the wall, will you?"

"Why is it I'm the only one in this house who isn't scared of creepy crawlies?" Daisy trapped the spider in a glass and held it up in front of her brother. "What's it worth?"

"If you want pocket money, take that thing out of here." Jack started to laugh again as Emma's bare feet slid around in the water. "And not a word of this to your brother."

Daisy teased him with the trapped spider before throwing it out the window. "You know, it's a good job I know you two are just mates."

"Why?" Jack asked curiously as Emma clung onto his arm.

"Because you've not been this happy in years. I'm almost beginning to like you."

CHAPTER 16

"It's a Pavlovian response," Flick said quietly. "He's a good-looking guy, intelligent and nice with it. Hold on, let me go downstairs."

Emma heard her sister close a door quietly and she imagined her creeping around, trying not to wake her nieces and grisly teething nephew.

"Are you sure you don't mind talking?" Emma made a cup of tea and sat outside on the doorstep of her piggery as the rooster announced the start of a new day.

"I've been awake since three this morning. I've read *The Gruffalo* fifty times and now I'm in desperate need of adult conversation. Believe me, we could be discussing fence paint and I'd be delighted. Carry on."

Emma placed a biscuit by her side and groaned. "I just make an idiot of myself every time I'm with him."

"I can't deny the spider incident will go on your wall of fame, but as for everything else, it's human nature to react to him the way you do. Your hormones are simply conditioned to jump when he's around. You'll stop doing it eventually."

"Yeah, you're probably right." Emma nodded, feeling relieved that her once crush wasn't about to repeat itself. "Hey, do you remember Jono, Jack's rugby mate?"

"I do. Sally's brother. Big bloke. A bit pervy."

"Was he pervy?" Emma frowned. "Anyway, he asked for my number once. Jack told me."

"Yeah, I remember that." Flick giggled. "Jack wasn't happy. We'd all been to the park one afternoon, and Jono kept trying to flirt with you. Of course, you being you, his efforts went unnoticed. We all thought it was hilarious, but Jack warned him off."

"I don't recall that." Emma furrowed her brow. "What was he doing?"

"In all honesty, I can't remember, but you were completely oblivious." Flick paused for a few seconds and Emma heard the intake of breath. "Actually, talking about Jono and his family, I wanted to tell you something. Sally and Sean…"

"They're seeing each other?" Emma suggested. In all honesty, she wasn't surprised. Sally had always had her eye on him, and Sean wasn't the sort of guy who liked washing his own clothes or getting up early to greet his hotel guests. If Sally wanted to be his new doormat, then good luck to them. "I'm relieved, to be honest. In fact, I hope they get engaged. It'll get the wedding planner off my back. She still rings me, asking what to do about the food and drink. If they can get a license in two days, they can have the buffet we should have been eating."

"Are you sad about not getting married?"

"No." Emma looked around at the sun-drenched rolling hills. "I don't regret leaving him and I don't regret leaving Redsworth. They were both the right choices."

"You know, it'll all come right in the end. You'll meet someone, fall in love, and get married one day. I know you will."

Emma touched the ridge around her empty finger. "Apparently, at my seventh birthday party, I asked Jack to marry me. He said I'd never be old enough."

"No, I was there. He said, *'I'll ask you when you're old enough.'*"

Emma laughed to herself. Twenty-seven years ago, to the day.

"I know the next few days will be hard, but I'm here for you," Flick said gently. "Happy birthday, sweetheart. Mum and Dad would have been so proud of you."

*

Taking advantage of the early hour, Emma walked to the summit of the farm and watched the sun rise over the villages and hills. Talking to her sister had helped to clear her mind and ease the guilt over her mixed feelings for Jack. In fact, she could use her birthday as a fresh start for putting him out of her head completely, allowing her to concentrate on her future instead of being held up by her past. As she sat in the long grass, watching a new day unfold, she allowed a sanguine smile to rest on her lips as she thought of the day ahead. Toby would no doubt make a huge fuss of her when he discovered it was her birthday. Maybe he'd insist on taking her for a drink in her dinner hour or bring her a cupcake with a candle in it. She imagined he'd be attentive and romantic, and maybe, just maybe, he'd kiss her. Hugging that thought to herself, she skipped back down to the farm, collecting fresh hen eggs on the way.

"You're early." Josh checked his watch. "Did our Jack's cock wake you up?"

"Josh!" Jack warned, putting his papers down on the table. "Language."

"What is it with you lately? Emma knows I mean the cockerel. Don't you?"

Emma shook her head with mock frustration. She could always rely on Josh to lower the tone.

"Since when did you get so prim and proper?" Josh continued. "You've been like this for a few days now. It normally happens when there's a new woman on the scene and you're trying to impress her by pretending you're a gentleman."

"I am a gentleman. Unlike you." Jack put down his papers and refilled his coffee cup. "Anyway, are we all set for swimming later?"

"I am." Josh cracked his knuckles. "I've got my trunks out ready. Do you have a costume, Emma?"

"Not yet." She frowned. "But I've noticed one of the village shops sells them. I'm hoping they've got my size."

"Or you could skinny dip."

"Josh," Jack warned, turning to his brother again. "Behave."

"Right, who is she?" Josh winked at Emma. "I bet it's the receptionist at the hall. I know she's got her eye on you."

Emma looked down at her hands and tried to ignore the feelings of envy. It's just a Pavlovian response. She needed to remember that. Anyway, she couldn't complain if Jack felt attracted to someone else. She had Toby.

"I'm not discussing this," Jack mumbled. "Anyway, how long did you spend chatting with Milly after we left?"

"I didn't stay with her." Josh's head jumped up defensively. "She went home."

"That's not what I heard." Spying his opportunity to get his own back, Jack sat opposite his brother with a cheeky grin. "Clive said you were outside her bakery when he walked past with the piglet for their night-time stroll."

"I walked her home, okay?" Josh tutted. "Just because I don't like her doesn't mean I'm not a gentleman. Stop changing the subject anyway. Who's this girl you're into?"

"None of your business." Jack's mobile rang, and he winced as he glanced at the screen.

"Is it her?"

"Yep." Jack sighed deeply before answering the call. "What do you want, Joanne?"

Emma picked up the dirty dishes and headed over to the sink, pretending not to listen. The fact he had a young son he wasn't allowed to see still astounded her.

"The money transfers at the end of the month, you already know that," Jack replied sharply as he turned to look out the window. "And I've already given you extra for shoes and a school uniform."

Plunging her hands into the hot soapy water, Emma concentrated on scrubbing the plates. This was none of her business, so she shouldn't be getting angry on his behalf. She quickly glanced at Josh, who signalled to his brother to cut the call.

"What do you mean he's moving in with you?" Jack raked a hand through his hair. "I knew you were seeing someone, but I didn't realise it was that serious. You told me you'd keep Caleb and your relationships separate."

"I'd better go," Emma whispered as she dried her hands on a towel. "I'll see you later."

"Yes, there is a woman standing next to me." Jack put his arm out to prevent Emma from leaving. "And no, she's not my latest fancy piece. Her name is Emma, and she's a friend of the family."

Emma dithered near the kitchen door. She really didn't want to hear how Jack would describe her next. Farm hand? A hindrance from his past?

"I don't care how much you like this new bloke, he's not getting involved with my son, and if you move him in with you, then I'll contact my solicitor and insist on visiting rights."

Jack slammed his mobile onto the table at the same time as Daisy peered around the door hesitantly. She looked at her brother with tear-filled eyes. "We'll never see him, will we? It's not fair. He's my nephew and I'm his aunty."

"Never say never." Jack held out a hand to his sister and pulled her against him. "It's just difficult at the moment. She's got me over a barrel."

"Why won't she let you see him?" Emma asked quietly. "What is she worried about?"

"She says Caleb will be confused if I enter his life and then leave it. The thing is, I'm his father. I'm not likely to turn my back on him, am I?"

"She's a bitch." Josh put his head back with a sigh. "Has she no shame?"

"Apparently not." Jack kissed the top of his sister's head as her face fell. "But it doesn't matter. Maybe when Caleb is old enough, he'll come to find us himself. Until then, everything I need is right around this table."

"I still think you should fight her for custody," Josh argued. "She can't stop you from seeing him. It's not legal."

"But she can turn him against me." Jack gave his brother a look to signal he'd ended the conversation. "Anyway, let's talk about something else. These bespoke hamper plans, for example."

"What hamper plans?" Josh looked at the papers before him. "Who's done these?"

"Emma has," Jack replied. "I think it will bring in some much-needed money. But we need Daisy's approval."

His sister flicked through the plans on the table. Emma watched her, keen not to interfere but at the same time wanting to guide the young girl through the intricacies of what would be involved.

"What do you think?" Jack asked. "These are only ideas. Nothing happens without your input or final say so."

Daisy chewed the end of her thumbnail as she re-read the pages. "Is this what Mum would have wanted?"

For the first time it struck Emma that she'd known Jack's mum for much longer than Daisy ever had, and even though that fact seemed cruel, it also seemed quite poignant that as her daughter grew up, she'd be surrounded by those who had known her mother best.

"I think your mum would want to see you doing something that would make you happy." Emma deliberately covered the plans and concentrated on the girl in front of her. "In all honesty, I don't think she'd care if you were working on this farm or in a zoo. Her priority would be that you were embracing every opportunity life threw at you. Your mum would want you to choose for yourself. Does that make sense?"

"Yeah, I think so," Daisy replied quietly as she looked at the plans again. "This is on a much bigger scale than I'd planned for. The barn isn't even ready to store stock in it. We'll need hamper baskets, a website; we'll need to link in with wine suppliers. What if I can't do it?"

"Emma's offered to help you." Jack ruffled his sister's hair. "But this is your choice. No one else's."

"Then yes." Daisy looked at Emma and nodded. "I think Mum would like this. Where do we start?"

"We need to chat with Milly first," Emma replied. "But it's important we tell everyone this was Jack's idea and not mine."

"Why?" Daisy asked curiously.

"Because posh boy won't like his girlfriend fraternising with the enemy." Josh grinned as Emma rolled her eyes. "He'll be jealous. So, the sooner Jack tells us who this new girl is, the better."

Jack sighed impatiently. "I've told you before, my private life is exactly that. Private."

"Come on, who is she?" Josh repeated. "You've been too happy recently. I know the signs when a woman is on the scene."

"I think it's Emma," Daisy replied cheekily. "They were both giggling in the bathroom last night because they found a spider on the floor, and he told me I wasn't to tell you."

“Did he now?” Josh grinned. “I can’t believe my big brother is scared of spiders. However, I think he’s got more common sense than to fall for the girl he grew up with.”

Jack simply picked up his boots and headed out the kitchen door, leaving Daisy chuckling at the table. Emma gave her young friend a warning glare in the hope it would stop her gloating. She hated to admit that being dismissed by Jack so quickly did grate on her. Not the perfect start to her birthday resolutions.

“Aren’t you going to work?” Emma pointed to the clock as Josh continued to sit at the table, still looking at the doorway his brother had just departed from. “You don’t want to be in trouble with your customers.”

Josh stared at Emma, his eyes flitting up and down her petite frame. He rubbed his chin thoughtfully before turning to look at the parlour.

“What’s wrong?”

“He’s got to be kidding. Surely not.”

Emma stared at Josh. “Are you okay?”

“I am, but he isn’t.” Josh closed his eyes and sighed deeply. “I think I’d better go and have a chat with him.”

CHAPTER 17

"Our favourite time of the day." The farmers laughed as they unloaded their vans and helped Emma into the farm shop with their goods. They stacked the crates for her as she plied them with coffee and muffins from Milly's bakery.

"And here's a little something from me." Emma reached under her counter and produced an iced celebration cake, passing it over to one of the farmers. "Your fortieth wedding anniversary, I do believe?"

"It feels more like sixty," the craggy faced man replied with a laugh. He lifted the lid on the cake box and licked his lips. "Fruit cake. My favourite. Tell me, are you married?"

Emma giggled at their high humour before turning to Toby as he entered through the barn door. "Morning. It's another lovely day, isn't it?"

"So, so." Toby shrugged as he opened a refrigerator and took out a bottle of lemonade.

The farmers passed Emma a sympathetic smile before closing the door behind them. She turned to Toby to see his face set in a deep frown. "What's wrong?"

"Nothing," he replied sulkily, then drank from the bottle.

Emma closed her eyes briefly. Petulant behaviour always wound her up. Sean had been a master of it. In this instance, however, she could guess where the moodiness had come from. "You're annoyed because I went out last night, aren't you?"

"Yes," Toby replied sullenly. "I thought you were watching a film with Milly."

"It was a last-minute change of plan." Emma felt her neck start to flush. "Josh wanted to go out, and I didn't want to let Milly down, so we all went out together."

"But you were prepared to let me down. I wanted to see you last night too."

Emma paused. She had no response.

"You were laughing a lot." Toby twisted the heavy gold watch on his wrist. "I've not seen you laugh like that before."

Thanking God he hadn't heard her giggling in the bath last night, Emma knew she'd need to offer Toby some reassurance, and herself too, because come to think of it, she hadn't laughed with Toby that much at all.

"It was something funny Milly had said." Emma knew better than to mention Jack at this point. "She's my sort of person."

"Just be careful around her. I've seen her in the Mouse a few times with different men and she dresses very provocatively at times."

"Does she?" Emma scrunched up her forehead. She'd only seen Milly in jeans or long sundresses. "Anyway, what she wears has no influence on me."

"But it does taint you with the same brush. I'm only trying to be supportive. Thornhill is an affluent village. People have standards and they are quick to criticise. Perhaps spending less time with Milly would be for the best."

Emma considered his words. Admittedly she wasn't the best judge of character, she'd lived with Sean for five years, but Milly didn't seem the flighty type at all.

"Be careful with the farmers, too. If you start giving them gifts, they'll read more into it, and you don't want that kind of attention, do you? I've also been thinking of a uniform for you to wear." Toby looked down at her tight pink t-shirt. "Something black and looser is more professional. Don't you agree?"

"Yeah, sure." Emma folded her arms across her front. "I'll find something black to wear tomorrow."

Toby's phone suddenly beeped, and he frowned as he read the message before lifting his head and smiling. "I'm glad we've got that sorted. So, tonight, what time shall I pick you up?"

"Tonight?"

"Featherby's, remember? They've just replied. We have a table."

Swearing under her breath, Emma tried to cast her mind back. She felt sure they hadn't arranged an actual date. Now what would she do about her plans to go swimming? Talk about sitting on a double-edged sword. No matter who she let down now, she'd be causing offence.

"Actually, I can't make it tonight." Emma scratched the back of her neck. "I made plans because I thought you were busy with your accountant."

"My accountant?" Toby's eyes narrowed. "Oh yes. I moved that to later in the week. So, who do you have plans with that's so important you can't cancel them?"

Emma shuffled her feet. She wouldn't lie to him. He deserved better than that. "I'm going swimming with Milly. Jack and Josh said they may come too."

"Where?"

Emma felt her throat dry up. She already knew she couldn't extend the invite. Jack and Toby together for a few hours with her sandwiched in the middle filled her with dread. "Some nearby lake that they know."

Toby's jaw ticked. "I know the lake you mean. All the boys I grew up with took their girlfriends there. It's got a reputation. Jack especially liked it. It cost him nothing and he got everything from it."

Tucking a curl behind her ear, Emma paused. Did she want to go somewhere Jack had favoured for his romantic dalliances? Somehow it made the evening feel tarnished. Maybe Milly wouldn't mind if she didn't go swimming. After all, if she went to Featherby's, she wouldn't have to try to squeeze herself into the tiny red bikini she'd bought earlier, the only swimwear she could find in the village at such short notice.

"The lake is also highly polluted."

"Is it?" Emma furrowed her brow. "I was talking to Clive the other day and he mentioned how clean the waters were around here."

"That old man needs putting out to pasture," Toby tutted. "You don't want to listen to him. He talks nonsense most of the time. So, Featherby's tonight?"

About to cave in and agree, Emma stopped herself. What had Jack said about her earlier, that she always entered situations on the back foot.

"I'll confirm our booking now." Toby smiled brightly. "You'll enjoy it. Trust me."

"I'm afraid I'll need to decline your offer of Featherby's tonight." Emma picked up an apple to prevent her hands from shaking. "I've made plans and I'm the sort of girl that sticks to them."

"Fine." Toby shoved his phone into his pocket. "Suit yourself. I hope you don't intend on drinking alcohol while you're there, and I sincerely hope you'll be respectfully covered up. Personally, I don't see the attraction of swimming in a murky lake when you could be having a nice meal."

Emma fixed her face into a supporting smile. "Let's not fall out over this. I'm really sorry I have plans for tonight, but I am looking forward to Featherby's. Shall we go tomorrow instead?"

"I suppose," Toby muttered, his eyes quickly flitting over her tight t-shirt. "Stay away from Jack tonight, okay? He's very quick to steal other people's girlfriends. What time will you be here in the morning?"

"I thought it was my day off," Emma replied quietly. "You said take the day off."

"Fine." Toby sighed deeply. "More time you'll be spending with the Seymours."

Emma chewed on her thumbnail as Toby left the barn. She hoped his mistrust of Jack would ease over time, otherwise she really would end up as piggy in the middle. As she started to unpack the crates, she realised she hadn't told him about her birthday. Not that it mattered now; it had already been rained on.

*

The afternoon arrived and once again Emma found herself rushed off her feet. Many of the tourists wanted her guidance and knowledge of the local food, which she'd taken the time to learn. Rivers the fish had swum in, the vineyards the wines had originated from, even the rich soils that had harvested the baskets of fruit and vegetables. '*Farm to Plate*' Emma doodled on her notepad. She quickly sketched a few ideas which she hoped she could discuss with Toby at Featherby's tomorrow night. This place would be a goldmine if they advertised it well.

"I love hot summer days, don't you?" Milly carried in a tray of freshly whipped desserts and opened one of the large refrigerators at the back of the farm shop. She paused, leaving the door open, obviously relishing the coolness that enveloped her long blue sundress. "These are selling like hot cakes, or cold cakes, depending on how you look at it. I figured I'd bring some over here as I'm running out of space in the bakery."

"I take it you're busy too. The sunshine certainly does bring them out, doesn't it?"

"Always." Milly glanced over at the revellers outside the Mouse, shaded under parasols as they laughed over cold beers and plates of food. "I just wish this place suited all pockets and not just deep ones. Toby has put the rents up again."

Emma's shoulders sank. Josh had warned her this might happen.

"Hey, I'm not having a go," Milly reassured her. "I just assumed you'd rather hear it from me instead of a disgruntled local. They're always complaining about money in this village."

"Talking of money, we've had an idea." Emma took out the notes she'd made last night and hoped they would help distract from the raised rents. "Daisy wants to restart her mum's cheese business. Jack will still supply and make the produce, but she wants to sell bespoke hampers with your breads and cakes included. What do you think?"

"I think that sounds amazing." Milly grinned excitedly. "It's exactly what I'm looking for. What do I need to do?"

"Just speak to Daisy, but if you could keep this between us for the time being. Toby doesn't know yet."

"It's nothing to do with him, is it? He owns the buildings, not the businesses."

"I know, but I think there's enough heat between Jack and Toby without me adding petrol to the flames." Emma paused as her friend fixed the headscarf in her hair. Now wasn't the time to ask about her army career, but she was curious about her other problem. "Do you have any more lodgers to interview?"

"Just one more." Milly accepted the dewy red apple offered to her and crunched into it thoughtfully. "If this one is no good, then I may need to sell the bakery or find somewhere cheaper to rent."

"You can't." Emma gasped, turning to face the newly designed window display of teapots and white rabbits. "It's one of the focal points in the village."

"I know, but I may not have a choice." Milly chewed on her apple dolefully. "Although, the Parish Council has finally sent my advert to the website I'd originally requested. Thankfully, the bloke I'm interviewing later seems normal."

"Unlike you." Josh grinned as he lolloped lazily into the farm shop with his t-shirt tied around his waist. "If he accepts, you'll need to hide your haemorrhoid cream and your cauldron."

Emma had to smile as Milly's cheeks started to redden.

"Oh, shut up, Josh. Do you actually own any tops, or do you enjoy walking around half naked like a werewolf?"

"I'm just giving you a sneak preview before we go swimming." Josh winked naughtily. "I know you're dying to see me in a pair of trunks. I won't disappoint you."

"As long as I bring my microscope," Milly muttered. "If you've nothing better to do, you can put a bolt on my spare bedroom door. No doubt my lodger will want privacy."

"If you ask me politely, I'll consider it." Josh picked a handful of grapes and popped them into his mouth. "Anyway, you need to be nice to me today. Apparently, I have to try and keep you afloat tonight."

"I'd come back and haunt you if you didn't," Milly replied as she headed for the door. "I'd be your worst nightmare."

"You already are." Josh threw a grape into the air and caught it between his teeth, a wide smile on his lips. "What?"

"Nothing," Emma replied, hiding a grin as they found themselves alone. "Don't they always say boys who act horrible normally fancy you."

"I'd need a lobotomy to fancy her," Josh muttered as he pushed an envelope towards her. "This came in the post. It looks like a greeting card. Oh shit." Josh slapped the front of his head. "It's your birthday, isn't it? I should have remembered the date."

"Hey, it's fine," Emma replied brightly, keen not to give away her disappointment over the lack of fuss she'd received so far. "It's been a long time since we celebrated those kinds of days together."

"I know, but I should have remembered. I'm so sorry. I hope Toby has showered you with expensive gifts. That guy is loaded, and he does nothing for a living."

Emma decided not to reply. All those points unsettled her.

"I take it you still like him then?"

"Of course I do," Emma replied hotly, knowing her lack of belief in her own words had caused the sudden sharpness. "Why wouldn't I? Just because everyone else thinks he's a pratt doesn't mean I feel the same way. He's had a rough time of it, and I think we should show him some compassion."

"Hey, calm down." Josh looked at her with concern. "Are you okay?"

"Of course." Emma retreated behind her desk to reorganise papers. "Anyway, what was all that about this morning? Who is this girl that Jack likes?"

"Oh, as per usual with Jack, it's complicated."

"I don't know why," Emma tutted. "He could have any girl he wants. Surely."

"Let's just say he's picked one he can't have." Josh suddenly gave a small smile. "I think things are going to get quite interesting around here."

"Well, good luck to him." Emma sniffed before stalling. "I mean, genuinely, I hope he's successful in attracting her. Aren't you?"

"I'm coming around to the idea, slowly." Josh rubbed his eyelid, a trait that Emma knew signalled his discomfort. "Can I ask you a personal question?"

"You can ask me anything. You know that."

"During high school, you had a crush on Jack, didn't you?"

Emma heard her own intake of breath before she felt it. "Oh my God, how did you know?"

"Process of elimination, really. You went all gooey when you were out with us and started wearing makeup. I figured it wasn't for my benefit."

Putting a hand to her red cheeks, Emma cringed. "I didn't think you knew."

"I had a pretty good idea, but don't worry, Jack never knew, or if he did, he never commented on it."

Steepling her hands against her lips, Emma knew she had to come clean. If she couldn't trust Josh, she couldn't trust anyone. "I never told you about this, but the night before you left Redsworth, I did something stupid. I wrote him a love letter."

"A love letter, to Jack?" Josh furrowed his brow. "Nah, he'd have told me."

"Well, I did." Emma turned her door sign to 'closed' and bolted the door. Given the lateness of the afternoon, she didn't expect much more customers. "Biggest mistake of my life."

"Why?"

"Why?" Emma looked at him incredulously. She adored Josh, but sometimes his emotional immatureness made her want to hit him with a brick. "How would you have felt if I'd told you I had romantic feelings for you? Knowing that all the time we were hanging around together, I'd have been thinking—"

"Whoa!" Josh held up his hand. "Believe me, I don't want to know."

"Exactly." Emma leant wearily against her counter. "You'd be mortified, and so was he."

"Was he?" Josh shook his head in confusion. "This letter. When did you give it to him?"

"Technically, I didn't give it to him. I pushed it through your front door."

"Ah." Josh nodded. "Yes, it's all coming back to me now. I remember it."

"So, there you go." Emma knew she'd regret this next question, but she had to ask. The truth would hurt, but sometimes you had to examine and clean a wound before it would heal. "What did he say when he read it?"

"Nothing," Josh replied, straightening up. "He never got it."

"Sorry?"

"Look, I knew you had a crush on Jack, and I guessed what the letter was. I didn't want it to cause any friction on our last day in Redsworth, so I pocketed it and never gave it to him. Do you know, I'd forgotten all about that letter until you just mentioned it."

Emma heard the catch in her throat. "You…" She swallowed deeply to erase the squeak. "He never got it?"

"Nope. I never read it either. So, whatever you wrote in there was for your eyes only."

Emma knew if she wasn't leaning against her counter, she'd fall. Her world had just spun on its axis. Talk about changing her road map. So, the reason Jack hadn't shown up for their date was quite simply because she'd never invited him.

"Oh, God." She wiped her hands down her pale face. "So that means, the second letter…"

Josh screwed his face up with thought. "I remember that vaguely. You gave it to him as we got into the car. He went really pale and looked like he'd been kicked in the balls. Was that another love letter?"

"Oh, bollocks."

Josh looked at her in confusion. "What's the matter?"

Emma felt the contents of her stomach rise as another realisation hit. When he'd said he didn't think she had closure on that letter, he meant the second letter. He had asked if she still hated him. Emma put her head in her hands and groaned. "Oh, what a mess."

"Earth to Emma." Josh waved a hand in front of her face. "I've no idea what you're going on about. Look, simple question, do you still have feelings for Jack? Do you still like him?"

Looking out the window, Emma watched Toby cross the village green, head low, as local gossipmongers gathered together.

"Of course I don't," Emma replied, less sharply this time. "You can tell him from me that I harbour no romantic designs on him. He'll be very relieved to hear that."

“Fair enough.” Josh narrowed his eyes. “Just one thing. When you were younger, you always said you wanted to be with someone who made you laugh. I don’t see you laughing with Toby, but I do see you laughing with Jack. All the time. Why is that?”

“Because we know each other so well,” Emma replied, her mind still swirling from the recent revelations. He’d never got her letter. How much did that change anything? Admittedly, it altered her past, but did it change her present or future? “Anyway, I’m with Toby now, and Jack’s attracted to someone else. End of.”

“Oh, it’s gone way beyond attraction.” Josh smiled at Emma’s uncertain expression. “My brother is in unfamiliar territory and I’m looking forward to watching him flounder. But Scout’s honour, your secret is safe with me.”

“What secret?” Daisy skipped into the farm shop with a carton of eggs. “These are from Jack. He said he’ll deliver more tomorrow.” She leant against the counter, pushing her brother out of the way. “What’s the secret?”

“It’s Emma’s birthday today,” Josh replied cheekily. “She’s been keeping it to herself.”

“Oh, happy birthday!” Daisy clapped her hands excitedly. “That explains the card that came in the post after you left. Oh, Josh, talking about cards, this is your order number for the dry cleaners for your purple jacket. Your pockets were full of junk, so I emptied them. Some old letters from Redsworth high school, a detention slip and there was an envelope in there for Jack, a pink one with a heart doodled on it.”

Emma’s eyes widened as she recalled her signature teenage flourish. “What did you do with it?”

“Oh, I gave it to Jack before I came out. Why?”

Oh bollocks!

*

Emma bent over to catch her breath as she stood outside the kitchen door, her legs shaking with exertion and nerves.

"What on earth have you been doing?" Jack opened the door, causing her to jump in fright. "I thought I heard someone outside. You look knackered."

Holding onto the drainpipe, Emma tried to gauge his expression and breathe at the same time. He didn't look like a man in shock after reading the out-pouring of a teenage girl. She quickly glanced at the kitchen table and saw her envelope, partly hidden under his accounts book. Had he read it or not?

"Why aren't you at the farm shop?" Jack frowned at her red face. "Are you okay? Do you want a glass of water?"

She glanced at his concerned expression and berated herself for not having worked this out sooner. Jack had always looked out for her. She'd been a fool not to consider that he simply hadn't read the letter.

"It's my birthday. I've come to get this card from my sister."

"I didn't know it was your birthday." Jack put his head back and sighed. "But I should have guessed, with it being the summer holidays. I feel awful now."

"No need." Emma reached for the greetings card and the pink note. Capturing both, she headed for the door.

"Is that not for me?" Jack nodded towards her hands. "That letter has my name on it."

"Oh." Emma shuffled her feet on the tiled floor. "It's a mistake."

"What's a mistake?"

Emma scratched her head. She couldn't think of an excuse and now he was staring at her in that sympathetic way.

"Did you write that?" Jack asked. "I thought I recognised the handwriting. Why are you trying to hide it?"

Feeling cornered, Emma stood in the middle of the doorway. She sat upon a double-edged sword. If she walked away with no explanation, she would look sly and underhanded, and if she gave it to him, she would die of shame. She closed her eyes and tried to think of what she'd written all those years ago. She vaguely remembered the cringeworthy poem, but not the rest of it. Maybe it wasn't too revealing. Her sixteen-year-old self couldn't have been so expressive for it to be taken seriously.

Realising he wasn't about to back down, Emma decided to treat it as light-hearted as she could. "It's just a load of waffle I wrote when I was sixteen. Certainly nothing that you'd want to read now."

"Why not?" Jack's eyes glistened with amusement, and she struggled to pull herself away from his gaze.

"Oh, you remember me when I was sixteen." *Pavlovian effect. Keep remembering that.* "I wasn't exactly mature, was I?"

Jack mused on her response. "I'd say you were. Okay, let me rephrase my question. What would I gain from reading it?"

Emma lowered her head. "You'd have a good laugh at my naivety and most likely be annoyed with me."

"Then I have my answer." Jack nodded to her letter. "Let sleeping dogs lie. Isn't that what we agreed to do? I take it this is about the barf bag comment, and if so, then I don't want to reopen wounds. We're getting along just fine at the moment, and I don't know about you, but I like it this way."

Feeling like she'd just reached the top of a roller coaster, only to find out that the ride offered nothing but a flat track, she pocketed the note with a mix of confusion and slight disappointment.

"You look stunned. Are you sure you don't want to talk about it?"

"I'm sure." Emma's legs shook as she leaned against the doorcase. "I need to get back to the farm shop and lock up properly before we go swimming. Can I just go and freshen up first?"

"Yeah." He pointed to the stairs. "As long as we don't end up in the bath together again."

In the privacy of the farmhouse bathroom, Emma gently unfolded the note. The familiarity of the neat, curly writing almost undid her.

Dear Jack,

I'm going to miss you so much when you leave. You've always been so kind and caring to me and my days will now feel so long and dark without you around. Before you leave, I want you to know how I feel about you because I'll never be brave enough to say it any other time.

You make my spring fresh, my summer warm, my autumn golden and my winters cosy. You make my school days go faster and my holidays last longer. I count down the minutes before I see you and treasure every second I'm with you.

I want you to know that my heart is breaking because you are leaving. Josh is my best friend, but you hold my heart. I've always been in love with you, and I think I always will. I know you will never love me back. I'm not pretty or funny and I know that I get on your nerves, but I hope our friendship has meant something to you because it's meant the world to me.

Tomorrow evening, I'll be at the cinema. Would you like to meet me? I just want a chance to say goodbye to you because I don't think I'll ever be happy again without you in my life. Without you, there is nothing.

My heart will always be yours, forever and always, no matter what distance is between us.

Yours forever,

Emma Francis xx

Emma leant her hot forehead against the cold glass of the bathroom mirror and cried for the young girl who had written those heartbreaking words. She also cried for the woman who now stood alone on her birthday, with a towel against her lips, so no one would hear her sobbing.

CHAPTER 18

"Wow, this lake is stunning." Milly looked around in astonishment, taking in the expanse of clear blue water nestled in the deep valley of the luscious green hills. "It's like a secluded paradise."

"Hidden treasures of the Cotswolds." Josh plonked his picnic bag on the grass and sat down, looking out over the calm waters. "How did the interview go with your potential lodger?"

"Great, actually." Milly sighed with relief. "He works in a bank and is keen to move in as quickly as possible. Having the extra money will be most welcomed."

"I hope you've got references from him," Josh warned her. "There's plenty of freaks around these days."

"Don't worry, I know what I'm doing," Milly replied sharply as she tied back her hair. "You're here to teach me how to swim, not how to live."

As the group settled in with their bags and blankets, Emma walked along the wooden jetty and looked down to the bottom of the clear lakebed. Jack was right, it wasn't too deep at all. She put her head back and inhaled the fresh scents of honeysuckle and wild garlic. They soothed her mind, much needed after the stress of the past few hours.

"So, are you ready for your first swimming lesson?" Josh hopped around on one foot as he removed his canvas shoes and denim shorts, revealing a pair of black swimming trunks that complemented his tanned skin.

Milly hesitated as her fingers touched the hem of her long dress and she looked around to see who else may be watching her.

"What are you worried about?" Josh teased. "Believe me, your body can't be as bad as your character. Anyway, like I said, I ain't interested in your figure, so get your kit off and let's get this lesson over with."

Gingerly lifting her dress over her head, Milly bit her lip as vivid red scars on the tops of her right leg were revealed. She looked at Josh to check his reaction as she held her discarded dress close against her.

Josh gave them a cursory glance before shrugging. "Come on, let's see if you float better than you can bake."

"I think my little brother has just discovered tact," Jack whispered to Emma as the couple made their way into the water. "Are you going in?"

"You know, I think I'll sit here for a bit." Emma pulled her knees under her chin as Toby's words rang in her ears. "Do you come here often?"

"Sorry?" Jack looked at her in confusion. "Was that a chat-up line, because it's fairly old?"

Emma rolled her eyes at her lack of thought. "I've heard this place is popular with couples. I just wondered if you liked it too."

"If you mean, did I bring women here in my youth to seduce them, then no, not my style, which hopefully you'll already know. Anyway, the rumours about this place aren't true." Jack stood up and stripped off his t-shirt before unbuttoning his shorts and climbing out of them. "Come and join me in a bit."

Her jaw dropped of its own accord. Of course, she'd seen Jack in shorts before, as a teenager, when his shoulders hadn't been as broad and his legs as muscly, not to mention that perfectly toned behind. Trying not to stare, she glanced over at Josh, who looked straight at her with a knowing smile on his face. He'd spotted her reaction. Damn.

Milly's squeals of laughter as the cold water blanketed her filled the valley. Her happy, carefree demeanour set the perfect image of people living their life, taking advantage of their health, youth, and freedom. Even Jack, as his strong arms glided him through the waters, the sun shining on his brown back and shoulders, looked the epitome of flawlessness. So why was she sitting here and not joining in? Surely on her birthday she should be having fun, and Jack would definitely not be affected by her freckled skin in a small red bikini. Toby had got that wrong.

Jack turned and lifted his head, wiping droplets off his face before waving to her. His relaxed attitude being all the encouragement she needed, Emma pulled her sundress over her shoulders and walked towards the lake. Life was too short to sit on the sidelines, as she'd found out to her disadvantage.

Josh's wolf whistle echoed around the valley, and she lowered her head and smiled shyly, glad Jack had chosen that exact moment to swim under water. The gravelly lake floor bed felt rough on the soles of her feet and she stepped gingerly across the shale to avoid cutting herself. Taking a bobble from her wrist, she tied her hair away from her face and relished in the evening sun warm on her bare shoulders.

The coughing and spluttering brought her attention back to the water. She shielded her eyes and headed towards Jack. "Are you okay?"

"Sure," he gasped, his eyes fixed upon her before coughing again. "I just swallowed a bit of water."

"You alright, mate?" Josh shouted from the shallow edge, a huge grin on his face. "Is it getting warm over there?"

Jack gave his brother a black look before swimming towards Emma. He stopped a few feet in front of her, his dark eyes glistening. "Need a hand?"

"No, I'm okay." Emma took the plunge and hoped the tiny straps on her top would hold against the gentle lapping water. "It's not too cold."

"Told you." Jack's eyes centred on hers. "Let's see if you're still a good swimmer."

Emma set off after him, their bodies gliding through the clear lake as the sun cast sprinkles of diamonds across the surface, dragonflies dancing in their wake. Despite her years out of the water, she surprised herself with her fitness, and with only seconds between them, they reached the other side. Panting slightly, she accepted Jack's hand as he pulled her onto the slip of shoreline. They sat side by side, their bodies glistening as they gently caught their breath. Aware of her lack of clothing, Emma folded her arms across her front and then uncrossed them for fear of appearing childish.

"Do you think those two will ever get along?" Jack signalled towards his brother, tutoring Milly as she floated on her back.

"It's hard to tell. They're both very defensive. They need to put the past behind them and move on."

"What's the story with the scars on her legs? Has she mentioned them to you?"

"Never." Emma frowned. "But it does explain the long summer dresses she wears. She's the sort of girl who will be honest with you, but she won't always offer up the explanation. Josh and Milly would be good influences on each other, if they could get along. She'll ground him and he'll pull her out of her shell."

"I agree." Jack looked at the couple thoughtfully. "I wouldn't be surprised if he wants to move out soon, back into the village."

"Does that bother you?"

"Not really. It was just Daisy and me after Joanne left. Josh said he moved back in because he couldn't afford the rent, but I know that's a lie. It was to help with childcare and to keep me sane."

"You're still very close, aren't you?"

"Yep." Jack bit his lip. "I couldn't cope without either of them. My family is my world. Although, I need to accept that one day Daisy will fly the nest too, and then it'll be just me."

"Unless you marry again." Emma batted away a lazy bee before turning to face him. "Do you think you will?"

"I dunno." Jack looked out over the water, where his brother and Milly were arguing over floating techniques. "I'd have to meet the right sort of girl. Someone who will take me, my lifestyle, and my little sister on board. I come with a lot of baggage."

"So do most people." Emma picked up a handful of shale and let it fall through her fingers. "I need to think about moving out too."

"You don't have to." Jack turned to look at her, his dark eyes intense. "Unless you're planning on moving in with Toby. Are you?"

"No, there's no plans to."

Jack nodded as he looked out over the water. "What did he buy you for your birthday?"

Again, Emma paused as she wondered what to say. She felt too embarrassed to admit that her morning with Toby had been spent cajoling him into a good humour and then reassuring him she'd no designs on Jack. "He's taking me out for a meal to Featherby's."

"Wow, he must be keen. It's an expensive place. Joanne liked it, but I couldn't afford to take her very often. She liked the finer things in life. Clothing, shoes, being seen in the right kind of place."

"Have you spoken to her since this morning?"

"No, there's no point. I don't think she wanted me to know about this other bloke. I think it was a slip of the tongue. She barely tells me anything about herself."

"And it hasn't put you off?" Emma probed gently, wondering about this girl he felt attracted to, and why he hadn't mentioned her.

"It put me off serious relationships for a long time, but now I'm ready to bring someone else into the fold."

Emma rested her chin on her knees and tried not to feel jealous of the woman who got to share his bed and his troubles.

"How about children? You must feel wary after what happened."

"It's made me less trusting, I admit. Caleb will always be in my thoughts even if I have a house full of kids, but I do want the chance to be a daddy. Dirty nappies, sleepless nights, building dens and teaching them how to fish. I want them to have the childhood we had." Jack smiled for a few moments. "How about you? Do you think you'll have kids with Toby?"

"Good God, no." Emma shook her head and then paused, surprised at her own vehemence.

"I thought you two were getting along?" Jack furrowed his brow. "Is everything okay?"

Emma lifted the strap of her bikini as it slid off her shoulder. "Yeah, we're fine. I guess it's early days. We're still finding out things about each other, plus we're not that serious. I mean, there's an attraction, but we've not taken things further. We've not … you know."

"I know." Jack smiled lightly. "And is that what you want? Something uncomplicated?"

"I think so." Emma lay back on the grass, no longer caring if Jack saw her pale, freckly skin or not. She felt comfortable with him. "I like Toby, but I don't want to talk about settling down."

"With anyone?" Jack's eyes twinkled as he lay by her side.

"With someone, eventually." Emma readjusted her bikini top as Jack turned to her again. His eyes followed her fingers momentarily before meeting her gaze and looking away, abashed. She stared at his side profile, feeling slightly amused by his awkwardness. "Would you rather not be over there with those two?"

"You mean watching them kill each other?" Jack laughed lightly at Milly's scream as her head disappeared under the water. "At least they seem to be getting along a bit better. It's a good job he's no designs on her because she can't stand him."

"And if he did like her, what advice would you offer him?"

"Me?" Jack looked at her in surprise. "What makes you think I'm best placed to help him? I've not exactly been successful in love myself. In all honesty, I'd sit back and watch him struggle. It's called watching and learning."

"Hey," Josh shouted from the other side of the lake. "Are you planning on abandoning us?"

"I suppose we should head back." Jack offered his hand to help her up. "We've brought a barbeque and beer so we can toast your birthday."

"You didn't have to do that." Emma walked with him towards the lake before joining him in the water. "I wasn't expecting anything."

"I know you weren't." Jack's eyes glistened against the evening sun as they swam gently towards the jetty. "That's why I did it."

Emma watched the strong muscles in his back move as he glided effortlessly through the water, and she averted her eyes guiltily. Toby would be sitting at home now, alone, no doubt wondering what she was up to. He certainly wouldn't be expecting her to be swimming in a tiny red bikini while the burnt embers of the setting sun bathed everything around them in a warm blanket of promise.

"Well, we have a swimmer." Josh grinned as Milly showed off her new floating technique. "Kind of."

"I'm still alive, I'll give you that." Milly doggy paddled towards them, straining her neck to keep her mouth above water. "Did you two have fun?"

"Yep," Jack replied, shielding his eyes as he looked around the hills. "I forgot how beautiful this place was."

"I caught you admiring the view." Josh winked cheekily at his brother. "I've got to say, Emma, you've changed a bit since I last saw you in our paddling pool."

"Shut up, Josh," Emma replied good naturedly as she splashed him. "You've not changed at all. You're still weedy."

"Right." Josh splashed her back, catching Milly in the middle as she squealed. "Water fight."

Closing her eyes against the thrashing water that hit her face and loosened her curls, Emma started to laugh, not just a giggle, but a full laugh, something she hadn't done in years. She fought back as hard as she could against the torrents of water, causing her feet to slip on the lakebed. Her head disappearing, she felt large hands around her waist as Jack lifted her up and held her close. The skin-to-skin contact burned into her despite the coolness of the water and she couldn't help the shudder that went through her, causing Jack to hold her closer.

"I think we need to celebrate with those beers now. It's getting cool." Josh led Milly back to the shore before turning to his brother with a mischievous smile. "Although I think someone's glad of the cold water at the moment."

*

"I can't believe I can swim." Milly sat down on the soft grass and drank her beer. "I feel quite proud of myself."

"I wouldn't call it swimming," Josh mumbled as he flicked the top off a bottle of beer. "But I'll admit you did okay. A double celebration then. To Milly's water arms and Emma's birthday."

"Cheers." Emma raised her bottle before putting it back down. She didn't want to go completely against Toby's wishes. She pulled Jack's fleece closer around her, inhaling his familiar fragrance. This evening had taken her back to her childhood when they'd frolicked in the shallow river until the sun started to set, their fingers shrivelled from the water and their hair in a matted mess. Back then, she'd never really appreciated how liberating it felt to undress in the outdoors, quickly drying yourself while trying to remain hidden. Towels had covered a lot more then, as she'd discovered whilst dressing behind her chosen tree.

The smell of cooking steaks and fried onions filled the air as Jack threw more twigs into the fire pit. The crackling wood and distinctive smell of campfires comforted her and, as the final rays of the sun set beyond the lake, she sighed with happiness.

"Has it been a good birthday?" Jack smiled at her, wrapped up in his fleece as she ate a burned piece of meat from their makeshift barbeque. "I know it's not Featherby's, but it was the best I could muster up in a few hours."

"It's been perfect," Emma mumbled around her mouthful of food. "This is delicious, by the way."

"Naturally," Jack replied, looking pleased with the comment. "Although it would have been better if I'd remembered to bring cheese as well. It could have been a taste test for Daisy's hampers."

"Are you sure you don't mind me being a part of this project?" Milly looked at Jack. "Yours is a family business, after all."

"I think we can handle you, if you can handle us?" Jack placed more slices of steak onto the fire. "We're not exactly conventional."

"Conventional is boring." Josh opened another beer, cursing as the froth spilled onto his shorts. "And seeing as we're not boring, how about playing campfire games? Quick fire questions. They're always quite revealing."

"How do you play?" Milly asked. "Don't forget, you all have the advantage of knowing each other. I don't."

"And that's the beauty of the game." Josh shrugged. "It doesn't matter if you know each other or not. The truth always comes out when you have to respond quickly. Basically, you ask three probing questions, and the other person must reply in under three seconds, otherwise it's not the truth. Want to play?"

"Sure." Milly shifted on her blanket to face Josh. "I'll go first. What's your proudest achievement?"

"Setting up my business." Josh nodded straight away. "I did it from scratch. Not bad for someone who left school with barely any grades."

"I didn't know you'd set it up yourself." Milly frowned. "I thought Toby employed you."

"Nope, I'm a freelance joiner. I can pick and choose my commissions. The boutique hotel in town, for example."

"You helped to build that?" Milly asked with surprise. "It's quite iconic."

"Actually, I worked with the architect to design the roof," Josh replied. "Next question."

Milly cocked her head to one side and bit her lip. "If you're a successful joiner, why are you still living on your brother's farm?"

Josh held his hand up as Jack started to speak. "Because I'm lazy and can't be arsed doing my own washing. Hence why I walk around half naked. Less laundry."

"At least you're being honest." Milly rolled her eyes in frustration. "You strike me as someone not housebroken. I bet you survive on microwave meals and pot noodles, don't you?"

Josh simply smiled in response. "What's your last question?"

Milly tapped her lip thoughtfully. "What's your biggest regret?"

"Not being with Mum when she died." Josh suddenly looked up, his eyes hurt and confused. "I can't believe I just said that."

Jack put his bottle down and stared at his brother as an eerie silence fell across the crackling fire. "You okay, mate?"

"Yeah." Josh shook his blond curls as if ridding himself of bad vibes. "Course I am. So, it's my turn with Milly."

“We don’t have to play,” Milly said quietly as she bit the side of her thumbnail. “I was being bolshy. I’m sorry, I genuinely am. I didn’t mean to dredge things up. I was just trying to be fun and…”

“I’m having fun.” Josh held his arms out. “I’m outside with a beer in one hand and food in the other. What’s not to like?” He bit into his steak, sloping marinade down his chest. “It’s a good job we didn’t bring those king prawns with us tonight. Are you still allergic to seafood?”

“I didn’t know you were allergic to seafood.” Emma reached for a slither of onion. “Is it severe?”

“Not life threatening, just unpleasant. Itchy eyes, swollen lips, and lots of vomiting and other bodily extractions that I won’t discuss in front of you all. Calamari has the worst effect on me.”

“Calamari is an onion ring.” Josh frowned. “Are you allergic to onions too, because if so, you need to stay away from Emma. She just ate some.”

“Calamari is seafood.” Jack laughed out loud at his brother’s confused expression. “I can’t believe you still believe that. Mum used to tell you they were onions, so you’d eat them…”

“Ah.” Josh bit his lip nervously. “Okay, this is slightly awkward. Why did you never correct me?”

“Too many words, too little time.” His brother grinned. “Why are you looking so guilty?”

Josh cringed as he turned to Milly. “Please don’t hit me. I didn’t do it deliberately to make you sick. I genuinely thought calamari was an onion.”

“Oh my God.” Milly squealed as Josh’s confession suddenly dawned on her. “You ate seafood on our date and then kissed me?”

Jack laughed loudly. “Only my brother could do that. That’s hilarious.”

“Yeah, very funny,” Josh mumbled as Milly and Emma fell over in the grass laughing. “I’m glad I’m causing you some amusement.”

"Well, at least now you know you're not a crap kisser." Emma wiped her eyes as she attempted to calm her mirth.

"Oh, he was a crap kisser," Milly replied as she stared at Josh mischievously. "But I can forgive him for that."

"Thanks," Josh replied through gritted teeth. "Anyway, my turn for questions, and I've no intention of going easy on you. Why the scars on your leg?"

Momentarily taken aback, Milly stopped laughing. She rearranged her long dress around her ankles and took another swig of beer. "Wrong place, wrong time."

"Nope, I'm not accepting that," Josh replied as he ate the last of his steak. "You paused; you're lying. What happened?"

"Despite you thinking I'm a boring person who gets excited by new icing techniques, I was in the army. I did serve as a doctor, and these scars are from a nail bomb that went off."

Josh leaned forward, a deep frown on his face. "Are you actually being serious?"

"Yep. I was discharged with Post Traumatic Stress Disorder. I was a Sergeant Major. That's why I now lead a very boring life sorting my cupcakes in colour order surrounded by teapots and white rabbits. It's called therapy." Milly pulled a blanket around her shoulders, as if protecting herself. "Pass me another steak, if you don't mind. This marinade is amazing. Did you buy it?"

"No, I made it. Despite not being house broken, I can cook." Josh rubbed his chin. "I'm really sorry I didn't believe you about the doctor thing. I was a bit of an arse with you."

"I've encountered worse than you," Milly replied with a slight smile. "Actually, you remind me of my first drill sergeant."

"Really?" Josh flexed his biceps.

"I meant he was a knob head too." Milly grinned as Josh rolled his eyes and tutted.

"I think my little brother has just met his match with you." Jack threw another log onto the fire, which missed by a few inches. Reaching forward, he nudged it into place.

"Drunk, by any chance?" Josh asked, raising an eyebrow. "It's not like the school rugby captain to miss a throw. Let's see how you deal with quick fire questions. Come on, Emma, what are you going to ask my drunken brother?"

Emma giggled as Jack threw a piece of charred meat in response. There were so many things she wanted to ask him, but they were all so personal. Aware of Josh watching her intently, Emma knew she needed to think of something generic.

"Okay, worst fear?"

"Apart from losing my family?" Jack scratched the back of his head. "Probably losing the farm. I know most people would say it's only land, but it's so much more than that. It becomes a part of you. Without this farm, I'd be nothing."

Keeping a poker face, Emma tried not to show how affected she felt by his admission. It took guts to be able to share your feelings instead of hiding behind them, something she was slowly learning to do. Aware of the sudden silence around them, Emma decided to go for something lighthearted. "Blondes or brunettes?"

"Or redheads," Josh added. "Don't forget those."

"I don't have a type." Jack threw an unopened beer towards his brother. "It's all about personality."

"If you say so." Josh grinned as he raised his bottle. "Never anything to do with boobs or bums. Come on, Emma. Last question. Make it a good one."

"Who would you give your last rolo to?"

"You, of course." Jack tweaked her nose as he threw more wood on the fire. "Who else?"

Smiling at his platonic reply, Emma opened another beer and clinked it against his.

"Before any more questions, I know what I need to do." Milly stood up and looked around her. "Too much cold beer."

"Same here," Josh brushed grass from his shorts. "Come on, I'll show you where the thicker bushes are."

Watching Milly and Josh walk by the lake shore and into the trees, Emma turned to look at Jack as he lay on his back, his arms under his head. "Are you okay?"

"Yeah." Jack looked up at the star-studded sky. "Just a little drunk."

Emma hugged her knees to her chest and watched the slight rise and fall of his chest. The last few hours had been an emotional whirlwind. Knowing he had never read her love letter had brought down the wall she'd built between them, and it left her feeling extremely exposed. She had a future to build here, but how would it feel knowing Jack would always be around the corner, reminding her of how life could have been?

"I've got some questions for you." Jack turned over to face her, his eyes illuminated by the brightness of the moon casting off the water. "First crush?"

You. Emma paused. She couldn't say that.

"Tick tock." Jack turned his finger clockwise. "You see, this is the good thing about this game. If you don't reply in three seconds, I know it's not the truth."

Emma lowered her head and laughed. "Someone from junior school. I can't remember his name."

"I'll let that one go." Jack narrowed his eyes. "Love or money?"

"Love," Emma replied instantly. "I have very little interest in money, or fashion, as you can probably tell by this cheap bikini."

Jack glanced at the discarded swimwear out of the corner of his eye and grinned. "I think I'm meant to compliment you on how you looked, but I'm not sure that's allowed when the girl wearing it is someone you grew up with."

"I think at our age, we can make the rules up. We know each other well enough by now."

Jack rested his head on his hand and stared at her, as if trying to reach into her thoughts. "You say we know each other well, but do you not think we're discovering new things about each other every day?" He patted the grass by his side, encouraging her to lie down. "I think we should sleep here. Don't you think this is perfect?"

"I do," Emma replied quietly, slightly amused by his drunken rambling. She watched a shooting star make its way over the lake, unfettered by problems, relationships, or worries.

"We could stay here; no one would bother us. Just two people laid side by side." Jack continued to stare at the sky, his jaw ticking. "My last question. Hall or Farm?"

"Hey, you two." Josh waved with Milly from the other side of the lake. "We need to get back. Clive said he'd stay with Daisy for as long as we need, but we can't leave it too late."

"Yeah, course." Jack sat up quickly. "I lost track of time." He dampened down the fire, extinguishing the heat and flames.

Emma watched as he gathered their things together, his actions swift, as if distracting himself. She wanted to know what he'd mean by that last question, but the moment had gone.

"Come on, Worzel." Jack pulled her up. "Your birthday's over."

CHAPTER 19

The rain beat hard on the roof of the piggery as Emma lay under her warm duvet, thinking about last night. Thankfully, due to the fresh air and exercise, she'd slept well, but the minute the rooster started to crow, her thoughts reverted to their conversation at the side of the campfire. What did he mean by *'Hall or Farm?'* What did he expect her to choose from? Her career. Her allegiance? Or something else? Making herself a cup of tea, she thread her arms into Jack's fleece and stood on the doorstep, trying to avoid the heavy raindrops as she wondered what to do with her morning. Jack's generosity of giving her a day off from milking didn't help either. Without working in the parlour or having to open the farm shop, she felt at a loss.

Admitting she needed something pro-active to do, she put on her raincoat and headed into the woods at the side of the stream. The canopy of trees protected her from the rain as she collected handfuls of wild garlic and juicy blackberries. She could make a creamy risotto and a crumble for dessert. She could even try out a recipe for homemade custard with the fresh eggs from Jack's farm.

Happy with her foraging, Emma headed back into the farmhouse kitchen and added more logs to the large fireplace as she prepared her cooking. She didn't envy Jack working on the top fields today, repairing the dry-stone walls in this weather. He'd be tired and hungry when he returned and no doubt in need of comfort food. As the rain continued to batter against the window, she turned up the heat on the Aga and diced the mushrooms. Saucepans bubbled as delicious smells permeated the air, filling her with a sense of homeliness and comfort. Happy with her preparation, Emma cleaned all the worktops and swept the floors before checking the fridge for white wine. Her search proving uneventful, she glanced at the mid-morning hour. She had plenty of time to head into the village to buy some from the farm shop.

The gardens of the chocolate box cottages reminded her of a freshly washed blanket after the morning downpours. Streams of water raced towards the drains and ducks took advantage of the worms and insects that were brave enough to raise their head above ground. Driving towards the barn and the village car park, Emma braked as Toby flagged her down from the side of the road. He opened the passenger door and flung his wet umbrella onto her back seat.

"Do you have a few hours to help me out with something? A business thing at Featherby's?"

Emma quickly glanced at her watch. The risotto wouldn't come to any harm for the next hour or so. "Yeah, sure, if you think I'd be of assistance." She concentrated on the road ahead as their tyres swished through the deep puddles. "I can't believe the change in weather from yesterday. I'm sure this place has its own climate. Last night was so warm."

"Did you drink last night?"

"Erm, no." Emma hesitated at his harsh tone. "I didn't."

"I hope that's the last time you put me second to the Seymours. Did he try anything inappropriate with you?"

"Of course not. I told you he wouldn't." Keen to avoid another argument, she attempted to turn the conversation back around. "What's this meeting about so I can try to prepare?"

"Erm, just Parish Council stuff."

"Like the farm shop?" Emma probed as she navigated a cattle grid. "Are they wanting new ideas for expansion, because if they are—"

"For God's sake, Emma," Toby tutted. "They'll have an agenda. Have you attended a business meeting before?"

Emma halted at a crossroads in the middle of a deserted country road. "What's the problem, Toby?"

"Nothing." Toby's expression suddenly softened as she sighed with exasperation. "I'm sorry. I guess I'm just a bit worried about this meeting. I still need to come up with ways of making money and it's stressing me out. Come on, let's get there before we're late."

Fifteen minutes later, they entered the doors of Featherby's, where diners stood in the reception area surrounded by wet coats and umbrellas as they waited to be seated. Emma strained her neck to look inside the restaurant area and bit back a gasp at the elegance of the high ceilings and the art déco staircase that led to an intimate mezzanine level. No wonder the waiting list for tables went into weeks. To her left, a conference room had already been prepared and Emma looked down at her wet jeans, feeling very much out of place. Heading to the ladies toilets, she made use of the complimentary toiletries to tame her hair and take the shine off her damp nose. After spraying herself liberally with the thoughtfully left perfume, she headed back out into the empty reception area.

"Where is everyone?" Emma asked the woman behind the desk. "I came with Toby Montgomery. Should I head into that conference room?"

"Oh no, dear," the woman replied as she placed her spectacles on the end of her nose. "The room is over here. I'm glad you've offered to help. I always find the rain adds a damper to the day, don't you think? Even though you're inside and dry, no one wants a reminder of the outside weather."

Emma followed the receptionist through a bare corridor, feeling confused. "Aren't I meant to be in that meeting?"

"With the Parish Council?" The woman looked at her disbelievingly. "You need a formal invitation to attend that. You can't go in there. This is where you're needed. There's a charity auction going on today in the main restaurant. They're raising money for impoverished children. Such a deserving cause, don't you agree?"

Emma stood in the middle of the sparse room and stared open mouthed at the racks of coat hangers. Surely not?

"It's a simple process." The receptionist handed her a ticket book. "Give them one half of the ticket and put the second half with the garment. Oh, and here's a tip box. We normally share the contents. Any questions?"

Shaking her head, Emma looked around the windowless room. How had this just happened? She couldn't say no to such a charitable cause. She thought back to her conversation with Toby as they'd driven here. Had he mentioned her attending the meeting or had he simply said she'd be of assistance?

"Two coats, both Armani. Treat them with respect." Emma looked up to see a queue of guests waiting impatiently to hand in their wet belongings. Feeling numb, she took the garments from the man in question. She didn't even register the clang of the pound coin hitting the plastic tips box.

An hour later, as she sat alone with a room full of steaming umbrellas, she realised that no mix up had occurred. If she'd have been invited for her professional input, Toby would have come looking for her by now. Hunger and humiliation filled her as sounds of laughter and applause from the busy restaurant echoed down the uncarpeted corridor. Is this how he viewed her? As someone willing to give up her day off to attend to other people's belongings.

Whispered voices pulled her out of her reverie, and she stiffened as urgent footsteps could be heard approaching the coat room. Expecting to be handed a ticket, Emma felt surprised to see a young man and woman enter the room, their arms and lips entwined in a passionate embrace. About to cough to alert them to her presence, she realised moments later that they'd gone far beyond being interrupted. With the man's hand firmly under the dress of the woman, Emma pushed herself into the coats and plugged her fingers into her ears to drown out the sounds of their frantic kisses and groping. Feeling underhanded and sly, she crouched down and prayed their activities would be over quickly. The cavorting couple, once happy with their illicit explorations, giggled like a couple of school kids before running back up the corridor to eat the remainder of their no doubt expensive meal. Breathing a sigh of relief, Emma started to stand up as she heard Toby's voice and the faint echoes of a female from the other side of a phone line.

"I told you I'm signing nothing," Toby said, his voice clipped. "It was your stupid fault you got yourself into this situation. I didn't ask for this, did I? If I sign that form, then I'm admitting to it, and I told you from the start I wanted nothing to do with this. And a word of warning, if you go ahead and blab, you know what will happen. Am I making myself clear?"

Toby paused as he spied Emma crouched amongst the coats and he quickly ended his call before looking at her strangely. "What are you doing on the floor?"

A million questions flooded her brain as she looked up at him before dusting off her knees.

"I thought you'd gone to the ladies or something. I couldn't see you in here."

"I was hiding." Emma's eyes blinked speedily as she tried to process the last few minutes. "Who were you just speaking to, and why the hell am I in here?"

Toby frowned as he looked in her pitiful tips box. "I was talking to a colleague."

"About?"

"This place." Toby looked around him as he pulled at the collar of his shirt. "I've been asked to review it for a Michelin star. What time can you leave your post?"

"My post?" Emma replied angrily, her eyes flashing dangerously. "You seriously brought me here for this?"

"No, of course not." Toby headed towards her and tutted sympathetically. "It's been a very unfortunate mix up. I didn't know it was a closed meeting until I got here. I had visions of you being seated in the restaurant, dining on oysters and champagne and being flirted with by the waiters."

"Well, I haven't been." Emma crossed her arms forcefully. "I've been dealing with everyone's wet belongings and watching a couple attempt to copulate. Believe me, it's not the day off I envisaged."

"Poor you." Toby took her in his arms, his breath smelling of garlic and citrusy wine, causing her stomach to rumble. "How can I make this up to you? How about I bid for you a piece of jewellery from the auction, something special?"

"I don't need jewellery." Frustrated, Emma picked up her bag. She'd stayed sober on her birthday just to please him, yet he'd spent the afternoon on fine food and alcohol and expected her to drive him around. "Did you invite me just for this? So you could drink?"

"Of course not." Toby's lips gently touched behind her ear, and Emma immediately felt her body tense at the unexpected intimacy. "You're worth much more than that."

His lips slowly moved to her jawline before hovering near her mouth and Emma held her breath as she realised the significance of the moment. All week she'd wanted him to kiss her, but not now. It just didn't feel right.

"This is quite private, isn't it?" Toby whispered as his hand moved up her arm to explore her bare shoulder and, more importantly, the strap of her bra as he lowered it. "I can see why that couple came in here."

Aware that his fingers had started to take liberties underneath her t-shirt, Emma pulled back, just in time to see a well-dressed lady standing near the hatch. Her mature eyes failed to hide her disapproval as she played with the pearls in her ears.

"Mine is the red coat." The pearls lady placed a pound coin in the tips box, giving Emma the sort of look she'd expect from her own mother. "Most guests are starting to leave, just in case you planned on taking your dalliances any further."

Emma lowered her head as she handed over the wool coat. Considering she stood in a five-star restaurant at the side of a village squire, she'd never felt so cheap. Or so dirty.

*

She didn't have the heart to stay and eat the mushroom risotto and blackberry crumble she'd prepared earlier. Instead, Emma headed straight to her piggery, feigning a headache. Neither had she admitted to Jack or Josh the events of her supposedly relaxing day off. If they discovered she'd visited Featherby's, she would let them believe what they would naturally assume, that she'd been wined and dined and treated like a princess. She still flinched when she thought about the look of disapproval the pearls lady had given her as Toby removed his hand from under her top. Why had she let that happen and, more importantly, why hadn't she walked away from that coat room as soon as she'd arrived there? What had she feared? What could possibly have happened if she'd stood up for herself?

Feeling disheartened and annoyed with her wasted day, Emma opened a bottle of wine and attempted to calm her raw emotions. However, the alcohol tasted as sour as her thoughts. Feeling caged by her own frustrations, she eventually pushed away her blankets and left the comfort of her fire to step outside. Looking up at the twinkling sky, she wondered, not for the first time, if her parents watched over her. Concentrating on two bright stars, she nodded to herself. Of course they were. With that in mind, she closed her door and prepared herself for bed. Tomorrow she'd start to be more forceful. After all, she'd nothing to lose.

CHAPTER 20

The sunshine glistened onto the courtyard as chickens clucked around, picking at the last of the crumbs Emma had thrown after breakfast. With Clive and Jack busy in the parlour, Emma headed into the small barn and studied the detailed plans she'd drawn up with Daisy. They both agreed the cheese hampers would sell mainly online, but once word spread locally, they expected a high footfall onto the farm. She bit her lip thoughtfully. Customers liked to see where the produce had been prepared. Maybe photographs of the cheese dairy, some of Jack and the family working together. Personal touches always helped, and once they'd decided on a name for the business, they'd be able to order printed bags, baskets and wrapping paper with their chosen logo. That was the exciting part; however, they first had to pass the hard work hurdle of getting everything moving.

Aware of Daisy's growing lack of interest in the project, Emma opened a tin of paint and loaded her paintbrush with the soft grey emulsion. This morning's breakfast had been the push she needed to move things along. Only seconds after they'd sat down to eat, Jack's phone had started to jingle. His ensuing conversation with Joanne had been heated and extremely vocal. Not only had she asked for more money, but she'd also refused yet another request for him to meet with his son. Jack slammed the kitchen door, his booming words echoing around the courtyard, threatening his ex-wife with legal action, regardless of the cost. Emma didn't need it spelled out to her. Jack needed more money.

Sitting down on a hay bale in the early sunshine for a much-needed rest, she smiled as the little piglet trundled over to her and sniffed her hands for treats. Picking him up, she placed him on her lap while she gazed ponderously at the overgrown patio at the back of the barn. From her vantage point, she had the sprawling vista of the Cotswolds at her feet. Rolling hills, patchwork fields, church bell towers, and charming thatched cottages. She couldn't deny it, of all her viewpoints on the farm, this had to be her favourite. Feeling inspired, Emma pulled out her plans again. Tables, a few well-placed comfy chairs, patio heaters and parasols to accommodate any weather. It would be a lot of work. The cracked flags would need replacing, and the shrubbery would need cutting back, but if she had the time and the money, this would be the perfect spot for a café. Scrutinising her plans again, a thought came to mind. Milly may not be able to expand her bakery, but a seating area could be set up here, offering the delights the bakery had to offer. Keen to talk it through with someone, Emma stood up and approached the parlour. About to make her way inside, she paused as she heard Jack mention her name. Knowing she shouldn't, but at the same time feeling her feet glue themselves to the floor, Emma pressed herself to the wall and pinned back her ears.

"She's too nice to have her feelings played with." Clive's words floated through the doorway. "You need to tell her."

"I know," Jack replied, slightly out of breath, and Emma imagined him hurling sacks of feed into the troughs. "But it's just so hard. I've known her all my life. As a kid, I always wanted to protect her, and I still do now. What if this hurts her? What if we're never the same once she knows the truth?"

"What does Josh think?" Clive's voice petered in and out as he moved around the parlour. "He knows her best, doesn't he? Has she said anything to him, or him to her?"

"She knows I'm attracted to someone; that's all she knows."

Emma strained her ears, her heart banging against her chest. This felt like the cliff-edge of a tense movie.

"The thing with Emma," Jack continued, his breath huffy. "She's extremely clever and her business mind is second to none, but she's not exactly worldly."

"I don't know about that. She knows a lad like you needs a woman in his life. Are you telling me you go to bed at night thinking about the farm, or do you dream of who you could have your arms wrapped around?"

Jack's light laugh carried on the warm morning breeze. "I've needed a few cold showers lately, I'll tell you that much. However, I can't act on anything while Emma is living in the piggery. It would make her feel uncomfortable, and she needs support right now."

"Well, don't let too much time pass," Clive replied over the noise of the holding gate being opened. "Love doesn't hang around, and Emma will understand that."

Creeping slowly away, Emma wished she'd never overheard the conversation. Her heart constricted at the thought of being a nuisance to Jack and his love life. Did he inwardly groan at each of her mishaps, knowing each one took him a step further away from romance? It had certainly thrown her a curve ball. Ten minutes ago, she'd been preparing strong conversations to have with Toby, but if standing up for herself went tits up, where would she turn? Jack didn't have the money to support her financially. Yet, for as long as she lived on the farm, she'd be holding up his sex life, and from what she remembered of Jack, he wouldn't be happy with that. Perhaps she needed to try harder with Toby and swallow back some of her pride.

*

"Hey, where are you heading to? A funeral?" Jack looked askance at her black skirt and equally dark shirt. "What's wrong with your shorts and t-shirts?"

"I fancied a change." Emma looked down at her sensible shoes, feeling foolish. Still, Toby was the boss and if he wanted her to dress more appropriately, then she had to. She touched her tightly wound bun, already feeling a headache coming on from the tension of the pins.

"I was going to ask you for a favour." Jack bit back a grin at her stockinged legs. "I think the fan belt is slipping, but I don't think madam would appreciate driving my tractor for me while I listened to the engine."

Emma glanced at her watch. She knew the farm shop would open late today out of respect for the passing of one of the elderly villagers. She had intended to go in and take advantage of a few hours cleaning, but in hindsight that was more to do with occupying her time rather than necessity. "Okay, I can help. What do you want me to do?"

"You'll need to hitch that skirt up for a start."

"Pardon?"

"The steps." Jack grinned as he put his hand on her shoulder and pointed to the high cab. "Have you got a girdle underneath that or is it just your outer garments that give you the look of a strict librarian?"

"Very funny," Emma mumbled as she lifted her skirt, exposing a slight glimpse of her peacock blue knickers. She quickly glanced at Jack to see him laughing. "Do you intend on standing there watching me struggle?"

"Nope, just enjoying the view," Jack teased as he put his hand on her behind and pushed her into the seat. "Just turn on the engine. That's all you need to do."

Remembering driving the tractor last week, Emma followed his instruction and watched him listen to the loud rumbling. He hadn't shaved today. She liked him like that. The ruggedness suited his dark complexion. She wondered if his girlfriend felt the same. Cocking her head to one side, she watched him bend over and admired his rear view. There was no way he'd keep his hands off a girl for much longer. Jack had a reputation for not holding back.

"Are you turned on?" Jack shouted.

"What?" Emma gulped loudly and put both hands on the steering wheel. "No, of course I'm not turned on."

"I said, are the hazard lights turned on?"

"Oh." Emma put a hand to her neck, feeling flustered. She looked around on the deck and shrugged. "I don't know."

Rolling his eyes, Jack navigated the steps with his long legs and jumped into the cab. He plonked himself by her side and turned off the engine. "Can you hear me better now?"

Straightening her sensible skirt, Emma nodded.

"Why are you dressed like that? Be honest with me."

Emma groaned. She may as well be truthful. "Toby said I needed to dress smarter."

"And do you always do what Toby says, because you sure as hell don't do anything I ask?" Jack gave her an amused smile before sighing. "Sorry, I'm being facetious again. Go on. I'm listening."

Emma toyed with changing the subject. This wasn't his problem, but she'd started now. "I don't have anything else to wear that's sensible. He thinks my t-shirts are too tight and inappropriate."

"He's complaining about that?" Jack laughed before biting his lip. "Sorry."

"The thing is," Emma replied, trying to ignore his twinkling eyes. "I did have a wardrobe full of clothes, but I couldn't fit them all into my suitcase."

"Okay, come on." Jack jumped out of the cab and helped her down the steep steps.

"Where are we going?" Emma asked as her flat shoes caught in the grass sods.

"I might be just a farmer, but I do know what women look good in." Jack took hold of his car keys and directed them towards the Range Rover. "I've had plenty of practice at this."

Half an hour later, they found themselves rifling through racks of clothing in one of the town's shopping departments. Jack held up a pair of thigh-high leather boots and even the woman behind the desk started to smile as he hummed the '*Pretty Woman*' theme tune.

"How about a pair of lacy stockings, or a basque?" Jack grinned at the lingerie set on the mannequin by his side. "I'd love to see Clive's face if he saw these hanging off our washing line."

"Shut up. You'll get us thrown out. Anyway, I can't afford any of these." Regretfully, Emma stroked the material of a cream summer dress before picking up a plain black one from a cheaper rail. "Come on, let's go before we get arrested for being disorderly."

"Excuse me." Jack put his arm around her shoulders and held the cream dress up towards the shop owner. "Do you have this in her size?"

Emma glared at him as she felt herself being led off to a large changing room with the silky outfit swinging from a padded hanger. Slipping the dress over her head, she watched the soft folds of fabric fall onto her knees as the discreet zip pulled in her small waist. Looking at herself in the mirror, she loosened her bun and allowed a few curls to frame her face. The thin straps showed off her toned arms and shoulders while the tiny flowers sewn into the delicate silk glinted each time she moved. This dress had been designed for the type of girl who knew she would be adored each time she wore it. It wasn't for her.

"Hey," Jack whispered, peeking his head around the door. "Does it fit?"

"You're not supposed to be in here." Emma gave her reflection one last glance before unzipping the back. "It's too big."

"Let me see," Jack tip-toed towards her, his face a picture of mischievousness. "This is like sneaking in the girls' toilets at school. Come on, open the door."

Emma held the back of the dress together as she crept out of the cubicle, her head low to avoid his gaze. He'd dated many girls who would have suited this dress. In comparison to them, she felt like a cheap gift wrapped up in expensive paper.

"Turn around." Jack tenderly zipped the outfit back up. "Look at yourself. What's not to like? Toby would love it, don't you think?"

Glancing at her reflection, Emma shrugged. How could she tell him that she didn't lead the type of life he envisaged? She may be dating someone who had the ability to spoil her, but so far, he hadn't.

"The thing is, because you're fuller…" Jack lifted his hands and then dropped them. "You know, on top."

Emma looked at his flushed cheeks in amusement. "You mean my boobs? You can refer to them. You're meant to be the farmer, the one not embarrassed by nature."

"I'm also a man," Jack whispered as he reversed out of the cubicle. "I was trying to say that the style suits you. Have a think about it."

Alone once again, Emma gave the dress one more cursory glimpse before searching for the sombre outfit she'd arrived in; however, the hanger she'd left it dangling from contained nothing. Sighing deeply, she knelt to check under the door before accepting her fate. Jack Seymour may look like butter wouldn't melt. He was anything but.

"You took my clothes." Emma crept out of the changing rooms in time to see him paying for the dress she still wore and the black one she'd chosen herself. She followed him outside into the bright sunshine. "Why did you do that?"

"Because this morning you helped me with the tractor and worked on the hampers, and you've given Daisy a new lease of life just by being around. Basically, it's my way of saying thank you."

Emma stroked the silky fabric, accidentally bumping into a young man, his appraising looks unmistakable as he passed her by.

"Plus, you need to dress well for your job, which brings in a much-needed income to the farm, so I consider it an investment." Jack pushed her stockings into the back of his jeans. "Come on, you're going to be late, and if you get sacked, we're all in trouble."

"What are you doing with my tights?"

"Fan belt replacement." Jack grinned. "What do you think I'm going to do with them?"

*

Jumping out of the Range Rover, Emma approached the farm shop five minutes late. Holding the heavy keys in her hand, she felt surprised to find the door already open. Tentatively pushing against it, she walked inside and peered into the familiar coolness.

"Where have you been?"

The deep voice made her jump and she turned around to find Toby standing in the window, his black-shirted frame in shadow against the bright sunlight, giving him the look of a sinister silhouette.

"And why are you wearing that, after being with him?"

Emma placed a hand against her chest. The truth at this point wouldn't help. She knew him well enough by now.

"Well?" Toby asked, his voice higher and sharper. "Why are you dressed up for him?"

"I got this for you, actually." Emma could hear the tremor in her voice, and she hated herself for the evident weakness. She'd never found jealousy or possessiveness a good trait, but she had no idea how unattractive it could be. "Jack just drove me here because I was running late. That's all."

"Why are you still living on that farm? Don't you think it's about time you moved off it and found yourself somewhere proper to live?"

With what funds? Emma thought to herself as she placed her handbag on the floor near her counter. Since earning, she'd insisted on paying for her piggery, but after that, it left her very little for luxuries. The whole barn seemed to fill with his oppressive mood as his eyes followed her around and it settled on her shoulders like a dark blanket of coercion. As he shifted through the papers on her counter, determined to find fault, Emma debated her choices. She could massage his ego, or she could let him fester.

"These accounts are a mess." Toby pointed to her meticulously ordered book. "Where are the remainder of the incomings?"

"The accounts are not a mess," Emma replied patiently. "I studied all this as part of my hospitality—"

"If I say these accounts are in a mess, they are in a mess. Did you put the prices up like I asked?"

Emma wiped her sweaty palms down the front of her new dress. "No, I didn't."

"Why not?" Toby glowered at her. "Do you think you're better than me? Answer me one question. Who is your boss?"

"You are," Emma replied quietly.

"So, if I say increase the prices, what do you do?"

"I increase the prices," Emma whispered as she spied a bunch of tourists heading into the shop, their light-hearted chatter a huge contrast to the corner she inhabited.

Tapping his foot on the floor, Toby watched the customers peruse the stands, picking things up and examining their prices before putting them back down again. "Time wasters," he said none too quietly.

Wishing the floor would open up and swallow her, Emma continued to look down at the accounts. She felt sure the group had heard the sly comment as they approached the counter with a small bag containing a variety of homemade jams. Already knowing the price, Emma keyed it into her till.

"I'm afraid my assistant has priced everything up wrong today." Toby reached over her, deleting the amount on the till before re-entering it, adding on another few pounds. "Haven't you?"

"I … erm…" Emma sought her head for her hospitality advice manual, but she had nothing to go off as a suitable response. No course would ever prepare you for your manager embarrassing you in front of customers. "Yes, I'm afraid there's been an issue." Emma bit her lip with shame. "I can put it back for you, if you like?"

"No, it's okay, dear," the older lady replied with a sympathetic smile. With a heavy heart, Emma remembered her as the pearls lady from Featherby's, the one who had caught her with Toby's hand up her top. "Everyone makes mistakes. I'll pay what's due."

Shaking out a carrier bag, Emma put the gift inside, aware that her cheeks would be as flame red as the raspberry chilli jam just purchased.

"It's a pound per bag." Toby held out his hand rudely. "Or you can take it without a bag?"

"Without the bag," the pearls lady replied sternly. "Every penny matters at my age."

As the elderly group headed outside, Toby passed her the pricing gun. "And what happens if you don't do as I say?" He looked down at her meaningfully as she stared up at him. "You lose your job. Simple as that."

Toby spent the remainder of the day over her shoulder, criticising her moves. She understood his game. This was her punishment for arriving with Jack. In any other situation, she'd walk away, but once again she'd found herself mixing business with pleasure. If she said goodbye to him, she'd say goodbye to her job, and as Jack had said earlier, her wage coming into the farm at this point in his life was vital. She would have coped better if Toby's jibes were professional only, but when he bought himself dinner and ate it in front of her, knowing full well she had nothing herself, that had hurt. Sharing the sanctity of her shop with him didn't help either. As the afternoon progressed, she watched him dismantle her carefully organised displays, turning them into orderly sets of formalness. The vases of fresh flowers and twinkly lights were removed and shoved under her counter, along with her confidence. By the time she closed the farm shop and entered Milly's bakery, she felt weary and in need of a friendly face. Looking around the bijou interior for signs of life, she eventually headed upstairs.

"Hey, what's wrong?" Emma recoiled at the sight of her friend's swollen lips as she leaned over the toilet. "Is this something you've eaten?"

Milly nodded as she wretched again. Wiping her mouth, she put her hands to her damp forehead and groaned. "It must have been the pasta sauce I bought. I didn't know it had seafood in it."

Trying not to panic, Emma quickly recalled her basic first aid before remembering her friend's medical background. "So what do we do?"

"Hospital," Milly slurred as her tongue started to swell. "Quickly."

*

Emma breathed a sigh of relief as Milly's lips started to return to normal following her adrenaline injection. The junior doctor who administered it gave them both an admiring glance before spieling off all the reasons why pre-bought meals were dangerous for people with her condition. Seemingly happy that he'd impressed them, he checked his bleep and made some comment about patients who really needed his attention.

"Don't you miss this?" Emma asked, hoping to drown out the sounds of someone vomiting in the next cubicle. "The fast pace."

"Nope." Milly sat on the edge of the hospital bed, her dark hair trailing over the straps of her pale-yellow sundress. "I have no desire to go back. I've been there, seen the movie and bought the t-shirt."

"What happened when you were bombed?" Emma looked at her friend hesitantly. She looked so tiny and vulnerable. "It's obviously had a huge effect on your life."

"I survived," Milly replied quietly as she stroked the sterile bedding underneath her. "Someone didn't. His name was Ronin. He saw army life as an adventure. People described him as full of life. Smart mouthed, mischievous, a hit with the ladies. He had everything to live for. I made him come with me that night to check the stock on the emergency vehicles. He realised what was happening before I did. He pushed me back, and in doing so, he took the full blow of the blast himself. They call it survivor's guilt. Someone as vivacious as him should have lived. If I hadn't encouraged him to come with me, he would have."

Emma recognised the brick wall Milly had built around herself. After all, she'd lived within a similar fortress herself until she'd arrived here. She hesitated over her next question and then decided to simply ask, "Is that what you're doing now? Pushing him away?"

Milly looked up and frowned before sighing deeply. "I take it you mean Josh. He reminds me of Ronin, I can't deny that. Both meandering through life with no commitments or worries. The thing is, I need someone dependable now. Someone mature. Josh should come with a warning. 'For one night only, not for keeps.'"

"But he's also very loyal," Emma added. "And extremely caring."

"No." Milly shook her head forcefully. "I need a man, not a child. I need someone who can protect me and understand my moods. I still wake up screaming some nights."

"Oh, Milly." Emma put her hand out and touched her friend's arm. "Do you want me to stay with you tonight?"

"I was about to suggest that." The young male doctor swung back the privacy curtain without warning. He examined Milly's throat again, making noises of approval as he moved his torch around. “Anaphylactic shock isn’t something to be taken lightly. Thankfully, my swift actions saved you this evening, but I do recommend that you carry with you an adrenaline auto-injector. Now don’t panic. I appreciate you may find all this medical terminology overwhelming. I’ll explain what it does.”

“I know what it does,” Milly muttered. “Can I go home now?”

“Not until I’m completely happy with your recovery.” The young doctor checked his quiet bleep again. “You’ll be pleased to know I have a few minutes spare for any questions you may have for me.” He sat on the edge of the bed confidently, his white smile as dazzling as the sheets below him. “Fire away.”

“Seeing as you’ve kept me here for the recommended six hours, administered a 0.3 intramuscular dose of Epinephrine and repeated that after five minutes, and also added an Intravenous fluid bolus to ensure that my A,B,C’s were responding normally, then I guess you are confident I’m fit and well.” Milly picked up her own hospital notes and lazily flicked through them. “Death normally occurs quickly after a trigger, with food reactions taking approximately thirty to thirty-five minutes before respiratory arrest typically occurs. Insect bites and stings normally quicker, ten to fifteen minutes, but very rarely do people die six hours after a trigger. Do you have any questions for me?”

The young doctor’s smug smile slipped off his face. “Who are you? Do you work here?”

“Nope.” Milly jumped off the side of the bed. “I’m just someone who sorts her cupcakes in colour order. I’m no one special.”

Looking discomforted, the young doctor checked his bleep. “Well, I’ve got other patients to see. Do you have someone who can stay with you tonight?”

“I’ll stay with her.” Josh peeked his head inside the cubicle, looking at Milly with undisguised surprise. “Do you need a lift home, Milly Parks, or should I refer to you as Sergeant Major?”

The doctor's spine immediately straightened, and he nodded to Milly respectfully before turning to Emma, giving her cream dress an admiring glance. "I take it he's not your husband?"

Not being able to help herself, Emma gave a nonchalant shrug. "We're a threesome. He's our sex toy."

*

"Serves him right for being patronising." Milly giggled as they left the Accident and Emergency Department. "I've got at least ten years of medical knowledge on him. Cute dress, by the way. Please don't tell me you had a romantic night planned with Toby?"

Emma shook her head. This wasn't the time or the place to regal them with her awful afternoon.

"So, what do I need to know for staying with you tonight?" Josh turned up his windscreen wipers while navigating the country lanes back to Thornhill. "Do I need to learn how to inject you with that pen thing?"

"I've had enough of pricks tonight, thank you," Milly mumbled. "I don't need anyone to stay with me. Anyway, I've got my lodger moving in tomorrow morning. I don't have time to sit down and be pampered."

"I had no intention of pampering you." Josh changed gears as they reached the incline of one of the many rolling hills. "What do you know about this bloke who's moving in? What checks have you done on him? Someone with your background should be tight on security."

"What is your obsession with this?" Milly replied sharply. "The agency does the checks. I'm busy enough, and that's why you staying with me tonight isn't necessary."

"I'm not thinking entirely just of you. I thought it would kill two birds with one stone. You wanted a lock on your spare bedroom, and I've got that shelf you wanted hanging. Staying with you gives me an early start. I'm busy too."

From the back seat, Emma glanced at Milly, rolling her eyes via the rear-view mirror, then smiling to herself. They were both so stubborn. Someone had to give in, but so far there didn't seem to be a clear winner. Leaning her head against the cool window, she watched the greenery glide by, lit only by their headlights as the couple in front continued to argue. Approaching a secluded lay-by, she raised her head and stared at the familiar yellow sports car. Toby sat in the driver's seat as expected, but the passenger intrigued her. A tall, dark-haired woman got out. Her shiny hair, as equally long as her legs, swung around her shoulders as she slammed the door and gave Toby the fingers. Emma craned her neck to get a better look as they drove past, but the speed of their travel and the now heavy rainfall soon distorted her view. Sitting up straight, she pondered on what she'd just seen. Who was she, and why had they stopped to argue in the middle of nowhere?

"Emma can stay with me tonight." Milly turned her head. "Can't you?"

Frowning to concentrate on the conversation in-hand, Emma caught Josh's eye through the rear-view mirror. Even in darkness, she recognised his disappointed expression. "Actually, I can't."

"What?" Milly turned around sharply. "Why not?"

One small white lie in the aim of romance wouldn't do any harm. "Because I lied to you earlier. I do have plans tonight. I'm meeting Toby for supper, so I'm afraid Josh will need to be your night nurse."

"Great," Milly huffed as she turned around to face the window. "Another large prick I have to endure."

CHAPTER 21

The overnight rain had finally given way to sunshine. By the time Emma had changed into her new black dress, the sky had turned a deep, promising blue and the grass had a just-cut scent that no washing powder would ever come close to. A complete contrast to how she felt inside.

Despite the cosiness of her piggery, she had barely slept, and the little sleep she did manage had been dominated by dreams of being trapped. Now her eyes felt heavy and gritty.

Tying up her curls, the gentle knock on her window surprised her. With only thirty minutes before she needed to be at the farm shop, she hadn't expected a visitor.

"Have you got a few minutes?" A red-eyed and wobbly lipped Daisy stood on the doorstep of her piggery. "I need to talk to someone."

A few minutes later, they were cosily ensconced on Emma's sofa bed as the roof of the piggery creaked under the warming sun. The young girl had so far not said much, but with a hot cup of tea in her hands, Emma knew the dam was about to burst.

"I'm letting her down." Daisy's strong lip finally gave way to heaving sobs. "She wanted me to have a good life and now she's gone, and I don't think I'm doing enough to make her proud. What if she is watching me and wishing I'd tried harder? I've never made cheese. I don't even like cheese."

Emma sat next to the sobbing child and pulled her close, glancing at the clock. Toby would have to wait. "I take it you mean your mum?"

Daisy nodded as her sweet-smelling hair fell over her face. Emma pushed it back behind her ears, something her own mum had done many times. "I thought I'd be able to cope, but I can't. There's so much to do." Daisy pulled at the leather bracelet around her wrist. "And the farm needs the income. Jack's trying to train me up so I can take over the farm when he's too old, but I want to go to University first. I want to party and do all the things Jack did, and maybe when I've done all that, I'll come back here, like he did, but I want the choice."

"Does Jack know how you feel?"

"No, of course not," Daisy replied, looking aghast. "He'd hit the roof. University fees are astronomical. I've been saving all the money I've earned, but it's nowhere near enough. I just don't know what to do, and on top of all that, I don't think I've done well in my school exams, and now I'm worried Jack will be disappointed in me, and then my mum will be too."

"Oh, Daisy." Emma kissed the top of the girl's head. "Has Jack ever been disappointed in you?"

"He's never said so." Daisy wiped her nose on the back of her hand. "But I know his marriage broke up because of me."

"No, it didn't." Emma offered the young girl a tissue and continued to stroke her hair. "Why would you even think that?"

"Because I heard them arguing about having to stay in to look after me. Joanne always wanted to go out and have fun. On some nights, she went out without him, and I could hear them shouting when she came home late." Daisy's chin wobbled again. "He was so happy when she told him about the baby. I remember him making loads of plans for a nursery and a tree house. If it hadn't been for me, perhaps she'd have stayed, and Jack would be with Caleb instead of having to look after his stupid sister."

"You are not stupid." Emma held the young girl's shoulders and forced eye contact. "Jack loves you very much and he's extremely proud of you. Every day he talks about your achievements. As for Caleb, that was Joanne's decision to walk away, not yours. She must have had her reasons, but you are not one of them. Okay?"

Daisy nodded as she lay her head on Emma's shoulder and twisted one of her curls around her finger. "I like you living here. Please don't shout at me, but do you like Jack, as in want to snog him?"

"What?" Emma looked at the young girl in surprise. "Where'd that come from?"

"Just wondered." Daisy shrugged. "It would be nice if he met someone I actually liked, that's all. Plus, I don't think you're Toby's type. He's always bothered about his looks and what he's wearing, and you don't."

Emma had to smile at the comment. Only kids could get away with such brutal honesty.

"Will you come with me for my exam results tomorrow?" Daisy looked at her pleadingly. "Jack will listen to you if my grades are bad."

Emma's heart fell into her shoes. She knew Toby wouldn't give her time off, not in his current mood, but how could she let this young girl down?

"Please?" Daisy looked at her with tear-filled eyes.

"Of course I will." Emma nodded. "I'll be there, one way or another. I'll find a way."

The young girl exhaled deeply. "Why is life so hard?"

"Because it teaches us to appreciate when it's good." Emma kissed the top of Daisy's head. "My mum used to have a saying. *'Life is amazing and sometimes it's awful, and in between it's mundane. Breathe in the amazing, hold on through the awful, and breathe during the ordinary. Because it's all life and it's breathtakingly beautiful.'*"

*

"Toilet seats work both ways," Milly tutted as Josh replaced a light fitting in her window display. She grabbed hold of her tea sets and moved them onto the counter. "How come you can aim with that hammer but you can't in the bathroom?"

"Because this hammer is small and my—"

"Oh, shut up." Milly bit back a smile as Josh winked at her. "Has he always been this full of himself?"

"I'm afraid so." Emma laughed as she filled her baskets with loaves of fresh bread. "I take it you're feeling better this morning. Did Josh look after you?"

"If you mean, did he put his feet up, eat crisp and belch a lot, then yes, he did it very well. How was your supper with Toby?"

"Oh, I decided on an early night instead." Emma looked towards the hall, wondering what time Toby would arrive in the farm shop. She'd spent most of the morning on her own and she couldn't deny not having him around had been extremely liberating. "Nothing to do with you, I promise. It was my choice."

"How's my big brother?" Josh asked with a screwdriver between his teeth. "Has he spoken to you yet?"

"Spoken to me?" Emma frowned. "Well, we chatted over breakfast. He said the milk tanks were playing up again, but that's it. He milked alongside Clive again, while I carried on painting the other barn with Daisy."

"And Tilly Mint, is she okay? Is she nervous about tomorrow?"

"She'll be fine," Emma replied, not wanting to betray her young friend's confidence. "I'll be honest, I've been more worried about you two. I thought you'd have killed each other by now."

"There's time yet," Milly muttered as Josh tripped over the rabbit display in the window. "At least he got to sleep in a bed with a soft mattress, a thick duvet, and soft bouncy pillows. I had to squeeze up on the sofa in case I started being sick again."

"That was your decision, not mine," Josh replied as he checked to make sure the new lights worked. "You could have used a bucket. I wouldn't have judged. In fact, that reminds me." He balanced himself against his ladders as he lifted his foot. "I stood on a screw this morning. Those sanitary towels in your bathroom cabinet are a perfect fit for my shoes. Excellent first aid bandages. I had no use for your waxing strips though."

"You didn't go through my personal things!" Milly looked at him in shock. "That cabinet is private. Do you not know the meaning of privacy?"

"Yeah, of course I do." Josh blew his blond curls out of his eyes. "I didn't look at you behind the shower curtain when I crept in the bathroom."

Milly opened her mouth to protest before seeing his cheeky grin.

"Got you." Josh winked. "You're so easy to wind up. Don't worry, I'm a lot of things, but I'm not a pervert. I even covered you with another blanket last night to protect your dignity. See, I'm not all bad."

"Last night?" Milly furrowed her brow. "You slept in my bed last night."

"I slept in the chair opposite you, actually."

"Why?"

Josh shrugged. "I promised I'd look after you. I can't do that from another room, can I? Plus, you were talking in your sleep. You seem unsettled."

"Was I?" Milly paused. "Did I say anything?"

Josh hesitated slightly before replying, "I think maybe you had a bad dream, but you settled when you realised I was with you. It was no big deal. Don't sweat it."

Milly stared at him, her head to one side thoughtfully as the bell above her door jingled.

She turned around to find a middle-aged man carrying a large overnight bag. He looked around the small bakery with approval, his grey eyes flitting over Emma and Milly.

Attempting to make more room, Josh folded his ladders, accidentally knocking over a pile of plates in the process. They smashed immediately onto the hard floor.

"No, my best tea set." Milly groaned as she bent down to pick up the broken shards. "Josh, you are a total knob head."

"Allow me," the man said, gathering the cracked plates quickly together. He turned to Milly with an unruffled smile that complemented his suave suit and perfectly cut dark hair. "I'm Sebastian, your new lodger, and one of you pretty ladies must be Milly, my landlady, and already, the pleasure is all mine."

CHAPTER 22

Why was he doing it? Emma watched Toby as he stood by the farm shop window. Didn't he realise jealousy was an unattractive trait? For the past forty minutes, she'd listened to all the reasons why Jack Seymour should be burned on a stake. He was a womaniser, a bully, too smug, too proud, too successful. The more he went on, the more she sided with Jack, and in all honesty, of late, she didn't need the encouragement.

"Was he always this pompous as a kid?" Toby's lavender eyes flashed with envy as he read the Parish Council's latest magazine with a page dedicated to the success of dairy farming in Thornhill. "Some people think they have it all, but they don't. I know for a fact that guys like him can still have the rug pulled from under their feet. They are not invincible."

"What do you mean?" Emma shook her head in confusion. This had gone way beyond a feud for Toby. It had become an obsession, and that worried her deeply.

"All I'm saying is that no one is perfect." Toby eyed her closely. "If you don't like him, move off his farm."

Emma closed her eyes momentarily as she thought of the excuse she'd come up with last night. "I can't. I signed a contract for the piggery and paid upfront. I have no more spare cash."

"So, move in with Milly."

Once again, Emma had considered this would be his backlash. "Her new lodger moved in this morning, and Josh stayed with her last night. She was poorly in hospital and he didn't want to leave her."

"Are you telling me you shared the farm with Jack alone?" Toby's eyes flashed dangerously. "I didn't know that."

"We weren't alone. His sister was there." Emma's hand shook as she checked the sell by dates on the stock in the refrigerator. Why did she always feel like she needed to defend herself around him? As if she needed permission for every move she made.

"Mark my words, he'll come to nothing. Jack Seymour is a chancer. At some point in the near future his farm will fail. He's that cocky, he'll out-do even himself. If you want my advice, move off now and get away from him before he takes you down with him. There's no money in dairy farming despite what this article says, and he can't expand into anything else. It's a dead-end business."

Emma mouthed the next words as he said them.

"Or find yourself another job."

Continuing to restock the orderly no fuss shelves of the dressers she had lovingly painted, Emma felt her optimism for life drain away.

"We're closing early today." Toby ushered a group of customers away from the gifts section and back onto the village green. He turned to Emma with a satisfied smile. "Jack Seymour doesn't get these kinds of perks. I can close my business at whatever time of day I please. I'm not governed by weather or cattle, simply by my own actions. Don't you think that's liberating?"

Or stupid, Emma thought as she viewed the family of tourists now standing near the duck pond with nothing to eat for their dinner. It would be unlikely they'd return to her barn any time soon. "Do you think it's a good idea to close early?" Emma asked quietly. "It's forecast to be a nice day. There'll be a heavy footfall."

"I realise you think you run this place, but you don't." Toby picked up his car keys. "I do, and the reason I'm shutting shop is because we are going to Featherby's."

Emma inwardly groaned. She couldn't cope with another cloakroom humiliation.

"They are hoping to get a Michelin star, and I'm one of their reviewers. If you stick with me, you'll live the high life."

Emma found herself thrust into her seat as Toby sped away from the hall, his tyres causing gravel and dust to rise behind them, and drinkers in the aptly named 'Dusty Mouse' to turn their heads in annoyance. The roar of the vehicle and the wind against her face prevented further conversation, and for that she felt grateful. Just being in his company made her feel uneasy.

Her ears throbbing from the noise of the engine, Emma unplugged her seat belt and reluctantly followed Toby as he strode quickly to the main entrance of Featherby's.

"Ah, good, you've brought her back." The efficient receptionist pointed at Emma. "He said you'd be good at organising the cloak room and you were, but this time, please don't leave your post while we still have property in there."

Emma clenched her fists as she stared at Toby's retreating back. So, he had engineered her to work on that day. She knew it.

"Here's the ticket book." The receptionist fixed her spectacles on the end of her nose. "At least you're dressed better today. Jeans are okay for the pub, but not for here."

For one split second, Emma considered working in the cloakroom if it would prevent her from having to sit opposite Toby. About to follow the receptionist, she paused as Toby's angry voice infiltrated the reception area. Watching him by-pass the patient line of diners, Emma held back, pretending to examine the art hung around the walls.

"Excuse me." A well-dressed lady from the orderly line tapped him on the shoulder. "There's a queue."

"I don't queue," Toby replied arrogantly before turning to the head waiter with no pleasantries. "I want your best table in the mezzanine."

The young man licked his lips nervously. "I'm afraid, sir, all our mezzanine tables are gone."

"That's your problem, not mine." Toby turned to Emma as she did her best to disappear into the artwork. "Come over here and stop loitering."

"I'm sorry, sir," the head waiter continued. "We already have diners seated, perhaps we can arrange seating in our new conservatory, it has wonderful views over the—"

"I am Toby Montgomery." Toby brushed his lapels. "Landlord of Thornhill. *Land. Lord*," he emphasised each word slowly. "If you want this place to have a Michelin star, it's me you need to impress first. Where's your manager?"

As the flustered waiter picked up the phone, the well-dressed old lady tapped Toby on the shoulder again. "Perhaps you could stand to one side so we can be served, or do you charge a pound for me talking to you?"

Groaning, Emma recognised the pearls lady. She turned to Emma with a smile that cut her to the core. When had she become someone who people pitied? Even after leaving Sean, she had kept her pride. At what point had she put Toby above her own dignity and self-respect, and what kind of wanker expected that?

Obviously familiar with difficult guests, the manager stood in a discreet corner, where he nodded politely as Toby gesticulated angrily between the head waiter and the restaurant. Staring at her sensible shoes, Emma prayed for the floor to open up and swallow her whole.

"Follow me," Toby signalled after a few minutes. "We have our table."

Their arrival in the busy restaurant coincided with the obvious uprooting of an agitated couple. The look of contempt from their neighbouring diners didn't go amiss as she followed Toby up each stair. To add insult to injury, their table now overlooked where the pearls lady had been seated with her family. If ever she wondered how the accused felt in the dock, now she knew.

Her white knuckles clenched in her lap, she thanked the waiter for the menu and buried her head inside the list of dishes.

"I'll choose the wine." Toby shook out his own napkin and laid it on his knee before looking around proudly. "It's free because of the embarrassment caused in the reception." He clicked his fingers at a nearby waitress as he pointed to the bottom of the wine list. "A bottle of that one, please. Two glasses and this place will be footing the bill today, am I right?"

"No." Emma shook her head. "We'll pay, like everyone else here."

"I don't think so." Toby looked at her incredulously as the waitress scuttled away. "Anyway, most of these people pay rent to me. They should show their landlord some respect."

Oh God, so the people dining below were worse off in pocket because of him and his increased rents? Could this scenario get any more awkward? She peered down to see the pearls lady looking up, and she saw herself through her eyes; a weak-willed girl being dictated to by a pompous git.

"Two foie gras, followed by two ribeye steaks, medium rare with dauphinoise potatoes. Quickly please, we are hungry."

"Hold on." Emma put down her menu. "Don't I get to choose my own food?"

"It's what I always order when I come here." Toby waved the waitress away. "Are you vegetarian?"

"No, but I don't agree with how foie gras is prepared. I think it's unethical."

"So are you, sharing a farm with that man?"

Emma sat back and sighed angrily. She may have to work for him, but that didn't mean he could control her. "Why are you being like this with me, Toby?"

"Because you need to know I won't stand for you fraternising with the Seymours. You belong to me, not them."

"Actually, I don't belong to anyone." Emma felt white anger start to burn from her toes upwards. How dare he be so presumptuous. It was time to turn the tables. "So, what did you do last night?"

Ripping a piece of bread with his teeth, Toby paused. "I stayed in. Why?"

"Just curious." Emma watched his ticking jaw closely. "When I came back from the hospital last night with Milly, I saw some dodgy characters parked up by the side of the road. I wondered if you'd heard of undesirables in the village."

Toby's eyes flitted momentarily. "Like who?"

"Oh, I don't know," Emma replied, enjoying seeing his cool front slip. "Maybe a female. Someone tall, dark haired. Sticking two fingers up at you."

"What do you know about that?" Toby hissed. "Have you been following me?"

"Would you have anything to hide if I had?" Emma took a sip of her chilled wine. The coldness in her mouth contrasted with the heat in her head, helping to clear her mind. "Who is she?"

Toby shrugged nonchalantly. "That's nothing to do with you."

Emma stared into his shifty lavender eyes. How bigoted could this prick get? Did he have any shame at all? The white anger in her toes moved up into her stomach and she experienced the same surge of adrenaline she'd felt when she discovered her empty wedding account and the Ferrari parked on their drive.

"Did you know Jack's selling luxury food hampers on his farm?" Emma took another sip of her deliciously cool wine as she added a match to the bubbling fuel. If she was going to do this, she'd do it spectacularly. "I've been helping him set it up. The website looks amazing and the market research I've done for him is watertight. It can't be anything apart from a huge success."

"Please tell me this is a joke," Toby growled with a low voice. He slammed his drink on the table as their foie gras arrived. "You've been helping him set up another business? One that I could have benefited from. Luxury food hampers?"

His outburst coincided with the change in music and his words echoed around the large room. Feeling many eyes upon her, Emma sat perfectly still, allowing him to take centre stage. *How dare he swear at me in public!*

"I can't believe your betrayal." Toby's lip curled as the restaurant remained silent. "You're my girlfriend, not his."

"I'm not your girlfriend, and neither do I want to be." Now her mind had been made up, Emma's mission became impossible to stop. Weeks of domination and manipulation rose to the fore. "You're jealous of Jack and with every good cause to be." Emma knew her voice had risen, and she also knew it had attracted the attention of many diners, both below and by their sides. Instead of intimidating her, their curiosity spurred her on. "You may have money, but you are a first-class dickhead. You're also a bully and a pathetic businessman. Perhaps you should look at Jack to see where you're going wrong."

"I'm not standing for this. You're sacked, with immediate effect." Toby pushed his chair back with a force that sent it tumbling into the couple behind him. "You weren't worth the money I paid you anyway."

"You can't sack someone after they've resigned." Emma moved her own chair back calmly, positioning it neatly under the table. "People warned me you were a wanker, but I was drawn in by your fake charm." She drank the rest of her wine and thanked the waitress who had delivered their first course. "Enjoy your meal. I'm going home to get pissed in a piggery and it will be infinitely more enjoyable than sitting with a wanking tosser like you." Heading to the mezzanine stairs, she delved into her bag and threw the heavy farm shop keys that landed in the remainder of his starter. "If you find time tomorrow, aside from comparing yourself to someone you'll never live up to, perhaps you can open up your own shop."

As Emma walked down the last few steps, the pearl lady stood up and started to clap. By the time she reached the door, she had a standing ovation.

And no job. Again.

CHAPTER 23

"Knock on," Jack shouted from the edge of the field as Daisy ran squealing with a rugby ball under her arm, Josh chasing her. "Hey, you can't carry on playing."

"I can do what I like," Daisy bellowed as Josh caught her. "I'm a girl. We make the rules up."

"Don't I bloody know it." Jack turned around and frowned as Emma walked across the field to join them. "What are you doing here?"

The simple sight of a group of people who cared for each other playing something as light-hearted as rugby made Emma feel strangely safe. As if they were a unit, bonding in the same team. She had spent the last hour walking from Featherby's, resulting in burned and blistered feet caused by her new shoes. Along the way, she'd reverted between a great sense of pride at her retaliation and a desperate need to cry. Now, in the safety of the farm, she struggled to keep the tears at bay.

"Emma?" Jack approached her quickly as he lifted the bottom of his t-shirt to wipe a sheen of sweat off his forehead. "Aren't you supposed to be at work?"

"Work?" Emma shrugged, her voice cracking with the effort of trying not to sob. "I don't have a job anymore. I've resigned or been sacked. Depends on how you look at it."

"Toby has fired you?" Josh kicked the ball towards Daisy as he joined his brother. "Why?"

"Because he's a wanker." Emma gave them a watery smile. "It just took me a while to figure it out."

"What's he done?" Jack folded his arms, his dark eyes fixing on her. "Has he hurt you?"

"Not physically." Aware of Daisy playing alone, Emma aimed to keep her explanation simple. "He's just very possessive, and of late, he's been making my life quite unpleasant."

Josh sighed. "I knew it. I knew something wasn't right. What's he been doing?"

Emma swallowed deeply to keep her tears in check. "He doesn't like me living here with Jack." She looked at him, feeling embarrassed by her confession. "He thinks there's something going on between us and he's jealous. Basically, he keeps asking me to move off the farm, but I don't want to."

"We don't want that either," Josh replied as his brother swore under his breath. "What else has he been doing?"

"Just using me. A few days ago, he took me to Featherby's, and he said it wasn't planned, but I ended up working in the cloakroom on my day off."

"Why did you not tell us about any of this?" Jack suddenly pinched the bridge of his nose as he answered his own question. "Because I've been teasing you about him. Shit, I'm so sorry."

"No, it's my fault." Emma rolled her eyes at her own stupidity. "And to add insult to injury, I think he's seeing someone else. I saw him with another woman last night when we picked Milly up from the hospital, and when I questioned him, he said he hadn't gone out. I'm so sorry. I should have listened to you both, but he threatened to sack me, and I needed that job. I thought I could handle him, but his unpleasantness and the way he's so unprofessional, I wasn't prepared for it. It's hard to defend yourself when you don't know how low a blow they're going to pull next."

"I feel like killing him." Jack raked a hand through his hair. "Controlling bastard. He's always been the same."

"Shall we go and have a quiet word?" Josh suggested.

Jack shook his head. "No, I don't want him in our lives. Tempting as it is to land him a thump, and believe me, I'm pretty close to doing it, I'm not going to give him the satisfaction of seeing he's wound me up. I think we should let him sweat."

"He's not happy about the hampers." Emma cringed. "I'm sorry, I told him about them."

"It's okay, I understand," Jack replied patiently. "I've known him for a lot longer than you have."

Emma's toes curled inside her tight shoes. She really should have listened to them both from the start. "I'm also really sorry I no longer have a wage coming in. Do you want me to move out?"

"Absolutely not. You leaving the farm shop couldn't have come at a better time. Daisy spoke to me earlier. She said she doesn't want to run the cheese business. I'm kind of hoping you will."

"Me?" Emma took in an audible breath. "You mean to set it up?"

"No, I mean to run it. Permanently."

Feeling her jaw drop, Emma repeated his words. "Permanently, as in, forever?"

"That's what it means in my dictionary." Jack bit his lip hesitantly as his brother ran back to resume the rugby game. "Unless you have plans to move on."

Emma's thoughts spun around like laundry mid-cycle. How did she feel about staying here? Forever? She looked around the hills bathed in the early evening sun, at the thatched farmhouse and her cosy little piggery. She would be living her best life. At least until Jack met someone or re-married, then it would quickly become a nightmare.

"You don't have to." Jack's deep eyes softened. "I'll understand if you don't want to be around Toby anymore. I know how much you liked him. His actions have hurt you, haven't they?"

Emma nodded. There seemed little point in hiding that fact; it must be written all over her face. "I'm a bit worried how he'll react to me running the hamper business from your farm. He'll see that as a betrayal."

"As long as we don't give him any ammunition or let him into our circle, there's nothing he can do other than dance around on the periphery like a prat." Jack ran a hand through his hair before biting his lower lip. "Does that mean you're going to stay?"

Her thoughts went back to that moment at the side of the lake. *'Hall or farm'*. Is this what he meant? Where did her loyalty sit? Regardless, she'd be a fool not to take the lifeline.

"Of course I'm going to stay." Emma smiled, feeling a little embarrassed. "But I also need you to know that he thinks we are … well, he thinks you and I…"

"Are having wild passionate sex in the back of my parlour." Jack grinned at her flushed cheeks. "Yeah, I've heard the rumours."

"Rumours?" Emma gasped. "You're joking?"

"It's a small village, Emma." Jack laughed at her wide eyes. "Why, is it that unbelievable? Us, I mean?"

Emma looked up into his smiling face. Just like his brother, he'd always enjoyed a good wind up.

"Come on, we're trying to distract Daisy from her exam results tomorrow and we also need to take Josh's mind off a certain newcomer to the village."

"Ah." Emma nodded as she walked across the field to join the other two. "Sebastian. Milly's new lodger."

"He's a banker, apparently." Daisy kicked the ball into the air and deftly caught it. "I saw him today in the village. One of the women said he's a dish and very charming. She said he could be the new James Bond."

"He's a wanker," Josh muttered. "With lots of blarney. Three suitcases turned up after him. Who the bollocks needs three suitcases, and I ended up carrying two of them for him. And do you know what he did?"

Jack bit his lip and quickly glanced at Emma to judge her reaction.

"He tipped me. Five friggin' pounds. The cheeky bastard. Do I look like a bloody bellboy?"

Emma put a hand over her mouth to smother the laugh.

"He's got more oil than our chip pan. I'm telling you, Milly won't like him at all. I'll give it two days and she'll throw him out."

Jack smiled. "You hope."

"Yeah, well, it's nothing to do with me anyway." Josh took the ball off Daisy and kicked it angrily across the makeshift goal line. "She doesn't mean anything to me. So, are we playing this game or not?"

Abandoning her formal clothing in favour of shorts and a t-shirt, Emma headed back onto the field with a new sense of light-heartedness. Jack was right, Toby couldn't hurt her, and neither could he stop her running the cheese and hamper business. He had no power over her anymore.

Watching the small group play for a few moments, Emma felt her love of the game return. Without thinking, she ran forward as Daisy passed her the ball. Seeing a clear run, she held it under her arm as she sprinted, head down, while the warm summer breeze threaded through her curls. Risking a quick look behind her, she sped up to increase the distance between her and a determined Jack, close on her heels. Her legs burning, she sped up, but couldn't outrun him. Collapsing with laughter as he grabbed her, they tumbled to the ground.

"I've got you," he panted. "At last."

CHAPTER 24

"How are the new milk tanks?" Emma asked as she filled the troughs with hay. "Are you glad you invested in them?"

"I didn't really have a choice. They've set me back a few thousand, but I needed them." Jack led a herd of impatient cows into the stalls, keeping an eye on Emma at the same time. "Another reason I couldn't afford to give Joanne more money. If I don't keep up to date with regulations, I could lose this farm. Although, after talking to Daisy last night, I don't know why I'm bothering. I'm not sure she'll come back after University."

"I can tell you're disappointed." Emma smiled at him sympathetically.

"I'm not disappointed in her decision; after all, she needs to choose her own future. It's just that this farm has been habited by Seymours for generations and it's typical it dies out when I take over."

"Unless you have more children?" Emma shrugged, pretending to act like she couldn't care less about his response. "This girl you like, does she want kids, or have you not spoken to her about it?"

"Let's say we've not reached that stage yet."

"Still at first base?" Emma laughed, trying to sweeten her own bitter pill.

"Believe me, first base would be a welcome relief right now." Jack grinned as he slapped a cow on its hide, hurrying it along. "I'm still waiting to get picked for the team, if you catch my drift."

"You've not even kissed her?" Emma put her hands on her hips in astonishment while at the same time feeling a mix of guilt and happiness at the revelation. "Is it because of me?"

"Pardon?" Jack turned around swiftly. "What do you mean?"

Not wanting to admit to earwigging, but at the same time hoping to clear the air, Emma went for a mid-field approach. "I don't want to be the reason you're not being, you know, yourself. I'm not completely innocent. I know you're a man and you want to do stuff."

"I'm glad you've noticed." Jack's lips lifted as he continued to herd the cattle around the parlour. "However, I'm also capable of controlling myself, so in answer to your question, you being around isn't the issue."

"So what is?"

"Let's just say she's a bit of an enigma. Anyway, what help will you need with the hampers and the café? I think it's a brilliant idea, by the way, to extend Milly's seating area here on the farm."

Emma realised the conversation about his love life had been abandoned. Although to be fair, he'd never discussed his girlfriends around her when they lived in Redsworth. Did he still see her as the kid with the Ribena mouth? Someone you didn't discuss the big S word with. If so, he'd be shocked at the thoughts running around her head lately. He'd also be shocked to discover that in six hours' time, she would have been saying the big '*I do*'. She rubbed at the bare ridge around her finger. That had been one lucky escape.

"Also, I forgot to tell you, my mate in Chester is selling up his bistro business to move abroad. I've asked him for a decent quote on some of his furnishings and equipment, and he's said I can pick the stuff up tonight. I'll go after evening milking."

Emma frowned. "That's a long drive. Four hours, at least. Are you sure you're up for that after working all day?"

“Needs must.” Jack sighed. “I don’t have the money to buy brand new.”

“Do you want me to come with you and share the driving?”

“If that’s okay with you.” Jack put his arm around her shoulders. “A long drive is always shorter with company.”

They headed into the kitchen as Daisy made her way sheepishly down the stairs, her swollen eyelids a telltale of the tears that had soaked into her pillow. Emma immediately reached out to the young girl and kissed her sleepy head, relishing in the sweet smell of sleep and soap.

Daisy’s bottom lip wobbled as she leant her head against Emma’s soft curls. “I can get my results online, but I want to go into school instead. That way, if they’re bad, I can get advice straight away.”

“We’re all coming. Clive is staying on the farm to keep an eye on things, and Josh will meet us there.” Jack smiled at the sight of Emma and Daisy wrapped up together. “And if your results are bad, we’ll make you paint the fences, and if they’re good, we’ll still make you paint the fences.”

Daisy’s lack of retaliation to the teasing caused Emma’s heart to swell for the young girl. “Come on, you need to eat.” She fried up a pan of omelettes and laid them on the kitchen table. “Food is fuel for the brain.”

“My mum used to say that.” Daisy sat down and picked up her knife and fork.

“I know she did,” Emma replied softly. “She said it to me enough times too.”

“She was a wise woman.” Clive headed into the kitchen, closely followed by an inquisitive Pickles, who immediately headed under the table to examine the floor for potential crumbs. “How are the new milk tanks?”

“Worth every penny.” Jack nodded. “Did the cows behave for you going back to the fields?”

“They always do around me.” Clive pulled a plate of food towards himself and tucked into it eagerly. “Unlike young Emma. She was the talk of the Mouse last night. I believe Master Montgomery got a mouthful from you in Featherby’s.”

Emma sighed as she put down her knife and fork, her appetite suddenly gone. “Go on, are they all laughing at me?”

“Actually, they thought you were extremely brave.” Clive picked up his large mug of tea and slurped from it noisily. “The farmers have your back around here. You’ve built a lot of loyalty in this village. I’m not sure what will happen now that you’ve left.”

“They’ll carry on supplying Toby, surely?” Emma replied. “What else would they do, and what would he do if they stopped?”

“I don’t know.” Clive picked up the tea pot and refilled his cup. “I guess we’ll have to wait and see, but Toby is nothing if not hot headed.”

Carrying the empty plates to the sink, Emma paused. That comment sounded like it had come from personal experience. “Is there something I don’t know?”

Jack tipped his head to one side. “I deliberately didn’t tell you this because the past is the past, but Toby made life a bit difficult for me after dad left. Just petty things, like asking the Parish Council to consider sourcing dairy from other farms, scaremongering about foot and mouth, that kind of thing. He soon got bored of it.”

“Oh God.” Emma sat down with a thump. “I’ve been a complete fool, haven’t I?”

Jack shrugged. “He’s very charming and knows what to say to disarm you. We’ve all been there with someone like him. The important thing to remember is not to give him any ammunition.”

Feeling like a ten-year-old reminded about crossing the road without looking, Emma returned to the washing up. Trust her to go and bring Toby’s unpleasantness into the Seymours’ life. She just hoped Jack was right and that his frustrations would be short-lived.

*

Daisy's friends crowded around each other in small groups, legs twisting, and fingernails bitten to the quick as they waited for the school doors to open. Emma remembered the feeling well, only she'd had her mum and dad by her side, whereas Daisy just had her brothers. *Not that their appearance seems to be a disadvantage*, Emma thought wryly as the schoolgirls looked towards their group, tittering and giggling behind their hands.

"It takes you back, doesn't it?" Josh crossed his arms and leant against the bike shed. "I remember getting our exam results a few days before we left to come here. I knew I hadn't done well, but you were sick with nerves."

"I was just thinking about it." Emma narrowed her eyes as the memories took hold. "We went back to your house for a party, and your mum made me this massive sandwich because I hadn't been able to eat all day."

"And then you threw up in the garden behind the rose bushes." Jack laughed. "Too much food, I presume."

Emma smiled to herself. It had been nerves, mingled with sadness and apprehensiveness. That afternoon she had written her love letter and it had sat in her shorts pocket, along with the slip of paper containing her exam results, both equally precious. She had tried to capture every second of that day, knowing their time together would soon come to an end. Later that evening, she'd popped her note through their letter box, and the rest, as they say, was history.

"I don't know who's more nervous." Jack steepled his hands over his mouth as the doors opened and the group of teenagers gathered in an orderly line as their teachers gave them all words of encouragement. "What if she's not done well?"

"Then we'll support her." Emma stalled. "Sorry, that was a bit presumptuous of me. I meant, you'll support her. Anyway, does it matter what her results are?"

“To me? No, absolutely not.” Jack swallowed deeply as Daisy finally disappeared through the doors. “However, I’m aware she feels like she needs to prove something to us, and because of that, I want her to get the results she deserves. I’m proud of her already.” Jack stopped and looked up, exhaling loudly. “Jesus, this has really got to me.”

Emma took his hand and rubbed it gently. It should have been an act of solidarity and comfort, but she couldn’t ignore the zings that shot up her arm, nor could she ignore the tightening of Jack’s fingers around hers. He was obviously more nervous than she’d realised.

Thirty minutes later, Jack had resorted to pacing the school grounds like an expectant father. Grabbing fistfuls of his hair, he eventually stopped. “Where is she? It’s not good news, is it? She’s going to be gutted.”

“We’ll find out any second,” Josh replied as the school doors burst open and a group of giggly girls escaped like air out of a burst balloon. Amongst them stood Daisy. She shrugged gently before walking over with a sheepish smile.

“Sorry.” Daisy bit her nails. “I genuinely am.”

“Hey, it’s okay.” Jack pulled her into a giant hug as Josh ruffled her hair affectionately. “I told you, it’s not about marks on paper, it’s about passion and motivation.” Jack closed his eyes tightly for a few seconds. “I know I don’t say this enough, but I love you.”

“You soft git.” Daisy smiled mischievously as she waved a piece of paper in the air. “I’m sorry … I made you wait so long for this!”

Josh snatched the exam results off her before whooping and lifting her up in the air. “You absolute beauty!”

Jack read the grades before gripping her in a headlock. “You total minx. You’re painting fences all day after this.”

“I will.” Daisy skipped excitedly. “After my party.”

“Party?” Jack looked at his brother. “Seriously?”

"Oh, come on." Daisy rolled her eyes. "I know you're winding me up. You're pretending you thought I'd do badly so you didn't need to bother with a celebration. Well, you can't fool me."

Recognising the genuine look of fear in the men's faces, Emma stepped in. "We can't pull the wool over your eyes, can we? We thought there'd be about ten of you, am I right?"

"Yes." Daisy jumped excitedly. "We're going to do our makeup and hair, and Josh can take our photographs."

"Wonderful." Josh widened his eyes before turning to Emma. "I wish she'd failed. Help."

*

"There's a dozen cupcakes in there all decorated, a good selection of sandwiches and a large celebration cake." Milly placed everything gently on her counter. "I take it she's over the moon?"

"Absolutely buzzing," Emma replied with a smile. "They're all at the farm now, having their photographs taken. Josh has to keep stopping while they re-glue their false eyelashes, but he's keeping his temper under control." Emma paused as her friend suddenly frowned. "What's the problem?"

"My ring has gone." Milly bent down and looked under the counter. "I normally leave it near the oven when I'm baking. I'm sure I left it there yesterday."

Emma helped her look around the small bakery. "Is it not upstairs?"

Milly ran up to her bedroom before heading back down. "No. I can't find it. Unless I left it in the bathroom. I'll check later when Sebastian has finished showering."

"How is Sebastian?"

"He's really nice." Milly cocked her head as she listened to the water running. "And very polite. After all those disastrous interviews, I've finally found someone normal, and you know what I really like about him?"

Emma raised an eyebrow, already feeling sorry for Josh.

"He's mature and sensible. He's obviously very intelligent, and he has this calmness about him that's quite sexy."

"So you like him?"

"I think I do." Milly paused as she served a few customers before returning to her counter. "Anyway, enough about me. Have you driven down?"

"No, I didn't think I'd get parked this late in the morning. Josh is picking me up." Emma nodded towards the farm shop where Toby could be seen standing near the window. "Has he said anything to you?"

"No, but a few other customers have." Milly smiled playfully. "I've heard all about the roasting you gave him. How are you feeling about it?"

"Nervous, and a bit sad," Emma admitted. "Toby's very possessive and hot-headed. I'm a bit concerned about how he'll retaliate, and obviously I'll miss the farm shop."

"So, he's definitely sacked you?"

"That's how he'll portray it, and it's not worth me arguing with him over it. I'm working on the farm now, and if you like my ideas on extending your café up there, then I won't have much time to dwell on Toby. There's so much to do. Daisy has made a start on building a website and she's already got all the licenses, but preparing the small barn to sell the produce will be down to Josh and me, with Jack at the helm, of course."

"It seems Jack and you are the perfect partners."

"Stop it," Emma warned. "I don't want those types of rumours starting."

"It's a bit late for that." Milly grinned. "There's a lot of villagers who want to see Jack settle down with a nice girl, especially after Joanne, and I think they're hoping you'll be the one."

"They'll be in for a long wait," Emma mumbled as Josh appeared at the bakery window. She signalled for him to come through. "How did the photo shoot go?"

"They're all on my laptop, adding special effects." Josh nodded politely towards Milly. "Are you ready to go?"

"You just need one more box." Milly headed into the back of the bakery. "I have some canisters and helium balloons you can have. Give me a few minutes. I need to find them."

"Ah, I thought I heard a male voice." Sebastian ran lightly down the stairs, buttoning up his shirt. "James, my good man, how are you on fixing toasters?"

"My name is Josh, not James, and I'm afraid I'm not working this morning."

"Ah, shame." Sebastian pursed his lips. "If it's faulty and sets on fire, that becomes a bigger problem."

Emma stared at Sebastian's dark lashes. "Are you wearing makeup?"

"Of course not." Sebastian took a pristine white handkerchief from his pocket and wiped under his eyes. "My pen burst. So, this toaster. Who do I go to if you're not working?"

"It's just me in this village." Josh glanced at Sebastian's expensive watch before looking down at his own work-worn hands and dirty nails. "I can come tomorrow afternoon, or I can give you a fuse. That's normally the issue."

Sebastian reached into his suit pocket and extracted a ten-pound note. "Would this change your mind?"

"Actually, Josh is busy with his sister's party," Emma interrupted. "Perhaps he can—"

"It's okay, I'll do it."

Josh trudged upstairs, leaving Emma alone with Sebastian. She smiled at him politely before heading behind the counter to have another look for Milly's ring. Bending to see under the worktops, she turned her head slightly and immediately stiffened. Working in hospitality had taught her how to deal with many types of people, including ones like him. The men who liked to ogle. She'd learned early that firm eye contact and a stern look normally did the trick.

"It's fixed. It was the fuse." Josh traipsed back down the stairs, his jaw tight with annoyance. "I had a spare in my pocket."

Sebastian cleared his throat while Emma continued to focus on him. "You're a good man to know, James. I appreciate your help."

"Here we go." Milly struggled through the doorway with a large box. "Balloons, bunting, and a few party poppers." She placed the package on the counter and looked around at the stiffly standing group. "Is everything okay?"

"Absolutely perfect," Emma replied breezily, in the hope it would lighten the tense atmosphere. "Thanks for all this, but we'd best be going. We have ten sixteen-year-olds to feed and entertain."

Climbing into Josh's van, Emma slammed the door with force. Judging by the way Josh tugged on his seat belt, he felt as disgruntled as her.

"He's smarmy." Emma folded her arms tightly. "Why did you do that work for him? He could have waited."

"I can't afford a bad reputation." Josh turned on the engine and threw the van into reverse. "Believe me, I'd rather have stuck the toaster up his arse. Speaking of arses, there's one in the farm shop staring right at you. Don't turn around. Keep looking ahead."

Emma felt a shiver down her spine as Josh maneuvered out of the space. She had no one else to blame. She'd brought this unpleasantness on herself.

"Fancy a drink at the Mouse later?" Josh asked as they began the short drive back to the farm. "I think I need to unwind."

“I’m sorry, I can’t.” Emma screwed up her nose apologetically. “I’m going to Chester, sharing the driving with Jack.”

“Speak of the devil.” Josh pulled over and answered his dancing phone. “We’re on our way, don’t panic.” Josh furrowed his brow as he listened to his brother, his hands tightening around the phone. “You’re kidding me? Joanne can’t do that without speaking to you first. Can she?”

Emma folded her hands in her lap and concentrated on the glove compartment in front of her while her ears strained to catch the murmurings on the end of the line.

“Shit.” Josh ended the call and thumped the steering wheel before re-starting the van. “We need to get back. Joanne is getting remarried.”

Emma bit her lip questioningly. “That doesn’t sound too bad. Or is it?”

“It is when she wants him to sign some papers so her fiancé can adopt Caleb. He’s devastated.”

CHAPTER 25

"The traffic is heavy tonight." Jack checked his wing mirror as Emma changed lanes on the drive to Chester. "I didn't expect this after rush hour."

"It's a busy motorway," Emma replied as she shifted gears. "I don't think it's ever quiet."

Emma knew his navigation efforts were covering up his upset. She couldn't even begin to comprehend how he must be feeling, his own child a complete stranger to him, and receiving another man's name. Slowly, bit by bit, Joanne appeared to be cutting him out of the child's life, and Jack had to live with that, knowing his own flesh and blood walked this earth unaware of his existence.

With his head in his hands, he'd sat at the kitchen table for hours, and despite Josh's calm support, he'd refused to discuss it. Between them, they'd tried to talk him out of the drive to Chester so soon after Joanne's news, but he'd made his mind up and refused to be challenged on it. Emma recognised his stubbornness came from a desire for things to appear normal, just for now, until the dam burst.

"You'll need to move lanes." Jack squinted at the motorway signs through the rain. "We come off in a bit."

"I know," Emma replied, watching the traffic up ahead slow down as their windscreen wipers struggled to cope with the downpours. "Trust me. I know what I'm doing."

"Sorry, I do appreciate you coming tonight to share the driving." Jack sat back in his seat and rubbed his eyes. "I guess I'm used to being in control."

Waiting for him to continue, Emma pretended to concentrate on the calm voice of the satnav as it directed her through a myriad of country lanes.

"Are we nearly there yet?"

"What, are you like five years old?" Emma risked a grin as she navigated water-filled potholes and cattle grids. "You're going to tell me now that you feel sick."

"I wouldn't be surprised after all the coffee you plied me with." Jack put his head back on his seat. "At least we didn't spoil Daisy's day. She's none the wiser. Her results are great, aren't they?"

"I never doubted her." Emma held the steering wheel, wondering when his diverse tactics would run out. "She's a bright kid."

"I know. I also know when her friends start going to college, she'll want to join them. She has an old friend from Spain, Adam. He's back in England and going to a college nearby."

Emma nodded. She hadn't the heart to also tell him that in two years' time the call of University would be too much for a girl like Daisy to ignore. Someone popular, pretty, and intelligent would be off without a by or a leave. It didn't seem like the right time to address that.

"I think this is the place." Jack pointed to a small café overlooking the village cenotaph. "Let's get this done quickly so we don't get soaking wet."

An hour later, they were back on the road again, the steering in the large van feeling heavier for the equipment stacked behind them. As the rain continued to pelt on their roof, Emma prayed the traffic would be kind to them on their journey back. She didn't fancy being stranded on these remote country lanes with no access to food, water, or blankets.

"That's not good." Emma squinted at her phone in the darkness of the car. "They've shut the major road that leads us back to the motorway. "Do you want to pull over and we'll check the other routes?"

Pulling into a muddy layby, Emma squinted at the satnav. "There's only the main highway or tiny country lanes." She peered through the windscreen at the land ahead of them, barely visible under sheets of water. "What do you want to do?"

Jack checked his own phone and grimaced. "I could do with a coffee, something to eat, and a little boy's room." He entered an address into the satnav. "If you're okay with my plan, I think we should head back to the village we've just driven through and see if there's anywhere we can stop for a few hours."

By the time they reached civilisation, it became obvious to Emma that any further travel wouldn't be a sensible approach. Not only were the roads flooded to a point where they risked their engine cutting out, but the rain battering so hard against the windscreen made visibility almost impossible.

"This place looks okay," Jack shouted above the worsening weather as they drove down a tree-lined driveway towards a manor house, its large frontage lavishly draped with honeysuckle and roses. "We can have something to eat, a warm drink, then hopefully the situation will have improved."

Agreeing seemed the only plan, they parked their van and ran inside. The richly stained panelled walls and thick sumptuous carpet immediately alerted Emma that this wasn't the kind of place that welcomed a farmer and a bedraggled waif to pitch in a corner sharing a coffee and a cheese baguette.

She pulled Jack to one side. "This isn't a pub. It's a hotel."

"I think you might be right. However, going off the local news updates, we may need to stay. All major routes are closed."

Stay? Emma's eyes widened at the steep room rates. Did they have single rooms? They had no spare clothes, no nightwear.

"Are you okay?" Jack bent his knees slightly. "You look flustered."

"I'm fine." Emma fiddled in her bag for her purse. "I've got enough money for my own room."

Jack glanced at her flushed cheeks and wild auburn curls with amusement. "If that's code for you're not sharing with me, I've got the message. It was never going to be part of my suggestion."

Emma couldn't reply. The thought of sharing a room with him rendered her speechless.

"It's a race meeting, sir," the hotel receptionist replied sympathetically. "I can offer you one room, but we have nothing else."

"Any nearby hotels?" Jack asked hopefully. "We just need two single rooms."

"Nothing, sir." The young woman frowned at her screen. "I've just checked the nearest one and it's also full. You're lucky we've got this one free. It's a last-minute cancellation. Do you want it?"

Emma's legs started to wobble as Jack turned to her and shrugged. *One room. One bed. Oh, dear God.*

"Hold fire for just one second." Jack guided a stiffly shouldered Emma towards a quiet corner. "These rooms normally have a sofa in them. I know it's not ideal, but I can ask for extra bedding. What do you think?"

What do I think about sharing a room with you? Emma swallowed to ease her dry throat. *My thoughts are currently not appropriate.*

"It's okay." Jack nodded at her silence. "I understand. How about you take the room and I'll sleep in the van?"

The clouds above them chose that exact moment to burst with such a force that even Jack cringed. Emma watched him zip up his fleece and rub his hands. No one could sleep in a van in this weather.

"Book the room," Emma heard herself muffle. "It's fine. We'll share."

"Are you sure?" Jack frowned at her hesitancy. "You don't have to, but if it's any consolation, I don't snore, and I promise to be the perfect gentleman."

"Shame," Emma muttered, and then looked up in shock as Jack stared at her. "I mean … just book the room."

*

Touching the key card to the pad, Jack pushed open the heavy bedroom door and stood to one side, allowing Emma to walk through.

Deliberately not looking at the four-poster bed, she headed towards the full-length windows and pulled the voile curtains to one side. The gardens twinkled up at her, the subtle lighting shimmering against the fresh droplets of rain. She breathed in deeply, allowing the floral notes and smell of dewy grass to relax her. They were both adults. She needed to behave with maturity and confidence. It was just a room, a place to sleep. No doubt Jack had shared rooms with many girls. None of them would have been gibbering wrecks.

"I've never stayed anywhere like this." Jack joined her at the window. "There's even a television in the bathroom. What do they call these kinds of rooms?"

"Executive," Emma replied quietly. They also called them honeymoon suites, but he didn't need to know that. Quite apt considering this would have been her wedding night. Heading into the ensuite to give herself a chance to breathe normally, she sat on the end of the jacuzzi tub and stared at the bottle of champagne and two flutes. She could do this. One bed. One sofa. One night.

"Guess what?" Jack leaned against the bathroom door and shrugged. "No sofa, but I can sleep on the floor. The carpet is thick enough. Come on. Let's eat while the restaurant is still open. I'm starving."

The waiter poured them both a glass of wine and placed the bottle back in its ice bucket. Emma looked around the warm panelled room, lit by the many tea candles scattered on tables and shelves. Her second meal in a high-end restaurant. She imagined this one would run a lot smoother.

"I'm sorry, Emma." Jack looked at her closely. "You're probably sick of posh eateries."

"I can think of worse places to be." Emma raised her glass against his. "As long as you don't order my meal for me, or send me to work in the cloakroom, we'll get along just fine."

"Look at the pair of us." Jack sat back and sighed. "Both suckers for immoral lovers."

"Speak for yourself. I never slept with mine." Emma glanced at Jack's pale complexion. "You know, I've ignored the elephant in the room all evening. Now it's time to talk."

Jack shook his head. "I'm not ready. Not yet."

"Well, I am." Emma leaned over the table. "You're not getting away with this, Seymour. I've got you all night and I will hound you until you speak."

"And I believe you would." Jack bit his lip hesitantly before taking a drink of his wine. "Basically, she's a bitch," he whispered. "A complete and total bitch. What more do you want me to say?"

Emma shrugged. "You can say what you like. I'm not involved, so you don't have to protect anyone's feelings."

Jack seemed to muse on her words, his jaw clenched.

"Come on, spit it out," Emma encouraged him. "Just say it. Say what's in your head."

"Fine." Jack put his glass down on the table firmly and leaned towards her, his voice low and full of hurt. "Four years, four whole friggin' years she's denied me contact with my child. I mean, how cruel, vindictive, and downright cold can you get? Half the time he's with her parents, for God's sake. He's not even living with her at the moment so she can spend time with her new fiancé."

Emma sipped her wine and continued to listen.

"I went without food some nights so I could afford to pay child maintenance." Jack pointed at the table angrily. "She's got me exactly where she wants me, hasn't she? What if I need to carry on paying each month, knowing the money is supporting their extravagant lifestyle, because let's face it, she isn't going to marry a man who isn't financially secure?"

Thanking the waiter for their cheese tartlets, Emma gave him the briefest of eye contact. He needed to do this. He needed to vent, cry, or both, without judgement.

"What if I never see him?" Jack pushed his untouched plate away. "What if she tells him I'm a waster, a drunk, a rundown farmer who's best out of his life? He'll grow up believing that. He'll hate me. Do you think I should apply for joint custody?"

Emma smiled at him gently. "It's not my place to say."

"I just hope to God Caleb benefited from all that money." Jack picked up his wine glass and then put it back down again. "I found out about Caleb's birth via a mutual source. Not only had I been denied any chance to bond with him physically, but I couldn't feel it emotionally either. Does that make me a horrible person?"

"No, it makes you human. It takes two to make a baby, but it takes love to make a family."

"I guess you're right." Jack paused for a few moments as the waiter took away their starters and served their main meals. "You're a good listener, Emma."

She shrugged. "It's one of my positives. I'm also a good shoulder to cry on if you need it."

For the first time that evening, Jack smiled. "I'm not about to break down on you. Don't worry."

"It wouldn't bother me if you did. It's good to cry every now and again. You should try it sometime." Emma thought back to all the years she'd known him. She'd never seen him cry. Ever.

"I don't think this is the place for a six-foot-three farmer wearing a mud-stained t-shirt to have a meltdown. But thank you. I do appreciate it." Jack took a deep sip of his wine and closed his eyes, as if releasing himself of bad vibes. "Look, you've had a tough time too lately. You shouldn't be sitting here, listening to me moaning."

"Hey, what you've been through is a big deal. Don't underestimate your emotions. We can talk about this as much as you need to. Listening is therapy for me too. Like I said at the summer ball, it's good to know someone else can make a hash of their life. Look at it this way, at least you've only done it once, whereas I didn't learn my lesson the first time. I had to travel two hundred miles and repeat the same mistakes and lose my job. Again."

"I've been wanting to ask." Jack bit his lip thoughtfully. "Why did you stay with Toby if he was being so horrible to you?"

"Many reasons." Emma sighed, putting down her knife and fork. "I felt sorry for him and a bit defensive of all the bad press he was receiving, especially as he'd been so supportive when I arrived, but mostly I wanted to keep my job so I could pay my way on the farm."

"So you stayed with him to help me?"

"Partly, but there were selfish reasons too that played a big part in it. Rebound from Sean, a wish to be seen as desirable, and he took away some of my vulnerability." Emma shrugged before looking up as a small wedding party made their way into a side room. She smiled to herself. How apt.

All her life, she had dreamed about her special day. A full-length white silk gown, fitting at the waist and flaring out into a long train, complete with a veil ethereally skimming her shoulders while she glided down the aisle towards her handsome groom. She inwardly rolled her eyes as she thought of the plain cream viscose dress left hanging in Sean's wardrobe. It had been a far cry from her fairytale dream, as had the man. How ironic that on what would have been her wedding day, she sat opposite part of that dream, yet he'd never been as far away.

"Are you okay?"

"Yeah, sure." Emma lifted her head and nodded. "As you say, the last few days have been stressful. It's catching up with us both. If our mums were still alive, they'd be boxing us around the ears and telling us to sort ourselves out."

"Did I ever tell you that my mum was always match-making you and Josh?" Jack laughed lightly as Emma looked at him in surprise. "She used to say, '*Don't let her slip through your fingers.*' I don't think she believed you had a platonic relationship. Although, to be honest, I think she just wanted us both to marry well."

"I love Josh dearly, just not in that way." Emma ran her finger around the top of her wine glass. "Apparently, I once asked you to marry me."

"You did." Jack's eyes twinkled for the first time that evening. "It was your birthday. Your dad had blown up a paddling pool, and you insisted on wearing a two-piece swimsuit. You walked up to me brazen as anything with your hand on your hip and asked me would I marry you."

Emma bit her lip as she searched his face. "And what did you say?"

"I said I'd ask you when you were old enough." Jack turned as the remainder of the bridal party made their way into the side room. "When you said Sean had stolen your money, did you have a date booked for the wedding?"

"Yes." Emma drained her glass. "It would have been today, which means tonight would have been my wedding night."

Jack stared at her, his eyes wide as he knocked back the rest of his wine. "Jesus, so no pressure then?"

CHAPTER 26

The heavy rain ceasing, they headed towards a twinkly lit pergola trailing with highly scented sweet peas. In the distance, they could hear the faint bars of music as the newlywed couple shared their first dance, their joined frames just visible through the window.

"We're not talking about Sean or Joanne anymore tonight." Jack reached into his fleece pocket and pulled out a whisky tankard. "Always be prepared."

"Did you bring that with you?" Emma asked as he took off the lid and offered her a drink.

"No, it's Josh's. He must have borrowed my fleece and left it in." Jack grimaced as he took a deep drink. "Do you think Sebastian has his sights set on Milly?"

"I think so. He certainly seems keen to impress her." Emma felt the whisky pleasantly reach her toes, and she wriggled them inside her trainers. "Milly keeps her cards very close to her chest though. Sometimes I wonder if she likes Josh, and then they start arguing again. He's another one who's being very guarded. I wish he'd open up to me like he used to do and then I could give him some proper advice instead of the flirty rubbish you fill his head with."

"Pardon?"

Emma giggled at his astonished expression. "You never had to work at getting a girl to like you. You just did your eye contact thing and they'd be putty in your hands."

"Eye contact thing?"

Emboldened by the alcohol, Emma leaned towards him. "Like this, big brown eyes all soft and flirtatious. I mean, it's cute but it doesn't fill a girl with confidence that you'll hang around."

"I don't believe I'm hearing this." Jack laughed as he took another sip of whisky. "You're insulting my chat-up techniques on the one evening I need confidence and support."

"It's called being a critical friend." Emma sat back, feeling relaxed. "Everyone needs one. What I'm trying to say is that Milly and I are very alike."

"So how should my brother handle it?" Jack leaned forward on the bench and offered her the tankard. "Go on, I'm interested."

"She needs to be wooed, in a non-obvious way."

"Wooed? In a non-obvious way?" Jack looked at her and frowned. "There's no such thing."

"Of course there is. Flirting can be a turnoff." Emma laughed at his confused expression. "Do you not believe me?"

"I'm not saying I don't believe you. I'm just wondering what sort of guys you've dated that have turned you off with their flirting."

"Flirting can be cheesy."

"Nope, find the right guy and flirting is fun."

Emma rolled her eyes with frustration. "This is why you've not reached first base with this girlfriend of yours. You're going about it all the wrong way."

Jack leaned towards her, his eyes twinkling. "So, what should I do instead?"

"Does she even know you like her?"

"I'd say that's a definite no."

"Then there's your problem." Emma huddled further under the pergola as the rain started to fall again. "Flirting can't always be taken seriously. You need to be more direct, in a non-obvious way. Basically, you've not wooed her enough. Dangerous game."

"Apparently so," Jack murmured as he sat closer to her to protect her from the worst of the weather. "Who'd have thought I'd be getting love lessons from Worzel."

Emma shivered again as their breath clouds mingled, disturbing the cobweb dreamcatchers above them.

"Come on, let's go back inside." Jack pulled her to her feet and pretended to dance with her as they passed the window of the wedding party. "I don't know about you, but I think a hot cup of chocolate is just what we need right now."

"I can't go back in the bar looking like this." Emma wiped her hands across her wet bottom. "I look a mess."

"You look like you." Jack gave her a wide smile. "I'm actually thinking about room service. What do you say?"

This time, Emma sat in the room, feeling calm and relaxed as she listened to the rain pour through the open patio doors.

"Here…" Jack took off his shirt, revealing a faded black t-shirt that clung to his arms. "…put that on and let those wet jeans dry. It'll come way past your knees."

In the ensuite, Emma looked in the mirror as she brushed her hair. She barely recognised herself. Her eyes sparkled, her tanned cheeks glowed, and her curls fell softly around her face. She looked like an advert for someone who had just discovered the secret to happiness. Slipping her arms through Jack's shirt, she relished in its warmth and familiar fragrance. Tonight, somehow, he seemed different, and it couldn't be blamed entirely on the bombshell that had hit him earlier. There was something else. A side to him she hadn't seen before.

He stood tactfully by the window, providing Emma with the opportunity to slip under the silky sheets and cover her bare legs before passing her a frothy cup of hot chocolate with marshmallows.

"Aren't you cold?" she asked, as he made himself comfortable on top of the bed.

"Nope, quite warm actually."

"Is that why you're on top of the covers?"

"Partly."

She turned as he faced her at the same time. "This feels weird, doesn't it?"

"A bit." Jack chased the melting mallows as they oozed into his drink. "So, do you think Josh should tell Milly that he likes her?"

"I think he needs to make his feelings clearer to her without coming on too strong. I'm worried Sebastian will win her over because Josh doesn't seem interested."

"And what if he's wrong? What if Milly doesn't like him? Then he's made a pratt out of himself and ruined a potential friendship with her."

"That's why he needs to be more upfront. Ignorance prevents choices. It closes doors. It doesn't open them."

Jack seemed to muse on her comment. "When did you become so knowledgeable and grown up?"

"I was grown up when I arrived here." Emma took a sip of her drink and laughed as Jack dabbed cream on her nose. "You just didn't see it."

Jack laced his hands around his cup and bit his lip, a nervous trait she'd come to recognise. "Whatever I did to hurt you all those years ago, I never meant it."

"I know you didn't," Emma replied, taken aback by his sudden reference to her letter.

"And if I could take it back so that you'd never had to write it, I'd do it tomorrow."

Emma closed her eyes. Maybe one day she would tell him, but for now, her love letter remained in her piggery, and would do until she knew for sure their relationship would withstand the truth. It felt ironic that to tell him the contents of her letter, she would have to make sure she'd lost him first.

Resting against her pillows, she held her breath as Jack suddenly leant towards her. His eyes centred on hers, and she felt her heart skip a beat as he whispered in her ear. "Of all the farms in all the towns in all the world, she walks into mine."

Breathe, breathe, breathe, Emma instructed herself as she struggled to compute his meaning.

"See." Jack smiled impishly as he watched the reaction on her face. "I told you flirting works."

Laughing nervously, Emma almost dropped her hot chocolate. She held it tightly, her fingers almost white in their efforts.

"It's late," Jack said quietly. He took the cup from her hands and pulled the covers over her as she rested against the pillows. Her body immediately reacted to his touch, every nerve ending awakened, waiting to feel him closer.

"Are you okay?" he asked.

"Of course," Emma whispered back. Glad her voice hadn't betrayed her nerves.

He lay by her side on top of the sheets. Despite the width of the bed, she felt acutely aware of their intimacy, to the point where their little fingers almost touched. She could feel the heat from his body, and wished she had the courage to move her hand and let him know she felt his closeness. She could tell from Jack's breathing that he hadn't relaxed either. Even without touching him, she could feel the tension in his body. Sleep, it seemed, wouldn't come to either of them easily tonight.

CHAPTER 27

"Sebastian bought it for me," Milly added casually as she touched her glossy lips. "I seem to have mislaid a lot of my makeup, although saying that, I don't tend to wear much of it these days, but I do like this lipstick he's bought me. It's very thoughtful of him."

"I'm surprised he didn't tip you instead," Josh mumbled as he measured a wall for a shelf above her worktop. "Isn't that what wankers, sorry, bankers do?"

"Why don't you go back to what you're good at." Milly smiled sweetly. "Banging and screwing."

Emma sat in the window seat of the bakery and aimed to keep a poker face. She had no intention of getting involved in this little spat, but she did wonder how long they could keep up this pretence. The attraction between these two felt so tangible she could chew on it.

"How high do you want this shelf?"

"As long as it's higher than your morals, it'll do." Milly added strawberries and crumbled meringue into a bowl of whipped cream and mixed them luxuriously. "Actually, talking of morals, are you going to see that arsehole?"

"I think I'll have to." Emma could already feel lavender eyes boring into her from across the village green. "If I'm going to continue living in Thornhill, then I'll need to clear the air with him."

"Do you want me to come with you?" Josh plugged in his drill and grabbed a handful of screws. "Make sure he behaves?"

"He'll behave," Emma replied, before berating herself for once again trying to defend him. "In all honesty, he's got a right to be annoyed. I did make a fool out of him."

"Don't start trying to find excuses for him," Josh replied with a knowing look. "He wouldn't protect you if the roles were reversed. You don't still have feelings for him, do you?"

"Of course not." Emma looked up in surprise. "I simply don't want to deliberately poke fun at him. I'm trying to be positive about the whole thing, not negative."

"Someone's feeling favourable towards the world. I take it you got out of the right side of the bed this morning; in fact, a very expensive bed according to my brother."

Milly put down her bowl. "What have I missed?"

"These two were stuck in a flood last night. They had to stay over in a hotel. One room. One bed."

Emma flushed lightly at the teasing. She wondered how much Jack had told his brother. Not that there had been anything to report. Under the canopy of the romantic bed, they'd eventually fallen into a deep sleep and woken up to Jack's alarm, their arms and legs entwined as if they'd spent the night intimately acquainted with each other's bodies. What had prompted their closeness, she had no idea, but she knew Jack felt uncomfortable with it. He'd delicately untangled himself before heading for a shower, and the event hadn't been mentioned since.

"One bed?" Milly leant on the counter and faced Emma. "Tell me more."

"There's nothing to tell." Emma picked up a piece of flapjack and crammed it into her mouth in the hope of ending the conversation. She chewed away furiously as the flush on her neck deepened. Had they guessed her feelings for Jack? She hoped not.

"Did your clothes get all wet in the rain and you had to take them off?" Milly gave her an impish smile. "Hotel rooms are notorious for being hot."

Josh put down his spirit level and turned in surprise. "Milly Parks. This is my brother and best mate we're talking about. I don't want to hear details."

Her cheeks full of cake, Emma could only sit and listen to their playful banter and pray they didn't hit the nail on the head.

"Don't you think hotel rooms are erotic?" Milly popped a strawberry in her mouth. "Forbidden nights in a strange bed, no interruptions—"

"Hey, do you want this shelf going up or not, because if you carry on talking like that, something else will be—"

"I don't want to know." Milly plugged her fingers into her ears. "You are incorrigible. Do you have any filters?"

"Nope." Josh grinned. "I say what's in my head. Although I can be diplomatic when needed, and I'm great at keeping secrets." He turned to Emma and winked. "Even the ones no one has told me yet."

Inwardly, Emma groaned. She'd never been able to hide anything from Josh. She should have known he'd figure it out. The remainder of her thoughts were drowned out by the high-pitched squeal of the drill as a shower of dust covered them all, followed by a cracking in the plaster.

"You absolute knob head." Milly stared at her bowl of Eton Mess covered in powdery dirt. "Now look at what you've done." She stared at the hole in the wall and the large chunks of debris now scattered across the floor and on her patisseries. "What the hell are you trying to do?"

"I dunno." Josh frowned at the hole. "I thought your wall was brick, not plasterboard."

"What's all the noise?" Sebastian came running down the stairs in a long silk robe. "Will someone please tell me what just happened?"

Josh rubbed his eyes. "I was sure I'd checked that wall earlier."

"Well, you obviously didn't, and that's a very foolish mistake to make." Sebastian shook his head disapprovingly. "And look at the mess you've made of Milly's pudding. You've caused her extra work and great embarrassment when customers come through the door." He turned to Milly and smiled affectionately. "I told you yesterday, I can afford to increase my monthly payments if it means you can have a better standard of living. In my line of work, I liaise with many property surveyors who link in with good, reliable tradesmen. Highly qualified too. Just say the word and I'll bring them in."

"It's okay," Milly mumbled as she opened a cupboard and took out a dustpan and brush. "It's just an accident."

"An accident where you could have been hurt." Sebastian put his hand on Milly's arm possessively. "Has James apologised?"

"Of course I have," Josh replied defensively. "And my name isn't James, and I didn't do it on purpose. I made a mistake."

"Well, it's a good job you're only dealing with shelves and not money." Sebastian pulled his robe tighter. "You should be doing the sweeping up, by the way. Not my good landlady."

"Oh no." Milly jumped into action as Josh stood in the middle of the room, glaring. "I can clear it up. It's not an issue."

"Let him. You paid him. Why buy a dog and bark for yourself?"

Emma watched a new form of awkwardness descend upon the small group. At least prior to Sebastian's arrival, the atmosphere had only been tinged with harmless banter; now it felt tainted with a heavy oppression. She helped Josh sweep up the remainder of the plaster and throw it into the bin outside. Casting a quick glance at Milly, she wasn't surprised to see her looking uncomfortable.

"And there we go, all clean again." Sebastian nodded before heading back upstairs to his room. "Give me a shout if James causes any more problems. And please try and keep the noise down."

"I'd better go," Josh said quietly as he packed his drill. "It sounds like Sebastian knows people more trained at this trade than me. Perhaps they can finish this job off for you."

The bakery door banged, rocking the white rabbits in the window display as Josh headed across the village green. Emma watched his hunched shoulders as he negotiated the happy groups of families sitting together in the sun. She turned to see Milly stare sadly into her dust-covered pudding. "Are you okay?"

"Sure." Milly shrugged. "I mean, I know Sebastian was a bit harsh, but Josh has made a mess of the wall, and he was noisy."

Emma stayed tactfully quiet as she wiped down the grit-covered counter.

"Sebastian is only trying to look out for me. He's very sensible and mature. He just wants me to feel safe, whereas Josh…"

"Makes you laugh?" Emma suggested wryly as she picked up her bag. She knew she didn't need to say anymore on the matter. Her friend would figure her feelings out for herself. Eventually. "Anyway, are you going to wish me luck?"

"Pardon?" Milly replied absentmindedly. "Oh, of course. You're going to see Toby. Good luck."

Her window displays of wicker hearts and dried flowers had been replaced with plastic containers containing the dregs of old vegetables. Emma's heart constricted. She missed this place so much and the customers she'd bonded with. Ironically, she didn't miss the man who had made all this possible, but she did feel like she owed him some kind of apology. Bracing herself for attack, she opened the door to the barn and faced her nemesis.

Toby stood behind the plain counter and narrowed his eyes. "I take it you've come for your things?"

"Partly." Now faced with the man himself, Emma felt her fear start to drain away. What harm could he do to her that he hadn't already done? "I've also come to apologise for how I behaved in Featherby's."

"Well, go on then."

Emma swallowed back her annoyance as he casually folded his arms. She needed her life in this village to be as non-confrontational as possible, and if that meant momentarily bowing to this idiot, then she would. "I'm sorry for walking out on you and calling you a wanker in front of everyone."

"And for throwing your keys in my food?"

"Ah, yes." Emma had forgotten about that, and she silently congratulated herself on her accurate aim. "That too."

"You can't get away with talking to me like that in front of my villagers, and there will be consequences, but I'm prepared to accept your apology and try to see past your anger issues." Toby opened a drawer and passed her an apron. "No doubt it's women's problems and something I'll have to get used to, but we'll talk about it and set some boundaries that work for us both."

Momentarily flummoxed, Emma stared at her apron still dangling from his hands.

"I take it the grass isn't greener on the other side?"

"Pardon?"

"I knew you'd come back to me. Jack Seymour looks good on paper, but he can't keep his women. Even Joanne didn't want to go back to him."

"Whoa." Emma screwed up her eyes as she tried to take it all in. "What do you know about Jack and Joanne?"

"Nothing." Toby fiddled with the pens on the counter. "I know she left him and never went back. Now, I've written a list of things you need to do. There's new stock that needs unloading and these cupboards require a damn good cleaning. I need to get organised for the next Thornhill event, the autumn ball. My new business idea has been approved by my mother, which means I'll be taking over the reins fully."

Once again, Emma paused. They were definitely singing from different hymn sheets. Did Toby really think she'd come cap in hand for her old job back?

"Would you like to come to my apartment later?" Toby inched closer to her. "The best thing about arguments is the making up."

Emma stepped backwards as his lavender gaze fixed itself hungrily on her chest. Of all the scenarios, she hadn't expected this one. Tantrums, vindictiveness, even snarling, but not makeup sex.

"Toby, I think there's been some confusion." Emma held her hands out to halt his advances. "I've not come for my job back, and I don't wish to rekindle anything with you." Toby's body stiffened at her words, and Emma put her head in her hands and groaned. "I genuinely came to say I'm sorry, and that's it."

"Have you done this as some kind of joke?" Toby's lip curled angrily. "Has he set you up to do this? Where is he?"

"He's probably at the farm." Emma felt her patience snap. "For God's sake, he's got bigger things to worry about than you. He's knackered. We barely slept last night."

The minute the words were out of her mouth, Emma knew she'd played the wrong card. If things had been getting ugly before, they were about to get a lot worse.

"You had sex with him?" Toby hissed. "How dare you."

Seeing little point in trying to defend herself, Emma walked towards the door. "Would it matter if I did? As far as you're concerned, he's guilty before being charged. Your obsession in trying to get one over on Jack is an illness, and furthermore, it's futile."

"He'll pay for this," Toby shouted after her as she slammed the door. "Mark my words, I'll make sure of that. I'll destroy him."

“Whatever,” Emma murmured as she banged the door behind her. Walking across the village green on wobbly legs, she braced herself for war. Not only had she just crossed the enemy line, but she’d also thrown the first grenade.

CHAPTER 28

Emma cleaned out the chicken pen, throwing the dirty straw into the wheelbarrow with force, each shovel and thrust reminding her of what she'd like to do to Toby's head. Heart racing and a sheen of sweat on her forehead, she eventually headed into the small barn to calm down. Hands on hips, she breathed deeply to control her anxiety. This was a point in time; her arguments with Toby wouldn't last forever. He would eventually meet someone else and put this ridiculous feud to the back of his head. In the meantime, she needed to stay as far away from him as possible.

Feeling much calmer, she picked up her list of jobs for the cheese shop. There was still a lot to do to get the hamper business and café off the ground. Plugging in the coffee machines they'd brought back from Chester, she filled them with beans and prepared them for their first use. Finally happy with the strength of flavour, she poured herself a cup and sat down at the laptop. Daisy's prototype website had come on a treat, and she scrolled through the list of produce and hampers they'd agreed to sell. After writing down a few more suggestions, she set to work on the interior of the small barn.

Josh had installed a log burner for the indoor seating area to add a cosiness that would be much needed over the coming months. With autumn and winter approaching, Emma planned on attracting customers with seasonal afternoon teas. Milly had already suggested pumpkin pies, baked cinnamon pears, and rich vanilla beans, while a winter menu would entice festive lovers with sticky toffee mince pies, clove scented mulled wines, and brandy laced hot chocolates.

Feeling inspired by the warmth coming from her fresh coffee and the crackling of the logs, Emma ironed the plum-coloured curtains she'd bought for the café and hung them at the barn windows. After washing the many cups and saucers and setting up the small refrigerators, she sat back and admired her work. It hadn't totally removed Toby from her mind, but it had helped to prioritise her thoughts.

Noticing a wispy haziness flow through the barn door, she halted as her senses reacted immediately to the smell of burning. Trying not to panic, she headed across to the milking parlour where the trail became stronger. Fumbling with the keys, she unlocked the door, shooting immediately to one side as flames flew out, pushing her back with their heat and intensity.

"Keep back!" Clive wheezed as he approached her quickly, slamming the farm gate behind him. "Is anyone in there?"

"No, I don't think so. They're all off site." Emma choked on the smoke as she pulled the old man away from the flames. "We need to phone the fire brigade."

Emma finished the emergency call and then rang Jack and Josh, her legs shaking as she watched the flames shoot out of the parlour. The fire brigade would need to travel from the main town, a good ten miles away. If they didn't react quickly, they could lose everything. Grabbing the hosepipe, she attached it to the outside tap. Aiming it at the flames, it soon became obvious to them both that her attempts were futile. The fire had well and truly taken hold.

She pulled at Clive's arm, aware of his wheezy breathing. "Wait for Jack. I need to get inside the parlour."

"You can't!" Clive looked at her in shock. "You can't go in there. You'll die!"

They both shielded their faces and stepped backwards as sparks suddenly shot from the roof, sending thick black plumes into the air.

"I have to. The generators are in the parlour. They're full of gasoline. If they go up, we'll lose everything, the farmhouse included. I have to try. They're right near the holding gate and they're on wheels. I just need to grab them and run."

"Dear God." Clive grabbed a length of rope and passed it to her. "Tie this around your waist. I'm giving you twenty seconds. If you're not out, I'm pulling you out."

Emma's whole body shook as she rounded the flaming barn. With the stench of burn filling her nostrils and catching the back of her throat, she pulled back the bolts on the holding gates and attempted to look inside the blazing building.

Without further hesitation, she grabbed a towel from the washing line and soaked it in water before wrapping it around her mouth. With adrenaline pumping through her veins, she stepped inside the smoke-filled building and tried to get her bearings. Within seconds, her eyes began to sting and she quickly adjusted her towel to cover her nose as well as her mouth. With her arms held out wide, she felt around until her hands fell upon the rubber handle of a generator. Keeping an eye on the flames, she quickly pulled the machine outside and away from the searing heat.

Clive breathed a sigh of relief as he passed her a glass of water and checked her rope before she headed back inside. Even though only seconds had passed, the smoke had thickened significantly, and Emma could barely make out her hands in front of her face.

Working from memory, rather than sight, she headed towards her goal. The heat from the flames roared against her body and her eyes began to sting with such intensity that she didn't dare open them. Feeling for her waist rope, she tugged on it to test the tension. She'd tried, but this had now gone beyond anything she could tolerate. Panicking, she turned around to find her way back to the holding gate. She needed to get out of here. The second generator would have to take its chance. She felt her way along the tiled walls, coughing violently, until her hands fell upon the water basin. Her heart banged against her chest. She'd gone the wrong way. Trying to control her coughing, she turned around and got down on her knees to avoid the smoke and heat. Only then did she feel the slackness of the rope. Pulling on it, she soon had both ends in her hands and her breathing became more erratic.

Pulling the wet towel tighter around her face, she forced herself to calm down. The firemen must be here soon, and Clive would tell them she was inside. Crawling forward on jelly-like limbs, she dimly became aware of being lifted off the floor. Wondering if the smoke had affected her mind, she fought against the strong hold as she floated through the thick smoke. Fresh air eventually hit her face, causing her to cough violently as her rescuer placed her on the floor.

"You stupid woman! You absolute friggin' idiot!" Jack ran his hands through his hair as he stared at her smoke-stained face. "What the hell were you doing? Why did you do something so bloody stupid?"

Emma stared at him in disbelief as she gasped for breath. "I was getting your generators, you ungrateful sod."

She turned to see both machines on the grass. "How did that other one get there?"

"I dragged it with me as I carried you out." Jack rubbed a hand across his blackened face. "Clive is mindless with worry about you. Why the hell did you attempt such a brainless act?"

They both turned as sirens could be heard approaching the farm. Jack pulled her away. "Leave it to them. Clive is opening the gates. There's nothing we can do."

He stood for a few seconds, staring at the blazing building, his jaw tense as flames flooded from the doorway. He headed onto one of the fields and watched his parlour burn. Emma observed him anxiously as firemen dragged their hoses across the courtyard.

"Where's Daisy?"

"With you, isn't she?" Emma's eyes grew wide. "Josh said she was with you when I rang him."

"Shit, I sent her back here." Jack ran towards the kitchen, his efforts halted by the firemen, who listened to him before heading inside the smoke-filled farmhouse. Minutes later, they reappeared, shaking their heads.

"What the hell happened?" Josh bent over to catch his breath as he joined them on the field while staring in horror at the parlour. "You can see the smoke for miles around. What caused it?"

"I don't know, but I can't find Daisy." Jack grabbed a handful of his hair as he tried her phone again. "Where the hell is she?"

Emma felt the first stirrings of panic at Jack's reaction. She watched him rub a hand over his face as he held the phone to his ear, swearing under his breath as it continued to ring out.

"On a plus, she might not be on the farm." Josh took out his own mobile and dialled his sister's number. "You know what she's like. Anything to avoid hard work."

"We can't panic," Clive said shakily as the fire crew approached them for more details on Daisy. "She's a sensible girl. She'll have sheltered somewhere."

Emma thought quickly of the girl's favourite places to be. Not permitting anxiety to take over, she ran towards the piggery. As she pushed open the door, she allowed her mind the hope of seeing the young girl sitting on her sofa bed, completely unaware of the drama unfolding around her. However, looking at the empty room, Emma put her hands on her knees and tried not to cry.

With half the fire crew still searching, she joined the group on the smog-filled field for the longest wait of their lives. While Josh and Clive sat with their heads in their hands, Jack paced the ground like a caged animal. Wishing she had religion on her side, Emma sent up a silent prayer to anyone who would hear it. This family wouldn't survive a tragedy such as this.

"She's no reason to have been in the milking parlour." Josh fought against the wobble on his bottom lip. "She never goes in there."

"And she wasn't in the small barn because I've been there most of the morning." Emma squeezed her fists together and pushed them against her lips. She mustn't panic. She had to stay calm. "If Daisy smelt fire, what would be her priority?"

"Other than us…" Clive's red eyes looked around the smoke-filled farm. "…then it would be the animals."

"The cows are on the fields and the chicken pen is too far away to be affected." Jack threw his hands in the air. "I don't know what else there is."

"Pickles?" Emma asked, looking around the small group. "Where is he?"

"I fastened him in his crate when I let the fire crew in." Clive shook his head. "I didn't see Daisy."

"But she won't know that he's safe," Emma replied quickly. "Where's the piglet's favourite spot if he's not with you?"

"Rummaging for grain." Clive pushed himself away from the fence so quickly, he almost tumbled backwards. "He sleeps on the bags at the back of the milking parlour."

About to alert the fire crew, they halted as a bright torch flashed their way through the dense smoke. The signal continued as two other figures were seen near the small barn, carrying a limp form in their arms. Jack allowed a small groan to leave his lips as he ran over to his sister and threw himself by her side as they lay her gently on the dewy grass.

"I'm a doctor. Let me help." Milly quickly crossed the field and pushed everyone to one side. She nodded calmly to indicate her lack of concern as the sounds of sputtering and coughing echoed across the group.

"Is she okay?" Josh asked, his voice cracking with emotion.

Milly assisted the young girl into a sitting position and watched her carefully. "I just need to keep my eye on her. We need to watch for nausea and headaches. Keep asking her questions and let me know the minute you sense any confusion. She looks fine to me, but a trip to the hospital is advisable, just to check her lungs and oxygen levels."

"Why are you here?" Josh swallowed deeply to steady his voice. "Shouldn't you be in the bakery?"

"I saw the flames." Milly's hands shook as she spoke. "Someone said the engines were heading this way. I figured you might need some help. I just wasn't expecting this."

Jack winced as the sounds of creaking wood coincided with the roof of the parlour caving inwards. He stood up and closed his eyes while the white roar of the water hoses drowned out everything else. "I wasn't expecting this either. In my worst dreams, I didn't expect this."

CHAPTER 29

"What started it?" Milly asked quietly.

"I don't know." Emma's teeth chattered, and she gratefully accepted the warm woollen blanket Clive placed around her shoulders. With the flames now dowsed and the smog under control, they'd been allowed to sit inside the farmhouse if they kept the doors and windows shut. "I could smell burning. I went outside, opened the parlour door, and smoke was everywhere."

"That young bairn." Clive's lip wobbled as he sat down at the kitchen table. "I can't get her out of my head as they took her off in that ambulance, so pale and frightened."

"But unhurt." Emma moved her chair over to his and put her arms around him, strangely comforted by the rough fibres of his woollen jacket that tickled the sides of her cheek. "I just wish she hadn't gone looking for the piglet."

"She was probably disorientated." Clive wiped his nose on the sleeve of his jacket. "She inhaled a lot of smoke. I dread to think what would have happened if they hadn't found her sooner."

"Don't." Emma put her hands over her eyes so as not to picture the worst-case scenario they could have been facing. "I don't want to go there." She turned to face a pale and shocked Milly. "It took you back tonight, didn't it?"

Milly nodded as she fought against her tears. "I've only dealt with minor emergencies since I left the army. I surprised myself on how calm I stayed. I just wish it had never happened."

Car headlights in the courtyard caused Emma to lift her head. Aware of the fire crew still working, their blue flashing lights creating an eerie hue in the dark kitchen, she headed outside and tried to ignore the sickening stench of burned wood.

"How is she?" Emma asked quietly as the brothers trudged tiredly into the debris-filled courtyard.

"A few minor burns to her hands and some vomiting from the carbon monoxide, but otherwise she's fine. They're keeping her in overnight. I couldn't stay as she's not classed as a child." Jack stared wearily at his burned parlour. "Come on, let's go inside the kitchen."

Emma stood by the side of the table, feeling lost and bewildered. She switched on the kettle again for want of something to do, but her heart wasn't in consuming hot drinks. She wanted to hold Daisy close and comfort her. "Would they let me stay with her?"

"No." Josh wiped his eyes as he sniffed back more tears. "We asked. They said she needed to sleep. We can go back tomorrow and hopefully bring her home."

"Are you okay?" Milly asked quietly as Josh fought to control his emotions. "Do you want me to stay with you?"

"No." Josh angrily wiped his wet cheeks. "I'm fine. Just shocked. Don't let me stop you from getting back to Sebastian. He must be worried about you being with an idiot like me."

The hurt registered momentarily on Milly's face before she stood up and nodded. "I'd probably better go. I'll see you around, okay?"

"That was harsh," Jack said quietly as the kitchen door closed. "She didn't have to come."

"Don't tell me how to live my life," Josh mumbled. "You're no role model."

"Hey, come on, boys." Clive patted the men on their backs. "We've got enough to worry about tonight. Let's not fight.

Anyway, it looks like the fire crew are ready to speak to you. Shall I come with you?"

Jack shook his head as the moon attempted to make its way through the polluted sky, casting a grey gloom around the courtyard.

Emma watched his hunched shoulders as he disappeared inside the burned parlour. God only knew how he'd get through this on top of Caleb and almost losing Daisy. She hadn't been inside the parlour, but she already knew everything was gone. Despite her best attempts, he'd lost it all anyway. As the fire engines left, she pulled on her boots and crossed the courtyard. The small dairy door she'd unlocked so many times stood propped against the outside wall, its inner side warped and blistered. Making her way inside the normally spotless building, she swallowed deeply at the blackened walls. The stench of burn filled her nostrils as water and foam dripped down the tiles, covering the floor and gully, while the curdled contents from the new milk tanks mixed with the rubble, creating a grey, sticky sludge. Standing in the middle of the room, looking a complete anomaly in his t-shirt and jeans, stood Jack.

His back still to her, he kicked at the pieces of melted plastic. "They warned me they haven't ruled out arson."

"What? You weren't even here."

"It doesn't matter." Jack looked up at the skeleton roof. "The milk tanks are new and everything else was regularly tested. They've called for an investigation team to come in."

"Why?" Emma shook her head. "What's made them do that?"

"One of the generators was leaking. I noticed it when I dragged it out. The fire crew smelt petrol. I can't prove it wasn't deliberate."

Emma didn't know what to say. She watched as he continued to kick at the remnants of the milk lines. She couldn't comprehend how he must be feeling right now, but she guessed this would be one of the lowest points of his life. She approached him slowly.

"We'll get through this. Regardless of the outcome, we'll build another parlour. I know it will take time, but we'll do it."

"I'm finished." Jack shook his head slowly. "I haven't the finances to fund another parlour. It's over."

"No!" Emma tugged at his arm, convincing him to look at her. "This is our problem. Mine and yours. We'll deal with this together."

Jack's eyes bored into hers. He gently touched her cheek, stroking her damp hair away from her forehead. Then, amongst the rubble and charred remains of his parlour, he placed his head against her shoulder and wept.

CHAPTER 30

"No more heroics, Tilly Mint." Emma tucked the young girl into bed after washing her hair and drying it carefully to avoid blowing hot hair onto her face. Apart from sore hands, Daisy had escaped physical harm, but the emotional scars would be there for a long time to come. "I think you've got yourself out of manual labour for a few months, if not a lifetime. Your brothers are going to wrap you in cotton wool forever."

"Great." Daisy yawned as she rested her head against her fresh pillowcases and sipped from the hot cocoa at the side of her bed. "That's all I need. Jack watching my every move."

The past forty-eight hours had been like nothing Emma had ever known. The muck, rain, dirt, and debris fought against them at every opportunity as they struggled to keep the farm working. With the parlour of action still under investigation, they'd made do with a mix of hand milking and temporary equipment fuelled by the generators. Sleep came in the form of two-hour batches every morning and evening, but other than that, their burned and blistered fingers had kept the farm going. As for Jack, Emma had always known how protective he could be of his emotions, but he had clammed up over the last few days. His breakdown the night of the fire had stirred deep emotions within her. She'd never seen him cry. Unfortunately, his vulnerability had created a wall around him. Same as the night of the manor house, he now refused to discuss it and continued as if it had never happened.

"Your brothers have been worried sick about you." Emma winced as her calloused hands caught against the metal frame of the bed. "What's this?"

"Just a photograph album that Mum always kept. Her favourite moments, as she called them." Daisy stroked the cover lovingly. "I always feel closer to her when I go through it. Do you want to see it?"

Emma turned over the first few pages, marvelling at the pictures that evoked so many memories. Their old back garden in Redsworth, the bouncy castle Jack had burst his nose on; Josh's first grown up bike. She remembered it all with such clarity.

"Who's this?" Emma pointed to a very young Daisy with her arm around a boy of the same age, his hair all skewwhiff and his large glasses at a funny angle. "A friend of yours?"

"That's Adam." Daisy smiled fondly. "Like Josh and you, he was my best friend at school. He went to live in Spain with his parents when he was six. I keep in touch with him on social media. In fact, he's coming back to England to start his further education. I'll be going to college with him, hopefully."

As Emma turned over more pages, a photograph from the back of the album slipped out and fell onto the floor. Emma picked it up and found herself face to face with Jack in a groom's outfit, his arm around a tall brunette dressed in white. In any other situation she would have fixed her gaze on the handsome man she knew, but instead she stared at the familiar woman.

"It's a shame that picture didn't burn in the fire." Daisy snatched it and threw it back in the album. "Joanne was always a bitch."

Her mind going back to driving home from the hospital, Emma recalled the face she'd seen climbing out of Toby's sports car. She couldn't be sure, but the similarities were enough to cause her to ponder.

"I know about her getting remarried," Daisy said quietly. "Josh told me. We'll never get to see Caleb now."

Emma knew she'd need to phrase her next question carefully. "Did she mix with many of the villagers?"

"Not really. She suffered from delusions of grandeur. She always thought she was better than anyone else. I don't think Mum liked her very much. Why?"

"No reason, just curious." Emma tucked the young girl into bed and gave her back the photograph album. "You get some sleep while you can. I'll come and check on you in a few hours."

Emma headed downstairs with the now cold cup of cocoa, drinking it herself as a means of filling her empty stomach. Ignoring the kitchen table full of soot, wires, and nails, she sat down and tried to make sense of her thoughts. If it had been Joanne, why would she argue with Toby?

"I'm knackered." Josh wandered into the kitchen and sat down, his blond curls plastered to his head following the recent rainfall. "I don't see any end in sight and the weather is due to get worse tonight. I don't know how we're going to cope with milking during a rainstorm."

Emma tried to put the wedding photograph to one side as she sympathised with Josh over the cruelness of Mother Nature, a complete contrast to the loyalty from nearby farmers who came in hordes, offering food, milking equipment, and their hard labour.

"How's Jack?"

"Not good." Josh wrapped his chapped hands around a coffee cup. "He's worried sick about the fire assessment. The investigation team were in there most of yesterday, but he's no idea how long he'll need to wait for the final report, and he's dreading what the outcome will be."

"But it wasn't deliberate."

"We know that, but combined with Jack's financial problems, it doesn't look good. Plus, the insurance company doesn't know Jack has decided to fight for joint custody of Caleb. That'll cost a lot of money we don't have. If they found out, it would make a good case for an arson charge. It's something we need to keep quiet about. If that information got into the wrong hands, it would be like hanging him."

Emma closed her eyes. It made her sick just to think about Jack losing the farm.

"I know this isn't a priority right now, but have you spoken to him?"

"What about?" Emma asked, being deliberately vague.

"You know what about. I'm not an idiot, Emma. I've picked up on it, but he's no idea. He thinks you're nursing a broken heart over Toby and possibly on the rebound from Sean, but you're not, are you?"

Emma hesitated before nodding her head. If she couldn't trust Josh, she could trust no one.

"Why are you not doing anything about it?"

"Because I've made a pratt out of myself with two men this summer. I'm not going for a hat-trick." Emma folded her arms defensively. "I know he's your brother, but I need your discretion on this. I can't be hurt again."

"I've told you before, you have my word, and that still stands."

Emma smiled at him gratefully. "In the meantime, the priority has to be getting through the next few weeks. What can we do? How can we salvage this?"

"I'm thinking if we can get the cheese hampers selling, it'll help bring in some income. Not loads, but enough to tide us over until we know what's happening with the insurance report. I'll try and do more work on the smaller barn later."

"No." Emma shook her head forcefully. "I'll do it. Just pass me some instructions and I'll oversee it. The main carcass of the kitchen is already there."

Josh nodded. "I guess you know what you're doing. You did all this with the farm shop."

Emma licked her lips before swallowing deeply. "I've heard Toby is having a field day with all of this. Is it true?"

"I'm afraid so. He was overheard making fun of the situation, barbeque beef going free at the Seymours."

"You're joking." Emma's fury built at the cold and heartless comment. "I can't believe I actually liked him. He's abhorrent."

"He's a wanker, I'll give him that. But my mum always said what goes around comes around. I just hope it comes around before the autumn ball. I've heard rumours he's entering the village for a '*Foodie Cotswolds*' award with the theme of '*From Farm to Plate*'."

"Are you being serious?" Emma laughed incredulously. "Those were my ideas. Has he seriously passed them off as his own?"

"Yep, I take it you wrote the plans he submitted to the Parish Council too?"

"The cheeky bastard," Emma muttered. "I did those to increase custom to the farm shop and to explore possibilities of food tasting evenings. I've basically given him the reins to the village on a plate, haven't I?"

"One thing about Toby Montgomery, if you've got something he wants, believe me, he'll take it. He has no boundaries or morals."

Emma pulled on her bottom lip. *Didn't they say like gravitated to like?*

"Are you going to the bakery today?"

"Yes." Emma paused as she waited for Josh to say more. "Do you have any messages for Milly?"

"No, of course I don't. Why would I?"

*

"You've got your wall fixed, I see." Emma looked at the repaired plaster, already seeing the flaws in the finish, and she couldn't help thinking Josh would have done a much better job. "Who did it for you? A friend of Sebastian's?"

"No. He said his friend was inundated with work. I had to find someone on the internet." Milly glanced at the repairs with dissatisfaction. "Still, at least it's no longer a hole, and I should be grateful for that." She nodded briefly towards the stairs before continuing to ice a wedding cake with exquisite rosebuds. "He's working from home again today."

"He wears some strange clothing for a bank manager," Emma said quietly as she heard rapid footsteps above. "Didn't he have a silk robe on the other day? Does he never go into the office?"

"It appears not," Milly replied. "The room is full of computer equipment. I wish I could go in there and have a good look around, but I just get glimpses from the door."

"Does that bother you?"

"Kind of." Milly stuck her tongue out in concentration as she maneuvered her icing bag around the three-tiered cake. "Although, compared to some of the weirdos I interviewed, he's basically normal, and I can't complain about his cleanliness. He's always showering. In fact, thinking about it, I don't know what he does with his laundry because I don't tend to see much of it."

"A dream flatmate, then?" Emma questioned, checking her friend's face for reactions. "Do you think he could be boyfriend material, too?"

"I thought so at first. He's made it obvious that he's keen, but he's too weird for me." Milly stood back and admired her work before taking a photograph of it for her website. "Anyway, never mind my lodger. What do I need to provide you with for the hampers?"

Emma pulled a list from the pocket of her jeans. "We've had a flood of orders already. Are you sure you're okay with the name Daisy suggested?"

"I love it. '*The Happy Piglet Hamper Company*.' It has a good ring to it."

Emma had to agree the name did work and seemed very appropriate at the moment. Pickles had taken to sitting by her feet while she worked in the small barn, although Emma suspected the reason he stayed by her side had something to do with the regular handfuls of treats he received daily.

"So, artisan crackers and oat biscuits for the cheese, and a selection of petite fours for desserts." Milly nodded. "I can do those. Did you say you'll pick up the alcohol from the winery tomorrow?"

"Yep. They are more than keen to supply us. In fact, everyone has been so supportive."

"That's because it's Jack. He's helped many other struggling businesses in the past. How's the small barn after the fire? Still smelling of smoke?"

Emma sighed. "I've washed the curtains three times already. I can't afford new ones and I don't want to add to the company's claim. Ironically, the thing I'm more disappointed in is not being able to do anything with the patio at the back of the barn. It's full of rubble. I desperately wanted to turn that into an outdoor seating area. I know this sounds daft, but I felt at home there. Almost as if the trees and hills were built for my eyes. That view just epitomised everything I love about this place, but *c'est la vie*. We've got bigger problems. Jack's hardly slept these past few days. Sometimes he seems okay, and he'll sit down with us at the kitchen table, and other times he disappears for hours on end."

"That's understandable though, isn't it?"

"I guess." Emma shrugged. She worried more about Jack than she wanted to let on. He couldn't keep this up, the long hours, the worry over the parlour, Daisy, Caleb. At some point the dam would break.

"I take it he doesn't know you like him?" Milly smiled at her knowingly. "I've picked up on it."

"No, he doesn't know," Emma replied quietly. "And I want it to stay that way. He needs support right now. The farm is still a mess."

"You're certainly more cut out for country life than his ex-wife ever was, I'll give you that. The first sign of mud or hard work and you wouldn't see her for dust. She worked at Thornhill Hall for a while as Toby's Personal Assistant. She left that job when she fled the village. It was all very strange."

"I didn't know she worked at the hall." Emma frowned. "How long did she work there?"

"Only a few months. Why?"

"Just curious." Emma shrugged before staring at her friend as a thought gathered in her head. "How easy is it to find someone's address?"

"Depends if you know the right sort of people. I'm still in contact with old colleagues who can do it. What are you thinking?"

"I've got a favour to ask, but it's between us." Emma wrote a name on a piece of paper. "Can you find out where she's currently living?"

Milly raised her eyebrows as she read the writing. "Sure, I'll do my best." She suddenly cringed as Sebastian's bedroom door opened, followed by a loud yelp. She looked at Emma with confusion before making her way to the staircase. "Are you okay? Have you hurt yourself?"

"No!" Sebastian shouted. "Stay where you are. I'm fine."

Milly frowned at the harsh tones. "Are you ill?"

"No." Sebastian grunted before yelping again. "I'll be fine. Nothing to worry about."

Milly turned to Emma, her eyes questioning. "What do you think he's doing up there?"

"God only knows." Emma held back a laugh as another shrill wail floated down the staircase. "Sometimes ignorance is bliss.

Are you sure he's a banker? Did you check his references to make sure they were genuine?"

Milly grimaced. "I didn't, and before you start, I know I should have done, but he seemed so normal."

"You mean you didn't want to do what Josh suggested?"

Looking abashed, Milly turned away. *And so she should,* Emma thought as another muffled grunt came from above, and she reminded herself to keep a closer eye on Sebastian. She got the impression he wasn't as '*normal*' as he wanted Milly to think.

CHAPTER 31

The weather had worsened considerably by the time she got back to the piggery. Jack, Josh, and Clive had worked relentlessly on the cattle for their final milking of the day as Emma continued to clean the small barn. She had done her best to scrub the walls and floor of soot and debris, but no matter what she did, that unmistakable odour of burnt wood clung to everything. She tried to remind herself that she'd built the farm shop from scratch. That too had been in a state of disrepair, but it hadn't stood next to a burned-out shell of a parlour, or behind the muddy hooves of a hundred impatient cows, and that made all the difference.

As the wind and gusts sent debris scuttling across the fields, she put on her warm fleece and heated up the last of the lamb casserole. Mother Nature knew how to put on a show around here, so she may as well try to enjoy it. Leaving the curtains open in her piggery, she added more logs to the fire and waited for another illuminating fork of lightning. Never one to be afraid of storms, she counted the seconds before seeing the landscape light up again before her. About to view it from her window, she jumped out of her skin as a loud banging rattled her door.

"It's me." Jack shook heavy raindrops from his hair as he stood in the doorway. "Can you give me a hand? I've been trying to get the cows onto lower ground and into the shelter, but one of them has strayed near the stream and I can't get her back. The water's running too fast, and I can't risk leaving her."

Emma abandoned her food and quickly pulled on her raincoat. "Is Josh already there?"

"He's sparked out in bed, and I don't want to wake him. It's the first proper night's sleep he's had since the fire and, unlike me, he still has to hold down another job."

Grabbing her own torch, Emma battled against the strong winds as she followed Jack across the muddy field, her boots sinking into the rivets as she struggled to stay upright. The force of the storm pushed against them, and she shrieked as a strong gust blew her backwards, upending her straight onto the sodden ground. Jack pulled her up quickly and took her hand as they continued with heads down towards the stream.

Another fork of lightning lit up the landscape, and Emma held her breath as a large boom followed, shaking the ground as they walked. Keeping an eye on the firebolts above them, they hunkered down against the winds as they followed the path to the normally calm stream bank.

The roar of the water deafened them as they approached, and Emma's eyes widened, momentarily mesmerised by the swollen mass of froth and floating branches that engulfed the land before her.

"She's over there," Jack shouted, his hair plastered against his head. "Can you try and stop her from moving backwards?"

Emma wiped torrents of rain from her face as she walked calmly to the frightened animal. She knew her movements would need to be slow to avoid the cow from panicking. Not attempting to touch her, she simply spoke softly as Jack approached her from one side. The unexpected motion catching her eye, the spooked animal jolted, causing Emma to quickly step backwards. She looked at the surging water behind her. She needed to be careful or they'd both end up in there. Sensing the animal begin to calm, Emma spoke reassuringly but firmly. Comforted by the familiar voice and actions, the cow slowly headed towards the safety of the hedgerows.

Spotting the cattle's escape route, Jack threw Emma a piece of rope as another fork of lightning struck ahead. "We need to be quick. It's not safe out here. We'll use the rope to pull the shrubbery together. It'll do for tonight."

Half an hour later, with both of them drenched, they accepted they'd done all they could with their limitations. With the bangs of thunder increasing in frequency and intensity, Jack took her hand and guided her quickly down the fields. Her face stung from the rain and her bare hands throbbed with cold and pain from the thorny shrubs. Struggling to keep up with his pace, she concentrated on her breathing until they came to the safety of the farm gate. Jack led her through as he fought with its weight against the high winds.

"Power cut, typical." He grimaced at the blacked-out windows of the farmhouse. "At least the fires on. You may as well come in here because there'll be no electricity in your piggery."

Emma followed him inside on legs weak with cold and exhaustion. The heat of the kitchen contrasted warmly against her freezing skin and immediately her fingers and toes started to sting as they attempted to thaw. She held her hands under her armpits to ease the agony as she stood by the doorway, her wet clothes creating a pool of water around her feet.

"Get those wet things off. I'm used to weather like this. You're not." Jack threw more logs onto the fire and replaced the fireguard before turning back to Emma. "You don't want to catch hypothermia, do you?"

Emma grimaced as her fingers continued to throb. "I can't feel my hands."

Jack threaded her arms out of her sodden raincoat. Her jeans were caked in mud from falling on the fields and she fumbled with the fastenings to no avail, the numbness in her hands rendering them useless. Jack took over, undoing the top buttons before pulling her wet jumper over her head. The t-shirt underneath clung to her shivering frame thanks to the rain that had dripped relentlessly down her coat collar.

He stood back and took off his own coat and damp t-shirt. "Can you manage?"

"In all honesty," Emma replied, her teeth chattering with cold. "Probably not."

With the light from the fire highlighting his tense features, Jack peeled her t-shirt from her cold skin. Lifting her arms, she allowed him to pull it over her head, aware of her wet curls as they fell back around her shoulders. Kneeling at her feet, he threaded her damp jeans down her legs and helped her to step out of them.

He stood back and looked at Emma in her underwear as fire flames flicked over her bare skin. With his own wet jeans still stuck to him, he wrapped her up in a warm blanket, before gathering her wet curls and tying them up.

"Do you want me to leave you alone?"

Emma shook her head. That was the last thing she wanted. She felt his arms lift her effortlessly, his warm hands burning against her cold skin. He carried her towards the fire, his eyes never seeming to leave her face. Emma threaded her arms around his neck and savoured in the comfort of skin against skin. Instead of placing her on the floor, he continued to hold her, his breath warm against her wet hair. She relaxed in his strong hold, aware of his breathing as it became as irregular as hers. She lifted her head as he gently leaned towards her and placed the briefest of kisses on her lips.

Feeling like she'd been stung, Emma leaned her forehead against his, their breath mingling as they both accepted something had changed. He swallowed deeply as his hand gently touched her bare shoulder before their lips met again, this time with fire and intensity.

She felt her feet touch the floor as his arms wrapped around her body. The blanket slipped and pooled around her feet as he gathered her against him, his hands exploring her greedily before suddenly moving away, leaving her feeling cold and confused.

"I'm so sorry." His shoulders rose and fell with his breath. "I shouldn't have done that."

Emma stood in front of the fire. She'd never felt as vulnerable or as powerful. Despite his height, strength, and willpower, she knew she had caused his weakness. The passion in his eyes matching that of hers, Emma took his hand and placed it back where it had just left. He picked her up again, leaving her blanket on the floor, and carried her effortlessly upstairs. As he lay her on his bed, Emma wrapped her arms round him. She needed this. He needed this. Whatever would happen tomorrow, they'd deal with, but for tonight, they needed each other.

CHAPTER 32

Emma looked at her reflection in the mirror above the old copper bath. Did she look the same? She turned her head sideways to view her profile from different angles. Her hair remained the same colour, her nose the same shape, but emotionally, she'd changed.

She'd woken a few minutes ago to strange noises from the old farmhouse, early sunlight filtering through the unfamiliar bedroom curtains. Finding Jack in a deep sleep, she'd slipped his robe over her naked frame and crept down the stairs. Why hadn't she woken him first? In all honesty, she didn't want to see that look of regret on his face.

Eighteen years. He hadn't disappointed, but she knew where she stood. It had been a moment of madness. Their pasts had left them feeling raw and vulnerable, as if they'd failed in their abilities to be loved. Last night had been an accumulation of those feelings, a need to be reassured that the Joannes and Tobys of this world wouldn't destroy them. Despite what they thought of themselves, they were still desirable and capable of love. At least that's what Jack would be thinking. For Emma, her waters ran much deeper. Last night had changed her life. Forever. He'd been gentle, considerate, and caring, and he'd also held back, she felt sure of that, but it had given her an insight into how life could be to be loved by him, and now she couldn't go back.

Creeping gingerly across the bedroom, she picked up remnants of her underwear before heading down the creaking staircase. For those few hours, she'd allowed herself to be unfettered by inhibitions or worries. They were rare and precious moments.

"Morning, Emma."

Josh's voice and, more importantly, his knowing smile as he leant in the shadows of the kitchen, caused her to jump. Trust him to be awake at this hour and catch her in the act.

"I'm too much of a gentleman to ask, but I think I can put the clues together." Josh passed her a cup of tea served with an amused expression. "Am I right?"

Emma pulled out a chair and joined him at the table. He would pester her until he got the truth. She may as well be up front, with limitations, of course.

"So, what's going on?" Josh asked quietly as he sipped his coffee.

"I think you know the answer to that," Emma replied drolly as she steepled her hands under her crimson chin. "Are you shocked?"

"No, not really."

"Disappointed, or annoyed with me?"

"Nope, neither."

"I thought you'd be fuming. He's your brother. There's so much history between us, and we know each other so well…"

"I'd say you know each other a lot better now." Josh nodded to the bra in her hand before smiling apologetically. "Sorry, bad taste. I couldn't help it. Carry on."

"I just feel like a total idiot."

"Why?" Josh frowned.

"Because this will change everything. We can't go back to being just friends after this."

"And is that what you want, to be just his friend?" Josh lowered his head to look at her. "Come on, Emma. It's obvious your relationship with Jack has shifted."

"But it's never going to go anywhere," Emma whispered. "Jack's got his eye on another woman. You said so yourself. I'm just the red-haired, scruffy kid who used to wipe her nose on her sleeves. After this, he's going to be embarrassed and he'll start avoiding me, and then I'll have to move off the farm."

"Hey, calm down," Josh replied quietly. "I guess last night was a total impulse and you didn't do much talking? Actually, don't answer that. I don't want to know."

Emma allowed a small smile to escape as the morning sun appeared through the kitchen window, casting a warm glow across the table. "Does all this make you feel weird?"

"A bit," Josh admitted with an apologetic shrug. "But not as weird as I thought it would be. Three months ago, if someone had said you two would spend the night together, I'd have freaked, but now, it just seems like the next stage. Even Daisy picked up on it a few days ago. She asked me if something was going on between you both."

"She's very perceptive." Emma rolled her eyes at being caught out by a sixteen-year-old. "Kids pick up on much more than we realise. She mustn't know about last night though. I don't want her getting her hopes up. You can't base a relationship off one night."

"So, what do you want to base a relationship on?" Josh looked at her, one eyebrow raised. "Do you want a life with money within the walls of a Georgian hall, or do you want to be up to your armpits in cow muck every morning with my financially insecure brother?"

Emma laughed as she looked around the dusty and dirty kitchen. She wanted this. All of this.

"You need to sit down and talk with him." Josh pushed back his chair quickly as he heard footsteps on the stairs. "That's my cue to leave, but don't forget, listen to him, and for God's sake, be honest with him."

Emma's toes curled with every step that came closer to the kitchen and she glanced at the door, wondering if she could make a run for it.

"Hi." Jack looked at her hesitantly. "Are you okay?"

"Yeah, sure," Emma replied breezily, trying not to look at his hands, the same hands that had cocooned her last night. "I was thirsty, so I made myself a drink and, well, you know, just chilling." Clenching the sides of her chair, she willed herself to stop talking rubbish.

"I thought you might have been doing a runner on me." Jack sat in the chair just vacated by his brother. "I think we need to talk."

"It's okay, honestly. We're adults." Suddenly overcome with a desire to protect herself, Emma prepared her defence wall. "You don't need to worry. I'm not about to demand a marriage proposal or send you details of my dowry, if I had one, which I don't, because basically, I have nothing."

"That makes two of us." Jack bit back a smile at her nervousness. "Look, I know this is awkward, but I want you to know that I—"

"It's not awkward, really, it isn't." Standing up to turn on the stove, Emma took a pack of bacon from the fridge and fastened the belt of his robe tight around her waist. "We were both feeling a bit…"

Jack cocked his head to one side as he waited for her to continue. God, she loved him.

"A bit?"

"In need of comfort." Emma nodded to herself as she added bacon to the frying pan. That sounded platonic enough. "I guess we felt safe turning to each other for that … physical contact."

"Physical contact?" Jack mused on her words. "That's very clinical."

Emma cringed at the mess she was making of this. He must never know how much last night meant to her, but maybe she should be less formal. Only how do you do that when each time she looked at him, she had flashbacks of him kissing her.

Jack bit his lip at Emma's growing nervousness. "Do you regret it?"

"Do you?" Emma asked quickly.

"No, I don't. Not one bit. Admittedly, I never dreamed this would happen, but in all honesty, I enjoyed our … physical contact."

This time, Emma gave a proper smile as she saw his teasing expression. Maybe everything would be okay.

Jack stood up and took a carton of eggs from the fridge. "So, where do we go from here? There are no rule books for this."

"We don't need a rule book. I guess we go back to being normal, don't we?"

"Can we?"

Jack's deep eyes centred on hers and she turned quickly away. She couldn't go there, reading into things and seeing emotions that weren't for real. If they pretended it had never happened, they'd get through this. Admittedly, their relationship wouldn't fall straight back into place; like a woolly jumper, it had been washed and it would never fit the same again, but at some point, she'd stop thinking about last night. His hands. His gentleness.

"So, we put this behind us?"

"I guess," Emma replied quietly. "After all, we are friends, and friends don't do what we did."

Jack nodded slowly. "Friends certainly don't do what we did."

Emma turned back to the frying pan, feeling slightly miffed. Did he not want to repeat it? Had it been that unmemorable for him? She watched him set the table, the strong outline of his shoulders visible through his thin t-shirt.

Clothes were so overrated. Damn him.

CHAPTER 33

"I thought the Cotswolds was meant to be peaceful," Flick exclaimed as Emma transferred the call to speaker phone so she could work and talk at the same time. "Why does drama follow you everywhere?"

"You tell me," Emma mumbled as she heard a banging at the back of the bakery. She popped her head around the beaded curtain to see the pantry door slightly ajar. She kicked it shut with her foot before returning her attention to the phone call. "The loss assessors were hanging around the farm again today. I don't know what more they are expecting to find. They can't prove Jack committed arson."

"So why is he so worried?"

"Because he can't disprove it either, plus, you know how I told you about his son? He wants to fight for custody of him, which could run into thousands."

"Ouch. I get why he's so worried now. They could see it as an insurance claim. Well, all I can say is that it's a good job they don't know about his fifteenth birthday."

"Why, what happened?" Emma asked with a frown. "I don't remember anything."

"Josh oversaw the fireworks, and his dad put Jack in charge of the bonfire. I still have no idea if it was deliberate or not, but Jack built it near the old allotment sheds that always took the light off their garden."

"I do remember that." Emma giggled. "The fire brigade had to come out and the sheds were destroyed. Didn't he get a warning about that from the police?"

"Yes, but it was just a warning. The owner of the allotments tried to do Jack for arson, but it was never proved. Everyone thanked him though. Those sheds were an eyesore."

"Well, that's definitely information that shouldn't be in the wrong hands." Emma grimaced. "That event may still be on police record somewhere. If that got out, it would be the end of Seymour's dairy, which means the cheese business, the café, all that will go too. Thankfully, most people are being supportive about the fire, apart from Toby, of course."

"Is he being his usual obnoxious self?"

"Naturally. I'm keeping a distance. It's the only thing I can do." Emma looked over the village green towards the rustic barn, closed again for the afternoon. He'd not even watered the hanging baskets that she'd lovingly planted or kept the window shutters clean. No wonder the shop had shut early. It had lost its charm. "And there's something else bothering me. I thought I saw Joanne with Toby, arguing, but I can't be sure it was her."

"Did they know each other well?"

"I didn't get that impression; however, I found out she worked at the hall for a short while." Emma touched the piece of paper in her back pocket that Milly had given to her earlier containing the address she had asked for. "Do you think I should find out if it was her? Surely Jack would need to know, and I'd rather not fan the flames until I knew for certain."

"I'd stay out of it. Remember the saying, curiosity killed the cat. Don't get involved in something that doesn't affect you. You don't want Toby causing trouble while you're going through such turmoil."

"True, although he gets the reins to the village at the autumn ball on Friday and he needs to stay squeaky clean to keep the role. Not that he's earned it. He submitted my plans and passed them off as his own."

"You've definitely had a lucky escape. For once it seems I'm siding with Jack. By the way, did my explanation of the Pavlovian effect work for you?"

Emma sighed deeply. Ten days had passed since they'd slept together and so much had happened. Daisy had started at college, and each day she seemed to blossom from a giggly schoolgirl into a confident young woman, much to the worry of her overprotective brothers, who set unrealistic curfews and fretted when she rebelled against them. Even Josh had laid down some ground rules on how late she stayed out, although Emma secretly thought his grumpiness came from not seeing Milly every day.

As for the fire, Jack had managed to set up a temporary parlour. It didn't work as efficiently as their original one, but at least they could stop hand milking, which gave him time to cope with the demand for the cheese hampers. Orders were rolling in thick and fast, and they had bookings running well into the New Year. The success of the small business had astounded all involved, and Clive had already been roped into taking messages and replying to emails as well as learning how to gift wrap their produce. As for the café barn, that would take a little longer. The effects of the fire were still lingering, but Emma felt confident that in a few weeks they'd be in a better position to announce their grand opening. All in all, she had hit the mark professionally. Her love life, however, proved to be a different story. The minute she found herself in Jack's company, she'd revert to being a teenager. Stuttering words, jelly-like limbs and flushing cheeks were only half of the problem. Since sleeping together, she could barely meet his eye.

"Emma, what's going on? Why the silence? Are you not getting along?"

"Yeah, we are. I just wish I had a chance of closure on my feelings."

"You're living together and working together," Flick replied patiently. "No wonder you're always thinking about him. Some time apart would probably do you good. For as long as I can remember, you've been in love with Jack Seymour. You need a new distraction, like my four kids."

"Three kids," Emma corrected her. "Can you not count anymore?"

"No, I can count," Flick replied light-heartedly. "Although, technically, it's three kids and a quarter."

"Oh my God." Emma put down her oven gloves as a smile enveloped her face. "Don't tell me, number four is on its way?"

"Well and truly cooking," Flick replied, not quite concealing her contentment. "I know the usual signs by now. The minute I attempt to eat breakfast, boom, I vomit, and the test is positive. Mum was the same. You'll probably be very similar."

"Chance would be a fine thing," Emma murmured as she heard another loud banging, this time combined with a muffled shout. She headed behind the beaded curtain again and looked around the small room that Milly used for food preparation. Everything looked fine. About to head back to the front of the shop, she stopped as she spied a red feather on the floor near the pantry door.

"What are you doing?" Flick asked. "You keep fading out. Where are you?"

"In the bakery," Emma replied quietly. "Milly had a hospital appointment after her allergy episode. I said I'd cover the shop for her. Only I don't think I'm alone. Can I call you back?"

"Sure."

Emma tentatively approached the pantry door, her heart banging against her chest. She gasped as the handle started to jolt up and down. Grabbing Milly's rolling pin, she snatched the handle and pulled it swiftly back. Her jaw dropped at the sight that greeted her and she placed the would-be weapon back on the counter and stared in surprise at Sebastian.

"I can explain," he said, flustered, covering himself up.

"I think you better." Emma stared at his feet, encased in red high heels and elaborate fishnet tights. "Are those Milly's knickers?"

Sebastian's normally bolshy stance deflated like a plastic cup next to a fire as he pulled his red feather boa to hide his groin. "It's not what you think. I don't do this for fun. This is my job."

"Your job?" Emma forced her eyes away from his hairy chest and lace basque stuffed with napkins from the bakery. "You manage a bank, wearing that?"

"Well, the thing is…" Sebastian coughed awkwardly. "…I don't manage a bank. I tell people that because it's easier when I'm trying to rent accommodation. I'm what they class as an adult entertainer."

"You're a stripper?"

"No, of course not. How crass." Sebastian tossed his feather boa over his shoulder. "I own a website. It's mainly bored, middle-aged women, sometimes men. They send me their preferences and I wear and act as they request."

Emma wished she had Josh or Milly with her. Anything to break the silence of the refrigerators whirring quietly in the background. She didn't know if an etiquette existed for responding to such an admission.

"I needed an apron for my next call," Sebastian added unnecessarily. "That's why I was in the pantry."

"And does Milly know you do this?" Emma dragged her gaze away from the silk knickers stretched across a very full and hairy bottom. "Does she know you wear her underwear?"

"Of course she doesn't. Women don't like it when they find out what I do. My last landlady had a fetish for naked waiters. She logged onto my website. Needless to say, we were both shocked."

"Hi, I'm back," Milly shouted from the front of the shop. "Any news?"

"You mustn't tell her." Sebastian's head whipped around as he checked for somewhere to hide. "She'll kick me out."

"Who are you talking to?" Milly came into the back of the bakery and looked around. "Were you on the phone?"

Emma considered remaining silent before recalling Sebastian's patronising attitudes towards Josh. Instead, she motioned towards the pantry door. "There's a surprise in there for you."

"Really." Milly's eyes lit up. "I love surprises. Is it gift wrapped?"

"Oh, I think the wrapping is the best part." Emma stood back as Milly pulled open the door.

"What the bollocks?" Milly's face paled as Sebastian shuffled out, the ironing board wedged against his front to protect his dignity. He pressed himself against a wall before staring at the two girls cautiously.

"Is this some kind of joke?" Milly circled him as he attempted to cover up the overstretched knickers. "Are you going to a fancy dress party?"

"No, I am not." Sebastian's face turned puce as Milly put a hand over her mouth to stop herself from laughing. "Your advert in the 'Red Lace' magazine led me to believe you'd be open minded. Instead, I found a frigid spinster whose idea of fun is to mix bowls of cake mixture."

"With all due respect…" Milly snorted as she flicked his feather boa. "…you're not in the right position to be making fun of anyone else. Hey, is that my ring you're wearing?"

Before Milly could finish her sentence, the ironing board had been flung her way. As it hit the side of her head, she staggered towards the doorway and leant heavily against the frame.

Emma gasped as she saw her friend slump to the floor. Pulling her away from an equally stunned Sebastian, she ran into the front of the bakery and looked onto the village green for anyone who could help.

"What's the matter?" Josh threw a banana skin into the nearby bin as he passed the front of the shop. "You look like you've just seen a ghost."

"Worse." Emma grabbed his arm. "We need you."

Upon seeing Josh in his usual work outfit of torn jeans and equally messy t-shirt, Sebastian scuttled towards the pantry, his attempts thwarted by the door now being locked. Emma had to give Josh his due, he didn't react to the older man's dress-code, but simply crouched by the side of Milly and stroked the bruise on her head with the pad of his thumb.

"I'm okay," she said, standing up. "It was an accident. No harm intended."

"Regardless, you're hurt." Josh stood up and folded his arms as he turned towards a sweating Sebastian and his napkin-filled basque. "Any chance I can open a savings account with you? Or are you not working today?"

"You patronising bastard." Sebastian lunged towards Josh, who immediately ducked. "Trust you to look down on my kind of work. That's typical of the uneducated."

"Hey, I have no issues with whatever line of work you're in." Josh kept his hands in a karate chop as he eyed the older man's familiar jewellery with curiosity. "I'm as open-minded as the next guy. Even more so, I'd say. However, what I do have an issue with is you deceiving my good friend and, by the looks of your outfit, stealing her personal belongings. I think you'd better pack your bags, don't you?"

Josh motioned for Emma and Milly to leave the room. Glad of the escape, they ran upstairs and flung open Sebastian's wardrobe, their mouths agape at the array of flimsy outfits.

"Oh God, my makeup is here and more of my jewellery. I wondered where all my good stuff had gone." Milly winced as she picked up a pile of used wax strips full of dark hair. "Now I know what all that yelping was about, but how could I have not known about his job?" She gingerly touched the side of her eye where the ironing board had hit her. "I used to pride myself on being observant. It was my job to be aware of my surroundings. I really have lost my touch, haven't I? I should have checked his references."

"You could never have predicted this," Emma said quietly as she listened to the shouting downstairs and the scuffle of the two men. "And you'd never have known how reactive he could be when provoked."

They both paused as they heard the unmistakable thud of fist against flesh, and Milly put a hand over her mouth as she gasped. "Sebastian is huge compared to Josh."

"I doubt that'll bother Josh. Believe me, he can handle himself." Emma leaned over the banister as Sebastian sat on the bottom stair, stemming the flow of a bloody nose. "Let's get these suitcases out of here. You'll have to send his computer equipment onto him via another means."

Ten minutes later, the girls looked out the first-floor window to watch the older man crossing the village green with his luggage, wearing thankfully more than he'd had on in the pantry.

"I've just found his website." Emma searched through the freezer for a bag of frozen vegetables. "It's not exactly hard core, but it doesn't compliment an *Alice in Wonderland*-themed bakery."

Milly sat down on her sofa and put a hand to her swelling eye. "How is it that men always know how to strike right on the eye socket?"

"I wouldn't know. I've never hit a girl." Josh took the packet of frozen peas from Emma and placed it gently on Milly's face. "He's gone, by the way, and I very much doubt he'll be returning, but you're going to have a humdinger of a black eye in the next few days."

"Great," Milly groaned as she tried to sit up. "Just what I need. No lodger, no money, and a face like a boxer." She looked at Josh's hands. "I didn't know you could defend yourself like that."

"I have a black belt in Karate, and let's just say I watched a lot of Indiana Jones movies in my youth. It seems the two paid off. Anyway, is anyone going to tell me why he was dressed like '*Little Miss Muffet*'?"

Emma watched Josh lift Milly into a more comfortable position and place a blanket around her knees. She smiled to herself. Didn't they say that every cloud had a silver lining?

"Where are you going?" Milly asked as Emma headed for the door. "Are you not staying to have a drink? I think we need something after that shock."

Emma shook her head. The way Josh had stepped in to save Milly had highlighted to her how she desperately wanted to be someone's priority. Moping after Jack would do her no good.

"I've kind of got stuff to do." Emma smiled reassuringly. "I'll be fine."

Josh followed her as she made her way downstairs. "Will you be okay? Do you want me to walk you back to the farm?"

"No, but thanks. I think I need some time to myself. I've got some thinking to do."

Josh smiled hopefully. "About Jack?"

"Yes." Emma nodded as she straightened her back. "It's time I grew up."

CHAPTER 34

Pulling on her fleecy pyjamas, Emma shivered as the heat from the fire started to take hold. Making herself a hot cup of sweet tea, she curled up under her blankets and yawned. The events of the day had finally taken their toll, leaving her feeling shaky and tired.

The knock at her door when it came caused her to inwardly groan and she prayed it wasn't Daisy with yet another homework question. She stepped back in surprise to find Jack dressed in a smart shirt, his brow furrowed with confusion upon seeing her nightwear.

"I thought we were going out?"

"Out?" Emma asked.

"Yeah, Josh just rang me. He told me about Sebastian. He said you wanted to go for a drink and talk about something." Jack's dark eyes searched her face before stepping back. "I take it only I got the message. Hey, it's fine. I'll see you tomorrow, okay?" About to turn away, he looked down at the expensively wrapped hamper left on her doorstep and read the note threaded through the red ribbon. "Eat me, drink me. That's cute, I like it. I think someone has set us up."

Emma nodded with embarrassment. This had Josh and Milly written all over it. However, she didn't want another evening knowing Jack had been forced to stay in her company.

"It looks like they've chosen the best of everything." Jack read the contents as he handed it over. "One of your deluxe hampers, I presume. Let me know what you think of it. It will be good research if nothing else."

Emma balled up her fists as he walked away, determined not to call him back. She had to let him go at some point and inviting him in to share the hamper wouldn't do either of them any good. She closed the door on him and leant against it, trying not to cry. She needed closure.

After a few minutes, she looked through the window to see if he'd reached the farmhouse and gasped to find him still standing outside her piggery.

He shrugged apologetically and smiled at her reflection. Mentally berating herself for forgetting his recent upsets, Emma unlocked the door and stood to one side.

"We need to talk." Jack shoved his hands in the pockets of his jeans. "This is driving me around the bend."

Emma acknowledged his words with a nod as she closed the door behind him and watched him walk towards the log burner, his dark hair ruffled and his eyes intense with emotion. For as long as she stayed on this farm, she'd never get over him. Accepting her fate, she looked down at her pyjamas. If they were going to have this conversation, she needed to be more appropriately dressed. Picking up her jeans still on the floor where she'd left them, she looked around for somewhere to change.

"Emma, in case you've forgotten, I have seen you naked."

Momentarily stunned, she stared at him open-mouthed.

"All I'm saying is that you need to stop being awkward around me. We didn't do anything wrong. It's perfectly normal and natural to do what we did, yet you seem to want to forget about it."

"Normal and natural?" Emma swallowed to ease her dry throat. "To you maybe. You're a farmer. You see this kind of thing every day, but for me it's a bit more than that, and yes, I am feeling awkward and embarrassed."

"Embarrassed?" Jack smiled as she started to pace around the coffee table. "From what I remember, you've nothing to be embarrassed about."

Emma hid behind her hands, her emerald eyes peeking between her fingers. Had he really just said that?

"Okay, we're not ready for this conversation just yet." Jack picked up the hamper and opened the lid. "Come on, it seems a shame to waste all this good food. Let's try to relax. You can tell me about the flirty French maid you found in Milly's pantry."

His light-heartedness diluted the pressure and she found herself starting to smile.

"According to my brother, Sebastian deserved the burst nose. He's been stealing Milly's things, apparently."

"That's what annoyed her more than anything," Emma replied. "I think she may have come around to his job role, eventually. But not theft. Is Josh still with Milly?"

"Yep. According to him, she received a bad head injury and can't be left alone. Doctor's orders, I presume." Jack lifted a small bottle of elderflower cordial from the hamper and shared the contents between two tin mugs from her kitchenette. "It's been a long time coming."

Emma looked at him hesitantly as he rooted through the hamper. "Are we really going to eat? You can leave if you want. I don't mind."

"Well, I do mind. I'm hungry and I desperately need a distraction from the worry over the fire. Plus, they've used some of my best cheeses here. This could be my chance to show off. It's very rare I get the opportunity these days. By the way, do you know you've got a piglet sleeping in the corner?"

Emma viewed Pickles curled up in his basket with fondness. Clive had taken in a stray cat that evidently put the little piglet on edge. Plus, Pickles had got so attached to her of late that Clive had agreed it made sense for him to stay with her, and, in all honesty, she enjoyed his company.

“Do you know how to taste food properly?” Jack continued to unpack the hamper and lay the perfectly wrapped gifts on the rug. “And I don’t mean by sitting in posh restaurants surrounded by fifteen course menus.”

“Ha, ha.” Emma sat on a cushion by his side. Was he flirting with her, or aiming to help her unwind? Regardless, her hormones were scattering around like popcorn in a hot pan.

“Did you know you should taste food without the sense of sight?” Jack cut up a piece of cheese and held it between his fingers. “Okay, close your eyes and open your mouth.”

“I beg your pardon?” Emma burst out laughing. “That just sounds dodgy.”

Jack gasped with mock horror. “Emma Francis, I never expected that from you. Do you have any more inappropriate comments, or shall we carry on?”

Emma wiped her eyes as she fanned her hot face. She’d surprised herself with that remark. “I’ll behave myself. I promise.”

“Good, because if you wish to swap innuendo all evening, I’m your man.” Jack put the cheese down as she doubled over in another fit of mirth. After the stress of the past few days, this light relief had come at the right time. She looked back up, glad of the waterproof mascara.

“I’m sorry. Right, I promise to be good this time. It’s out of my system now. I’m going to be serious.”

He raised an eyebrow as she sat back and closed her eyes. Feeling his fingers gently touch her lips, she slowly opened her mouth and took the small cube of cheese.

“Keep your eyes closed and let your senses do the rest. What can you taste?”

Emma chewed the small sample and frowned. “Earthy, definitely creamy. Maybe peppery?”

She opened her eyes to see Jack smiling at her while nodding with approval. “Well done. It’s our version of a Stilton. Do you want to try another one?”

This time Emma closed her eyes without hesitation. He was right. Without vision, her other senses seemed to heighten. She could hear his rhythmic breathing, smell his familiar shower gel, and the hairs on her arms stood up in response to his closeness. No longer concerned about how she looked, she tasted the new cube sample and let it melt on her tongue.

"Grassy, caramel, lemon?"

"You're good at this." Jack gently wiped a crumb off her bottom lip, and Emma's body reacted immediately to the intimacy. She drew in her breath, conscious that their fingers were already reaching for each other.

"We can't keep ignoring this," Jack said quietly. "You know what I'm talking about."

Emma lowered her head, cursing her traitorous emotions for giving her away.

"I'm going to ask you a question and I want you to reply within three seconds…"

"Hey, that's not fair." Feeling breathless, Emma stood up to give them some distance. She didn't want to be another notch on his bedpost. She wanted more than just occasional lovers. She wanted it all. "You can't put me on the spot."

"I'm trying to find out how you feel," Jack replied patiently. "I can't read you at all. Since we slept together, you're so protective of your emotions and extremely defensive."

"I'm not defensive," Emma snapped.

"Do you want to sleep with me again?"

"Yes." Emma pulled at her curls in frustration at how quickly she'd replied. "Are you happy now? Your quick-fire question worked."

"Are you seriously asking me that?" Jack bit back a grin at her crimson cheeks. "Why are you blushing?"

"You know why I'm blushing." Emma cursed herself for wearing her palest pyjamas that clashed wonderfully with the furious heat rash on her neck. A complete contrast to the man opposite her with his cheeky smile and perfect cheekbones. "Yes, I like you. Yes, I'm attracted to you, but I've no idea how to play it."

"And you think I do?" Jack held out his arms as he laughed. "I've never felt as out of water as I do now. Do you think I expected this to happen? My little brother's best mate, the one who used to jump on my bed and leave the tops off my felt-tip pens. You arrived on my farm and gave me grief for weeks, and what happened? You turned up at that bloody summer ball looking like everything I'd been missing from my life, and not only could I not take my eyes off you, but you made me laugh from the minute I got there."

"I did?" Emma looked at him incredulously. "You enjoyed that night with me?"

"Josh said you'd be slow on the uptake, but I underestimated him." Jack steepled his hands and blew on them nervously. "You think there's another girl, don't you?"

As the pieces of the puzzle started to fit together, Emma sat down heavily by his side. She couldn't think. She could barely breathe. Surely, it couldn't be? Her heart banged painfully as she started to shake.

"My brother has had a field day over the last few weeks, teasing me about my feelings for you, and I've not had a leg to stand on because everything he said was true. I am totally and completely out of my depth with you. I can't chat you up because you'd take the piss out of me. I can't flirt with you because you said I'm naff at it, and I've certainly not been able to kiss you, because you're Emma."

"So, you slept with me instead?"

Jack paused at her unexpected comment. "A moment of weakness. You broke down my wall, what can I say?"

"Are you being serious?" Emma's voice shook with nerves and emotion as she looked into his eyes. "Because if you're trying to make me feel better after Sean and Toby, this isn't the way to go about it. If you want to be a good friend to me, just be supportive. I don't need your sympathy."

"Sympathy?" Jack tipped her head towards his. "I'm the one who needs sympathy. My brother wouldn't give me any clue to your feelings about me. He said I had to figure it out on my own. I've always prided myself on being a quick learner, but with you, I have no idea what you're thinking. Just put me out of my misery. Do you feel this pull between us?"

Emma sat on her hands to prevent them from shaking. He had no idea she'd experienced this pull for so many years. "Yes. I've felt it too."

"Thank God." Jack bit his bottom lip nervously. "Before we say anymore, I need you to know that I have nothing. All my money goes into this farm, and what's left brings up Caleb and Daisy, and if the insurance won't pay out, I won't even have this land. I know you're not on good terms with Toby at the moment, but he has money and status. He could buy you a million dresses and shoes to match…"

"I don't want a million dresses."

"Are you sure?" Jack searched her face for answers. "I know he didn't treat you right, but I think he genuinely cared about you. In his own way."

Emma looked at him. Properly looked at him. For the first time ever, she felt she had permission to absorb him. For years she'd taken sneaky glances. Even the night they'd spent together, she'd closed her eyes for fear of opening them and finding him gone.

"I'll need to put my fight for Caleb on hold for a while, but depending on the outcome, I still want to try for joint custody." Jack looked at her hesitantly. "More emotional baggage, I know."

"I think you're doing the right thing," Emma said quietly.

"It's all down to you. You've strengthened our family group. You've strengthened me. I've no idea if I'll be successful, but I need to try."

Emma leant her forehead against his. She felt like someone had just given her the moon and stars to hold. Never in her wildest dreams did she envisage she could feel so happy. Her mind went crazy with thoughts. He liked her. Jack Seymour. He wanted her. Lifting her head, she touched his face, outlining his jaw, his lips, all the features she'd gazed upon but had never been able to touch. She couldn't mess this up. She held something in the palm of her hand that felt too precious for words. Placing her lips against his, she kissed him, not as a friend, but as a lover. Jack groaned softly as she deepened her kiss, her hands moving to the buttons on his shirt.

"No." He captured her wrists gently, smiling at her furrowed brow. "Believe me, I want nothing more than this right now. Some days, I've barely functioned because I've thought of nothing else, but I want to do this right. I want to date you first. You've always been Emma, but I want to know the real you. I want a chance to practice my rubbish flirting on you for a start."

Emma laughed at his ability to help her relax during what could have been an awkward moment.

"It's the autumn ball on Friday." Jack stroked the side of her cheek. "Let's use that as the start of us being together. Our first date. After that…"

Emma cocked her head to one side and smiled cheekily.

"After that, I make no promises to behave." Jack pulled her closer to him and lay on top of her as he gently kissed her shoulders, just visible underneath her fleecy pyjamas. "First base has a lot of positives. I'm happy to stay here. For now."

CHAPTER 35

"It's not safe to leave someone alone after a head injury," Josh repeated as he drank straight from the milk bottle. "Everyone knows that."

"But no medical book says you have to take your clothes off to administer treatment." Jack looked at his brother's inside out t-shirt. "Unless nakedness reduces the dizziness."

"Okay, piss off," Josh grumbled, his cheeks turning as pink as the morning sunrise. "Yeah, we had sex. Are you happy now?"

"Oh my God, finally." Emma lifted her arms in celebration. "So, was it romantic? Did you take all the advice I gave you years ago? Did you play soft music? Light candles? Dance with her?"

Josh wiped milk off the top of his lip. "Don't be stupid. She's not into stuff like that. I just took her clothes off."

"Typical." Jack shook his head. "Have you no shame?"

"Nope. More importantly, are you going to do something about your own love life?"

"I already have." Jack reached for Emma and tenderly kissed the end of her nose. "She's agreed to date me."

Josh put the milk bottle down and stared at the pair with their arms around each other. He laughed lightly before lowering his head.

"Is this okay?" Emma cocked her head to one side and looked at her best friend. "I know it must be weird for you. I do understand."

“Actually, I was just thinking how good you look together.” Josh clapped his brother on the back before hugging Emma. “I’m really pleased for you both. Just do me a favour, no snogging in front of me, okay?”

“Or me.” Daisy giggled as she joined the group hug. “So, you finally plucked up the courage and told her. Honestly, every time you met up with Toby, he went into sulk mode.”

“Okay, leave me with some dignity.” Jack grinned as he held his little sister in a headlock. “Aren’t you meant to be helping Emma with the cheese shop when you’re not studying, or have you forgotten about your family commitments now that you’re at college?”

Daisy pulled a face before heading to the barn with Emma. “I hope you know what you’re letting yourself in for. My big brother can be very demanding at times. Hey, are you okay?”

Emma put a hand to her stomach and cursed the extra omelette she’d eaten this morning. She’d woken with a hunger like nothing else and now, an hour later, she regretted her overindulgence.

“Did you drink a lot last night?” Daisy asked as she logged into their website for the day’s orders. “Josh said he’d make you both a hamper, but I didn’t think he’d put alcohol in it.”

“I only had a small glass of elderflower cordial.” Emma grimaced at the bitter taste in her mouth. “Perhaps I’m allergic to your brother, after all.”

“Oh my God, Joanne will be so jealous when she finds out you’re a couple. I’d love to be a fly on the wall when Jack tells her.”

“I wouldn’t have thought that would be relevant to her.” Emma took a drink of water, thinking back to the address still in her jeans pocket. “She doesn’t speak to Jack, does she?”

“Not at the moment, but she’ll have to speak to him regularly if Jack gets access rights to Caleb. I’ll admit, I’m looking forward to being an aunty.”

"It might not work, Tilly Mint. You need to bear that in mind."

"I know, but I need some excitement. Do you think Josh and Milly will get married?"

Emma laughed. "Stop trying to pair everyone off. Let people enjoy where they're at. Anyway, when will your old school friend arrive? Didn't you say you were planning on meeting up with him?"

"Friday, just in time for the ball."

"So, will he be your date then?"

"Urgh, no way. Adam is just a friend."

"Ah, but time changes things." Emma smiled smugly. "Everyone deserves a second chance."

They both jumped at the unexpected figure menacingly filling the doorway. "And is that what you think you've got? A second chance with Jack Seymour?"

Daisy ran outside to alert her brothers as Emma folded her arms defensively. "What do you want?"

"Nice little set up you've got here." Toby looked around the small barn at the array of hampers already assembled. "Does everyone know you learned your skills working for me?"

Emma decided to ignore the insult. "What do you want?"

"Have you been telling all the farmers not to trade with me?"

"Why on earth would she do that?" Jack approached, flanked by his brother and Clive. "She's perfectly capable of building a business without having to threaten someone else's. If you've got anything to say, you say it to me. Anyway, you've got a nerve coming onto my land. I told you years ago, you're not welcome here."

"Tough," Toby replied with an uncharacteristic confidence. "I won't stand for you destroying businesses within the village. I may not own this land, but I do have a say in who we trade with, and if you make life difficult for me, I'll make it difficult for you."

"Whatever." Jack sighed. "Anything else? I don't want to think you've ruined your sheepskin slippers just to shout empty threats at me."

Toby nodded towards Emma. "You've got my cast-offs, I see."

"Whoa," Josh said quietly, putting a hand out to his brother's tense arm. "Leave it."

Seemingly pleased with the frustration he'd left behind, Toby pushed through the three men and headed back across the courtyard to his sparkling clean sports car. "It makes a change, doesn't it?"

"What does?" Jack asked, eyeing his nemesis closely.

"You, tasting failure." Toby looked around at the ruined parlour and the scorch marks still visible on the courtyard floor. "It would be such a shame if the insurance didn't pay out. Wouldn't it?"

"What the hell was all that about?" Jack winced as gravel sprayed in all directions. "What gave him the courage to come here, and what does he know about the insurance people?"

"Nothing. We've not spoken about the fire with anyone. He's just trying out his new crown for size." Josh kicked a bag of chicken food with force. He's a pratt. I should have let you thump him."

"He's worried, that's the problem." Clive shook his head knowingly. "I've heard from the head of the Parish Council that they're not happy with the lack of the trade in the farm shop since Emma left. It's evident he can't run a business. If he can't prove he's successful at making money, his mother will shift the running of the village to another family member."

"That doesn't bode well for us, him being pissed off." Jack rubbed his bristly chin as he narrowed his eyes. "His comment has made me nervous though. He doesn't have any moral boundaries."

Emma's stomach continued to churn. She deeply regretted the day she'd allowed Toby into her life. Would she ever learn?

Taking a deep breath, she tried to ignore the growing nausea from this morning's breakfast, but despite her efforts, she could feel the bile rise into her throat. Running outside, she bent over and brought up the contents of her stomach into a nearby drain.

"Emma?" Jack held back her hair, his forehead creased with concern. "What's wrong?"

"She said she'd eaten too much breakfast," Daisy stood back, looking worried. "Will she be okay?"

"Of course I will." Emma gulped in the fresh air. "It's nerves mixed with overindulgence. I'm sure it is." She nodded to Josh, who stood watching, his expression puzzled. "I'm okay, I promise."

"Regardless, I want you to rest." Jack led her gently into the kitchen and sat her at the table. "Daisy and Clive can take over the hampers for today. Go and lie down, and don't worry about posh boy. He's had his cage rattled and in turn he felt brave enough to rattle mine. He can have this one on me, but next time I'm ready for him."

Emma leant against Jack's chest and listened to the rapid beating of his heart. She'd never seen him riled before.

She just hoped he had no reason to be.

CHAPTER 36

Pickles watched her pace from one end of the piggery to the other before snuffling at her ankles for some much-needed attention. Emma lifted him into her arms and went through the pros and cons again. Hadn't Flick told her to leave this alone? However, something at the back of her mind warned her that she couldn't.

Sighing at her own indecision, Emma eventually made up her mind. She placed the piglet on the back seat of the Range Rover and pulled Joanne's address from her back pocket. Better the devil you know.

Following the satnav through valleys and tiny villages, she once again questioned her reasons for doing this. In theory, she should be staying out of this family feud. But then again, Jack would never risk doing this himself. He had too much to lose by contacting Joanne directly, especially at the start of a custody battle over Caleb. No, her reasons for doing this were founded. Taking a sip of water to help her dry mouth after her mornings upset stomach, she eventually arrived on the long street of identical town houses. Winding down her window, she peered at the peeling blue door she'd set out to find. Only problem being, now that she'd arrived, she felt too nervous to carry out her task.

Knocking back the rest of the water and patting the sleeping piglet for dutch courage, Emma picked up the parish church leaflets and threw them into her rucksack. It seemed as good an excuse as any to be walking around such a quiet street. Deliberately heading to the first house, furthest away from her destination, she meandered along the narrow dusty pavement and pondered on her agenda. What did she expect to find out? It would be unlikely Joanne would come to the door and explain if she still had contact with a squire from a privately owned village many miles from here. Then again, upon seeing the Thornhill leaflets, she might.

All other homes finally exhausted, Emma slowly approached her target. The wooden gate squeaked loudly, and she grimaced to see neighbouring curtains twitch. Unlike other gardens, the small patch of lawn under the front window appeared well maintained except for a few weeds spurting between the paving stones.

Suddenly losing her bravery, she'd just turned to walk back towards the gate when she heard a bolt being drawn on the door. Emma froze and slowly turned around. It felt on a par with being caught in your teacher's office. It wasn't illegal, but you needed a bloody good excuse for being in there.

The long dark hair and saucer brown eyes were unmistakable from the wedding photograph she'd seen, and the woman climbing out of Toby's car. This was Joanne, the girl who had captured Jack's adoration enough to marry him and then left his heart scattered in pieces. Emma felt in awe, not just of her beauty, but of her influence over the man she loved.

Joanne eyed Emma curiously before holding out a hand for a leaflet. "What's this for?"

"Oh, just advertising," Emma squeaked, coughing to remove the frog in her throat. "Funds, you know."

"I know this village. I also know it doesn't need to beg for charity." Joanne frowned at the piece of paper in her hand. "I used to live there."

Emma shuffled her feet. She hadn't expected this conversation opportunity so quickly. In fact, being honest with herself, she hadn't expected this meeting to happen at all.

"Do you live there?"

Crossing her fingers, Emma shook her head. "I just get paid for delivering leaflets. I take what I can. Money's short."

“Yeah, I know the feeling.” Joanne sighed as she leant against the doorway. “What are they wanting money for anyway? I’ll be honest, they’ve got a nerve if they’ve asked you to come to this side of town begging. Their scarecrows wear better clothing than most of us around here can afford.”

Emma laughed nervously. “I guess some people are just hard faced.”

“Well, they’ll get nothing from me. I have very little in the way of fond memories of that place, or the bastards that run it.”

“Montagues?” Emma narrowed her eyes in thought. “Is that their name?”

“Montgomerys.” Joanne’s lips thinned as she tossed back her glossy hair. “A bunch of lying bastards. I can only thank them for one thing, and the only reason that’s turned out well is because I’ve insisted on distance. So, sorry, but I won’t be donating anything to them.”

A sudden noise from the back yard distracted Joanne and her face softened as she craned her neck before looking at Emma questionably.

“I’ll be going,” Emma muttered, still none the wiser why this woman and Toby had needed to argue. If anything, this meeting had heightened her curiosity. About to leave, she stopped as a childlike voice came from the back of the house.

“Piggy?”

“It’s not a piggy.” Joanne rolled her eyes with fondness. “We’re still learning animal names. It’s a cat, Caleb.”

Emma froze. Wasn’t the child staying with her parents? She swallowed deeply, suddenly keen to leave. This wasn’t right. She shouldn’t be the first one to see Caleb. That should be Jack.

“No, piggy,” the small voice repeated, coming closer. “It’s a pink piggy.”

Her heart thumping, Emma remembered leaving the car window slightly open. Damn, talk about the pig being out of the bag, literally.

"I'll just go and see what he's on about." Joanne headed down the ginnel to the back of the property. "Oh my God. It's actually a pig. How the hell has that got in here?"

"I'll get my toy pig and then they can play." The body belonging to the small voice disappeared swiftly inside the house, leaving a stunned Emma and a confused Joanne alone in the paved yard.

"I hate farm animals." Joanne picked up a brush to herd the small piglet into a corner. "Horrible stinking things."

"Hey, the broom will frighten him," Emma said with alarm, as Pickles started to quiver under a patio table. She bent down and whispered to him, coaxing him gently out before placing him safely in her arms.

"Please don't tell me he belongs to you?" Joanne looked at Emma strangely. "Who are you?"

"Me, no one," Emma replied quickly, heading for the ginnel. "I'm going."

"I've got my pig," the small child ran towards her, his head down as he concentrated on navigating the flags with his tiny feet. "They can play now."

Emma looked at the soft toy in his chubby hands, before taking in his sun-kissed legs and plump little stomach. Caleb suddenly raised his head and gave her a beatific smile. Emma stepped back as if she'd been stung. She turned and fled, her heart banging against her chest, and those childlike lavender eyes imprinted on her mind forever.

CHAPTER 37

"I need to talk to you." Emma's hands shook as she looked up the ladder. "It's urgent."

"Yeah, sure," Josh shouted down from the thatched roof of the cottage he'd been working on. "What's it about?"

"It's about Jack," Emma replied quietly. "I really need to speak to you."

"Okay." Josh checked his watch. "Just give me twenty minutes. Go and have a coffee with Milly and I'll see you in the bakery."

Glancing at the deserted farm shop, Emma breathed a sigh of relief to find it shut. She couldn't face him. Not wanting to talk with anyone, she sat down on an empty bench and wished she could turn back time. She should never have gone there, but she had, and now she'd opened Pandora's box.

"So, you know?"

Emma jumped at the hissed voice from behind, his mouth so close to her ear that the hairs on her arms tingled with alarm.

"Joanne has just rung me. It wasn't too hard to figure out it was you."

"I'm going to tell Jack," Emma whispered between gritted teeth, not even turning her head. "You can kiss goodbye to your village role now, you bastard."

"You think?" Toby replied softly as he leant over her shoulder.

"I know so," Emma breathed steadily despite the anxiety running through her core. "You've let Jack bring that child up, knowing he's yours. He's struggled financially and emotionally every day to make ends meet."

"And what fun it's been to watch him." Toby sniggered. "He's not that clever, after all."

Emma clenched her fists in her attempts not to hit out. "As soon as your mother arrives tomorrow night for the ball, I'll be the first at her door."

"Are you sure?"

This time, Emma turned to face him, confused by the quiet confidence in his voice.

"If you go to my mother, I'll ring the insurance company about Jack." Toby's lavender eyes darkened with malice. "My family will eventually come around to the idea that I've sired a son and heir. Jack won't be quite as elated to lose his farm."

Aware of her eyes widening, Emma tried to stay calm.

"What will the insurance company say when they find out he's done this before?" Toby smiled at her cruelly. "You should be careful who you speak to. Enemies have ears."

Emma swallowed back her nausea. Sebastian. He must have overheard her conversation with Flick.

"Poor Jack. He's been fighting for a kid who was never his, and now the insurance company suspects he's set fire to his own parlour. Petrol? He can't get away with such a feeble excuse as a leaky generator. They'll soon see past that lie. Oh, and let's not forget his harassment charges against Joanne, combined with the fact he can't afford joint custody. All that is bad enough, but your careless talk about the bonfire from his fifteenth birthday has put the noose right around his neck. I can't wait to see him hang. Unless…"

Emma waited for him to continue; her stomach cramped with knots as a feeling of faintness overtook her.

"If you leave the village and take your secret of Caleb with you, then I may stay quiet about what I know about his past, and the petrol."

"No," Emma gasped. "I can't do that. My life is here."

"Not anymore, it isn't." Toby grinned mockingly. "I've waited eighteen years to destroy that bastard, and you've just handed me the weapon to do it. So, here's your choice. If Jack or my mother finds out about Caleb, I will make sure he goes to prison on arson charges. He'll lose his farm, his family, his self-respect, and his reputation."

Emma recalled Josh's words. Certain news in the wrong hands would destroy Jack. They all knew that.

"Whereas if you leave, the only thing he'll lose is you." Toby put his face right up to hers. "Which do you think means more to him?"

*

Her phone continued to ring but Emma ignored it. With the curtains to her piggery drawn and the doors and windows locked, she cowered beside the log burner and hugged her legs to her chest.

Jack would never forgive her. Daisy would never go to University. Josh would struggle to get work, tainted by association. The farmers were loyal around here, but no one would support someone who'd burned down their parlour, risking his sister's life in the process.

But she couldn't leave him. She couldn't. Especially not now. What would she do? Where would she go?

Rocking herself, she held the persistent ringing phone. They'd figure it out eventually that she'd hidden here, but she couldn't face them. Her fingers shaking, she sent back a short text, '*Feeling off, having an early night.*'

She glanced at her watch as the natural light started to fade. She couldn't sleep. She'd be the traitor, the one who sent them to the slaughter. Even if they said they'd forgive her, she would always have to live with the knowledge that she'd caused their destruction.

But if she left, she'd be taking a part of Jack with her. Her sister had been right. She suffered the same signs. She'd done the test. Which would be the lesser of the two evils? He may not want her, but could she take this away from him? Would he suffer this kind of loss twice? Could she survive without him in her life? No, she couldn't.

She put her head in her hands and sobbed. This was the hardest and the most heart-breaking decision of her life, and she still had no idea what to do. Curling up on the hard stone floor, she prayed for a sign from her parents. Anything that would guide her through. Anything at all.

CHAPTER 38

Her throat burned from vomiting and her eyes were swollen and painful from crying, but she'd made her decision. Feeling betrayed by the cloudless skies, Emma walked across the fields towards the kitchen. She didn't even notice the dew-filled grass or the way the burnt-orange trees glistened with cobwebs as the sun rose behind them.

"Feeling better?" Jack looked into her swollen eyes with concern. "Actually, I think I have my answer. Should you even be out of bed?"

"I'm fine." Emma pushed him away gently. She couldn't bear his sympathy. "I'll get started on the hamper orders."

"Whoa." Jack held her elbow. "What's wrong?"

"Nothing." Pouring herself a coffee, Emma sipped it gingerly. "Just tired."

"I hope you'll be feeling okay for the ball tonight. It's our first date." Jack put his arm around her, holding her against him. "Unless you want to stay here. In fact, I could try and free this table of clutter and cook us a nice dinner if you'd prefer. You could put your feet up and let me pamper you."

Emma willed him to stop. His supportiveness cut deeply into her, creating scars that would never heal. She felt sick at what she had to tell him.

"Josh and Daisy will be out tonight at the ball so it's just us." Jack added oil to the frying pan and started to prepare breakfast as the floorboards creaked above them. "Josh said you wanted him yesterday, but he couldn't find you. What was that about?"

Emma paused. The words wouldn't come.

"Actually, I think I know what's wrong." Jack placed a bacon sandwich in front of her. "You can't fool me. I spotted the signs yesterday."

Emma put down her cup as she held her breath.

"You're worried about the fire, aren't you? Well, so am I, but it can't be much longer before I hear something? I don't know what's holding it up."

Emma felt icy grips of fear around her heart. Had she made the right decision?

"I guess I just need to be patient. Until then…" Jack kissed the end of her nose. "…I've got you."

"Urgh, get a room." Daisy shuffled into the kitchen in her slippers. "I hope you two won't be snogging tonight at the ball."

"Less of the cheek," Jack replied with an affectionate smile. "And you'll be helping Emma in the barn again today. She's still not feeling well. These hamper orders have really taken off. What's your next expansion plan?"

"She's taking over Toby's role as village squire." The young girl giggled.

"Don't be so silly," Emma snapped before seeing Daisy's hurt look and sighing. This was no one's fault but her own. "I'm sorry. I think I'm best off being alone today."

"Yeah, sure." Jack cocked his head to one side as Daisy disappeared upstairs without breakfast. "Please don't worry about this insurance claim. No news is good news. If they suspected arson, I'm sure they'd have been in touch by now. I'm feeling more hopeful by the day."

Emma jolted as her phone buzzed. She read the text with a cold feeling in her heart.

'Tick-tock, tick-tock. What's your decision?'

*

The hours ticked on, each one a reminder of her task. She'd received three more messages from Toby by mid-afternoon. His threats were not idle.

Tying up the last of the hamper baskets, she sat down outside the barn and placed her head in her hands. This is how people must have felt before being taken to the guillotine.

"Hey." Jack fastened the jacket of his suit as he waved to her from the kitchen doorway. "The solicitors have rung; they want to talk to me. I'm trying to be positive."

Emma walked over to him and straightened his tie without giving him eye contact.

"Do you want to come with me?"

The request threw Emma and she momentarily paused. "I don't think that's a good idea. I'm busy."

"Okay." Jack's flitting eyes covered his hurt. "I shouldn't have asked. Wish me luck?"

"Good, you're still here." Milly pulled onto the courtyard and jumped energetically out of her van. "I've got your hamper orders, and you didn't pick the wine up, so I've done that for you too."

Emma nodded listlessly as she continued to stare at Jack's frame.

"Did Josh tell you he stayed the night?" Milly approached her discretely as she stood in the doorway of the kitchen. "Don't worry. I told him he could tell you both."

Forcing a smile, Emma nodded again.

"I never thought I'd say this, but I think I'm falling for him," Milly whispered. "He was so romantic. He made us both a nice meal, lit candles, and played soft music. He fed me my dessert and then undressed me so slowly. I honestly thought he'd be the type to just rip my clothes off, but he isn't. He just wants people to think he's like that. I don't want to tempt fate, but for the first time in a long time, I feel happy."

Emma smiled politely as thoughts ran through her head. Her decision would taint everyone.

"How's Daisy?" Milly shouted over to Jack. "Has she gone to college?"

"Yep." Jack picked up his car keys. "She's living the dream. Working hard and playing hard and already planning which University she's going to. At this rate, I'm going to need a second job just to fund her wardrobe."

"And I've heard about you two love birds." Milly winked. "Josh already told me. Life is on the up for you, Jack."

"It's about time." He laughed lightly as he stared at his ruined parlour. "I've had my fair share of bad luck. Fingers crossed today will be the fresh start I desperately need."

Emma watched him standing near the kitchen table as Milly drove away. Her Jack. The boy who had filled her dreams. She had visions of the three of them running around as children, innocent, free and unburdened. Birthday parties with their parents. Summers spent in the rivers. Christmas's sharing their gifts. Every moment of her childhood had been shaped by them. As the memories flooded her, she grieved for each one as she slowly said goodbye.

"I've decided to leave," Emma said quietly. "This isn't the life for me. I should never have come here."

"What?" Jack's face paled. "Are you being serious?"

Emma handed him the keys to her piggery. "I don't love you. I'm sorry."

CHAPTER 39

"What the frig are you playing at?" Josh asked angrily as he followed her around the piggery. "Is this what you wanted to talk to me about yesterday? Leaving him?"

Emma forced herself not to cry as she zipped up the remainder of her belongings. It had taken her three months to settle here and less than fifteen minutes to pack. "He was getting too serious."

"Too serious?" Josh laughed incredulously. "Isn't that what you wanted? I mean, aren't there things you need to talk to him about?"

"Like what?"

"Like, recent news."

"There is no recent news," Emma replied quietly as she checked the drawers for anything she may have left behind. She should have known he'd pick up on it.

"I'm struggling to believe you. You can't pull the wool over my eyes." Josh placed his hands on her shoulders. "Don't let this happen to him again. He's heartbroken, Emma. You've totally destroyed him. He didn't even go to the solicitors; he's still sitting at the kitchen table. He doesn't give a shit about this farm, not in comparison to what he has with you. He loves you and I know you love him; you always have."

Emma lifted her head slightly. And that's the reason she had to leave.

"I know if you talk to him, he'll listen to you."

"I don't want him to listen," Emma replied calmly, deciding to use her last remaining card, the one she knew would sever her relationship with the Seymours for good. "I love Toby. I have since the day I arrived. I never loved Jack. I lied."

CHAPTER 40

The village green filled up with the autumn ball revellers, taking advantage of the free champagne Toby's mother had put on for the event. In the middle of the well-dressed crowd stood the bastard himself, laughing with the few who had been forced to speak with him.

Emma walked alongside the shop walls, hoping to stay out of view. Her bus would be here soon and then she could try to rebuild a life for herself. If such a thing existed without Jack. To give Flick her due, she hadn't asked questions, but simply agreed to let her stay for as long as she needed, but she already knew she'd never recover from this. Closing her eyes, she allowed a tear to roll down her cheek. She could have had everything.

The rumbling bus appeared around the corner. Normally a familiar, welcoming sight, it now filled her with despair. She stood up and prepared to board. Grabbing the handle of her suitcase, she pulled it, feeling a resistance.

"We need to talk." Jack put his hand firmly on the case. "Now."

Aware of the driver glancing at his watch with frustration, Emma yanked her suitcase out of his hands. "I'm leaving, Jack. I'm sorry."

"Not yet, you're not." He pulled her and the case away from the bus before waving the driver on, the determination on his face reminding her of the day she'd arrived on his farm. He guided her across the green as Emma glanced nervously towards Toby, still distracted by the attention of the villagers as he strutted around like a parrot on a perch.

"So, the man you love is over there, go and tell him." Jack held her shoulders and pointed her towards the crowds. "He'd be delighted if you declared your love for him in front of me, so just do it."

Emma tried to turn away but her fight against Jack's hold was fruitless. She could feel herself shake from head to toe. She had to get away from here.

"Don't treat me like an idiot." Jack tipped her head towards his. "I don't believe for one minute that you're in love with him. What's going on?"

"I can't tell you," Emma whispered. "Please, just let me go. It's best for everyone if I leave."

"Why did you ask for Joanne's address?"

"What?" Emma lifted her head in shock. "How do you know about that?"

"Milly told me. She's just as confused by you leaving as we all are. Is this to do with Caleb?"

"Please, Jack," Emma pleaded. "Just leave it."

"No, I won't. What are you afraid of?"

Emma pinched the bridge of her nose. She hadn't expected this, for Jack to fight for her. In that one cruel second, she suddenly realised he truly loved her.

"Why won't you tell me the truth?" Jack grabbed her shoulders and held them tightly. "It's obvious someone has said something to you, and common sense tells me this is about my son. Whatever has happened or whatever you know, just tell me. Believe me, nothing is worse than letting you walk away from me."

His words almost undid her, but she used every bit of restraint to keep her composure. He'd find out one day about Caleb, of that she felt sure, but at least by that point, he'd still have his farm, his livelihood and his respect.

"Joanne?" Jack looked up, his grip on her shoulders loosening. "What the hell. What is she doing here?"

Emma's anxiety heightened as she turned to see the tall brunette walking determinedly across the green. If Toby saw either of them, it would be game over.

Jack strode over to his ex-wife, his face filled with confusion. "Where's Caleb, and why are you here?"

"I'm here because I'm sick and tired of being manipulated." Joanne eyed Emma cautiously. "I know who you are. Have you told him?"

"No." Emma shook her head as she glanced nervously towards Toby. "Please, let's talk about this somewhere else. Let's get away from here. There's something you all need to know."

"I'm done with talking," Joanne barked as she headed purposefully towards the gathering groups. "I want to start living my new life guilt free, and I can't do that with this hanging over me."

Panicking, Emma ran across the green. She needed to stop this. They needed to know the truth.

Toby looked around nervously as they approached before stepping away from the crowds. Emma didn't miss him flinch as Jack's jaw started to tick.

"Are you going to tell him, or shall I, because one thing's for certain, I am no longer scared of you." Joanne lifted her perfectly sculptured chin as she faced Toby. "Your toxic denials and your twisted control are finally over. In two weeks, I'll be married. I won't need support from anyone. I'll be free of you."

"Hey." Jack shook his head. "If you're getting married in two weeks, I'm the person you should be speaking to. There's things we need to discuss."

Emma willed Joanne to stay quiet, but she knew that point had already passed.

"Caleb's not yours," Joanne whispered. "I'm so sorry. I had no choice but to let you believe that."

Jack's head went back with shock and his face paled whiter than the pristine shirt cladding Toby's back. Emma watched his shoulders slump as all the fight in him gave way to defeat. She desperately wanted to comfort him, but she knew the hardest words and the true extent of this deceit and betrayal were yet to come.

"Toby is his father." Joanne winced at her own bitter words. "He's known from day one. He said he'd take Caleb away from me if I told you. I needed your money to stay afloat. He refused to give me a penny. I had no choice."

Jack put a hand over his mouth as his eyes filled with pain. "Please tell me that's not true."

"I'm so sorry." Joanne bit her wobbling lip. "I can't live like this anymore. You deserve to know the truth, and I need to be free of him."

Jack gave an anguished moan before bending over and putting his hand on his knees.

"I didn't want this." Joanne reached out for his arm. "The photographs I sent you were of my nephew. If you'd seen Caleb, you'd have known the truth. All this was never my intention. He didn't give me a choice."

"Don't touch me," Jack hissed as he shrugged off her hand. "I've crippled myself emotionally and financially to keep you and your child secure. I've had countless sleepless nights wondering if I'll ever get to hold him. I've cried for him, yearned for him, I've gone without food for him. And all because you slept with that slimy bastard? Of all the people in this village you could have turned to, you chose to leave my bed for a cheap piece of shit."

With each slump of Jack's shoulders, Toby's stature seemed to grow. Keeping a close eye on his mother milling around, he approached Jack with a twisted smile. "You can insult me all you like, but I had a lot of fun sullying your wife, and I'd like to say I had great difficulty in enticing her, but she came to me willingly."

Joanne slapped Toby's face as Jack's shoulders heaved with temper. Emma put her hand out to him. "Let's just go, Jack. Let's not do this here."

"I hope you've enjoyed rearing the next line of Montgomerys," Toby continued in his tormenting whisper. "I have to say, it's been very enjoyable watching you struggle."

Wishing she had Josh on hand to control the six-foot ball of rage, Emma pulled on Jack's arm. "Don't retaliate. Please, let's just leave. Toby, leave this alone. You've hurt him enough."

"Does your mother know about this?" Jack replied quietly as his fists curled tightly. "Does she know what a low life piece of shit she's brought into this world?"

"That's the best bit about all of this." Toby grinned as he watched the older woman laugh with the villagers. "You're not going to tell her."

Jack's eyes burned as he shook his head. "Try and stop me."

"Please, Jack," Emma whispered as she grabbed his hand. "Let's just go."

"Oh, I don't need to try and stop you," Toby replied, his eyes glinting menacingly. "Your girlfriend has already put the noose around your neck. Do you want to know why she's so keen to get you away from here? It's because I know all about your fire. I know the whole sorry story."

Jack flinched. "What about the fire? There's nothing to tell."

"What fire?" Joanne asked her ex-husband. "You've never mentioned a fire to me."

"That's because he's desperate for no one to find out the truth." Toby smirked at Jack's wary expression. "A smell of petrol. Finances in the red. An expensive custody battle and a warning for arson in the past. The courts will have a field day with this one."

Jack wiped a hand over his stubbly chin as his phone started to bleep. He checked the message, a deep frown on his face.

"You're talking nonsense. I don't know what you've heard or where you've got it from, but the fire wasn't my fault."

Emma hung her head in shame as Toby stared at her. "I'm afraid I got the information first-hand. She told me."

Jack looked at her, his eyes filling with a new kind of hurt. "Why would you do that?"

"I didn't." Emma wiped the flood of tears from her cheeks. "I told Flick. I thought I was alone in the bakery, but Sebastian overheard."

"And that's why you're leaving me? You found out about Caleb, and he blackmailed you?" Jack stood in the middle of the green, looking lost and vulnerable. "I don't know what to say. This is all too much."

"Tit for tat." Toby smiled maliciously as more villagers joined the growing crowds. "Arson's a bit more serious than fathering a child. I guess if this got out, you'd have a lot to lose. I think they call this having the upper hand."

Jack looked around him with a defeated expression. He closed his eyes briefly before his phone beeped again. He read the remainder of the message with a neutral expression before sending a quick reply. "Well, it looks like you've finally got something that means so much to me. You're Caleb's father. I guess I should offer you my congratulations."

"Hold on," Joanne interrupted quietly. "I don't want him in my son's life. I never wanted him to be a part of Caleb's upbringing. Ever. Not his money or his influence."

"He should be proud to be a Montgomery," Toby huffed. "It's better than being a farmer's son."

"And you think you're a role model." Jack shook his head in disbelief. "Do you seriously think your mother will be proud of you if this ever got out? You get a married woman pregnant, ignore your own child's existence, leave her to bring up the baby alone, and are happy to let someone else take care of his future? You are one despicable, spineless wanker."

Toby looked around nervously as Jack's voice rose. "Hey, I will ring the insurance company. It isn't an empty threat."

"Go ahead," Jack shouted. The crowds on the village green started to quieten as they sensed a drama unfolding in front of them. "Behave like the selfish bastard that you are. Why would anyone expect anything different from a Montgomery?"

"What's the problem?" Mrs. Montgomery approached the small group before eyeing Joanne suspiciously. "I don't know what's going on here, but you're creating a scene and tonight isn't the time for that."

Toby swallowed nervously, his Adam's apple bobbing around like a ballcock in a cistern.

"I hope you two aren't fighting. This role comes with great responsibility, Tobias. We talked about this. I expect maturity and the good name of this family returned. You promised me you'd work with me on that."

"Of course." Toby pulled at the stiffly pressed collar of his shirt. "We were just discussing his farm. He's going to sell it to us."

Mrs. Montgomery turned to Jack in confusion. "Why now, after all these years?"

"Jack, you can't sell the farm. Please, don't do this." Emma signalled towards Josh and Milly as they walked across the green towards them. She needed to get Jack away from here. Toby could still ruin him. "Please, let's all talk about this. No decisions need to be made tonight."

"I got your text about Caleb." Josh stared at Toby with barely concealed hatred. "Does he know about the fire report?"

"Who's Caleb?" Mrs. Montgomery looked around the small group. "Who is he?"

"I think we should concentrate on the fire report." Jack pulled the small group away from the prying eyes and ears of the villagers. "The assessors analysed every detail. The fire started because of a fault with the new milk tanks."

"What?" Emma stared at Jack in disbelief. "When did you find this out?"

"Just." Jack held up his phone. "Josh has been messaging me for the last hour with updates. He went to the solicitors for me. The company I bought the tanks from have admitted liability and offered me a very generous payout to keep this out of court. In a few days' time, I'll have enough money to rebuild fifty parlours if I wanted to."

Toby's face suddenly paled as he stared at the official document on Jack's phone.

"So, I'm afraid there is no arson charge. However, the report went into a lot of detail about the petrol they found. I expected it would. I could smell it myself near the generators. The assessors weren't too suspicious as that's what generators run off, but they did highlight the type of petrol they found. It's more commonly associated with sports cars."

Putting a hand over his mouth, Toby groaned.

"The petrol didn't start the fire, but it was the main reason I lost the whole barn. If those generators had gone up, I'd be grieving the loss of my sister too."

"Jack, what are you insinuating?" Mrs. Montgomery's eyes narrowed. "I'm warning you, I won't stand for accusations like this."

"It's no longer an accusation," Josh said quietly as he leant forward and supported the arm of the grey-faced woman. "Clive checked Toby's car earlier. It's the same petrol."

"Is this true, Tobias?" his mother asked weakly. "Did you try to set fire to Jack's farm?"

Realising he'd been cornered, Toby's strength dissolved. "I only wanted to cause a bit of damage. I didn't know his sister was nearby."

"You bastard!" Josh raised his fist as Milly placed a hand on his arm. "You could have killed her."

"I don't believe this," Mrs. Montgomery whispered as she slumped onto a nearby bench. "Over these past few weeks, I thought I'd seen a change in you, but you've inherited your father's obsessive hatred and jealousy of anything you can't have. You could go to jail for this. Have you considered that?"

"I don't want to go to jail." Toby's bottom lip quivered as he knelt at his mother's feet. "I'm sorry. I truly am. I thought the farm being damaged would force Jack into selling it. Please forgive me."

"Oh, get up, you pathetic idiot." Jack pulled him roughly onto his feet as Joanne approached, holding the hand of a small child. "You've got more explaining to do. Haven't you?"

The blond-haired child ran across the green, his plump legs jumping in delight at the ducks milling around the pond. Racing forward in eagerness, he suddenly tripped and fell onto the soft grass. Jack bent down and helped Caleb up, holding his tiny hand in his. He tenderly stroked the soft cheek as he smiled at the bright lavender eyes, full of innocence and possibilities. He then turned away, his own eyes burning with unshed tears.

"Come on," Emma said quietly as she led him away. "Let's leave them to it."

CHAPTER 41

"Where have the others gone?" Emma asked as she looked around the busy ballroom for Josh and Milly.

"Back to the farm." Jack craned his neck over the rest of the dancers. "Who was that bloke my sister was dancing with earlier?"

"Apparently, you used to let him play in Daisy's bedroom when they were younger," Emma replied with a grin. "It seems he's grown up over the last ten years."

"Adam?" Jack puffed out his cheeks. "He didn't have muscles like that when I last saw him. I don't like that at all."

"Well, it seems Daisy does." Emma giggled as she lay her head against his chest. "How are you feeling now?"

"A mix of emotions. I spoke to Joanne earlier. She's going to let Mrs. Montgomery see the boy whenever she wants to, and her fiancé seems a decent bloke. He'll look after them both."

"I meant you. How are you?"

"So, so." Jack shrugged. "Caleb has been in my life for four years. I've thought about him every day, and I think I always will, but I've decided I'm going to give myself some time to heal, and then I'll take up Joanne's offer and go see him properly. It seems ironic that to finally meet him, I had to lose him."

Emma smiled sadly. She knew how much the news had hurt him.

"At least I kept you. I can't believe you were prepared to leave so I'd keep the farm."

"I wasn't thinking straight." Emma sighed as she leant against him. "I just kept worrying you'd never forgive me if you lost your farm because of my stupidity."

"Hey, it wasn't stupidity. He was in the wrong, no one else. I'd rather lose seven farms than lose you. Just promise me the next time you have a secret, you tell me. I'm not sure I can go through anything like that again." Jack smiled as he kissed the top of her head. "I just hope Toby learns his lesson. Working in the kitchens at Featherby's will teach him about hard work. Joanne told me his mother has stopped his allowance. I agree with her decision on that, and Caleb will give him a second chance to make something of himself."

"It's very good of you not to press charges." Emma looked up at him. "Many people would have been pleased to see Toby behind bars for what he did."

"And what good would that do anyone? Plus, I've nothing to feel revengeful about. You get your farm shop back. The insurance will now pay out, and with the private compensation from the milk tank company, I'll build a bigger parlour and buy more cattle." Jack spun her around to the music before pulling her back close to his chest. "And my brother has taken the plunge and decided to move in with Milly."

"Really?" Emma smiled. "He's finally found the guts to settle down?"

"It appears so, but most importantly, I'm on a date with my girlfriend. I'm only eighteen years too late. It appears I missed the first one."

Emma stopped dancing and looked at him suspiciously. "What do you mean?"

"Do you want to know how I knew you were lying to me about leaving?" Jack reached into his suit pocket and extracted a small pink envelope. "You make my spring fresh, my summer warm, my autumn golden and my winters cosy. My heart will always be yours, forever and always."

Emma gasped. Her love letter. After all those years, he'd finally read it. She looked up into his twinkling eyes and groaned. "I had the almightiest crush on you as we were growing up."

"Yeah, I know," Jack replied, biting his lip. "I always knew."

"You didn't," Emma gasped. "Seriously, you knew?"

"Of course I did." Jack laughed. "You did a good job of hiding it, but I guess I knew you too well. Your letter though, I had no idea your feelings were that strong. If I'd have known…"

"You'd have died with embarrassment." Emma glanced at him and smiled shyly. "It's okay. I think Josh did us both a favour. It wasn't our time."

"If it's any consolation, I would have turned up. But I'd have made you promise to make a life for yourself, to let me go, and to fall in love with someone who deserved you."

"Instead, eighteen years later, I come straight back to you."

"Like I said…" Jack's eyes twinkled. "…of all the farms in all the world, you walked onto mine. I think sometimes things are meant to happen. Sean, Toby, Joanne, Sebastian, they've brought us together. I do think people enter our lives, make a mark, and leave it for a reason. We just don't always understand why at the time."

Emma thought about the pearls lady. She'd never seen her since. Had she been sent into her life to guide her through? Had her angels above been watching her all along?

Jack tenderly kissed her lips. "Come on, I'm fed up with being stared at. A negative of a small village like this, everyone thinks your love life is their business. Let's go back to the farm. I'm looking forward to some time alone with you."

*

The lights from the farmhouse shone welcomingly as they left the bank of the stream and Emma felt a deeper sense of love as she looked around the rolling hills and valleys. She belonged here.

"Someone has been busy this afternoon. She's been desperately waiting for you to come home." Jack encouraged her to close her eyes as he took her hand. "Follow me. I think you'll like this."

Emma allowed herself to be led across the courtyard, her eyes closed as Jack gently guided her.

"Okay, you can open your eyes now."

Emma looked around in amazement at the small patio area behind the barn. The flags had been cleaned and the shrubbery cut back to expose more of the patchwork hills she'd come to adore. The nearby trees and pergola, once neglected, now shimmered under strings of twinkling lights. In the middle of the enchanting enclosure stood a bistro table set for two. "Who's done this?"

"I did," Daisy said shyly. "With a bit of help from Clive and the others. I know how much this tranquil spot meant to you, and I wanted you to come home."

Emma wrapped her arms around the young girl and held her tight as tears fell onto her soft hair. She looked up to see Clive grinning from the other side of the patio and she mouthed a thank you to him. "I love it. I can't think of anything more perfect."

"Talking of perfect." Jack coughed nervously before turning to his brother. "May I?"

Josh nodded. "She's all yours, mate. However, I think she's got something to tell you first."

Emma smiled at him knowingly. For a guy who claimed to be out of touch with women, he was very astute when he needed to be.

"You know, when you said some things are meant to happen." Emma gently touched her stomach. "I kind of come with some baggage of my own."

“What?” Jack’s eyes widened as he looked down at her. “Surely not. You mean … that night?”

“Urgh,” Daisy pulled a horrified face before turning to Josh and gasping, “I’m going to be an aunty. You’re going to be an uncle.”

“We’re going to be a family.” Jack placed a hand tenderly on her front, his eyes filled with emotion. “Emma Francis, I’m going to ask you to marry me, and if you don’t reply within three seconds…”

“Yes,” Emma whispered as her family crowded around them. “My answer is yes. Forever and always.”

The end

Thank you for choosing to read "Second Chances." If you enjoyed it, please consider telling your friends or leaving a review on Amazon, Goodreads, or the site where you bought it. Word of mouth is an author's best friend and much appreciated.

ABOUT THE AUTHOR

Louise is a data analyst for the NHS which she has been for twenty-five years. An only child, she spent her childhood reading famous five and secret seven books in a makeshift tent in her garden. She adores rabbits which earned her the nickname of Rabbit Lou amongst her good friends. She loves gardening and being cosy in front of a fire with a glass of wine or a cup of tea, depending on the hour of the day! She's happiest when with her husband David and son Thomas. They are her world. While in her early thirties, she lost both parents very suddenly to terminal illness. The aching loss and feeling of being cheated worked to shape her book. She hopes they will be proud of her.

Also by Louise Mercer

Following the untimely passing of her godmother, Laura finds herself the benefactor of a picturesque seaside B&B.

She's soon plunged into the life of hospitality, catering for the needs of her eclectic guests, with help from her vibrant and fun-loving friend, Amy.

However, the cosy seaside lifestyle she hopes for is soon dominated by her mischievous pup, an unwelcome ex-boyfriend, seaside storms and the search for long-lost family.

If her new life isn't challenging enough, she also has a battle on her hands against her own emotions, as the brooding, handsome village vet upsets her cosy applecart.

Printed in Great Britain
by Amazon

84340557R00190